HEARTSTONE

HEARTSTONE

SEPARATED BY TIME.
JOINED BY FATE.

ROSE SARTIN

AWARD-WINNING AUTHOR OF *BOUND BY HONOR*

LAGAN
PRESS

an imprint of
THE OGHMA PRESS

OGHMA
CREATIVE MEDIA

Bentonville, Arkansas • Los Angeles, California
www.oghmacreative.com

Library of Congress Cataloging-in-Publication Data

Names: Sartin, Rose, author.
Title: Heartstone/Rose Sartin |
Description: First Edition. | Bentonville: Lagan, 2022.
Identifiers: LCCN: 2022948352 | ISBN: 978-1-63373-779-2 (hardcover)
ISBN: 978-1-63373-780-8 (trade paperback) | ISBN: 978-1-63373-781-5 (eBook)
Subjects: | BISAC: FICTION/Romance/Western | FICTION/Romance/Time Travel |
FICTION/Thrillers/Supernatural|
LC record available at: https://lccn.loc.2022948352

Lagan Press trade paperback edition, December, 2022

Cover & Interior Design by Casey W. Cowan
Editing by Gordon Bonnet, Anthony Wood, & Amy Cowan

Published by Lagan Press, an imprint of The Oghma Press, a subsidiary of The Oghma Book Group.

For my children, Melissa, Angela, and Faye.
And for their children, Dameian, Malaki and Alora.
I'm so proud of you.

ACKNOWLEDGEMENTS

I'D LIKE TO thank my critique group, Mid-south Writers, including Barbara, Susan, Prix, and Sherry. I would also like to thank the members of the Osage tribe and the curator of the Bushwhacker Museum who made my research fascinating.

Thank you to my publisher, Oghma Creative Media, including Casey Cowan, who designs my fantastic covers, Gordon Bonnet, my editor, Amy Cowan, Anthony Wood, Venessa Cerasale, and Cyndy and Gill Miller who have encouraged me every step of the way.

And a very special thanks to Susan Eschbach and to my children, Melissa and Roger, Angela and Dennis, and Faye and Honnah. You have enabled me to stay safe at home during the pandemic. You've picked up my groceries and medication, made sure my car stays in good condition, and kept my computer and internet up and running so I can keep in touch with the world. I am blessed.

AUTHOR'S NOTE

THERE IS A legend in my family, of a young Osage woman who had been taken captive and sold for a hand of tobacco to a white widower with several young children. He did marry her, and, together, they raised a large family.

At ninety-three, their youngest child, my late grandfather's uncle, told my mother and grandmother his parents' story. It was a secret, due I'm sure, to the fear of bigotry and prejudice. I believe he wanted our branch of the family tree to know the truth.

As I said earlier, this is only a family legend. Documents and public records are sketchy, confusing and at times, contradictory. None mention the Osage. Still, I remember him as clear-headed and alert. I have no reason to doubt his account of what his mother—my great, great grandmother—must have endured.

ONE

"LOOK ALIVE, WILL." Ben Jenkins pounded the bathroom door. "Central's called in a ten-fifty- J-four. Move it. This isn't a standby."

Willie swiped the cool cloth across her damp forehead and closed her eyes against the mental image Ben's words evoked. Another J-3. One more torn body to hold together until their air-vac unit made it to the hospital. Not again. Not this soon. She opened her eyes and stared into the mirror. Her usual healthy complexion was pale.

"Now, Will!" Ben shouted from a distance.

Drawing a deep breath, she pushed away from the sink and unlocked the door. "On my way."

She sprinted down the hall and through the hospital's emergency doors behind Ben—the same doors they'd entered twenty minutes before with their second accident victim of the night in tow.

"I've got a feeling about this one." Ben always knew the bad runs. They strapped themselves into the chopper's seats and he slipped the radio set over his head.

The pilot, Jeff Sterns, nudged the big machine into the air. "5-8 is on scene," Jeff shouted over the rotor's staccato roar. "We have a rollover on I-70 at the 54 access, east of Kingdom City."

Ben pressed the headphones closer to his ear to listen before looking up. "There's one female J-four. Subject was thrown from the vehicle and killed on impact. They have one male J-three with unknown injuries. He's jammed under the steering wheel. Fire rescue is working with him."

Less than five minutes later she and Ben took their first look at the crash site. Slow-moving traffic, northbound on Highway 54 and eastbound on I-70 created long undulating ribbons of light. Red and blue emergency lights and yellow flashers from at least a dozen private cars surrounded the glaring spotlights trained on the wreckage.

A half circle of cars, headlights on high beam, illuminated a wide, level area a hundred or so feet from the site. Jeff aimed the helicopter toward that spot.

At touchdown, calm settled over her. It always came, the wall protecting her emotions from the horror she'd soon face. But the wall had thinned lately, and sometimes the calm regressed into unease.

Jumping to the ground, she sprinted toward the crumpled blue sedan. It listed on its side and top like a capsized boat. Acrid gasoline fumes penetrated the air, burning her nostrils.

A blanket-draped body lay on the offramp incline twenty yards away. The J-four. It was easier to think of the concealed body as just a code name, not a person that someone loved and would grieve. The code and blanket allowed her to turn away, gave her permission to ignore the inevitable pain of death, and think only of the life to be saved. The screech of tearing metal drew her attention from the hidden form.

Fire rescue still worked to free the second victim. How many times had she waited as the jaws of life separated mangled wreckage to give her access to equally mangled bodies?

Ben touched her shoulder as he passed. "There's Scott. Find out what he has on the subject."

A tall man broke through the growing crowd, and moved toward her, his face grim. Her stomach tightened. In the years she'd worked with Scott Fielding, she'd never seen his stoic expression falter. Ben had been right. This was a bad one.

She expected Scott to fall in beside her as she passed, but he grabbed her arm and swung her to face him. "Willie, let Ben handle this one."

She understood his intention. Scott knew she was going through a rough time. This profession took its toll on emergency personnel. But she wasn't ready to give up her job. She was a good air-vac nurse. She saved lives. "I can handle this, Scott."

He grasped both of her shoulders, forcing her to look up at him. "Not this time, honey." Scott's eyes filled with regret. "There isn't any easy way to tell you this. It's your cousin, Josh."

Josh? Her knees buckled. Scott tightened his grip on her arms. "No. Josh and Trish went to a funeral in Nevada—the one for the deputy who was killed during a traffic stop last week. They planned to go on to our family's homestead in the Ozarks. It can't be him."

Scott shook his head. "It's Josh, no doubt about it. I've talked to him. Don't you recognize his car?"

She looked at the overturned automobile and refused to believe her cousin was trapped in that pile of twisted metal.

"Willie, come with me."

"No." She jerked back, but Scott's grip held. "Let me go." If Josh lay trapped in that wreckage, she had to get to him and make sure he lived. She refused to let him die.

"Sam's there." Scott's voice was low, smooth. He was using a common calming technique, one she'd used an hour ago on an accident victim. She wanted to laugh at the irony but knew it would end in tears.

"Come on, Will. Sam has the best fire rescue team in the state, and Ben's with Josh by now. Let them do their job."

She dug her feet into the grass. "It's my job too, and if you're right, my cousin needs me."

"Your job is to see he makes it through the chopper ride to the hospital."

"Please, Scott. He's the only family I have left. I need to be with him."

The pressure of his grip on her shoulders eased, and a flicker of understanding entered her friend's eyes. "All right, but if you can't handle it, I'll drag you out of there."

"I know." She broke from his loosened hold and ran, shoving her way through the crowd.

The jaws had opened a hole in the wreckage. Sam lay on a thick pad spread over the metal, his head and shoulders inside the upturned car's front passenger window. Ben knelt on a second pad, speaking softly to him.

She dropped to her knees beside Ben and tried to peer inside. "How bad is it?"

Ben looked up in surprise and frowned. "What are you doing here, Will? Scott shouldn't have let you—"

"How bad is it?"

"He's conscious. He knows you're on site."

Sam pulled out of the car and grabbed a thick cover from the equipment pile. "Josh is pinned between the seat and the steering wheel." The fireman scooted back into the car and was out again a few seconds later. "I've protected as much of his face and upper body as I can."

He nodded toward the slicker-garbed men attaching chains to the wreckage before turning to give her a hand up. "They're going to pull the steering column. We should be able to lower the seat to the ground, get him upright. Then we'll free him."

"How is he?"

Sam shook his head. "I'm not sure. His BP is 134 over 72 but his pulse is 128. We need to get him stabilized, but you won't be able to establish an IV until he's out of there."

The clank and rattle of heavy chains pulling taut gave them warning. "Let's give them room."

The three moved aside as fire rescue workers double-checked the chains connecting the steering column to the jaws and the second set of chains running from the jaws to the car's front end.

"Hurry... hurry," she chanted. Josh was running out of time. His blood pressure should have been higher given his pain and stress. That combined with his racing pulse indicated a serious blood loss. She needed to get to her cousin before it was too late.

"Get ready," someone called as a fireman crawled over the pad into the car to steady Josh. The chains drew tighter. Metal scraped against metal. The vehicle groaned and shuddered as the wreckage slowly pulled apart.

A long, agonized scream tore the air and gripped Willie's heart.

"*Medic!*" The rescuer scooted out of the car. "He's free and upright but his abdomen is punctured."

Ben rolled into the spot vacated by the fireman.

Seconds later he backed out of the car. "His stomach cavity is filling with blood. I think we have a torn artery, but the gash is too narrow. I can't get my hand inside to check. You'll have to probe for the bleeder, Willie. No one else has small enough hands."

She didn't hesitate. Ben barely had time to move aside before she grabbed a sterile glove and crawled through the hole, dread knotting her insides.

Her first glimpse of Josh turned her stomach. Her cousin's eyes were closed, his long lashes dark against too-pale skin. The left side of his face was discolored and swelling. His breath came in short gasps. Blood soaked his uniform. Ben had cut the shirt open exposing the jagged gash that bisected his navel.

"Josh, can you hear me?"

He tried to move and choked on a groan. "Will?" His voice sounded thin and raw.

"Yeah, hon, it's me." She used her cheerful, everything's-going-to-be-fine voice.

"It hurts."

"I know." She slipped the sterile glove over her right hand. "I'd give everything I own not to cause you more pain, but I have to stop the bleeding."

His fingers tried to close around her wrist. "I trust you, Will."

"I'll be as gentle as I can." She carefully slipped her gloved hand into the gash and Josh went rigid. "Don't hold your breath." Please help me God. How was she ever going to find the bleeder?

"Trish?" He gasped as she searched for the artery.

She stilled. Trish was out there, under the blanket. She didn't allow herself to think about it. "Don't talk, Josh. Trish is already out. Let's get you out, too. Hold on a little longer."

Hot blood pulsed over her fingers, and bile rose in her throat. The amount of blood Josh was losing terrified her. She found the damaged artery and pinched it closed. "Got it," she shouted to Ben. "Let's get him out."

"Willie?" Josh's voice trembled. She leaned closer. His lips looked waxy, colorless. How much blood had he lost? "Tell Trish I love her."

He coughed, and Willie felt the muscles spasm in his abdomen. Blood seeped from the corner of his mouth and trickled across his cheek.

"Ben! Hurry!" she screamed over the screech of the metal saws.

"They're working as fast as they can, Will. How is he?"

She looked down at her cousin. His head was tilted to one side, his eyes clouded. "He's unconscious. We have to get him out of here now. He's coughing blood."

"He's almost out." Ben's tone was calm, even.

Josh opened his eyes again. "I have to tell you about—" He coughed again. Blood spewed across his chest and spattered Willie's arm.

"Ben!"

The car vibrated, and she tried to cover her cousin's body with her own as the undercarriage peeled away from the inverted chassis.

With a gentleness that always amazed her, the rescue team removed her cousin from the car and placed him on the backboard, strapping him in place without disturbing her hold on the artery.

Ben squatted beside them and checked Josh's blood pressure as Scott stabilized his neck with a c-collar. Her partner looked up from his equipment, eyes full of concern, and raised the two-way to his lips. "Central five-twelve."

"*Five-twelve,*" crackled the receiver.

"Central, subject is unconscious, pulse rate 140. I've established two IVs, the first lacerated…."

Ben's voice and Central's reply faded as Willie's grip on Josh's hand tightened. Ben would take care of everything. She had to concentrate on keeping the artery closed and willing Josh to stay alive.

"Hold on a little longer. *Please,* Josh."

Ben placed a hand on her shoulder. "We're ready."

The men shifted the backboard to a stretcher. Her fingers still clamped the artery as they sprinted toward the helicopter.

She sat stone-still on the flight back. Ben monitored her cousin's life signs, updating Central as they drew closer to the hospital.

She held the artery, prayed, and remembered... Josh laughing, Josh teaching her to skate and watching over her high school years like an overprotective big brother, Josh standing beside her at her parents' funerals, urging her to look to the future, to concentrate on her dreams.

Her cousin roused again. "Willie... came back to warn you...."

His voice was so weak she could barely hear him. She brushed his hair away from his face with her free hand. "Don't talk now. We'll have time later."

"Important. Stay away from Nevada." He tried to reach for her. Willie took his icy fingers in her warm grasp and leaned closer. His words were barely audible now. "He's crazy." The last word drew out in a guttural sigh. Her cousin went limp.

"Josh!"

Ben slid the stethoscope over Josh's chest then dropped the instrument and replaced the headgear. "Central we have a code." He leaned toward the pilot. "Set her down fast, Jeff."

Willie didn't hear the trauma center's response. Her heart pounded in her ears. Still gripping the artery, she watched Ben toss the headset aside, stack his hands on Josh's chest, and begin CPR. "One, two, three, four...."

"No, please God, no." Her vision blurred. Tears rolled down her cheeks as she bent closer to her cousin's ear. She needed to be sure he heard her.

"I love you, Josh. Please don't leave me."

TWO

WILLIE SET THE shovel aside and paused to take in the spectacular view. From her vantage point on one of the highest ridge tops in southwest Missouri, she gazed out over fields and woods that flamed yellow, burgundy, orange, and red. The bright-hued hickory, dogwood, sassafras, oak, and maple blended with the dark green cedar and pine. Could any place be more beautiful than the Ozark Mountains in mid-October?

She'd grown up in the area but had moved to St. Louis to complete her nurse's training and expand her studies to include trauma. She'd been an air-vac nurse for nearly two years.

After Josh's death, she couldn't cope with similar rescue situations, so she'd taken a leave of absence, sublet her apartment for six months, and moved to her family's homestead in the Ozarks.

Ben and Scott had agreed she needed time off, but neither thought she had any business moving to what they considered a remote area of Missouri.

She looked at the pitiful hole she'd been digging and sighed. A ridge top might be great for the view, but the predominately rocky surface had so little topsoil, large trees had been known to topple simply because their roots grew too close to the surface. Digging had been a challenge. After nearly an hour, she'd only managed to hollow out a place barely deep enough to plant the tupelo sapling. The tupelo, or black gum as the locals called the tree, wasn't all that common, and her family's old homestead didn't have a single one. But Josh had liked their neighbor's massive old gum tree with its hard, dark blue berries and bright red fall leaves. He'd talked about planting a tupelo on the ridge close to the house. Willie touched the small sapling she'd begged from old Mister Johnson. This was for Josh, and maybe for her as well.

She knelt to scoop the loosened soil and rocks out of the hole with her bare hands. Dredging out a second handful, she jerked back. Blood poured from a half-moon gash on the tip of her finger and smeared across the dirt-encrusted piece of flint she held.

Bile burned her throat. Her fingers clenched spasmodically around the stone and the flint flashed hot in her grasp. She couldn't open her hand to release it.

Blood. She shuddered, suddenly back with Josh—listening to him scream in agony, feeling his life's blood pulse over her hand with every beat of his straining heart, smelling the stench of gasoline, scorched metal, and blood—always the blood. She yanked the red kerchief from her hair and wound it around her hand to hide the wound.

Josh was dead.

Despite everything she'd done, despite her promise to keep him alive, he'd died, leaving her alone—making her the last living member of her family.

She closed her eyes against the memory and waited for the familiar queasiness to abate. Cautiously, she opened them again.

And saw the man.

He stood on the far side of the meadow, near the line of trees marking her property's west boundary—too far away to be an immediate threat. But close enough. She blinked, and blinked again, her mind unable to make sense of what she saw. He was tall, at least six and a half feet, his body lean and well-proportioned, not lanky like most tall men. A blanket draped his left shoulder. A breechcloth and suede-like leggings covered his lower body.

He stared at her, unmoving, as if he'd walked out of America's past into her meadow specifically to watch her. She glanced toward the house. Could she beat him to the door with enough time to lock it? But when she looked back to judge the distance separating them, he was gone.

Her eyes swept the area. He had to have gone back into the woods. The meadow was wide and open with no place to hide. Until a month ago it had been used for pasture and the cattle had kept the brush down. There hadn't been enough time for him to go anywhere else.

Grabbing the shovel, she jogged toward the back of the house on unsteady legs. Her cell phone was in the kitchen. She'd gotten out of the habit of carrying it with her. Lurching through the mud room door, she slammed it closed, threw the deadbolt, and tossed the shovel toward a corner. Racing through the open kitchen door, she grabbed her phone and continued down the hall into the foyer to lock the front door. She made a sweep of the house, checking every window to be sure it was locked, looking out, trying to spot him. Even from the upper story, there was nothing to see. Where had he gone?

Lifting her cell to dial emergency, she hesitated, unsure. What was she going to tell them—a nineteenth-century Native American was stalking her? Even she had trouble accepting the bizarre concept. Her overreaction to the blood, and the angle of sunlight against the trees must have created the illusion. She shook her head. That was a pretty detailed illusion.

Had stress and grief pushed her over the edge? She fought against a half-sob that bordered on hysteria. She didn't know what to believe.

Shoving the cell phone into her pocket, she looked at her wrapped hand. At least her finger didn't hurt as much. She ran upstairs to the bathroom that adjoined her bedroom and removed the bloodstained bandana, tossing it into the wastebasket.

The flint was still in her hand. She hadn't been able to turn it loose—still couldn't. Her fingers felt welded in place. The cut continued to drip blood into the sink. She turned on the hot water, and held her hand under the stream. But the near-steaming water didn't release the tension in her fingers, and she had to pry them open to release the stone. It clattered into the basin. Soaping her hands, she scrubbed away the caked dirt, careful not to touch the wound. She rinsed and soaped her hands again before a long final rinse.

The flesh gaped open. It might need a stitch or two, but for now, she opted to douse the wound with disinfectant and use a butterfly bandage. If the cut didn't show any signs of closing by tomorrow, she'd make a trip to the clinic in town.

After bandaging her finger, she slipped a rubber glove over her hand to protect the wound while she cleaned the sink. Under the running water, the flint glowed a soft shade of silver-gray and pink. Her eyes were drawn to the stone's fluted edges, and she carefully picked it up, immediately recognizing the arrowhead. The artifact was expertly crafted and knife-sharp. Her abused finger attested to that.

The silver-pink coloration was uniform, except for a rusty stain on the point that looked like dried blood.

She shivered. Why did everything remind her of blood?

It wasn't the first time she'd seen this discoloration. Flint in this part of the country contained veins of rust-colored iron oxide.

How ironic that she would hallucinate a Native American and then discover she'd been holding an arrowhead at the time. Had she known somehow, and her aversion to blood triggered the image? It made sense.

She decided to brew a cup of tea to fortify herself before returning to the ridge top to finish planting the tree. After filling the kettle, she broke a fresh sprig of spearmint from the plant in her window box. Crumpling the leaf into a tea-ball infuser, she placed it in the cup and poured boiling water over the top. As the tea steeped, she walked to the window overlooking the meadow. Her stomach tensed at the thought of going outside again, even if the man was a figment of her overwrought imagination.

Two cups of tea later, she grabbed her work gloves and headed for the mud room to retrieve the shovel. Stopping suddenly, she glanced toward one of the drawers in her kitchen cabinet—the drawer containing the handgun Josh had convinced her to keep.

She hated guns, didn't like the noise or the smell when they were fired. But Josh was insistent. He'd walked her through the process of obtaining the necessary permits. He'd even taught her how to use it.

She stood worrying her lower lip with her teeth as she weighed her distaste for the weapon against the need to feel safe. She avoided acting on impulse, but then she'd never seen a strange man in her meadow before. Opening the drawer, she removed the gun and checked the chamber to make sure it was clear. She then pulled a canning jar from the top of the cabinet. Shaking a full magazine into her palm, she inserted it into the bottom of the pistol and pocketed the weapon before replacing the jar.

———————

HER GLOVES PREVENTED further injury and protected her wounded finger. As she worked, she constantly glanced toward the spot where her specter had stood. Her thoughts wandered to Josh and Trish. This should have been their home, the place they'd planned to raise their children. The old but sturdy rock house had been built on the crest of a wide ridgetop to take advantage of the view. The back porch, or mud room, sat at ground level, while the foundation at the front of the house rose nearly five feet into the air due to the sloping front yard. Six steps led to the wide, covered porch.

She carried the shovel and bucket toward the back of the house but stopped when she heard the crunch of gravel. A vehicle must have turned onto the lane leading to her home. She expected to see the UPS truck. Ben had promised to send the rest of Josh's belongings this week. There hadn't been room for the boxes in her car when she'd left St. Louis.

But the big brown van didn't emerge from the concealing tree line. A sleek black sedan navigated the potholes that dotted the lane. One person sat in the car. A man, judging by his size. She assumed he wanted directions. Since hers was the last lane before the road dead ended about twenty yards beyond her drive, she ended up giving a lot of directions. Most of the time, she sent them to her closest neighbor, Mrs. Calhoun, who knew everyone in the county.

Altering course, she set the tools at the side of the house and headed for the front porch. If she waited on the steps, the driver could simply roll down the window and ask for help.

The driver didn't roll down his window. The man who climbed out of the sedan appeared to know exactly where he was, and he looked official. His black suit was obviously tailored to fit his six-two-or-three broad-shouldered frame. He probably worked out—a lot. His five o'clock shadow gave him a rugged appeal, and she imagined he'd be more comfortable in a casual shirt and jeans. His eyes were brown, but not an ordinary brown. Definitely not ordinary. They were a soft sable—eyes a woman could gaze into forever. Her cheeks warmed. She hadn't found a man this appealing in a long time.

"Wilhelmina McAllister?"

She cringed at the use of her given name. She suspected her parents had named her after her father's aunt in hopes she would inherit the widow's vast fortune. They should have known better. Her great aunt left everything she owned to a homeless relief center and a no-kill animal shelter. That suited Willie just fine. Both were great causes and she didn't need anyone's help to achieve her life's goals.

Her only regret was being stuck with a name that conjured thoughts of lace doilies and formal tea in the parlor. She didn't own a doily, probably wouldn't recognize one if she saw it. And her parlor wasn't for entertaining. It was a sanctuary filled with comfy furniture, books, and music.

"I'm Willie McAllister. Can I help you?"

"Miss McAllister, I'm Marshal Stona Jordan." He pulled a leather wallet from the inside breast pocket of his suit coat and flipped it open to reveal a badge and ID card. "I've recently been assigned to the Josh McAllister case, and I'd like to ask you a few questions. May I come in?"

Josh's case? Since when had her cousin's accident become a case? She led him up the porch steps and invited him into the front foyer. Her living room lay to the left through a wide arched entryway. The door on the right opened into the parlor. A staircase against the right wall of the foyer led to three second floor bedrooms. She guided the marshal straight through the hall to the kitchen at the back of the house.

"Would you care for a cup of coffee or tea?"

He shook his head. "No thank you."

"Something cold?"

"A glass of water if it isn't too much trouble."

"No trouble. Please have a seat at the table." She nodded toward a small dining nook off the kitchen. The bay windows offered a beautiful view of the meadow and the wooded hills and valleys surrounding her family home. The marshal made her nervous and she decided another cup of tea might calm her. She turned on the electric kettle then filled a tall glass with ice and water.

"You said you're working on my cousin's case? Are you investigating the accident?" She handed him the glass.

"In a matter of speaking." He took a long swallow of the water.

She paused on her way to the cabinet. That was cryptic. Retrieving a mug from the shelf, she dropped a chamomile teabag into it and filled it with hot water.

"You had some questions for me?" She carried the cup to the table and sat across from him.

He placed his glass on the table. "Are you familiar with the events surrounding your cousin's death?" He pulled a notepad and pen from the inside pocket of his jacket.

She set her cup aside to cool. "Marshal Jordan, someone must have failed to tell you I was one of the emergency personnel called to rescue my cousin and his fiancée. Trish died immediately. I was with Josh when he…." She swallowed back tears and took a sip of tea to ease the tightness in her throat. She still had trouble talking about his death.

"Miss McAllister, I am aware of your presence at the scene and your flight back to the hospital with your cousin. I understand this is difficult for you, but I need to know if he was conscious during the flight, and if he spoke to you."

He wanted her to relive the nightmare. Didn't he realize what it would do to her? She took a deep breath. Of course, he didn't. He was only doing his job.

She brought the cup to her lips again, needing a few seconds to pre-

pare for the ordeal. "Josh was in and out of consciousness, and in considerable pain. He talked to me, but most of what he said didn't make
sense. That happens a lot with trauma."

"Do you remember what he said?"

"He asked about his fiancé, Trish. He didn't know she'd been thrown
from the car. I didn't tell him she had... passed. When we were in the
air, he became anxious." She took a deep breath. "I think Josh knew he
didn't have much time. He wanted to warn me about something, told
me to stay away from Nevada."

"Nevada?"

"Not the state. I wouldn't have any reason to go there. I'm sure he
was talking about the *town* of Nevada, between Carthage and Kansas
City. To be honest, I can't imagine why he would believe I'd go there,
but I think he made a special trip back to St. Louis to warn me away
from the place. They were supposed to come here before returning to
St. Louis. Josh wanted to show Trish this farm. They'd be alive today if
he hadn't changed his plans."

"Did he say anything else?"

"He said, 'He's crazy.'"

"Who's crazy?"

She shook her head. "I don't know. Like I said, he wasn't making much sense. He'd lost so much blood. I don't know how he even
stayed conscious."

"Anything else?"

"There wasn't enough time." She paused, caught in the memory,
and took another deep, shuddering breath. "He went into cardiac arrest
before he could say more." She looked up. "I've told you everything I
can remember. Will you tell me what's going on? Why are you here?"

"The highway patrolman who investigated the accident interviewed
several witnesses who saw the accident. When your cousin took the I-70
exit from Highway 54, his car's brake lights came on, but the vehicle didn't
appear to slow down. He swerved to avoid hitting the truck in front of
him, and the passenger-side tires caught the edge of the pavement. He
tried to compensate, but lost control and his vehicle rolled over.

"The patrolman in charge suspected something might have been wrong with the sedan's brake system and decided to have it checked out. The mechanic found a small slit in a brake line. It wasn't wide enough to allow the fluid to leak out immediately. We believe every time Mister McAllister applied pressure to the brake, a thin line of fluid escaped through the slit."

"You're telling me a broken brake line caused my cousin's accident?"

"Not broken, Miss McAllister. Someone tampered with the brakes. Your cousin and his fiancée were targeted."

She stared at him dumbfounded. "Targeted?"

"I'm afraid that your cousin's case is now considered a homicide. They were murdered."

THREE

HOT TEA SLOSHED over the rim of the cup Willie held, burning her fingers. The cup clattered to the tabletop. They both jumped up as tea splashed across the surface. Willie ignored the mess.

"That's impossible."

The marshal grabbed a dishtowel from the counter and dropped it on the table to soak up the liquid, then tossed it into the sink. "I'm afraid it's true."

"No. The car must have hit something in the road—a piece of metal."

"The slit was too precise, exactly the right position on the line, a place difficult to find. Fortunately, the inspector was thorough. According to the report, he almost missed it. If it hadn't been for a thin residue of brake fluid on the damaged line, we wouldn't be having this conversation. We were hoping you could tell us who wanted your cousin and Patricia Collins dead."

She sank into her chair. "No one."

He frowned as he took his seat again. "Someone did."

She denied him with a near-violent shake of her head. "Trish taught first grade. Everyone loved her. Josh worked as a sheriff's deputy in St. Louis. He was new to the department, had never even made an arrest yet. No one would have a reason to kill either of them."

The marshal leafed through the pages of his notebook. "Did anyone on the flight to the hospital hear Mister McAllister warn you about this crazy person?"

"My partner, Ben, was there. He monitored Josh's vital signs on the ride back. But he had his headphones on most of the time, talking to central. I doubt he heard Josh. Why?"

Marshal Jordon ignored her question. "I understand Mister McAllister was your only living relative."

"Yes. That's right. Our parents are dead and neither of us had siblings."

"And this property belonged to your cousin?"

She nodded. "He inherited it when his parents died."

"According to my notes, this property has belonged to your family for generations, true?"

"Our great-grandparents settled here."

"Did it bother you—that Josh inherited the family homestead?"

She frowned. It was an odd question. "There was nothing to be bothered about. Regardless of who owned the homestead, it was always understood any family member had access."

"And now it belongs to you." He paused to give her an assessing look, then thumbed through several more pages of his notebook finally stopping at one. "You inherited all of your cousin's assets, a considerable amount of property and money."

Was there a hint of accusation in his voice? "What does that have to do with the accident?"

"It wasn't an accident, Miss McAllister. It was a homicide."

She straightened, her back rigid. "Do you believe I killed Josh? Is that why you're asking me so many personal questions?"

"We haven't connected you to the homicide. If we had, I'd be reading you your rights, not talking to you."

"Don't you mean interrogating me?"

He laughed. "It's obvious you've never been interrogated. I assure you, we're only talking."

She stood so fast her jacket bumped the table with a slight clink. "I think we're done."

He stood as well, his gaze directed at her jacket pocket. "Are you carrying a gun?"

She glanced at him, surprised.

"Answer me. Are you carrying a gun?"

"Yes, a handgun. I don't like having it, though. I've dealt with my share of gunshot wounds in the past two years. I've seen what firearms can do. They make me uncomfortable."

"But you're carrying one now. Why?"

She had no intention of telling him about the odd man she'd seen this morning. He'd think she was crazy.

"Bears," she blurted out. "My neighbor spotted a bear in the area."

He looked incredulous. "You planned to take down a bear with a handgun? Lady, all you'd end up doing is making it mad enough to kill you."

"I wasn't going to shoot the animal—just make enough noise to frighten it away."

"May I see the weapon?"

"It's legal. I have a permit to carry." She started to reach into her pocket.

He clasped her wrist. "Let me." Slipping his hand into her jacket pocket, he retrieved the gun and clip, then released her.

"It isn't loaded" She rubbed her wrist, though his grip had been gentle.

He looked up from checking the weapon. "I can see that." He held it up. "Did you believe the bear—or whatever else is out there—would wait until you loaded this?"

Her shoulders lifted. "I didn't think about it."

"Obviously." He shook his head. "An empty gun can get you as killed as a loaded one. Why do you own a gun if you don't like them?"

"My cousin insisted I have one. There was an incident in the hospital parking lot. Two men.... If Ben hadn't shown up, I might've been in trouble."

"Did you report the attempted assault?"

"Yes."

He set the gun and magazine on the table. "I only have a few more questions."

She shook her head. "I'm not answering any more questions. The next time you want to talk, I'll have my attorney present."

He shrugged. "That, of course, is your prerogative. You do understand your lack of cooperation could make you a person of interest?"

"No. It makes me smart. I worked as a part-time legal assistant while I was in nursing school. I've seen a lot of innocent people spend an exorbitant amount of time and money on legal fees, attempting to unravel misconceptions created during questioning." Moving into the mud room she open the outer door, not caring that he would have to walk to the front of the house to get to his car. "Unless you want to wait for my attorney, you need to leave. Now."

The marshal followed her to the door. After replacing his notebook and pen, he pulled a card from his inner jacket pocket and handed it to her. "If you have any further information for us you can contact my cell. I'll be in town for a few days."

She took the card but didn't look at it. "If I have anything more to say, my attorney will contact you."

He nodded and stepped out onto the back stoop.

She closed the door and walked to the living room to watch the marshal get into his car. Murder was such an ugly word, an ugly concept. Other than the rare traffic ticket, no one in her family had ever been in trouble with the law. Marshall Jordan had been evasive. Did the authorities really suspect her of murder?

FOUR

STONA JORDAN CONTEMPLATED the door she'd practically slammed in his face. Wilhelmina McAllister was not what he'd imagined. Her dossier led him to expect her intelligence. His supervisor had called her a viable suspect, but he'd never mentioned her violet-blue eyes or long, auburn hair so dark it was almost black. The woman was breathtaking, even in her old jeans and faded flannel shirt. Red plaid had never looked so good, and he'd never felt such an instantaneous attraction.

He followed the path to the front of the house and his car. Sliding behind the wheel, he fired the engine and turned around. As he pulled down the lane toward the main road, he glanced into his rearview mirror toward the house. Ms. McAllister was standing on her front porch, hands on hips. She looked as defiant as she'd sounded a few minutes ago. Feisty was the description that came to mind. The thought made him smile.

The smile didn't last long. He'd been blindsided by the beautiful woman. It was unsettling. He paused before pulling onto the farm road, picked up the McAllister file and leafed through it again. The folder didn't contain a photo that would have given him a little warning. It didn't contain much information either, mostly notes about her job and friends. Her cousin's death left her without a family. He couldn't help feeling a pang of sympathy for her.

Bob Castillo, his predecessor on this case, had investigated the victims' friends and their acquaintances, as well as Trish Collins's family. According to his notes, Bob hadn't found any evidence connecting Wilhelmina McAllister to the murders. Stona pulled his car onto the paved road. Still, she was the only person with a motive.

TWO HOURS AFTER the marshal's visit, Willie heard an approaching vehicle. Josh's belongings had finally arrived. The driver made seven trips from the van to her living room, stacking the boxes against the wall.

Most contained family keepsakes, clothes and a few of Josh's personal items. A shoe box, or a boot box judging by the label and size, made a rustling sound when she moved it. The lid was secured by a giant rubber band. She'd packed the small box inside a larger one without looking at the contents. Curious now, she removed the rubber band and lifted the lid to reveal Missouri maps, several letters from people she'd never heard of, and two small paperback books—one on Missouri Native Americans and another on the Osage tribe. She also found a brochure advertising the Bushwhacker Museum in Nevada, Missouri.

Nevada.

Josh had spent his last breath warning her to stay away from the town. Did the contents of the box have anything to do with his warning?

She remembered the man she'd seen in the meadow—the figment of her imagination. Could he be real? Taking a deep breath, she shook her head. Time for a reality check. The Native American in her field did not exist. The only connection between the arrowhead and the man was in her mind.

But the contents of the boot box and Josh's warning about Nevada might be linked.

There was only one way to know for sure. She needed to find out everything she could about her cousin's trip to Nevada. She'd phone every number in the box if she had to and check the information available at the museum. Make a trip to Nevada if necessary.

She carried the box to the parlor and settled into the overstuffed chair in front of the hearth. It didn't take long to discover what Josh had been doing.

Looking for their ancestors.

Like her, he must have needed a sense of belonging—of family. Even before Josh's death, she'd experienced a sense of loss, no big family to help celebrate life's special events, no long line of Christmas cards on the mantel, no family reunions. She understood how discovering past generations would intrigue him.

So why the warning about Nevada? How could investigating your lineage be dangerous? She leafed through the books on Native Americans. The Osage seemed to have been the tribe Josh found most interesting. He'd earmarked and highlighted pages in one book about the Osage Nation. Another on a variety of tribes had a chapter dedicated to the same people. It also had highlighted passages. Had Josh believed their family descended from the Osage?

It was nine fifteen before she glanced at the clock—nearly time for bed, and she hadn't even had dinner yet. She'd been caught up in the contents of the box for hours. Setting the small container on her desk, she went into the kitchen, grabbed a snack-sized box of yogurt from the refrigerator, and checked to make sure the back door was locked.

She noticed Marshal Jordan's card on the table where she'd tossed it earlier and carried it back to the parlor, setting it on the desk beside the boot box. Should she tell him what she'd discovered? She shook her head. The man wouldn't be interested in genealogy.

But she was, and not because she wanted to discover her family's history. She was positive someone in Nevada had tampered with her cousin's vehicle, destroying what was left of her family. Josh had warned her away, but she needed answers, and she had a feeling the marshal wouldn't find them for her.

She showered and slipped into a warm nightgown. October evenings in the Ozarks got chilly. Spying the arrowhead beside the basin, she carried the artifact to the bedroom and sat on the edge of her bed to examine it under the lamp on the nightstand.

It was perfect, and she'd pulled it out of a foot-and-a-half deep hole. It was amazing her shovel hadn't damaged the thing. How old was it? Had its maker used it for hunting or in battle? The rust-colored tip still reminded her of blood, and she shivered. Had it also reminded the warrior who fashioned the weapon of blood? She turned the stone over in her hand. Had he believed the illusion made it more powerful, or gave it a truer flight?

Holding the smooth flint in her palm, she studied the surface. Some native tools and weapons could be identified by shape and design. The more primitive the workmanship, the older it was assumed to be. The design itself might tell an expert what tribe it came from. She'd take the arrowhead with her to Nevada and compare it with those at the Bushwhacker Museum. The brochure indicated they had a few artifacts on display.

She jumped up intending to put it in her purse and was caught off guard by a wave of nausea. Her fingers seized, closing around the stone. She couldn't turn the thing loose. Her hand burned, and she whimpered more from fear than pain. The room swirled into darkness.

FIVE

"HURRY, MAMA!" BETH turned from the front window. "They're on the ridge top, riding toward our cabin." She glanced at her four-year-old twin brothers huddled in the corner, their eyes wide with fright. Running to the boys, she picked up James and grabbed Tommy's hand, pulling him toward the bedroom where their mother was opening the window.

Naomi turned to her daughter. "They're on horseback? Osage usually raid on foot."

"They're not today."

Her mother climbed out the window and reached for her sons. Beth passed James into her arms and lifted Tommy's feet and legs over the sill. "Get them away from here while there's still time, Mama."

"You'll be all right?" Naomi's reed-thin voice shook as she stood one twin on the ground and reached for the other.

"I'll be okay, Mama. Go to the dry creek bed and follow it up the draw. Get as far from the cabin as you can."

Both boys were crying, but a sharp word from their mother hushed them.

Beth was frantic to see them gone. "Keep down so they won't see you. Hide in the brush if you hear them coming. I'll be right behind you as soon as I bar the door. Hopefully, they'll think we're still in the house." She began sliding the window down. "Don't wait for me. If you do they'll catch us all."

Beth prayed her family wouldn't be spotted as she ran to the front room and glanced out the window. The riders were bearing down on the cabin. She raced back to the bedroom to glance out. Her mother and brothers were still in the open—only halfway to the creek. The cabin blocked the riders' view, but if one of the savages circled the house he'd see them.

She was their only hope. Drawing the warriors' attention to the front of the house would give Mama time to hide the boys. Instinctively she reached for the rifle. Common sense stopped her. She'd have less chance for survival with a weapon in her hands. They'd use the rifle as an excuse to kill her outright.

Heart pounding so hard she could hear it in her ears, she stepped out onto the porch and faced the warriors who'd stopped their horses in front of the cabin. They sat astride their mounts, shoulders back, heads held high, their bodies rigid with barely suppressed anger.

Savages, her father had called them, and he'd taken pleasure in telling his family grisly stories of the Indians' hideous practices. Facing them now, she believed every word. One warrior carried a lance. The others had bows, their arrows notched and ready.

The men's heads were shaved, except for a wide line of hair running from above their foreheads to the back of their necks, a braid dangling at their nape. Paint and tattoos marred their faces. Most of the white men she knew wore beards. These men didn't even have eyebrows.

The lance carrier's rage poured over her like white-hot lead, encasing her body, restricting her breathing, bonding her in place.

She knew why he was here.

He wanted her father, the father who wasn't here to protect his family, who hadn't bothered to get them to safety before his greed brought Osage retaliation down on them. They were here for retribution. Would killing his daughter satisfy the warriors' bloodlust?

The man with the lance spoke to the rider beside him, his words clipped. That man gave an abrupt nod and directed his attention to her.

"Stone Shaper wants to know if a coward hides inside his lodge and sends a woman out to protect him."

Beth didn't have to ask who the coward was. She shook her head. "My father is away."

A sharp command from the leader sent two warriors into the cabin. The sound of shattering glass and breaking furniture told her they hadn't found who they were looking for. She was nearly knocked over by the warrior bolting out of the door, shouting. What he had to say didn't please the men waiting on horseback.

"Where is he?" Hatred distorted the interpreter's face.

"I don't know." Her own hatred threatened to choke the breath from her body. Hatred, not for these men—they had a right to be outraged. She hated the man who'd not only betrayed the Osage, but his own family as well. Her father was lucky she didn't know his whereabouts. She might just tell them.

"You lie to protect him."

"I'm not lying. I don't know where my father is."

"You will tell us the truth, or I will slit your tongue, and your throat." His horse danced in a half circle, sensing his rider's ire. Without warning the interpreter raised his bow and loosed the notched arrow.

The impact slammed her back against the porch post, pinning her shoulder to the thick slab of wood. Fear numbed the pain. Her father's beatings had taught her to hide any reaction in order to prevent more sadistic abuse. She lowered her eyes, expecting another arrow any second.

A snarl made her glance up. The leader drove his lance into the ground, backhanded the warrior who'd shot her, and jumped from his horse. He strode forward, his gaze locked with hers, and drew his knife.

Beth closed her eyes, unwilling to watch the deathblow fall.

STONE SHAPER STUDIED the small woman with hair the color of early summer corn silk and eyes grey like the soft down on a heron's breast.

Her eyes were closed in fear. She expected to die, yet defiantly lifted her chin giving his blade access to her neck. The fluttering pulse at her throat beat against her soft skin like a small bird fighting to escape a snare.

"I-shta'tha-btla."

BETH FLINCHED. SHE'D seen her own death in the warrior's eyes and prayed it would be quick. She felt his body's heat. His breath brushed her hair and skin. The pain in her arm was nothing compared to the terror he engendered.

"I-shta'tha-btla."

"Woman, Stone Shaper tells you to open your eyes and see."

She recognized the grudging voice of the man who'd wounded her. The leader's hand touched her throat. Her eyes snapped open and she was caught in his consuming gaze. He clipped another order over his shoulder.

"He tells you not to fight him."

Her stomach threatened to give up its contents. His hand glided from her throat to the arrow's shaft, grasping it close to her shoulder. The pressure of his hand against the wound brought beads of moisture to her upper lip, but she didn't take her eyes from his. He spoke softly to her, his voice calm, respectful.

His knife raised, and she knew she was going to die.

The blade sliced down, severing the arrow's shaft.

She clenched her teeth, determined not to make a sound.

Sheathing his weapon, he grasped her upper arms, pressing his body against hers, and lifted her away from the post. She couldn't suppress a whimper as the shaft slid out of the wound.

Blood soaked her dress, smearing the savage's bare chest as he lowered her to the steps.

His hand slipped inside the neck of her gown and tore downward, ripping the buttons, exposing her shoulder and the swell of her breast.

She screamed and slashed at his face with her nails. He grabbed her hands and forced her back against the porch floor. When she tried to kick him, he came down on top of her, his hard, muscular body restricting her movements. His dark eyes, full of anger and determination caught and held her gaze. She could barely breathe, but it wasn't from the crush of his weight. She'd read the truth in his eyes. He would do what he wanted, and she was powerless to stop him. Without breaking eye contact, he shouted something she couldn't understand.

The interpreter responded, his words harsh. After another exchange, the man on horseback called out to her, "Hold still, stupid girl. Let him bind your wound." He spat on the ground. "My knife would have found your heart, but Stone Shaper has decided you will make a useful slave. Obey him or die."

She closed her eyes and nodded her understanding.

The savage moved to her side, sat up and pressed his hand to her stomach, keeping her in place, then thrust his free hand under her skirt. She gasped and stiffened. He didn't give her time to fight him, but jerked down, ripping away a fistful of her threadbare petticoat.

He yelled something and one of the warriors tossed him a skin of water. The hand on her stomach glided up to her unwounded shoulder and he pressed her back against the floorboards. Using his teeth to pull the plug on the water pouch free, he poured the liquid directly into the wound. She jerked in reaction, air hissing into her lungs. He must've poured most of the skin's contents through the wound. When the torment was over the back of her dress felt soaked to the waist.

Hauling her upright, he bound her wound, then surprised her by pulling the torn gown back up over her shoulder. By the time he'd finished, all she felt was numb.

One of his men led Stone Shaper's horse to the porch. The warrior lifted her to the horse's back and vaulted up behind her. She prayed the war party would ride away from the clearing, but they remained where they were.

Two horses were ground-tied at the corner of the cabin. She leaned forward, frantically looking for the warriors they belonged to. Stone Shaper tightened his arm at her waist, cinching her to his body.

Moments later, two savages emerged from behind her home. One brute held a squirming boy under each arm. He was laughing at their struggles. Mercifully, her brothers didn't look hurt, but they were terrified. Another man dragged her mother behind him. Her hair was down, her dress torn and covered with dirt and leaves. Blood trickled from a gash in her lip. She looked dazed.

Beth strained against the arm at her waist. "Leave them alone. You have me, let them go."

The warrior's cold blade touched her throat. She thought her captor was reacting to her demand, but when he reigned his horse around, she saw her father.

"That's mighty noble soundin', daughter." Jackson LaRouche and two men emerged from the woods. All three had rifles trained on the Osage leader. Her father didn't seem concerned about the knife at his daughter's throat. "It appears we have ourselves a standoff, now don't it?" His attention and rifle shifted toward the warriors holding his wife and sons. "It seems to me we both have somethin' the other wants. Maybe we could do some tradin'."

The interpreter nudged his horse forward a step or two. "I do not see anything you have to trade."

"That's right, you don't see it, and you won't until we've come to terms." He angled his head back toward one of the men standing behind him. "My friend here will fetch what you're lookin' for when we get what we want." Jackson nodded toward his wife and sons. "Just because you have them don't mean I'll forget about the furs."

Stone Shaper spoke low, drawing her father's attention. The warrior at his side translated. "We will see that which we seek and talk after." To emphasize his position, her captor touched the knife to her skin. She felt his blade press closer to her throat and prayed her father's arrogance wouldn't end her life.

Jackson didn't blink. "That threat don't hold water with me, red man." He spat in the dirt. "Ain't no woman worth giving up what I want." She couldn't believe she'd heard him right. Not even her father would be that callous. The two trappers with him looked shocked.

The knife lowered as Stone Shaper shouted something to the warrior holding the squalling boys. That man dropped Tommy and held him on the ground with a foot while he grasped James by the hair and put a knife to his throat. Beth and her mother cried out.

"Whoa now!" Jackson took a step forward and raised the hand that wasn't holding the rifle. "I didn't say we couldn't come to an agreement, but if you lay a hand on my boys or my woman, you'll never see your precious sacred bones again. I have a man watchin' them real close, and if we don't come back in one hour, he'll crush 'em into dust. Now I figure three bundles of furs instead of two could persuade us to return your goods, leave this land you prize so much, and never come back. I want my boys and my woman too. A man needs his comforts."

Jackson looked from one warrior to another. "You get what you want, and we make a nice profit on the furs." He inclined his head toward Beth. "Seein' as how you're taken with my daughter, warrior, I'll give her to you as a present to show my good faith."

"Jackson, no!" Naomi cried. "You can't—"

"Shut up, woman. You want our boys to live or not? It's easy to see their leader wants her. Look at how he patched her up. He'd have put his knife in her to finish the job if he didn't. She'll be fine. And you'll be alive. Or would you like to go with her?"

Her mother blanched. "You'll burn in hell for this, Jackson."

"You think I got a choice? I'm tryin' to save you and the boys. Beth understands. Don't you, daughter?"

She allowed all the hatred she felt for her father to show in her eyes. He'd betrayed her.

Jackson shrugged and looked at Stone Shaper. "Is it a trade?"

The two warriors spoke in rapid heated words before the one who spoke English gave her father an answer. "It will be as you say. When the sun is highest in the sky, three risings from now, we will meet in this place to trade."

"And my family?"

"Your woman and sons are yours now. Take them from this place. The girl you have given to us."

"No!" Naomi struggled to free herself from the savage's grip. "Jackson, you can't let them—"

"I told you to shut up, woman." He turned to Stone Shaper. "Agreed."

With a nod from Stone Shaper, her mother and the twins were set free.

The boys scrambled to their mother, hiding their faces in her skirt. She looked from her daughter to her husband and back to her daughter. "Beth?"

The worry and confusion on her mother's face gripped her heart. "Get the boys out of here, Mama, before they change their minds. I'll be okay. If they were going to kill me, they would have done it already."

"Naomi, get over here." Her father bellowed the command. Her mother silently pleaded for forgiveness, before prodding the twins toward their father. In seconds, they disappeared into the woods.

Beth sagged against the savage, weak with relief for her family, and apprehension for her own survival. She hadn't believed a word of what she'd told her mother. Every horror story her father had ever told about the Osage raced through her mind. The best she could hope for was to be given to some old woman as a slave. The worst didn't bear thinking about.

Stone Shaper clipped an order to his men and kneed his horse into motion, carrying her away from the clearing, away from her family. The two rode alone for several miles before the other warriors joined them at the crest of a high ridge.

The men had taken a long time to catch up. Was her family still safe?

Stone Shaper swung his horse around and greeted his men. Her eyes were drawn to the black smoke darkening the sky beyond the woods they'd traveled through. Now she understood why the savages had been delayed.

They'd set fire to her home.

SIX

A PROFOUND SADNESS settled like a damp shroud over Willie. The thick fog of her semiconscious state failed to mask the subtle sense of danger lurking at the edge of her mind.

Reason insisted she was in her room, in her family home. But emotion resisted reason, and swore she was in another time, another place—a place filled with hatred, terror and betrayal, inhabited by strangers she knew intimately.

Gradually, the fog lifted. She was sprawled across the bed, her legs dangling over the side. Pushing up, she glanced at the clock on the nightstand. Six-forty-three. The lamp was on, yet the light filtering through the closed drapes was brighter.

She reached up to brush the hair from her face but couldn't open her fist. The joints in her fingers ached with the effort to loosen her grip. She glanced at her palm. The arrowhead. Last night she'd retrieved the flint from the bathroom and carried it to the bed to examine it. Then things had gone a little weird—the way they had on the ridge top. She couldn't remember much after that. Had she passed out, or simply fallen asleep? She didn't know, but she must've clutched the stone all night.

The artifact flashed hot in her grasp, and she dropped it. Glancing at her palm she stared at the perfect imprint of the arrowhead and remembered.

The images in her mind were vivid, every moment she'd spent with Beth and Stone Shaper sharp, focused.

Stone Shaper was the man in the meadow. She was sure of it. But he didn't really exist. Her throat constricted and she struggled to draw a breath. Had the hallucination in the field carried over into her dreams? She shuddered at the possibility. Was she losing her hold on reality? Her mind rebelled at the possibility.

She glanced at the arrowhead on the floor. It was real. So was Josh's interest in the Osage. And as desperately as she wanted to deny it, Josh and Trish's murderers were also a reality. It might border on psychotic, but she couldn't help but believe everything, even the artifact and last night's vision, were somehow related.

Vision. The word fit. Whatever had happened to her last night was more than a dream. She'd experienced a connection with the warrior—and with Beth. It was like being a voyeur, watching someone's life unfold, or unravel like an old knit shawl.

What a strange analogy—strange for her anyway. She'd never owned a handknit shawl, had never seen one old enough to fray.

But Beth had. She was sure of it.

She hadn't just watched what was happening. She'd been inside Beth and Stone Shaper's heads. She'd felt every emotion—Beth's terror, her feelings of betrayal, Stone Shaper's rage and determination to right a wrong.

And she'd sensed something else in Stone Shaper. The fierce warrior had respected Beth's courage, her willingness to sacrifice herself for her family. Despite the hatred for her father and all whites, he had been compelled to protect Beth. He couldn't help himself.

Cautious, she picked up the arrowhead and stood on shaky legs. Crossing the room, she pulled a Kleenex from the box on the dresser, wrapped the stone and slipped it into the coin pouch in her purse.

Though she'd slept without a blanket, her nightgown was damp with perspiration. She needed a shower—and coffee. She needed coffee.

The dual world sensation didn't abate until late morning. Stone Shaper and Beth were never far from her thoughts. She needed to visit Nevada—right away—despite Josh's cryptic warning.

Josh.... She choked back the tears that were always so close to the surface and took a deep breath. Her cousin would've told her to stop feeling sorry for herself and get on with her life. It was going to take a while. She couldn't even begin to heal until she got some answers. She wasn't even sure what the questions were but had a feeling those answers were in the town Josh had told her to stay away from.

The advantage of being on leave was the ability to get up and go anywhere you wanted when you wanted. Of course, there were always things that needed to be done first. Having her car checked out was on her list of priorities. A quick call to Benson's Auto Service garnered an eleven o'clock appointment thanks to a late cancellation. It was almost ten. After a quick shower she slipped into jeans and a yellow pullover sweater, then platted her still damp hair into a single braid. By ten-thirty, she was ready to go.

After leaving her car at the garage, she decided to risk the lunch crowd at the Come and Get It diner before picking up a few things at the mercantile. A couple were leaving a booth by one of the large windows, and she slipped into the seat. The waitress cleared the table and brought her a menu. After ordering a chef's salad and iced tea, she sat back to watch the people passing the restaurant. The mercantile across the street was busy today, and occasionally someone would enter or exit the real estate office and barber shop.

Halfway through her meal, she noticed the tall man leaving the real estate office. Though he wore jeans and a blue chambray shirt instead of his suit and tie, she recognized Marshal Jordan. He said he'd be in town, but why? And what reason would he have to visit a real estate office? She shrugged. If he was asking about her, he'd be disappointed. Only her close neighbors and a few people at her church knew her, and none of them well. Her family had lived in the next town, and she'd visited the family homestead often as a little girl, but when Josh's family relocated to St. Louis when she was ten, the visits had ended.

The marshal entered the barber shop next. He didn't need a haircut. His dark, thick hair had obviously received a recent trimming. He'd needed a shave yesterday afternoon, but he didn't look like a bar-

bershop-shave type of guy. Apparently, he was still looking for information. But why ask about her in a barbershop? After a moment she
grinned and shook her head. A small-town barbershop was as good a
place to go for gossip as the local beauty parlor.

Well, it was a waste of his time and the taxpayer's money. He wasn't
going to find some deep dark hidden secret in this town or anywhere
else for that matter. She hadn't done anything wrong.

Leaving a tip for the waitress, she picked up the bill and her purse,
walked to the register and paid for lunch. She stepped outside and took
a deep breath as she crossed the street headed for the mercantile. The
brisk fall air carried the earthy scent of autumn. She glanced through
the barbershop's plate glass window as she passed. Stona Jordan sat in
one of the straight-backed chairs lining the wall. He looked up suddenly, and their eyes locked. Unsettled, she looked away and continued on,
but sensed his gaze following her into the store.

———————

STONA TRIED NOT to be obvious as he leaned toward the window
to see where Ms. McAllister was going. When she disappeared into the
next building, he returned his attention to the conversation between
the barber and the man in the chair.

The barber grinned at him and nodded toward the window. "She's
a looker, that one. Comes to town every week or so since she moved
into her uncle's house."

He dropped a hot towel on his customers face and neck, ignoring
the muffled protest. "Guess it's her house now since her cousin died."
He shook his head as he stropped the straight razor. "Too bad about
Josh. His dad used to bring him into the shop for haircuts when he was
little. Always thought he was a real nice boy." Removing the towel, he
used a shaving mug and brush that looked older than he was to lather
the man's face.

"Lost track of the family when they moved to St. Louis. Did hear that Josh lost his folks in a car accident a few years back."

When Stona didn't comment he looked up from his work. "Guess you wouldn't know about Josh, you bein' a stranger here and all. He was killed in a car accident, too, not long ago."

The barber jabbed his thumb in the direction the McAllister woman had gone. "Left that little gal all alone." He paused after drawing the blade across his customer's cheek. "Can't imagine not having anyone to call family. Don't think she had any friends to speak of up there either, or she wouldn't have left them to come to this town. Nothing but memories for her here, and from what I understand, precious few of those."

Stona glanced out the window, then back at the barber. "She doesn't have friends here?"

The man shook his head. "Don't know of any. The only time she leaves her place is to buy supplies or go to church."

"She goes to church? Where?"

"The interdenominational, west of town. Go there myself on occasion. Good Bible-teaching church."

Stona nodded. "She must have friends there."

"Acquaintances, but I wouldn't call them friends." He used the towel to wipe residue lather off his customer's cheeks and neck, then removed the drape-cloth. "Don't get me wrong." He accepted the bills the other man handed him and nodded a goodbye. He turned to Stona. "She's nice enough, just keeps to herself."

He shook out the cloth and waited for Stona to take a seat in the chair. "Guess it's gonna take time for her to get over her cousin's death and settle in here."

Stona was climbing into the barber chair when he saw the subject of their discussion cross the street, grocery bag in hand. She had opted not to pass in front of the barbershop again but angled toward a point beyond the diner. Her jeans and light-yellow sweater fit snug enough to enhance her curves without seeming too tight. Ms. McAllister presented an enticing picture. Stona noticed he wasn't the only man watching her. Even the barber had fallen silent. He frowned at the man.

When she moved out of sight the barber held up the cloth again. "Yessir, she's quite a looker. Now, what can I do for you?"

Stona pulled a ten out of his pocket. "Sorry." He handed the bill to the barber. "I've remembered something pressing I need to take care of."

"Do you want another appointment?" Stona shook his head as he walked out the door. He had no intention of sitting in a barber chair listening to the man sing Willie McAllister's praises. He was working an open investigation, and he had no business being attracted to a woman he might have to arrest for murder.

The mechanic had pulled Ms. McAllister's Honda out of the garage and was handing her the keys when Stona stopped beside her. She looked over, saw him, and immediately frowned. She waited until the mechanic returned to the garage before glaring at him.

"If you want to ask me any more questions, you'll have to wait until I call my attorney. I'm not talking to you without him."

"How do you know I'm not here to arrest you?" He wasn't, of course. He was curious to see her reaction.

She only tilted her head and quirked an eyebrow but remained silent.

"You're not concerned over the prospect?"

She shrugged her shoulders. "I haven't done anything wrong. Do I need to call my attorney?"

He had to admit she was cool under fire. "No. I'm not here to arrest you."

"Are you here to ask me more questions? I'll say it again. Do I need to call my attorney?"

He laughed. She hadn't missed a beat. "No, I'm not here to ask any questions. Just thought I'd say hello as I passed by." He glanced inside her car. A small map, a couple of brochures and an envelope rested in the passenger seat. "Planning a trip?"

"I thought you weren't going to ask me any questions."

"Just curious."

She sighed and shook her head. "I'm taking a short day-trip tomorrow, to visit a museum. If you'll excuse me, I have groceries that need to go in the refrigerator."

He nodded and opened the door for her. She slid behind the wheel, snapping her seatbelt in place.

"Be safe," he cautioned before closing the door. She gave him a brisk nod and started the engine. He barely had time to step back before she gunned the motor, turned the corner, and drove out of sight.

Ms. McAllister bore watching.

SEVEN

WILLIE COULDN'T ESCAPE the uneasy feeling gnawing at her insides as Nevada loomed like a specter in the distance. Josh had tried to warn her about something or someone in the town. It was impossible to know for sure, but she suspected his death was connected to Nevada. His final words had been cryptic, understandable considering he'd been in excruciating pain and shock had set in. She blinked away the tears that misted her eyes and took a deep breath. He'd had so little time left to talk to her. Had he known the killer?

He wouldn't have warned her away if the threat wasn't real. Was her impulsive trip to Nevada a mistake?

Keeping her eyes on the road, she reached for her bag and rummaged through the contents for her coin purse. Unsnapping the pouch, she touched the tissue wrapped artifact, reassuring herself it was still there. Her connection to the thing bordered on obsession.

In her mind everything, the arrowhead, the Osage, the murders, seemed to revolve around Nevada. Logic told her Josh's interest in the Osage was unrelated to the murders, and the arrowhead had nothing to do with any of it. But she couldn't separate them in her mind.

From Highway 71, Nevada looked like an average Missouri town with fast food restaurants and service stations close to the highway exits. Suburbs nudged the businesses along the main roads and a water tower topped the hill.

But downtown Nevada resembled a Missouri town from the mid-eighteen hundreds. If it hadn't been for power lines, traffic, and the modern buildings peppering the business district, she might as well have stepped into the past. She half expected to see hitching posts in front of one of the impressive old granite structures. Two-and three-story, red brick, flat roofed buildings dominated the center of town. Probably built in the 1800s, most were well cared for. Many still housed small shops and businesses.

Her first stop was the Bushwhacker Museum. She was surprised to find it in the basement of the Vernon County Library, a modern single-story red brick structure. The museum could be accessed from inside the library or from a street entrance. She decided to use the library entrance since it was closer to the parking lot.

Downstairs, her attention was drawn to a buggy that held a place of honor in the main room. She stopped at the reception area located close to the outside entrance stairs. A middle-aged man sat behind what looked like a late 50s teacher's desk. Its oak finish had darkened to a rich patina. The man smiled and stood when she approached.

"I'm Greg Brandon, the museum director. If I can be of help, please let me know."

She returned his smile, paid the admission fee, then took the arrowhead from its hiding place. "Actually, I *do* have a question." She removed the tissue from the artifact. "I was planting a sapling the day before yesterday when I found this." She held up the arrowhead. "I'd hoped you might be able to tell me what tribe it's from."

He held out his hand. "May I?"

She drew her hand back, surprised by a swift burst of apprehension.

When the director tilted his head in question, she realized how paranoid she was acting. Giving him an apologetic grin, she placed the artifact in his hand. "I live in southwest Missouri, not far from the Arkansas border. From what I've read, several tribes hunted the area. I thought you might be able to tell me what tribe used it."

The director studied the piece, and then looked up, his face bright with excitement. "This is a wonderful find." He walked to a lighted exhibit and held the stone close to the glass for a better look. Almost reverently, he touched the fluted edge.

She stepped closer. "Be careful. It's sharp."

He nodded. "I can see that. The edges are nearly perfect. Its owner must have lost it soon after it was crafted. But this actually isn't an arrowhead. It's too large. Most arrowheads are half the size of this one, and bird points are considerably smaller. This is a spearhead." He handed the artifact to her. "Let me show you some examples."

Clutching the stone to her heart, she followed the director to a framed display of fluted stones on the wall beside the Native American cubical. The artifacts were arranged in an oval. The larger ones—what she now recognized as spearheads—lined the outside, with the smaller arrowheads placed inside the line of spearheads and the tiny bird points arranged in the center.

Two of the spearheads were larger than hers, wider and thicker. A couple of the spearheads were similar in shape to hers, and might've come from the same tribe, but they lacked the definition of her piece. The edges were duller, well used. The one in her hand could have been crafted yesterday.

"I don't see any made from silver-pink flint like this one."

"Your spearhead's unique. Small pockets of pink flint can be found in Oklahoma, though Missouri flint will occasionally have narrow veins of rose. He walked back to his desk. "It's just a guess on my part, but this looks like an Osage point. I have a friend who might be able to identify it. I'll give you his number." He took one of his cards from the holder on the desk, turned it over, and wrote a name and phone number on the back. "His name is James Sutton. He and his wife live in an old mansion built around nineteen hundred." He laughed. "Some of the locals claim it's haunted, but the Suttons have never mentioned anything unusual. You know how rumors get started."

She silently commiserated with the couple. A week ago, she might've considered the rumors as just that, rumors. Now she wasn't so sure.

He held out his hand. "This card is mine. If you need any further assistance, don't hesitate to call me." He cleared his throat. "Would you consider donating the spearhead to our museum?"

Willie's hand tightened around the flint and she fought the unreasonable urge to hide it away. Instead, she took the card. "Perhaps later. If I do decide to part with it, I promise to consider your museum."

He smiled. "Thank you."

She spent an enjoyable hour looking through the museum's displays. Small glass front cubicles lined the perimeter of the room, each offering a glimpse of history. Cookware, utensils, tools, weapons, and fashions gave insight to everyday life from early Native American to World War II.

That afternoon, during lunch at a local restaurant, she phoned the Suttons to ask if it would be convenient for her to drop by with the spearhead. Mrs. Sutton answered on the second ring. Willie introduced herself and explained her reason for calling.

"I was hoping Mister Sutton might be able to identify a spearhead I've found."

"Jim is at work, but he should be home around seven-thirty. You could drop by then. I know he'll be interested in seeing your artifact."

"I hate to disturb him so late in the evening. Can we arrange for me to visit another day?"

"Seven-thirty isn't late for us if it's convenient for you. Do you need directions to our home?"

"Seven-thirty's fine. Mister Brandon told me you didn't live far from Nevada." Setting the meeting later would give her more time to explore the Osage village site.

"That's right. It's about fourteen miles east on Highway 54. You'll see a white, two-story home on the right, with a large four-columned front porch. It sits about a hundred feet off the highway."

"That should be easy enough to find. I'll see you at seven-thirty then, and thank you."

Heavy gray clouds rolled in as she drove to the larger of the two villages mentioned in the brochure. Hopefully the rain would hold off.

For a state historical site, the Osage village wasn't easy to find. But with the help of a local mail carrier, she found the entrance and a small white-gravel parking lot. Hers was the only car in the lot.

A long uphill path led to a gazebo-like kiosk. Thunder rumbling in the distance drew her eyes to the southwest, and a gray green sky. Grabbing her umbrella, she headed up the hill at a brisk pace. Judging from the building storm clouds, this wasn't going to be a leisurely stroll through the historical landmark.

Had Josh visited the site? There was no way of knowing. But given the brochure and the fact that he had made a trip to Nevada, she assumed he had.

Small wooden plaques, mounted on four-foot angled posts, explained the different stops on the trail. One plaque pointed out a view of Blue Mound, the original burial place of the great Osage chief, Pawhuska.

She felt a connection to this place, a warm sense of belonging. Was it because Josh had been here? Another plaque caught her eye. The inscription indicated a chair-sized rock along the path. The Osage had used the small limestone outcropping to grind corn and other grains. The wide, shallow indentations in the rock evidenced decades—perhaps centuries—of use.

Reaching out, she touched the rough depression, picturing the generations of women grinding grain at this place. Without warning the stone flashed hot. She tried to jerk back but her hand wouldn't budge. She couldn't move her body. Her heart slammed against her ribs so hard it hurt—no, it hurt because she couldn't breathe.

Why couldn't she breathe?

EIGHT

WHY WAS IT so hot? Beth tried to push the quilt away from her face, but it kept coming back. Was Mama baking this morning? She shoved at the quilt again and kicked to free her legs, but the more she struggled the tighter the blankets became. They were suffocating her.

The twins were up. She could hear them fighting again, whooping and yipping like a band of wild Ind—

"Mama!" She surged forward but the blanket held her fast. "Mama, run, hide!"

STONE SHAPER PULLED the buffalo robe closer around the ranting woman as they rode through the village. No one heard her. The welcoming shouts of his people covered her weak cries. There was good cause for celebration.

The sacred bundle was once again with the Osage.

He caught sight of his cousin and called out to her. "Raven, find Brings Peace. Ask him to come to my lodge." She tilted her head in question but when he offered no explanation she nodded and made her way through the crowd toward the medicine chief's lodge.

His captive whimpered. The fever had come upon her in the night. The woman was no longer in this world. She fought the demons who claimed her mind.

Nudging his pony into a faster pace, he bypassed the curious crowd. There would be time later to give his own accounting of their raid.

He carried his captive into his lodge and laid her on the bed of furs beside the fire Raven had built. Since his mother's death last winter, he'd occupied the lodge alone. His cousin kept it clean and warm. Most of his meals were shared with her family.

Unwrapping the robe enshrouding the woman, he used his knife to cut the clothes away from her. Oblivious, she didn't protest, or try to hide her nakedness from him. Pouring water into an earthen bowl, he dipped a cloth into the tepid liquid and wiped the sheen of perspiration from her heated skin.

He had no qualms about touching her. She was his captive. He had the right of life or death over her, the right to use her as it suited him.

She mumbled and tried to push his hand away. He sighed. Her fate would be decided later. For now, his only concern was her survival. That he cared surprised him. She was white, and the daughter of his enemy. He should hate her. But he didn't. He respected her, wanted to know more about this woman with fear in her eyes and courage in her heart. He wanted her to survive. When she shivered, he pulled another robe over her trembling body and waited for Brings Peace.

The medicine chief entered Stone Shaper's lodge, took one look at the sleeping woman and shook his head. "Your captive will bring trouble to our people."

"She is mine by her father's words. His gift to appease us. There will be no retaliation from the whites."

Brings Peace squatted beside the girl and placed his hand on her forehead. She thrashed and muttered, calming only when he removed his hand. The healer's eyes were full of concern when he looked up.

"The fever has taken her mind. Few of only the strongest Osage warriors return to this world once they have crossed into the next. She is only a weak, white woman. She will not survive."

Stone Shaper seldom disagreed with his mentor, but he shook his head. "She is not as weak as you believe. This woman did not cower behind a barred door when we came for her father. She is little more than a girl, yet she stood alone facing six warriors to give her mother and brothers time to escape us." He turned the woman to her side, ignoring her weak protests, and bared her back. "If she were not strong, could she have withstood this?" Old scars, and recent welts and bruises marred her back. "I discovered these when I bound her wounds."

The older warrior traced his finger across a thin white scar that ran from under the bandage across her back. "This was the act of a coward. Your slave was only a child when she received this mark. Children are to be cherished and protected. Who would treat a child so?"

Stone Shaper eased the woman to her back and pulled the robe over her trembling body. "Her father."

The medicine chief bowed his head, slowly shaking it. "Many white men have no honor."

"Even as a slave she will find less to fear with us, I think."

Brings Peace glanced up. "I still fear her people will come after her."

Stone Shaper shook his head. "No one will bother to find her. Her father gave her to me with less concern for her welfare than he would have for a stray dog that irritated him."

"And her mother? Will she send people to find her daughter?"

"The woman was too afraid of her husband to stand up for the girl. My captive begged her mother to leave, promising we would not hurt her. She finally turned and followed her husband into the woods. Perhaps she too believes the girl is safer with us."

Brings Peace set his medicine pouch on the ground and removed the bloodied scrap of cloth that covered the wound, tossing it into the fire. After testing her red and swollen shoulder, he motioned for Stone Shaper to turn her again. He removed the dressing, discarding it as he had the other, and examined the ragged hole where the arrow had passed through. Retrieving a palm-sized strip of rabbit hide from his medicine pouch, he set it on the fur. He removed a smaller bag from the pouch and sprinkled half of the crushed leaves and herbs it contained onto the hide. Pressing the poultice to the wound, he secured it with wide strips of rawhide.

Stone Shaper rolled the still mumbling woman to her back, allowing Brings Peace to examine the entry wound more thoroughly.

"Her wound has festered." The medicine chief's tone indicated he held little hope for her recovery. Once more he reached into his medicine pouch and this time pulled out a flask.

Stone Shaper couldn't hide his surprise when he saw the metal container that held whiskey. Brings Peace chuckled. "Do not be concerned, my friend. I have not fallen victim to the white man's poison. Joseph tells me the spirits in the drink can stop the festering before it begins. He has used it many times to prevent the fever that often comes with such wounds."

Joseph had been what the whites called a missionary before he came to live in the village. A wise man, Joseph did not interfere in the struggle between the Osage and his own people. Brings Peace considered him a brother, and said his friend was more Osage than white. Only a few in the village were troubled by his presence.

Stone Shaper trusted his mentor's opinion, but trusting any white was not in his nature.

"Joseph is respected for his knowledge of healing, but the fever has already taken my slave. Can the spirits cure as well as prevent the festering?"

Brings Peace shrugged. "He never spoke of it, but I doubt it will hurt the girl."

Stone Shaper still had his doubts. "She is too weak to swallow and will choke."

"It is to be poured into the wound. We fight the arrow's poison directly with the white man's poison." He opened the flask. "You will need to keep her still. Joseph tells me the whiskey burns when it is poured on raw flesh."

Stone Shaper grasped her upper arms, pinning her against the furs as Brings Peace poured the liquid fire into the wound. The girl went rigid. She groaned, a deep guttural sound, and fought his restraint. Working quickly, Brings Peace sprinkled the remainder of the herb mixture onto a second rabbit skin and applied it to the wound, securing it as he had the poultice on her back.

Unshed tears sparkled on her eyelashes by the time they had finished.

The medicine chief studied his patient. "She did not scream."

"I believe she has learned to hide her pain. She did not cry out even when Bear's arrow pierced her body."

"It is a good lesson to learn." Brings Peace returned the flask and small bag to his medicine pouch before looking at Stone Shaper. "It is whispered you humiliated Bear in front of our warriors."

"Bear humiliated himself by allowing his anger to control his actions. This woman is little more than a girl, yet she faced us alone without weapons. Her courage demanded our respect, not the arrow Bear loosed.

"He acted without honor and might have prevented us from recovering and returning the sacred bundle to our people. My retaliation was justified."

"I fear you have made an enemy today. Bear will not forget this humiliation, or who caused it." He glanced at the sleeping woman. "Be cautious." Getting to his feet, Brings Peace walked to the lodge entrance. "I will return tomorrow and see if Joseph's medicine is as good as he claims."

Pausing, the medicine chief glanced from one end of the rectangular lodge to the other. "Raven keeps your lodge in order now, but she will soon accept a husband. You have mourned my daughter too long. She would agree with me when I tell you it is time to take another wife to see to your comforts. Tallgrass has three daughters who are yet unmarried. The third is young but still a woman. He would not be opposed to you as a son-in-law. His daughters are easy to look upon and gentle in temperament." The smile he bestowed on Stone Shaper was slightly teasing. "I have seen how they watch you. I believe you could have your choice, or make them all your wives. This empty lodge would soon be filled with children's laughter."

———————

BETH SHIVERED WITH the cold. She needed to get up and add kindling and logs to the coals in the hearth, but she couldn't seem to force herself to crawl out from under the covers. Her body shook so hard it hurt.

Why had Mama let the fire go out? "Mama, please light the fire. The boys will get cold."

She cringed when a burst of cold air struck her body. But suddenly there was new warmth. Mama must have started the fire, the heat seeming to radiate right under the covers. She was drawn to it, pulled into the warmth and held there. It was wonderful....

———————

STONE SHAPER FELT the woman relax against him and knew she slept once more. Three days and nights had passed since he'd carried her into his lodge. Three days and nights she had battled the demons that came with the fever. Brings Peace returned each day to care for her. Even Joseph had visited the girl. He had placed his hand on her head and prayed to the white man's God for her healing.

The fever left her before morning tinged the eastern sky with light. Her skin cooled, and she no longer battled monsters. She slept now, a healing sleep so deep she didn't wake when he slipped beneath the robe, pulling her against his warm body.

He didn't question the relief he felt. She was his slave. It was only natural for him to want her to live. A dead slave held no value. She sighed and snuggled closer, something she had become accustomed to doing while the fever controlled her mind. He curved his body around hers and rested his chin on top of her head. He intended to keep her, had made the decision when he'd seen the spark of defiance in her eyes. He needed a woman to clean his lodge and cook his meals—to see to his every need. Keeping her was logical. No one would question him.

NINE

AGAIN. IT HAD happened *again.* Willie pushed away from the large rock she'd been sprawled across—the rock she'd been touching before she'd—what—lost consciousness, gone into a trance? Climbing to her feet, she stood on wobbly legs and tried to sort out her chaotic thoughts.

She'd tried to shrug off the first vision, attributing it to stress, both physical and mental. But a second episode couldn't be explained away. The first occurrence had disturbed her. This one terrified her. It could happen again, with no more warning than a moment of dizziness. That was what frightened her the most, not knowing when or where she would succumb to whatever was going on in her brain.

What time was it? She glanced at the sky. Heavy clouds hid the sun, their dusky-green cast warning of the storm bearing down on the area. Fishing the phone out of her jacket pocket, she tried to turn it on. The battery was dead. How had that happened?

She needed to get to the car before the clouds opened up. Back-tracking, she followed the path, practically running toward the parking lot, but was forced to stop at the kiosk to catch her breath and rest her shaking legs. Apparently, the vision, or whatever it was, had taken its toll on her body as well as her mind.

From her position on the hill above the parking area, she watched an older blue pickup pull out of the lot. She hadn't noticed anyone on the walking trail. If anyone had been on the path, they would've seen her and offered help. The driver had probably been turning around. Or had he been checking out her car? Thankfully she'd remembered to lock her doors.

She waited until the truck was out of sight before leaving the kiosk. The only other vehicle she saw was a dark sedan stopped in front of a row of mailboxes.

After climbing into the car, she relocked the doors and scanned the area for anything suspicious. The dark sedan parked beside the line of mailboxes hadn't moved. The man behind the wheel was hunched over, apparently talking on his phone. There wasn't enough light to see his face clearly, and she was beginning to get nervous. Her phone wasn't working, and she was alone out here—really alone.

Leaning back against the headrest, she sighed.

The sky had darkened considerably. Starting her car, she turned on the headlights and checked the dashboard clock. Five minutes after seven. She'd be cutting her seven-thirty appointment close.

A few drops of rain hit the windshield as she pulled out of the parking lot, but not enough for the wipers. She didn't remember much about the trip back to Highway 54. Her mind was too caught up in what had happened at the village. She'd never felt so out of control, so vulnerable. Twice—the phenomenon had happened twice with no forewarning—as though her consciousness had been catapulted back in time. She'd been there, inside their minds, sharing their lives, their thoughts, feeling Beth's terror and Stone Shaper's concern for his white slave. Had she hallucinated it all? Could hallucinations happen while you were unconscious? She honestly didn't know what to think.

The rain began in earnest before she reached the highway. The wind picked up as she turned east. She wouldn't have spotted the old mansion without the aid of the Sutton's front porch lights. The storm was on top of her. Lightning flashed with thunder crashing simultaneously. The wind roared, and she fought to keep her lightweight car between the ditches. Hail stones the size of large marbles pelted the windshield as she turned onto the driveway. If they got much larger the glass wouldn't survive the pummeling. She shut off the motor, released her seatbelt and waited for the storm to abate. Lightning struck somewhere close by, sizzling like cold water on a hot skillet. Thunder shook the car. A huge oak tree silhouetted against the brightly lit porch whipped and bent like a willow in the wind. She held on to the steering wheel as gusts rocked the car.

The ancient tree she'd been watching groaned and shrieked in protest as it twisted free of the earth and plunged toward her car. She lunged across the seat, wedging herself between the gear shift and seat backs as the massive oak collapsed.

TEN

STONA JORDAN WHEELED into the drive seconds behind Willie McAllister, his car skidding to a stop directly behind hers. The pea green sky and hail had been the harbingers of a full-blown storm. They needed to find cover—fast. He hoped the occupants of the house were at home and had some type of storm shelter. They were about to receive guests.

Leaving his lights on bright, he shoved his car door open against the hurricane-force wind and climbed out. Pulling his suit jacket off he struggled toward Ms. McAllister's vehicle. It wouldn't give her much protection, but it would have to do. Hunching forward, he powered through the deluge like a quarterback driving through the opposing line. A fierce gust of wind knocked him off balance. Before he could re-cover, he was lifted off his feet, dropped onto the pavement, and rolled against a sapling that edged the drive.

Tornado. It really did sound like a freight train. He grabbed the small tree, anchoring himself against the very real danger of being sucked up into the storm's vortex. Thankfully, the funnel hadn't touched the ground yet and was moving away fast. The hail was gone, but the rain still pelted his body, washing away the mud and debris he'd picked up during the fall.

The huge tree in front of the house still whipped unnaturally. Suddenly time seemed to radically change. Everything slowed to a macabre ballet as the oak tilted and rolled in place, its roots tearing free of the sodden earth. He swore he heard the leviathan groan as it ceded the battle to stay upright.

Willie. He surged to his feet. "Willie, Get down! Get down now!" He fought the wall of the storm to get to her.

There wasn't enough time.

The tree thundered down on top of her car, the sound deafening. His car lights illuminated tree-sized branches engulfing her vehicle. Leaf-covered limbs hid it from his view. Heart slamming against his ribs, Stona battled the splintered oak to get to her.

His first look at the mangled vehicle nearly stopped his heart. One huge branch angled across the hood and windshield, crushing them. Another had mutilated the entire back half of the vehicle.

No one could have survived that.

He closed his eyes against the mental image of her broken, bleeding body being lifted from the wreckage. He remembered she had no one left to care whether she lived or died.

He cared. And suddenly it was important to him that she not be alone—even in death.

He climbed into the debris of the fallen tree, using the limbs to lever himself onto the crumpled hood of the car. Steeling himself against what he was about to see, he cleared the thick branch and peered through the crumbling windshield. His car's headlights focused mainly on the rear of her vehicle. Very little light penetrated the tree's yellow leaves at the front of the vehicle. The interior was dark. He needed his flashlight and was about to climb back over the branch when he heard the groan.

"Miss McAllister?" He leaned into the car. "Miss McAllister—Willie—can you hear me?"

A door at the house slammed. "Who's out there?" The man's voice was almost lost in the shrieking wind.

Stona pulled back and stood on the branch. Grabbing a limb for balance, he shouted. "Call 911 and bring a light!" He didn't take the time to explain. Leaning as far into the car as possible, he tried rousing her again. "Willie, can you talk to me?"

"I—what happened?" Her voice was shaky but strong, considering. His relief at her response took him by surprise. He'd failed to distance himself from the situation. Not good.

"Was I in an accident?"

"Not exactly. Do you remember the tree coming down on your car?"

"Tree? I—wait. It was storming."

He instinctively ducked when lightning cracked nearby. "It still is. Are you hurt?"

"My head hurts, and my side feels bruised, but I think I'm okay."

He was encouraged by the fact that she was feeling anything and was able to communicate coherently.

"Who are you?"

The question jarred him. "You don't remember me?"

"Should I? I can't see you, and I can barely hear you over the wind. Are you Mister Sutton?"

"No. I'm Stona Jordan."

"The marshal?"

He smiled at her incredulous tone. "Yes, that one."

"What are you doing here?"

He didn't think she'd like the idea of him following her. "We'll talk about it once we get you out of here." He thought he saw lights flitting through the branches and leaned up. The couple from the house were hurrying toward them, the beams from their flashlights bouncing as they ran. He stuck his head back into the car. "I'll be right back."

He climbed down and intercepted the man and woman. "You probably shouldn't go any farther. There's broken glass and torn metal everywhere. You could get hurt."

The man seemed uneasy and kept glancing at the gun holstered at Stona's hip. "I'm Marshal Stona Jordan." He was about to reach into his suit coat when he realized he wasn't wearing it. He must have lost it when the storm tossed him against the sapling. Hopefully, it hadn't been blown away.

He turned to the man. "May I borrow your light?"

"Of course." He handed Stona the flashlight.

It took no more than a couple of sweeps of the light to locate his coat. The wind had plastered it against the inside of the front passenger tire. Bending, he pulled it free, then returned to the couple to show them his badge and identification.

The man, who looked to be in his mid-forties, extended his hand. "I'm James Sutton, and this is my wife Mary."

Stona nodded to the middle-age woman before returning his attention to her husband. "Were you able to contact the authorities?"

"Yes. The sheriff's on his way and fire rescue won't be far behind. The nearest paramedics were just finishing a call. They'll be here soon. Is there anything we can do to help?"

"I'll need to move my car. Is there a place I can park it where it won't be in the way?"

"You can pull on the front lawn. Don't worry about the grass. It won't be the only vehicle out there tonight. I imagine there's going to be first responders all over the place."

"Thanks."

Mary Sutton touched his arm to stop him when he started to walk away. "Is that Miss McAllister in the car? She was supposed to meet with us this evening."

At a nod from Stona, she clutched her throat. "Is she okay?"

"As far as I can tell she'll be all right. If you'll excuse me, I need to move my car and get back to her."

"Of course, Marshal."

He pulled his car close to the base of the uprooted tree, locked it, and pocketed the keys before returning to the couple.

Mrs. Sutton shoved a couple of heavy quilts into his arms. "I thought you might need these."

"Thank you, ma'am. I'll see you get them back." Mr. Sutton offered his umbrella. Stona shook his head. "You keep it. I'm already soaked. You might want to wait on the porch where you can stay dry." They nodded and sprinted toward the house.

Clutching the quilts to his chest, he climbed back into the wreckage, the flashlight's beam his only light now. Directing the beam at what was left of the car, he was amazed she had survived. If the massive tree hadn't twisted on its way down, the largest branch would have landed directly across the front seats. She would've been crushed.

"Marshal?"

He bent toward the windshield and aimed the light into the vehicle's interior. "I'm here." His first good look at her situation was disheartening. The car had wrapped around her like a cocoon, the seats bending to offer a buffer between her and the torn metal. She wasn't climbing out of there without more help than he could give her.

"What's happening?"

"Emergency crews and paramedics are on their way." Unfolding the blanket, he draped it over the top of the car, across where the windshield used to be to keep the rain out of her face. He ducked under the makeshift tent. "We'll get you out of here as soon as possible. How do you feel?"

"Like the middle part of a sandwich."

He laughed and raised the beam of light to her face. When she blinked rapidly, he moved it out of her eyes. Blood trailed into her left eyebrow from a small gash in her hairline. He reached into the back pocket of his slacks for the folded handkerchief he kept there. It was as soaked as his clothes, but clean. Squeezing the excess moisture out of the material, he reached in and carefully wiped the blood away.

She winced when he placed the cloth over the cut. "I didn't even know that was there."

"It isn't deep, but you've got a good-sized bump on your head." The high-pitched wail of a siren drew his attention. "Looks like the sheriff's here. I'll go talk to him."

MAYBE THE SHOCK was wearing off, but suddenly she was terrified at being left alone in the darkness, in this metal coffin. With unbridled clarity, she knew what every person she'd ever helped extricate from a demolished automobile felt—what Josh had felt. She struggled to free her arm and, reaching out, grasped his hand. "Don't leave me, please."

His fingers closed around hers. "Okay, I won't. Stay calm."

Stay calm. He had no idea what he was asking of her—or maybe he did. His firm grip on her hand was like an anchor holding her in place through a storm that not only raged around her, but within her as well.

The light he held illuminated his face, giving her a glimpse of his concern. They hadn't parted on friendly terms. She was surprised by his attitude, and grateful.

He lifted the cloth from her forehead. "The bleeding stopped. From the size of the knot, I imagine your head still hurts."

"You never told me why you were here."

"We don't need to talk about that right now."

"It's better than wondering when they're going to get here with the can opener. I'm beginning to feel like a sardine. So, why are you here?"

He admired her tenacity but right now it was inconvenient. "You probably won't like my answer."

"Try me."

"I was following you."

ELEVEN

"YOU WERE WHAT?"

"I was follow—"

"Marshal Jordan?"

Stona squeezed Willie's hand before letting it go. "I'll be right back. I won't go far."

He climbed out from under the blanket before she could protest and glanced toward a sheriff's vehicle parked where his had been, its emergency lights still flashing. The car's headlights cast the man standing in front of the car in silhouette.

"I'm Marshal Jordan."

"Marshal, I'm Sheriff's Deputy Roberts. Mister Sutton tells me there's a woman—a Miss McAllister—inside the vehicle. Is she all right?"

"She's conscious, and claims to be unharmed, but she's trapped."

"Fire rescue is right behind me. It's gonna take them a while to get her out, though. They'll need to cut part of that tree away before they can get to her."

"She's an air-vac nurse, so she's familiar with how long rescue efforts take."

The shrill wail of sirens and foghorn warning blasts from a fire truck heralded the arrival of fire rescue.

The deputy moved out of the headlight's beam. "I'll let them know what we have here."

"Good. I'll let Miss McAllister know what's happening." He ducked back under the blanket. "Fire Rescue is here."

"Yes, I heard. Will you stay with me?" She seemed calmer now, but her voice still trembled.

"I'll stay as long as I'm not in the way." He directed the light to her face again. "You're awfully pale."

She tried to laugh. "Most people trapped in cars are pale. I just have a headache—and a strong desire not to be left alone in here."

"You're sure you're all right?"

"I'm sure. Stop worrying about me." He smiled over the irritation in her voice.

He stayed with her while the crew used chainsaws to cut away the limbs and branches blocking access to the car. After nearly an hour they were ready to get her out.

"It's almost over." He squeezed her hand. "They need room to work, but I'll be close. I'll see you again as soon as you're free."

———————————

SHE WAS ALONE again.

But not for long. No more than a minute passed before a fire rescue worker leaned as far into the car as he could.

"Hi, I'm Jake—Jake Arnold. The marshal says you're an air-vac nurse, so you probably know the routine better than I do."

Willie tried to shake her head. "Not from this angle, I don't."

The man laughed. "Then maybe you won't be bored." He unfolded a large thick pad. "The roof has to come off so we can get you out of here. We'll use cutters and combo-tools to free the roof from the front half and middle of the chassis. It'll be loud, but not too bad. The back half of your car is crushed. We'll have to use a rotary saw to cut across the roof behind the front seats. You probably know it's going to be loud."

"Yes. What about fire?"

"Your car's gas tank is intact, so there shouldn't be a risk of fire. Once we lift the roof off, we'll be able to get you out pretty quick." He spread the blanket over her. "I know this'll feel a little claustrophobic, but we shouldn't take long."

He was right. Once the blanket cast her in darkness, she fought the urge to gasp for breath. She wished the hands covering the top of her head were the marshal's instead of her rescuer—wished the voice soothing her as the firefighters worked was his. She couldn't understand it, but she needed him.

"Marshal?"

Jake answered her call. "He's right outside the car, about ten feet away. He can't hear you for the hydraulics generator. We've cut through the window and door frames. There's only a foot or so to go with the saw." A few minutes later she heard the roof break free and the grunts of her rescuers as they lifted the top away from the chassis. They used the jaws to pull the seat backs away from her.

She sat up before anyone could stop her, shoving the blanket away from her head. Jake nearly panicked. "You need to stay still and let us put you on the backboard."

"I don't need a backboard. I just want out of here."

"But, ma'am, you should wait for the paramedics."

"I appreciate your concern, and all of your help. You are as good as any team I've ever worked with. But my back and extremities are fine. If you'll help me out of here, I'll prove it to you."

Strong arms came around her shoulders and under her knees. She was eased away from the steering wheel and lifted out of the car. Grabbing the man's neck for balance, she glanced up to see Stona Jordan's eyes narrowed on her.

"I've heard doctors are difficult patients. Apparently, nurses are too." Nestling her against his chest, he walked to the waiting ambulance.

"Put me down. I'm not hurt."

"The knot on your head is beginning to discolor and the gash needs to be seen to." He lowered her to the waiting gurney. "Let the paramedics check you out."

She gave in semi-gracefully, scowling at him but turning a smile on the EMTs while they checked her vitals. After cleaning and bandaging the wound on her head, one of the men suggested they take her to the hospital for further tests. She shook her head and winced when the action escalated her headache.

The older of the two paramedics gave her a concerned look. "Your eyes seem fine, but you could still have a mild concussion."

"I know the symptoms. I promise I'll get help if I need to."

"Is there someone at home to take care of you tonight?"

"No, but I'm fine."

"If you won't go to the hospital at least find someone to stay with you tonight."

"I will, thank you." When she started to climb off the gurney Stona was there to lift her down. She didn't protest the arm he slipped around her, since she was still a little shaky from her ordeal.

The EMT tilted his head toward her but spoke to Stona. "I'm serious. She doesn't need to be alone tonight."

"I'll make sure she calls someone."

Did they suddenly forget she was there? She glanced at the younger paramedic. "Are we finished here?" At his nod, she turned to Stona. "I need to talk to Mister and Missus Sutton."

He glanced toward the house. "The deputy's talking to them right now. I don't know how long they'll be. You can wait in my car, and I'll have them come to you when they're finished." She didn't argue. The temperature had grown markedly cooler after the storm. By the time they reached his vehicle she was shivering.

After settling her in the front passenger seat, he reached into the back, grabbed a light blanket and wrapped it around her shoulders. "Are you sure you're okay?"

"I think I'm just experiencing aftermath."

He smiled. "I don't doubt it."

One of the firefighters sprinted over to them. She recognized Jake. He held her purse out to her. "Miss McAllister, we found this in the floorboard of your car."

Accepting the purse, she returned his smile. "Thank you again for helping me. Please let everyone know how much I appreciate what they've done tonight."

"I will. We're all glad you walked away from this one. We're packing up to head back to the station. The paramedics have already left." He shined his light toward her destroyed vehicle. "Is there anything else you need from the car before we go?"

"The papers in my glove compartment."

"They're in your purse. We figured you'd need them."

"Yes, I will. Thank you again."

The fireman paused, then cleared his throat. "I guess you'll be staying in Nevada tonight. I drove my own car here. I can wait until you're ready to go, then drive you back to town and help you find a place to stay. After you're settled in, maybe we could have a late dinner."

"Miss McAllister won't be staying in Nevada tonight." Stona's voice was mild, but his words were clipped.

She gave Stona an incredulous look. They hadn't discussed her plans. His assertion and the way he'd spoken to Jake were almost territorial, which was a ridiculous assumption on her part. They barely knew each other.

The marshal caught her expression and relented. "The medics don't want her staying by herself tonight. I'll see her home and make sure someone stays with her."

Jake shrugged and nodded before turning to run his light down the trunk of the fallen tree. "It's gonna look different around here without that tree."

The light's beam slowly drifted to the base of the uprooted oak and the hole it had left behind. Willie's gaze followed and caught a reflection. Curious, she stepped out of the car.

"There's something in there." She walked closer to the fallen tree for a better look. Both men followed, Jake aimed the beam toward the hole.

She gasped and stumbled back against Stona. "Is—is that what I think it is?"

The light wavered, and so did Jake's voice. "Yeah, is that what she thinks it is?"

TWELVE

THE SKELETON SEEMED to be climbing out of its ancient grave. The oak's roots were tangled in the chest cavity and under the pelvic bone as though boosting its long-time companion to the surface. Bony arms reached above the grinning skull, embracing a gnarled root. One knee lifted high, seemingly frozen in mid-jump. The other foot was submerged in the thick, murky puddle at the bottom of the hole.

Jake turned to Stona. "Are we looking at a crime scene?"

"If we are, it's an old one. You'd better call the deputy."

The fireman didn't bother walking to the front porch. "Deputy Roberts, get over here, fast!"

Willie jumped at the unexpected shout and might have joined the skeleton in the hole if Stona hadn't grabbed her arm.

The deputy and the Suttons hurried toward them, as did the fire crew. Stona took Willie's hand and returned to his vehicle. Opening the driver's door, he reached in and switched on the high beams, spotlighting the grisly scene.

She was inexplicably drawn to the macabre form. She pulled free of Stona's hand and moved into the light. The past few hours, the storm, nearly being crushed by the tree, the bones—even the growing crowd seemed surreal. She took a deep breath, needing to alleviate her anxiety.

Stona put his hands on her shoulders and she flinched. The man moved like a cat. She hadn't heard him come up behind her.

He bent close. "Careful. The dirt's loose and muddy. You could slip."

His presence comforted her, and the next deep breath she took was in relief. "How do you suppose he came to be buried here?"

Deputy Roberts and the Suttons had only just arrived. The deputy was close enough to hear her question. He removed his hat, finger-combed his hair and put the hat back on his head.

"That's a good question." He glanced at Stona. "I wonder how long it's been there."

Stona shrugged. "Longer than the tree, I'd guess. Care to estimate how old it is?"

The officer scratched the five o'clock shadow on his jaw. "Couple hundred years, maybe longer. That was a mighty big oak."

"Call your boss and let him know what we have. The sheriff will know who to contact."

Willie looked up at Stona. "Can we cover him with something? He wouldn't want to be gawked at."

"That's a good idea."

"I've got a tarp in the garage." Mr. Sutton circumvented the downed tree and pulled a set of keys from his pocket. He activated the garage door remote and a few minutes later handed a folded blue tarp to Jake, who climbed the horizontal tree trunk and draped the plastic over the bones.

Stona turned to the deputy. "I suggest you tape off the area. As soon as word gets out, you'll have a crowd to contain."

The deputy nodded. "Marshal Jordan, would you mind staying until the sheriff gets here? I might need some help."

Stona hadn't released Willie's shoulders, and could feel her trembling. He bent to her ear. "Can you wait a little longer?"

Mrs. Sutton glanced over. "She can wait in the house. It's warmer."

She shook her head. "Thank you, but I'll be fine in the car."

His fingers tightened. "This could take a while. You may as well be comfortable. I'll let you know when we can leave."

She followed Mrs. Sutton into the front foyer of her home where a grand staircase drew the eye to the second floor. They continued through a short hall to the spacious kitchen. The modern appliances couldn't reduce the historical feel of the room. Cabinets and cupboards mimicked the pattern of the nineteenth century moldings. A large round oak table took up the center space.

"Have a seat, dear, while I put on some coffee." She laughed. "Actually, all I have to do is push a button. I had the coffee maker ready for breakfast."

"Thank you." She slipped into a chair facing a bank of windows.

"Call me Mary." Having pushed the button, she shuffled through a cabinet for paper cups. "I imagine the men out there would appreciate a hot cup of coffee." She retrieved two thermos bottles from the bottom of the same cupboard and set them on the counter before placing two mugs on the table. "Do you take anything in your coffee?"

Willie smiled. "No, black is fine, thank you."

A couple of minutes later, Mrs. Sutton filled their cups and poured the remaining coffee into one of the thermoses before putting on the second pot. When that one had finished brewing she filled the second thermos. "I'll take these out for my husband to pass around, then come back and keep you company."

Willie nodded, and her hostess left the room. She was about to bring the coffee cup to her lips when a scratching noise in the corner by the bank of windows caught her attention. She set the cup down and listened. There it was again, like a tree limb scraping against the glass. Leaving her seat, she walked to the window.

She rested her hands on the counter below the window frame, and leaned forward, her face nearly touching the pane. Night was a solid black wall beyond the light radiating from the kitchen. She couldn't see anything moving, couldn't even hear the wind or rain. So, what had made the noise? The door at the front of the house opened, then closed, and she heard Stona's voice. She glanced over her shoulder, but immediately turned back to the window.

And screamed.

A stark, pale face hovered inches from her own.

She pushed away from the counter, her heart surging against her ribs. The ethereal visage seemed frozen in the night, unmoving, simply staring at her with hollow sad eyes then faded until only dark remained.

Arms grabbed her from behind and she grappled with her assailant.

"Willie, it's me." Stona pivoted her to face him. "What's wrong?"

"Someone—" she turned and pointed toward the window. "Someone's out there. I saw him through the window."

He pushed her toward Mr. Sutton. "Stay with her." Releasing the safety on his gun, he sprinted toward the back door. "When the sheriff arrives, send him out."

The sudden anxiety she felt for him was palpable. "He should've waited for the sheriff. It's dangerous to go out there alone."

Mr. Sutton urged her into a chair at the table. "You don't need to worry about him. He looks capable of taking care of himself, and he won't find anyone." He glanced at his wife. "We never do."

THIRTEEN

WILLIE GLANCED FROM husband to wife. "What do you mean you never do? How often does he come around?"

James Sutton shrugged. "We lost count years ago. He seems to be a restless spirit. But until now we've been the only ones to see him—that we know of. I have to say, though, the people we bought this place from were anxious to sell it. An agent handled the sale and took care of all the paperwork. The asking price was so low we assumed the property would need a lot of work. But it didn't."

Mary brought her a glass of water. "It wasn't until we moved in and became acquainted with folks in the area that we understood why it was such a good deal. No one wants a haunted house."

Willie's eyes shot back to Mr. Sutton "Restless spirit—you think I saw a... a...."

"*Ghost*, dear." Mary patted her hand. "You saw a ghost."

"That's not possible. Ghosts don't exist."

Mr. Sutton took a seat across the table from her. His wife dropped into a chair beside him. "A lot of people would argue with you about that. A few years back I would've agreed with you, but seeing is believing, isn't it?"

She thought about the bizarre man in the meadow. The mind didn't always play fair, and it could be influenced by chemical imbalances or outside sources like drugs or alcohol.

Stona reentered the kitchen and pulled a chair over to sit in front of her. "Are you okay?"

Her cheeks warmed. "I'm fine. I don't know what made me act like that."

"Don't be embarrassed. You were just cut out of a car. I'd say you're entitled to a scream or two."

"Did you find him?" She glanced at the Suttons for their reaction to her question. James Sutton simply raised an eyebrow. Mary gave her a knowing smile when Stona shook his head. Neither mentioned their take on the face in the window. She was grateful for their silence. She wasn't up to a debate on the existence of spiritual beings.

"There wasn't a sign of him." Stona turned to her. "Can you describe him?"

"He was old, and pale. His eyes were… haunted."

"What about his hair? Was it long or short?"

She sucked in a breath and exhaled quickly. "I don't remember his hair. Right now, I can't be sure of anything."

"With what you've been through today, it doesn't surprise me."

He didn't know the half of it. "I can probably tell you more when my head clears. This headache makes it impossible to concentrate."

Mary stood. "I forgot about your headache, dear. I have some Tylenol in the cabinet over the sink." A minute later she shook a couple of tablets into Willie's palm and handed her the glass of water sitting on the table.

Willie downed the pills and smiled up at the older woman. "Thank you so much."

Stona touched her hand to bring her attention back to him. "Were you planning to spend the night in Nevada?"

Mary patted her shoulder. "You can spend the night with us, dear."

The thought of sleeping in this house sent shivers down her spine. "I appreciate your offer, but I need to get back home."

Mr. Sutton sat forward. "I can make a few phone calls and arrange for a rental car to be delivered here. It shouldn't take long."

The marshal shook his head. "She isn't in any condition to drive, I'm afraid. I'll take her home tonight and make sure she gets a rental car in the morning."

Before she could protest, Mr. Sutton spoke up. "I'll call our insurance company first thing in the morning. Then take care of the rental cost. It might take a day or two before an adjuster can come out to assess the damage." He glanced at her. "Your car's obviously totaled. The company will pay for a replacement. You'll probably need to return in a couple of days to sign the claim forms."

"Yes, I can do that."

"And we'll talk about the spearhead when you come back. If you'd like to leave it with me, I can make some comparisons with what I have."

She clutched her purse to her chest as though he might snatch it away, experiencing the most insane fear of being separated from it. It bordered on obsession. "That's okay, I'll bring it back with me."

Standing, Stona pushed his chair to the table, and took Willie's hand. "You look exhausted. We can leave when you're ready."

"I'm ready now, but you don't have to drive me. I can use a rental."

"Okay, provided I drive you to the hospital first and let a doctor decide whether you're up to the drive."

"There's nothing wrong with me."

"You have a headache and a good-sized knot over your eye." When she started to argue he shook his head. "Either I drive you to the hospital or I drive you home. It's your choice."

"You can't tell me what to do." She closed her eyes. Now she sounded like a five-year-old.

"Have you forgotten I'm a Marshal?"

"You still can't—"

She was halted by the hard look in his eyes.

"Try me."

Her shoulders slumped. She couldn't fight him, not when she knew he was right. But spending the next couple of hours alone in a car with a man who thought she was capable of murder....

At least he didn't gloat. Removing a card from his shirt pocket, he handed it to James. "Let the sheriff know Miss McAllister has gone home. He can contact me if he needs to speak with her."

He pulled her to her feet and took her arm as they headed through the house to the front door. The Suttons followed and said their good-byes before she and Stona skirted the barricade ribbon surrounding the skeleton.

She paused to stare at the blue tarp. "It seems so disrespectful to let him hang there. Someone should take him down."

Stona shook his head. "They can't. The tree roots and the bones are entwined. It will take an expert to untangle the body without damaging it."

She nodded. "At least he's covered."

Mary rushed up to them. "I thought you might need this for your trip home." She handed Willie a light blanket. "You can return it when you come back." She gave her a quick hug before sprinting back to the house.

When they reached the car, Stona opened the door for her and placed his hand on top of her head as she slid into the passenger seat. He closed the door before she realized what he'd done. Despite the horrendous day she'd had, or perhaps because of it, his action struck her funny. By the time he circled the car and climbed into the driver's seat, she was laughing.

He gave her a cautious glance before starting the car. "Are you okay?"

She laughed harder, tears brimming in her eyes.

He turned the car around but didn't pull out of the drive. "What?"

She could barely answer between gasps. "I'm surprised you didn't cuff me and put me in the back seat."

It took him a minute, then his grin told her he'd figured it out. "You're having a good time at my expense, aren't you?"

She tried to look innocent. "What makes you think that?"

He reached over and wiped a tear from her cheek. "Just a hunch." His smile broadened as he pulled onto the highway, and they headed for Nevada. "I've never heard you laugh. It's a nice sound."

A compliment? Her cheeks warmed with pleasure before she reminded herself the man giving it suspected her of murdering her cousin.

He must have sensed her irritation. Saying no more, he gave his full attention to the road. The silence as the miles passed was anything but comfortable. After an hour or so, she shook out the blanket and draped it around her shoulders.

"Cold?" He reached over and kicked the heat up a notch, then aimed the vent in her direction.

"Just a little chilled. The heat helps. Thank you."

"No problem. How's the headache?"

"Better."

"We're still about forty-five minutes out. Why don't you try to rest?"

It sounded like a good idea. Snuggling into the blanket she closed her eyes.

"Willie?"

His voice startled her awake. "What?" She sat up, the blanket falling from her shoulders to her lap. "What's the matter?"

"It's okay. I thought you'd want to know we're just coming into town."

"Oh. Thanks." She brushed the hair back from her face and glanced out the window at the familiar surroundings. "I didn't think I'd fall asleep."

"I'd say it took you all of about a minute and a half after you closed your eyes."

"Did you call me Willie?"

"Is that a problem?"

"No. It's that—when did you start calling me Willie?"

"When I held your hand while they cut that car away from you. I don't remember you calling me Marshal after that either."

She nodded. "I guess we'd moved beyond formality at that point."

"I guess we did." They stopped at a red light, and he glanced over. "I'd like your permission to look through your cousin's possessions. I assume since you were his next of kin you have them."

"Yes." She immediately became defensive. Did he think there was something in Josh's belongings that would incriminate her? Then she came to her senses. He was doing his job, and his job was to find the murderer and bring him to justice. It was what she wanted him to do, and if looking through her cousin's belongings helped, she would cooperate.

"I haven't gone through anything except the small box containing the information about Nevada. You're welcome to look at anything you need to." She took a deep breath and exhaled slowly, trying to ease the flutter of tension in the pit of her stomach. "It's going to be difficult—opening those boxes and seeing his personal belongings. It isn't an experience I want to share with a stranger."

"We may discover something that will lead us to the person responsible for your cousin's death."

"I know." She looked at his profile as he concentrated on the road. His expression gave nothing away, but he'd talked like they were looking for someone else. Did he finally believe her? She hoped so. "Where do you want to start?"

"You said you've opened the small box. We'll look in it first and see if you missed anything. He glanced at her. "We can put it off for a day or two."

He turned onto the farm road that led to her lane. "You need to call someone to come and stay with you tonight. I'll wait until they get here."

She shook her head. "That isn't necessary. I'll be fine."

"The EMTs were adamant. You shouldn't spend the night alone."

"I'm a nurse. I'd know if I needed a babysitter."

He didn't argue. But he did pull into the next driveway and start to turn around.

"What are you doing?"

"Taking you to that hospital we passed a few minutes ago. We'll let their ER doctor decide if you're ready to spend the night alone."

"That isn't necessary."

"Are you going to make that call?"

She heaved an exasperated sigh. "My friends all live in or around St. Louis. I don't have anyone to call. And I'm too tired to go through the emergency room routine."

"I see." He paused, and she was sure he was contemplating taking her to the hospital anyway. But he backed onto the farm road and continued toward her property. Neither spoke until he'd navigated the lane to her house. "Do you want to go in the front door or the back?"

"The back. I don't think I can handle the front steps tonight." Nodding, he pulled around, and shut off the motor. "Wait here where it's warm while I open the house and make sure everything's okay."

She fished in her purse and held out the back door key. Watching him enter her house and methodically turning lights on and off as he checked the rooms was unsettling. She consoled herself with the assurance that he was, after all, in law enforcement. He wasn't intruding. He was securing.

When he returned, he opened her door to offer a hand out, then opened the rear door and grabbed a duffel bag.

"What's that?"

"My clothes. I noticed you have a couple of extra bedrooms. I'm spending the night."

FOURTEEN

"YOU'RE WHAT?"

Stona took Willie's arm and walked her toward the back door. "I'm spending the night."

She dug in her heels. "Wait. No."

"No?" He tilted his head. "Why not? You need someone to stay with you tonight, and I'm the only person available."

"I don't even know you."

"After today we know each other pretty well. We're on a first name basis. I've even held you in my arms."

"You were carrying me to an ambulance."

He shrugged, and grinned. "Some first dates can be intense."

She'd been subtly aware of his good looks, but that smile could stop a heart. And he was teasing her—not the actions of a U.S. Marshal bent on arresting her for murder. She didn't know how to respond.

He must have taken her silence for agreement. Grasping her hand, he walked her into the house. "Which room is yours?" They were climbing the stairs when he asked the question in a no-nonsense tone.

He was back to being the unflappable lawman—the one she found more comfortable— which made no sense at all.

She caved, giving up on dissuading him. "The first room on the right."

"I'll take the room across from yours."

"Okay." She was immediately grateful he hadn't chosen the second bedroom on the right—the one that connected to her room. At some point in time, a bathroom had been built between the two bedrooms with an adjoining door opening into each bedroom. She'd assumed one of her not-too-distant ancestors had redesigned the two rooms to accommodate a nursery. It would've been perfect for Josh and Trish if they'd....

Stona tossed his duffel in front of his door, then opened hers and switched on the light. "How are you feeling?"

"I'm fine." She started to walk past him, but he wouldn't let go of her hand. He lifted her chin with his free hand and leaned close to look into her eyes. For a moment she thought he was going to kiss her.

"Your eyes are still a little dilated."

She was glad he couldn't read minds.

"Are you sure you're feeling all right?"

Flustered, she pushed his hand away. "I told you I'm fine. All I need is sleep."

Nodding, he stepped back. She was closing the door when he stopped her. "Leave it open so I can hear if you need help."

"You're kidding."

"I'm not asking you to leave it wide open. Just crack it enough for me to hear if you call."

She nodded. "You can use the bathroom at the end of the hall. It's the last door on the left." She shrugged. "I guess you already know that since you went through my house."

He tilted his head. "Did it bother you—my going through your house like that?"

"It wasn't necessary. I keep my doors locked."

"It doesn't hurt to be cautious."

She folded her arms in front of her, suddenly ready for a fight. "Why would I need to be more cautious than I am?"

"Your cousin was murdered."

"And you think I'm responsible."

"I've never said that."

"You implied it. You've even admitted to following me."

"Did you ever stop to consider I might have more than one reason to follow you?"

That brought her up short. "What other reason could you have?"

"The same reason I had for checking out your house. Technically you're a person of interest, but you could also be a potential victim."

She hadn't considered that possibility. The man in the meadow and the face in the window immediately rushed to mind and were as quickly dismissed. Anyone bent on hurting her wouldn't dress in a Native American costume to do it. And the Suttons were already familiar with their apparition, whatever it was.

But at the Osage village site…. "There was a blue pickup at the historical site today."

"I saw it."

"How?" Suddenly the light dawned. "Wait a minute. You were in the dark sedan by the mailboxes."

He nodded.

"I didn't see you following me."

"You weren't supposed to. You took a long time on the trail and I was about to check on you when the pickup pulled into the parking lot beside your car. The driver never left his vehicle and pulled out of the lot when you started down the hill. I didn't follow him because—"

"Because you were following *me.*"

He shook his head. "Because after watching him, I was afraid to let you out of my sight." He crossed the hall, picked up his gym bag and carried it down the hall to the bathroom. "Get some rest," he called over his shoulder. "I'll see you in the morning."

She waited until after he'd gone into the bathroom, then closed her own door. Retrieving a fresh nightgown from the chest-of-drawers, she headed for her shower. The hot water soothed the tension in her muscles.

She winced when she inadvertently brushed over the bump on her forehead while drying her hair. Glancing in the mirror, she saw the bluish bruise above her eyebrow. At least it was on her head and not her cheek. She wouldn't have a black eye.

When she returned to her bedroom, the hall door was cracked open. She peeked out and saw his door was also open—neither wide enough to be intrusive.

She padded back to the bed and climbed in, knowing he wouldn't invade her privacy. Was it because he was in law enforcement? That helped of course, but she also trusted him as a person. She pulled the blanket over her shoulder. Why she felt that way was a mystery.

The events of the day had waited until she was relaxed before rushing in on her. The outcome of her own investigation had been enlightening and a little scary, but not productive as far as her cousin's murder was concerned.

She'd had another blackout, which was disturbing. She'd also fought a storm, gotten trapped in her car, had to be rescued, discovered a skeleton, and possibly seen a ghost. But she'd found no reason for Josh to warn her away from Nevada.

She was also finding it difficult to hold on to her grudge against Marshal Jordan—Stona. He'd been her lifeline tonight when she'd been trapped in her car. The terror of seeing the huge tree toppling toward her, of knowing she might die in the next moment, was traumatic enough, but to be entombed in the wreckage had brought on a degree of panic she'd never experienced before. Hearing him calmly tell her help was on its way, knowing she wasn't alone, that he wouldn't leave, had sustained her through the ordeal. And tonight, here at home, his concern for her well-being had been genuine.

Stona. She turned to her side and punched her pillow before smiling. If he honestly thought she could kill her cousin, why would he make himself vulnerable by leaving his door open?

STONA LAID HIS badge and holstered gun on the nightstand beside his bed. He'd heard Willie moving around earlier, but her room was quiet now. He stretched out on the bed and stacked his hands behind his head.

The trip had muddied his concept of what had happened to Josh McAllister and his fiancée. Willie McAllister had motive—she would inherit everything the family possessed plus a hefty insurance payoff. As for opportunity, she could've hired someone to tamper with her cousin's car.

The slit brake line was the reason federal marshals had become involved in the McAllister investigation. This accident fit the MO of an assassin they'd dubbed The Surgeon. A killer for hire authorities had been unsuccessfully tracking for the past decade. He'd gone to ground two years ago. There was speculation he retired. How old did an assassin have to be to retire? Fifty? Sixty? Maybe as young as forty-five?

Did an assassin crave killing like a serial killer? Was that why he'd accepted one more job? And who had paid him to murder Josh McAllister and Patricia Collins?

Not Willie.

After meeting and spending time with her, he was convinced they were investigating the wrong suspect. There was an innocence about her that was hard to fabricate. If her demeanor was contrived, she was a pro. He'd investigated a lot of men and women who pretended innocence. But there was always a flaw—something not quite right about their responses to his questions. He was good at picking up on the small mistakes that eventually found them out.

Willie was different, genuine. Her every action and reaction seemed straightforward, honest. She'd tried to hide her vulnerability, but he'd seen the veiled sadness in her eyes when she talked about her cousin, heard the pain. That kind of devastation was nearly impossible to fabricate.

He moved off the bed and walked out into the hall to make sure she'd left her door open. She had, and her room was silent. Pushing the door a little wider, he peeked in. After a moment his eyes adjusted to the darkness and he was able to discern her sleeping form. Satisfied, he returned to his own bed and pulled up the light cover. He was finding it increasingly difficult to distance himself from his lovely person of interest. He'd be glad when this assignment was over.

―――――――――

WILLIE CAME AWAKE with a start. Where was her purse? The spearhead was in her purse. She couldn't remember where she'd had it last.

Slipping out of bed, she hurried to the dresser where she always kept her things. The purse was there, half open and leaning against the mirror. Exhaling the breath she'd been holding, she grabbed the bag in both hands and scurried back to climb on top of the bedspread. Heart racing, she switched on the bedside lamp and upturned the purse, scattering the contents across the cover. A quick scan yielded nothing. Where was the spearhead? She tossed her billfold out of the way. It bounced off the bed onto the floor.

When she'd tossed every item to the floor and still hadn't found it, tears filled her eyes. She couldn't lose it. It was too important, too dear.

It had to be in the purse. Frantic now, she shook it out again. Nothing. She was about to tear out the lining when she felt something in the small zippered compartment on the inside wall of the bag—and remembered zipping the tissue-wrapped flint inside for safekeeping.

Retrieving the bundle, she practically shredded the tissue to get to the stone. The moment her fingers touched the smooth flint she felt the familiar wave of dizziness. Her hand clamped around the spearhead as it flashed hot. Her heart pounded in her ears. Dark stars swirled in her vision, absorbing the light as she felt herself falling. She whispered a familiar prayer.

"Please, God, not again."

FIFTEEN

THE SMALL FIRE was only a few feet from where Beth lay on the furs. A campfire? She vaguely remembered the campfires, but they were in the woods. She was inside a structure of some kind. Where? Her muddled mind couldn't focus. Patches of memory—all of them frightening—vied for clarity, but no single thought prevailed.

Awareness came with two sudden realizations. One, she wasn't wearing any clothes, and two, the man next to her was as naked as she was. Their bodies touched, his curving around hers, his arm hooked over her waist. They were as close as the spoons nesting in her mother's treasured silverware chest. She knew who he was, and knew the Osage warrior was awake, watching her.

Long ago she'd learned you were never alone in the wilderness. It was only a question of how big and how dangerous the creature watching you was.

Short of a bear, she couldn't imagine anything deadlier than her captor. He frightened her, even more than the man who'd wounded her. She understood that man's kind of brutality, knew how to cope with it. Her father was brutal. But she couldn't predict this warrior's actions. She couldn't protect herself against someone she couldn't understand. He yawned, and she tensed waiting for his next move.

"Sleep, girl. It is not yet time to greet the morning."

He spoke English? Why hadn't he spoken directly to her father?

His drowsy voice assured her she had nothing to worry about for the moment. Then he rolled her to face him, grasped her hip in his big hand, and pressed her more intimately against his soft flesh. He grunted his satisfaction with their new position and closed his eyes.

Her face went up in flames. She'd helped care for her brothers from the moment they were born. She still helped with their baths. She knew exactly what he was forcing her to cuddle. His deep even breathing convinced her he'd gone back to sleep. A reprieve? Hopefully, he was more interested in finding his rest than in tormenting his captive.

At least he didn't smell like her father's friends. Even from a distance they stunk of unwashed bodies and sour whiskey. Her mother used to air out the house after one of their visits.

This man smelled of the outdoors and woodsmoke. His clothes probably carried the scent of his horse. Unfortunately, he wasn't wearing them.

Her bare breasts rubbed against his smooth chest with every breath he took. Her nipples hardened. The tingling fluttered to her stomach, then moved lower. She squirmed against the tension it caused. Heaven help her, it felt—nice.

What was *wrong* with her? No decent woman would feel anything but revulsion. Did it make her a loose woman, like the one who lived over Soddie's bar near Cedar Valley?

No, of course she wasn't. Loose women were supposed to like men enough to let them take liberties with their bodies.

She didn't much care for men at all, had avoided her father's friends—hid from them if they'd had too much whiskey. Her pa hadn't let any of the young men from the settlement close enough for her to get to know them.

When she turned fifteen, her mother took her for a walk and explained what happened in the marriage bed. The marriage act, she'd warned, always hurt. She'd also said it wouldn't hurt as much if she stayed still and let her man have his way. If her husband wasn't bent on beating her and he liked kissing, she might find some pleasure before he rutted with her. Sometimes it made the chore less painful. Her mother didn't explain exactly how a man and woman mated, but she figured it wasn't much different from how animals rutted.

Uncomfortable with her thoughts, she tried to ease away from her captor. His hand brought her hips right back against his soft flesh. But it wasn't soft now. It had grown long and hard and thick. It pressed against the junction of her legs, seeking a deeper intimacy.

Gasping, she tried to clamp her legs shut. "Get away from me, savage." She screamed and screamed again.

He put his hand to the back of her head and pushed her face into his chest, cutting off the harsh sound. His scent filled her nostrils. His taste shocked her innocent senses. He wouldn't let her move. She could breathe, but that was all.

He pushed her back against the soft furs and came down between her thighs. "Continue to struggle against me, girl, and you'll learn what it is to become a woman—*my* woman."

He didn't have to explain his meaning. Even in her innocence, she knew he'd positioned her for his invasion. The firm tip of his engorged flesh nestled against her. She stilled and so did he, both aware of his slight penetration. She tensed against the pain she knew was seconds away and glanced between them. Her heart jumped to her throat. He was bigger than she'd imagined. It was going to kill her.

Shaking uncontrollably, she drew deep gasping breaths of air. But she couldn't catch her breath, was suffocating. Even now black swirled before her eyes as she sucked in more useless air.

She couldn't stop herself.

———————

"BE STILL, WOMAN unless you want to finish what I had not intended to begin." When she didn't heed his warning, he realized something was wrong. Pressing her hips to the furs, he ignored his body's demands, and pulled away from her.

Kneeling at her side he watched her strain for breath. Brings Peace had told him fear brought on this craving for air. He'd also told him how to cure it. Touching his mouth to hers was a foreign concept, the idea mildly repulsive, yet he did not hesitate. Grasping her jaw, he forced her mouth open. Drawing a deep breath, he pinched her nose shut, slanted his mouth over hers, and blew his own breath into her body. He released her nose, letting her exhale, but pinched it closed before she could draw a breath. Keeping his mouth on hers he drew air through his nostrils and repeated the action. The only air he allowed her was from his own body. She fought him, her fists flailing against his chest and back. Relentless, he continued filling her lungs with his breath. Finally, the tension drained from her body and she stopped fighting him.

He let go of her nose, but his mouth lingered, softened as his tongue traced her lips and he experienced his first taste of a woman. Far from repugnant, her sweet mouth stirred his manhood, made him want more. He slipped his tongue into her mouth, rubbing it against hers, enjoying the raspy stimulation. When he lifted his head, she stared at him, her eyes full of questions.

His fingers covered her lips. "Shh, I only wanted to taste you." He stretched out beside her on the furs and pulled the cover over them both, then leaned above her. "By your father's words you belong to me. You will grow used to my touch and learn not to fear me."

Bending, he touched his lips to her shoulder—just above the healing wound. "When you've recovered your strength, you will see to the care of my lodge and fire and prepare the meat I provide." He pulled her back against his body and nuzzled her neck. "Only when you are strong again will I mate with you."

The arm he curved around her waist snuggled her closer. His hand glided up her belly to cup her breast. When she tensed, his hand tightened in warning and his lips touched her ear. "You will allow my touch. It is my right."

———————

SHE STARED INTO the flames. Had her father truly given him the right to touch her? She blinked back resigned tears. Did it really matter?

She forced herself to relax and his hand loosened, but his thumb began to softly brush her nipple. She endured his touch, suspected he was teaching her a lesson in obedience. Her nipple once again puckered and tightened into a hard nub. He grunted his satisfaction. Her cheeks burned with humiliation. He was teaching her another lesson, proving he had more control over her body than she did.

"Why didn't you speak my language before—when you talked to my father?" It was all she could think of to distract him.

"I do not like using the white man's words. You will learn my language, so I am not forced to use yours."

"Who taught you English?"

"A white man who is now Osage. There are many in our village who speak your language."

He yawned, then nuzzled her ear. "Sleep."

She had distracted him, but she was too aware of the man that slept beside her, too confused by her conflicting emotions to sleep. He was a savage. Why hadn't he raped her?

Mama said no man could control his baser instincts when he craved a woman. Men took what they wanted. Her father did, especially when he and his friends had been drinking. He'd drag Mama to the bedroom while his friend shouted lecherous encouragements and leave the door open—most likely to show them what they were missing.

She hated him for humiliating her mama and for leaving his only daughter alone with his drunken friends. Even as a child, she'd seen to her own safety, making sure they knew she had her father's pistol in hand when she climbed into the loft. They may have outnumbered her, but none of them was brave enough to be the first up the ladder.

Mama was wrong when she put all men in the same category. Her captor had been so close to taking her virginity she'd seen the heat in his eyes and the beads of sweat on his brow. Yet he'd pulled back. The savage had been the exception to Mama's rule.

His hand plumped her breast and slowly glided over her belly, his fingers slipping into the curls at the junction of her legs. She bit her lower lip, tasting blood, and reminded herself it was his right.

SIXTEEN

STONA WASN'T SURE what woke him. He lay still, listening for any unusual sound, but the house was silent. Rolling out of bed, he adjusted the band on his sweatpants, grabbed his gun and stepped into the hall. Willie's bedroom was quiet but there was a light on. He pushed the door open enough to lean into the room.

"Willie!" The door bounced against the wall as he lunged through. Her head and one shoulder dangled over the edge of the bed. She groaned when he lifted her back against the pillows. Taking her wrist, he found a pulse—her heartbeat was rapid but strong. She was cold. He pulled the covers out from under her, then slipped them over her shoulders. How long had she been like this?

He took in everything at once, the empty purse and its contents strewn across the bed and carpet. Had she been robbed? No. He would've heard anyone in the hall.

"Willie, can you hear me?"

She groaned again. Her face was flushed. He put the back of his hand against her cheek. It didn't seem overly warm, but a damp cloth for her forehead wouldn't hurt. He headed for the bathroom, stepped on something hard and hopped the rest of the way muttering a few words he was glad she didn't hear.

When he returned, he sat beside her on the bed and smoothed the cloth over her cheeks before placing it over her eyes.

"Willie, honey, wake up for me." He was about to retrieve his cell phone from the other room and call for an ambulance when she dragged the cloth from her face.

"I'm not your *honey.*"

He was so relieved he wanted to kiss her. It wasn't the first time he'd had the urge. Picking up the cloth she'd brushed aside, he put it back on her head. "Okay, you're not my honey. How do you feel?"

————————————

LIKE SHE'D JUST been snatched back from another time and place. And while it was comforting to have someone there in case she needed help, it was also disconcerting. It was going to take time to process what had happened to her.

"Willie, answer me. How do you feel?"

She sat up. "A little fuzzyheaded. I'll be okay, give me a minute."

"Are you able to get dressed on your own?"

"What time is it?"

He glanced at the clock on her nightstand. "A little after two."

"In the morning?"

"Of course in the morning. Do you need help getting dressed or not?"

"Why would I want to get dressed in the middle of the night?"

"I'm taking you to the hospital, like I should've done last night."

"I've told you before, I don't need to go to the hospital."

"A few minutes ago, I found you hanging off the bed, unconscious. You can't tell me nothing's wrong."

She sighed. "I really don't feel up to arguing with you about this. I'm tired. I dozed off. That's all." Even she found it hard to believe that excuse, and from the look on his face he wasn't buying it either.

"Would you like to tell me what happened with the purse?"

"I was looking for something."

"Do you always throw the stuff in your purse on the floor when you're looking for something?"

"I was upset. I thought I'd lost it."

"Lost what?"

She started to swipe the hair away from her face and realized she still clutched the spearhead. "This." She held it up for him to see but couldn't open her hand.

"What is it?"

"A spearhead."

He reached out. "May I see it?"

She instinctively pulled her hand back, unwilling to let him touch it. "I'd rather you didn't."

He tilted his head. "Why?"

She lifted her shoulders in a half shrug. "I don't feel comfortable letting anyone else touch it."

"Do you believe I won't give it back?"

"No, of course not. It's hard to explain. It just feels like I shouldn't let it out of my possession. I know it sounds crazy."

"A little obsessive maybe, but not crazy. Can I at least look at it while you're holding it?"

She nodded. He waited for her to open her fingers and again tilted his head when she didn't immediately do so.

"I can't let it go."

"Can't or *won't?*"

"Can't."

He cradled her hand in both of his and drew her arm closer to the light. "Your knuckles are white. You've probably cut off the circulation. Does it hurt?"

She shook her head. Lack of circulation was as good an excuse as any. She wasn't about to tell him this had happened once before. When he began to briskly rub her forearm she pulled back.

"I'll be fine once I get my fingers open."

"Here, let me help." Her knuckles burned as he slowly forced her hand open. The spearhead fell into her lap but neither paid any attention as he massaged the ache out of her fingers. Holding her hand palm up he examined the fluted impression left by the artifact.

"You must have had a death grip on that thing. Did it cut your hand?"

"I don't think so. There isn't any blood."

He nodded toward the bandage on her index finger. "What happened there?"

"I cut it on the spearhead."

He traced the near-perfect imprint on her palm. "I'd think you'd want to avoid it, considering."

She shrugged. "You'd think so. It makes no sense, but I can't seem to let it go. The impression goes away in an hour or so."

"It's happened before?"

Too late she realized the implication of what she'd said. And he would have to pick up on it. "Maybe," she hedged.

"It either happened before or it didn't. Which is it?"

"Okay, it happened."

"How many times?"

His voice was hard, and she was beginning to understand the difference he'd mentioned between simply talking and an interrogation. "Four times altogether."

"Did you black out each time?"

"No." When she didn't say more, he caught and held her gaze. The man was getting irritated and she didn't feel up to yet another browbeating session. "The first time it happened, I didn't black out. I only got dizzy."

"So, you've blacked out three separate times."

"Yes."

"Tell me what happened."

"I blacked out twice while I held the spearhead. The time before this, I wasn't holding it, but it was close to me."

"How long ago did that happen?"

"Yesterday, at the Osage village. I was standing beside a large rock the Osage used for grinding grain. I touched the stone and experienced a wave of dizziness before blacking out. When I woke, I was sprawled over the stone with no idea of how much time had passed."

"You were out there totally helpless? Anyone could have found you. The man in the pickup…."

"But I wasn't alone, was I? You were following me, and if the man in the pickup had taken the trail, you would've followed him too."

"And if I hadn't been following you, and the driver of the pickup had taken the trail?"

The possible outcome gave her chills. "I wasn't being careless. I never suspected it would happen again."

"What about last night? Did you suspect it might happen again when you insisted I leave you here alone?"

She pulled her hand from his and held it up to forestall him. "I feel fine within an hour of waking. I'm fine now. I don't need a babysitter."

"Willie, you're a nurse. You've got to know how crazy that sounds. If you were fine, you wouldn't be passing out. Get dressed. I'm taking you to the hospital."

"No."

"Okay, you don't have to get dressed. You can wrap a coat around your nightgown. They see lots of nightgowns in a hospital."

"I'm not going with you, and you can't make me." Oh great, now she sounded like a six-year-old.

"Try me."

"Short of throwing me over your shoulder like a Neanderthal, you can't make me leave this house."

"As intriguing as that sounds, I won't have to throw you over my shoulder. I'll arrest you and drag you to the hospital."

"On what charge?"

"I'll make one up on the way. I've even got my handcuffs in my duffel."

"You can't do—wait. You carry handcuffs in your suitcase?"

He laughed. "Rein in your imagination, Will. They're usually in my glove compartment, but since I'm driving a rental, I stuck them in my overnight bag. Do you want an up-close look at them, or are you going to cooperate and let me take you to the hospital?"

She really hadn't been given a choice. And since when had he started calling her Will? "All right. I'll see a doctor, but can we please wait until morning? It isn't an emergency, and I'm exhausted. All I need right now is sleep."

He appeared to consider her request and finally nodded. "Okay. We'll go in the morning provided you sign a waiver allowing me to see the results of your tests and talk to your doctor." When she opened her mouth to argue he held up a hand. "You're not getting a rental car until I know it's safe for you to drive."

She couldn't argue with his logic, and gave him an exaggerated sigh. "Agreed."

He gathered the contents of her purse from the floor and put them on the bed. Returning the items to her purse, along with the spearhead, she closed her bag and set it on the nightstand. That's when she saw his gun.

"You brought your gun in here?"

He shrugged. "When I woke up, I sensed something was wrong."

"What do you mean?"

"I occasionally feel when something's wrong. I've learned to trust my instincts."

"Josh used to get those feelings. At his funeral, several of his friends in the department told me they'd grown to depend on his ability to know when something wasn't quite right." She yawned and immediately apologized.

He shook his head. "It's all right. You're exhausted. Try to go back to sleep."

She scooted down, fluffed the pillow, and turned on her side. He surprised her by pulling the cover up over her shoulder. She hadn't been tucked in since she was a little girl. It felt nice to be pampered. It could've felt awkward, but it didn't.

He bent closer and she thought he might kiss her forehead before leaving the room. He didn't, of course. She wouldn't have known how to act if he had.

He'd left his gun behind. How long would it take him to remember it was in her room?

Apparently, not long. After a few minutes, he knocked on her door and waited for her permission to come in. When she gave it, he came through the door carrying the blanket, sheets and pillow from his bed.

"What are you doing?"

"I'm spending the night."

It was déjà vu all over again. He was spreading the sheets and blankets on the floor next to her side of the bed. "Stop. You can't sleep there."

"I'll be fine. The rug's thick and the floor isn't cold."

Was he obtuse? "You know what I mean. You can't sleep in my room."

"I'm sleeping on the floor, Willie, not in your bed."

He had the gall to sound exasperated.

SEVENTEEN

WILLIE SWORE STONA was the most aggravating man to ever walk
the earth. Not only had he insisted she go to a doctor, but he'd managed
to get her an appointment and then gone with her. His reasons had
been valid, but she still didn't like it.

"You've given me permission to be informed of your test results. I
intend to talk to your doctor about them, so I may as well be there when
he talks to you."

Stona sat in the waiting room, while she was poked, prodded,
x-rayed and scanned. She joined him an hour and a half later, and together they waited to join the doctor in his office.

Dr. Conklin was a distinguished-looking man, probably in his late
fifties or early sixties. He stood and shook their hands before motioning them to the two chairs in front of his desk. "I'm sorry for your
wait, but I wanted to look over your test results before we spoke. He
looked at Willie. "You had a rough time of it yesterday. How are you
feeling this morning?"

She smiled. "Better, thank you."

He turned to Stona. "And you are Marshal Jordan?"

"I am."

"Marshal, I see that Miss McAllister has signed a waiver allowing us to share her test results with you. Does that mean you're here in an official capacity?"

Willie tensed. She wasn't acquainted with many people in the area, but she didn't want anyone in the community to know she might be a suspect in her cousin's death.

Stona glanced at her and smiled before giving his attention to the doctor. "Miss McAllister is my friend. I insisted she come see you after her accident."

The doctor took a moment to glance at the papers in front of him. "By *accident*, I assume you mean the tree falling on her car." He looked up at her. "That must have been traumatic."

Willie nodded. "A little, but I was fortunate."

Stona sat forward. "She still has a good-sized bump on her head."

Frowning at Stona, she turned to the doctor. "It was a little bump. I told him I was all right."

The doctor glanced between the two of them. "I'm afraid I have to agree with the Marshal. It's more than a little bump. Tell me, do you still have a headache?"

She wasn't going to lie to the doctor. "A slight one. It isn't too bad."

Dr. Conklin nodded. "You're a tough lady. Most people would be in bed. You have a mild concussion. You'll need to take it easy for a day or so—until the headache's gone. If it gets worse, let me know."

"Should she drive?" Stona gave Willie an I-told-you-so look when he asked the question.

"I wouldn't recommend it. Not for another day at least." He glanced at Willie. "Your scans and x-rays will be sent to another facility for analysis. We'll contact you with the results."

A few minutes later, she and Stona were on their way to his car in the parking lot. He took her arm when they stepped off the sidewalk. It was a courteous gesture, but when he continued to hold onto her elbow she wondered about his motive.

"You didn't mention your blackouts to the doctor."

"I didn't think it was necessary."

He stopped in the middle of the parking lot and pulled her around to face him. "Willie, you know better than to keep something like that from your doctor."

She would've taken a step closer to confront him if they hadn't been toe-to-toe as it was. "I spent over an hour taking every test they could come up with. Dr. Conklin looked at the results and found nothing unusual." She held up her hand when he opened his mouth to argue. "I'm not hiding my head in the sand. The tests I took should indicate a problem even if it isn't conclusive. If that happens, the doctor will contact me, and we'll discuss possibilities and further tests."

"Will you tell me if there are problems?"

"Why? My blackouts have nothing to do with Josh's death. They didn't start until I moved back here. In fact, the first blackout didn't happen until after I met you."

A car turned into the lot and he pulled her with him out of the way. "How long after?"

She lifted her shoulders. "That night."

"You were upset after our talk and you were traumatized yesterday. The blackouts could be stress-related."

Except for the incident at the Osage Village site—but it was as good a theory as any, so she nodded.

He walked her toward the sedan. "I still want to know your test results." He opened the passenger door once they'd reached the car and waited until she'd gotten in and snapped her seatbelt before closing it and walking to his side of the vehicle.

She changed the subject. "This town is too small for a rental agency, but Peyton Motors keeps a few rentals on hand. It's only a couple of blocks from here."

He shook his head. "I know you haven't eaten anything today. Let's have lunch. Do you like barbecue?"

The Station, as the locals called it, sat a block off the square along Main Street. A tall, attractive young woman with blonde hair greeted them as they came into the main dining area. "Hi, Marshal." She pulled fresh gloves from a box on the side counter and put them on. "What can I get for you today?"

"Hi, Angie." What do you recommend?" He turned to Willie. "Angie manages the Station. They serve some of the best barbecue I've ever eaten."

"Joel's taking a rack of chicken out of the smoker right now. How about a half chicken and two sides?"

"Sounds good to me." He glanced over. "Willie?"

She nodded toward a sign on the counter. "The brisket stew, I think."

Angie smiled in her direction. "It comes with fresh-baked cornbread—my grandmother's recipe. Go ahead and get your drinks and find a table. We'll bring your food out to you."

Stona insisted on paying for lunch and they took a seat at one of the smaller tables. Willie glanced around the room. The decor was unique—a stuffed turkey in the corner, multiple mounted deer heads, trophy fish. Rows of old license plates from practically every state in the union lined the walls.

Pigs were the main theme. There were pigs on signs, in paintings, pigs wearing chef's hats, piggy banks—one clear, with shredded money inside—pigs that squeaked, squawked, and whistled and, dangling on a string attached to the ceiling was a small pink pig with gossamer wings. Apparently, pigs *did* fly.

Angie brought their meal, and Joel and his wife, Tammy, the restaurant's owners, stopped by the table to say hello before leaving.

After they'd left, Willie looked over at Stona. "How many people in this town know you're a marshal?"

"Only a few. I've been in here a couple of times with Sheriff Devenson, and he introduced me."

"Does the sheriff know you suspect me of killing Josh?" She couldn't hide the worry in her voice.

"First, you're *not* a suspect. My office still has you listed as a person of interest. And second, I've never mentioned you."

"I appreciate that."

They ate in companionable silence and told Angie goodbye before heading back to the car. He pulled out of the lot into the late afternoon traffic, ignoring the directions she gave him to Peyton Motors.

"You're going the wrong way. The car lot's west of here, not South."

"I'm taking you home."

"But I need a car."

"You heard what the doctor said. You're supposed to rest at least one more day and no driving until tomorrow. I'd like to go through the boxes that belong to your cousin this afternoon if that's all right."

She guessed their talk about the car was over. "I thought I was supposed to rest."

"You can put your feet up on the couch and take it easy while I go through them. It shouldn't take long."

She grudgingly nodded. The sooner he looked through the boxes the sooner he could head back to St. Louis. The thought didn't sit well with her. Events of the past two days had elevated him to the position of her protector. The feeling of impending abandonment was probably natural. She tried to shrug it off.

He parked behind the house and once again ordered her to stay in the car with the doors locked while he made sure everything was secure. She noted with a sense of relief the duffel he'd carried to the car this morning was resting in the backseat. He returned a couple of minutes later, opened the door for her, and took her arm as they walked into the house. Was he always such a gentleman, or was taking her arm ingrained after years of hauling perpetrators in for questioning?

They walked into the living room, and he nodded her toward the couch. "I'll be right back." He left the room, and after no more than a minute or two returned carrying a pillow and light blanket. Motioning for her to put her feet up, he placed the pillow behind her back and covered her with the blanket.

"We'll take this a box at a time." He pulled the first box from the stack, and carried it to the couch. Scooting the coffee table out of his way, he sat on the floor, leaned against the couch and situated the box where she could see into it.

The first container was filled with financial statements, receipts, paid bills, and tax papers. None of the information pertained to Nevada or his interest in the Osage. The next two boxes were filled with clothes she intended to donate. Her cousin's shirts and jeans were so familiar she had to swallow back the lump in her throat.

The last three boxes were filled with Josh's books and photo albums. Those were the hardest to look through. Josh loved his books and had shared that love with her. The books in his collection were as familiar to her as they had been to him. Memories of the time they'd spent debating the merits of one book over another were sweet but sad.

Stona made it a little easier. He didn't drag out the process, but checked through each book with care and efficiency, noting where bookmarks had been placed, reading the occasional Post-it note Josh had written.

She grabbed the first photo album, almost possessively, and opened it. Josh's face smiled up at her. Stona turned page after page, revealing images of her mom and dad, Josh and his parents... her entire life lay between the covers of these albums. When she saw the most recent photo of Josh and Trish, her loss knotted her stomach, the pain restricting her breathing.

"I can't do this." She jumped to her feet, dragging the covers to the floor.

She left the room and the house at a run and kept going until she stumbled to a stop beside the tupelo sapling. Sinking to her knees, she rocked forward and back, hugging her midsection, keening. They were never coming back. She'd never hear their voices again, never listen to their laughter.

The sob caught her off guard. She thought she was through crying, had shed enough tears to drown in—tears she had only allowed herself in the privacy of her bedroom during long, sleepless nights. She swiped an angry hand across her wet cheeks but couldn't stem the flow of emotion. And she couldn't stop the pain. It tore at her insides, shredding her spirit, exposing her soul to the agony of total loss. In that moment there was nothing left. God help her, she was so alone.

EIGHTEEN

STONA MOVED TO the window to keep Willie in sight. Knowing her history of loss, he wasn't surprised by her reaction to the photos. He was concerned, though. He should have suspected going through Josh's possessions might trigger such a response. He'd tried to make it quick and impersonal, but when she picked up the top photo album and opened it, she'd looked devastated. He doubted she'd realized her fingers caressed every photo, her body rigid, and she flinched when each new image was revealed. Not the reaction of someone capable of ordering the death of another. Watching her now, he fought the urge to go to her, wanting to respect her privacy.

Until she fell to her knees.

He heard her guttural, wrenching moans before he reached her, the sound almost animalistic, primitive. He bent, lifted her to his chest, and carried her toward the house. Throwing her arms around him, she buried her face in his neck and sobbed her agony.

"Put me down." Her whispered order was at complete odds with the tight grip she had on him.

"No." He doubted she'd be able to stand if he did. Her entire body shook with emotion.

The front door was open. He hadn't taken the time to close it when he'd gone after her. He walked through, kicking it shut behind them on his way up to her room.

When he placed her on the bed she rolled away from him, facing the opposite wall and curled into a fetal position. The message was clear. She wanted him to leave her alone.

It wasn't going to happen.

Her tears had soaked his shirt and she was still sobbing uncontrollably. He wasn't about to walk away. Sitting on the edge of the bed, he reached for her. She stiffened and tried to jerk away from him. Everyone had their breaking point, and he feared she was dangerously close to hers. He refused to let her isolate herself. Dragging her into his lap, he held her tight against his chest until she stopped struggling, then simply held her until the sobs subsided.

She took a deep breath and then another. "I'm sorry."

"You don't have anything to be sorry about."

Sagging against him, she shook her head. "Going through his things…. It was like losing him all over again."

He was forced to bend close to hear her whispered explanation. If he'd had any doubts about her innocence, they'd been dispelled. She was experiencing honest, wrenching sorrow. He waited until her breathing returned to normal, then brushed her hair out of her face and tilted her chin up until their eyes met.

"Better now?"

She nodded and leaned against him. Neither said a word, as the minutes passed in healing silence.

She was the first to speak. "Don't we need to finish looking through the boxes?"

"It can wait."

"No." She took a deep breath. "I need to do this, then put the boxes away. Someday the memories will comfort me, but not now." She slipped out of his arms and stood on wobbly legs.

He got to his feet, grasping her elbow to steady her. "Okay, but we'll stop whenever you need to." He didn't let go of her as they slowly descended the stairs and walked into the living room. Leading her to the couch, he motioned for her to put her feet up. Once she was settled, he pulled the cover over her legs.

Her compliance bothered him. He'd expected an argument, might even have looked forward to it. As a marshal, he'd seen people who'd been beaten down by the challenges of life. Her body language looked a lot like theirs, listless, failing to make eye contact—almost obedient. He knew he was partly to blame for her condition. He had to remind himself that she was a strong woman and even the strongest person, man or woman, had their moments of despair. Sitting at the end of the couch, he pushed the cover off her feet.

"What are you doing?"

"Taking your shoes off so you'll be more comfortable." She didn't protest as he removed her shoes and pulled off one of her socks. When she still didn't object, he began massaging the arch of her foot with his thumb.

"Remember when I told you last night about my ability to sense certain things?"

She'd closed her eyes. "Mmmm."

He took that for yes. "Well, I've sensed something about you." Her eyes opened, and she tried to pull her foot away. He held fast, continuing to rub his thumb from toe to heel. "I don't believe you had anything to do with your cousin's murder."

"I didn't have anything to do with it."

He welcomed the hint of defiance in her voice. "You need to know you're not alone in this. I'm going to do my best to find the real killer."

He lifted her other foot into his lap, pulled the sock off, and began to massage the arch. "My superiors and the FBI will continue to consider you a person of interest. My opinion isn't going to change their minds. Right now, you're their most obvious suspect. Investigators can be tenacious if they believe they have their perpetrator, even if there's no hard evidence of a connection to the crime. They'll insist on definitive proof someone else killed your cousin. I intend to find that proof. I just wanted you to know I'll be working this case with the intention of proving your innocence, not your guilt. I'm determined to find the real murderer."

She sighed, and he wasn't sure if it was because of the foot rub, or what he'd told her. He didn't have to wonder long. She pulled her feet out of his lap and sat up. "So, I *am* a suspect?"

"Not officially, though I'm sure a few in the department feel they have your cousin's case wrapped up."

"They believe I'm guilty until proven innocent?"

"I'm afraid so, but they're not a court of law. They might have established motive, but they can't prove opportunity. They know you didn't personally tamper with the car. You were either at the hospital, or with your coworkers all day. We checked. And they can't connect you with the person who slit the brake lines. They don't even know who he is yet."

"Could you get into trouble for telling me this?"

He shrugged. "I could get a verbal reprimand from my immediate superior, but I doubt it. I'm not giving away any secrets. An attorney would tell you the same thing."

"Why are you taking the chance of damaging your career?"

"I'm no hero, Willie. I'm not risking my future to help you. My instincts tell me you're innocent. I'm acting on those instincts. I can't ignore them."

"You didn't have to say anything to me."

"No, I didn't, but you needed to hear it. You're vulnerable right now. You lost the last member of your family. Then I show up, tell you he was murdered, and you're the only person with motive. I imagine you feel you're already on trial, alone, against the system. It isn't true, Will. You aren't alone. We'll get through this together."

NINETEEN

HE'D SAID HE wasn't a hero. That depended on how you defined a hero. Willie watched as Stona closed a box and picked it up.

They'd spent the last hour going through the photos. Stona kept the mood light, asking about the places they'd visited in the vacation shots, and teasing her about her knobby knees in several childhood pictures. The easy banter turned what might have been an arduous task into an almost pleasant evening. But the pain of loss always lingered beneath the surface, and it was a relief when they'd finished going through the final album.

He stacked the box with the others against the wall, then faced her. "You're pale. The doctor wanted you to rest. Put your feet up again." He pulled the cover off the back of the couch where she'd tossed it.

She probably looked like one of the walking dead, though he was too much of a gentleman to tell her so. Did being unconscious, in the throes of a nightmarish vision, for who knew how long, qualify for a good night's sleep? She lifted her feet onto the couch and leaned back against the pillow.

He tucked her in, even straightening and fluffing the pillow behind her head. After setting her shoes and socks at the foot of the couch, he pulled the coffee table closer, then went into the kitchen. A few minutes later he returned, balancing a cup and saucer in one hand and a glass of water and bottle of ibuprofen in the other.

"I thought you could use something hot. I hope chamomile tea is all right. It was the first box I found."

"Yes, thank you."

He set the teacup on the coffee table and handed her the glass of water. Opening the ibuprofen, he shook out a tablet and offered it to her.

"Take this first, and then drink all of the water. You're probably dehydrated."

She nodded, opening her palm for the medication. After downing the tablet and finishing the water, she set the glass on the table. "I appreciate your help, but you don't have to wait on me."

He picked up the glass and handed her the teacup. "I only made a cup of tea. I'd hardly call that waiting on you." He started toward the kitchen. "When you've finished your tea, try to rest. Nap if you can. I'm going out to the car, but I'll be right back. I need my laptop to finish some paperwork."

"I didn't know you had a laptop with you."

"It's in the trunk with my briefcase." He turned to leave.

"Stona, wait." She set the cup on the table. "It isn't necessary for you to stay. I'm fine, really."

He shook his head. "You thought you were fine yesterday, but last night proved you weren't. I don't have to be back in St. Louis until the day after tomorrow. By then, you should have recovered enough to be alone. But I'm staying tonight." He walked away without giving her a chance to argue.

Leaning back against the pillow she closed her eyes. He was right. She needed one more day to recover.

The smell of food cooking woke her. Was Stona fixing supper? She didn't think she'd made any noise, but as soon as she sat up, he walked into the living room. He'd changed into a faded blue T-shirt that emphasized his wide shoulders and muscular arms and a pair of equally faded jeans that hugged his lower body. His tennis shoes had also seen better days. He looked good... really good.

She pushed the hair away from her face and glanced out the window. It was dusk. "What time is it?"

"Nearly six o'clock."

She'd slept most of the afternoon away. "Something smells good."

"It's almost ready. If you'd like, I can bring you a tray."

Her headache was finally gone and hopefully wouldn't return. "Thanks, but I'd rather eat at the table. Any more rest and I won't be able to sleep tonight." She took the hand he extended and got to her feet. "Give me a minute to go upstairs and splash some water on my face."

"Can you manage the stairs on your own?"

"I think so. The nap helped my headache." When she saw the doubt in his eyes, she smiled reassuringly. "If I need help, I'll call, I promise."

The meal wasn't elaborate, but the chunky beef soup from a can and grilled cheese sandwiches were good and the conversation light.

She swallowed the last spoonful of soup in her bowl and grinned at him. "You give a whole new meaning to the phrase protect and serve."

He wiped his mouth on his napkin and laughed. "Wrong department, but I'm glad you enjoyed the meal." He carried their dishes and silverware to the sink rinsing them under the tap.

She got to her feet. "I can clean up. You cooked."

"Too late." He rinsed the last bowl and stacked it in the dishwasher.

"Did you find anything useful in any of the boxes?"

"I'm afraid not. But at this point in the investigation we don't know what we're looking for. I've made a few notes on the contents of each box in case we need to go through one again. You marked a couple of them for donation. I'd appreciate it if you'd wait to give them away."

"Of course."

"Do you have a place for the boxes?"

"I've cleared out one corner of the storage area off the mud room."

"I'll carry them." They returned to the living room. When he nodded toward the couch, she shook her head but compromised by settling into the overstuffed chair and slipping her feet on the ottoman. He grabbed the blanket from the couch and draped it over her legs before lifting the box of books. They had to be heavy, but he didn't seem to notice.

She noticed. The snug T-shirt stretched over his taut muscles like a second skin. The suit jacket he always wore had hidden his obvious attributes. When he caught her looking and grinned, her entire body went up in flames. He'd had an arrogant swagger in his step when he'd disappeared through the kitchen on his way to the storage room. Perhaps the unflappable Marshal Jordan was human after all.

Stona returned to the living room after putting away the last box, but immediately excused himself and went to her study. She read for a while but, despite the long afternoon nap, she was ready for a hot shower and her bed by ten o'clock.

Out of habit, she made sure the front and back doors were locked before stopping by the study. He looked up when she hesitated at the entrance. "I'm sorry to bother you. I just wanted to let you know I'm going to bed. I'll see you in the morning." She turned to leave.

"Willie?"

She stopped and looked around at him.

"Leave your door open wide tonight. I'll do the same. If you get in trouble again, I want to be able to hear you."

She nodded, relieved to know he didn't intend to spend another night on the floor in her room. "Good night."

He smiled. "Sweet dreams."

She returned his smile and headed up the stairs. He'd wished her sweet dreams. She could only hope.

The hot shower made her even more drowsy, but when she went to the door to open it wider, she heard him coming up the stairs. Like a child caught sneaking out of bed, she scurried back to hers and practically dove under the covers. He stopped to push her door a little wider, then went into his own room. A minute later she heard him go into the hall bathroom. She dozed off listening for him to return to his room.

She wasn't sure what had awakened her. The room was shadow-dark, the only illumination from a nightlight plugged into the wall above the sink in the adjoining bathroom. Goosebumps shivered over her arms and she tried to rub them away. Someone was watching her. She could feel the intense gaze and swallowed back the need to cry Stona's name. Was she having another vision? No, of course not. This was her room, not a primitive cabin or an Osage lodge. She glanced around half expecting her world to suddenly change.

And then she saw him.

Stone Shaper stood less than ten feet from the end of her bed. Her room was dark, but he seemed to be standing in a pool of light. He was bare-chested and wore only a breechcloth and leggings. He carried a lance—the same weapon he'd carried the day his war party attacked Beth's home. The warrior was close enough for her to see the red-stained tip of the spearhead. *Her* spearhead.

He glared and shouted at her as he brandished his weapon. At least she thought he was shouting. No sound passed his lips. It didn't have to. His rage washed over her without words, his eyes promising a quick death.

TWENTY

THE FEAR-CRAZED screams jolted Stona awake. Rolling out of bed, he grabbed his gun and raced across the hall to Willie's room. He hit the light switch. She sat up in bed, staring straight ahead, eyes wide and glazed. She was still screaming.

"It's okay, Will, I'm here." He moved to the closet, nudged the door open, and checked inside. Nothing. Gun raised he checked the bathroom next. It was empty and the inside bolt on the door to the adjoining bedroom was locked. No one could've gone through into the other room.

Returning to her, he laid his gun on the nightstand and sat beside her on the bed. She crawled into his lap, wrapping both arms around his waist. He pulled her close and rocked her as though she were a child. His lips touched her ear.

"It's okay, Will. I'm here. I promise I won't let anyone hurt you."

She had a death grip on him. He could feel her heart slamming against his chest.

"It was him. But this time he was angry. He came after me. I thought he was going to kill me, then he... he disappeared." She looked up at him, her eyes wide with fright. "I know it sounds crazy, but he just disappeared."

"Willie, no one was here. I would've seen him. I was in the hall before your first scream ended. You must have been dreaming."

She violently shook her head. "No. He was too real to be a dream. He had a weapon."

Stona tensed. "What kind of weapon?"

"A spear. He was carrying a spear."

He relaxed. "Think about it, Will. No one's going to break in armed with a spear. Put it together. You've been under a lot of stress. Think about what you've gone through—losing Josh, the tree on your car, and the skeleton. It's the stuff of nightmares. And they came together in your dream, honey. It was only a dream."

———————

THIS TIME SHE let him get away with the endearment. He'd been worried about her. It was comforting, knowing someone cared. Sure, Ben and Scott cared. They were her best friends, and she allowed them to occasionally call her honey, but they weren't here—and Stona was.

He pulled her closer and rubbed her back. "You're shivering. You should get under the covers."

He lifted her away from him, but she grabbed his neck, fiercely hugging him. "Don't leave me. Please. I can't be alone right now." If he left her, she might not survive whatever waited for her to close her eyes.

"Okay I'll stay here tonight." He reached up to pry her arms away from him. "Let me go so I can get my blankets and pillow."

She wouldn't release him. "No, not on the floor. I need you close to me so he... I mean the dreams won't come back."

"Willie, that's not a good idea. You don't know what you're asking."

"I trust you. I know you won't try to take advantage of me. I don't understand how I know but I do. Please sleep with me tonight—and leave the light on, too."

He pulled back and looked down at her. "You're that frightened?"

"I'm terrified." He didn't say anything. His pensive silence worried her. She wasn't sure she would survive the night alone.

"All right." He stood with her in his arms and shoved the covers back with his knee before climbing into bed with her. Dislodging her arms from his neck, he settled her against his shoulder and reached down to drag the covers over them both.

Cocooned in his warmth and safety, she relaxed and snuggled closer to the heat radiating from his body. "Thank you," she whispered. "Good night."

"Good night, Will. Try to rest." His voice was strained, almost gruff.

———————

STONA HAD NO one to blame but himself. He could've said no—*should* have. He'd told her it was a bad idea, snuggling together in this bed, her warm soft body pressed against his. No, it hadn't been a bad idea, it had been crazy—and he'd be certifiable if she didn't stop wiggling her sweet little behind against his groin. He grabbed her hip and put a little space between their bodies. Maybe it had been crazy, but he couldn't say no to her. Not when he'd seen the fear in her eyes.

All he wanted to do right now was pull her closer than she was already, stroke her silken hair... and kiss her. Out of the question. She was physically and emotionally vulnerable. He had no business allowing himself to be attracted to her, much less wanting her. And right now, he wanted her more than he'd ever wanted a woman.

So, what was there about Wilhelmina McAllister that drew him like a magnet to north? She was sweet and feisty, caring and tough, and right now she was vulnerable.

He inhaled. He liked the way she smelled. Not good. Not good at all.

———————

STONA HAD FINALLY relaxed against her. Willie lay listening to his deep, even breathing before rolling away from him. He immediately grasped her waist, tugging her so close her face rested against his hard chest. Even in sleep, he held her as though someone might try to snatch her away from him. He made her feel safe, but she couldn't stop thinking about the warrior in the meadow, the same warrior who'd stood at the foot of her bed tonight.

Stone Shaper.

The Osage warrior in her visions had really never been limited to that dreamlike state. Was she the only one who saw him? If he appeared again tonight, would Stona see him, too? She didn't think so.

She was beginning to question her own sanity. Others would question it, too. If she told anyone, even Stona about what was happening to her, they would believe she was delusional.

Josh's death was the catalyst for what was happening to her. She'd loved Trish and missed her, but Josh was family, and what was happening to her was somehow linked to their past. It was crazy to believe that, but the episodes hadn't started until Josh's death. She'd always had her feet firmly on the ground, had never believed in ghosts, or UFOs or anything supernatural for that matter. Did she now? Her sigh was deep, heartfelt and wistful.

Stona's arm tightened around her and his lips touched her forehead in a butterfly-kiss. "It's okay, Will. I'm here. I've got you." His voice was a sleepy whisper and she knew he wasn't awake enough to know what he'd done. Still, it felt like a caress.

What was she thinking? She couldn't let herself take comfort in his presence. It had been pure cowardice on her part when she'd begged him to spend the night with her. She couldn't continue to depend on him.

He'd told her he believed she was innocent. As soon as he convinced his superiors she'd had nothing to do with Josh's death, he'd be reassigned to a different aspect of the case, or maybe to another case altogether. An ache gnawed at the pit of her stomach. She'd never see him again.

She couldn't stop him from leaving, but she could find out what had happened in Nevada. What had frightened Josh enough to send him home to warn her away from the small town?

The hand at her back began a gentle circular motion with just enough pressure to ease the tension from her neck and shoulders. His cheek pressed the top of her head. "Sleep, Willie. You're not alone."

She would be tomorrow or the following day.

But tonight, she had a protector and a friend. For the moment she wasn't alone. It would have to be enough.

TWENTY-ONE

WILLIE OPENED HER eyes and knew she'd overslept. The early morning sunbeams that usually streamed through her east-facing window had already come and gone.

A quick glance at her clock confirmed her assumption. Almost ten. She glanced at the pillow beside hers and saw the indentation. She hadn't dreamed it. Stona had been in her bed last night—at her invitation.

And she didn't think she'd dreamed the reason he'd been there. Slipping her feet to the floor, she reached for her robe at the foot of her bed and put it on. Had Stone Shaper really appeared in her room last night? Common sense said no, but every ounce of her being screamed yes. She hadn't dreamed him.

Stona believed she'd had a nightmare brought on by weeks of stress, complicated by her concussion. She wouldn't disagree. His theory freed her from trying to explain an occurrence she didn't understand.

She made up her bed, gathered the black dress pants and green, long-sleeved silk blouse she'd laid out the night before, and headed for the bathroom to shower and change.

Twenty minutes later, after a quick once-over in the mirror, she decided she was ready to face the day, if not the man waiting for her downstairs. Unplugging her cell phone, she slipped it into her pocket, walked across the hall, and glanced into the guest room. Stona's bed was made. Nothing in the room indicated he'd ever been there. He must've carried his overnight bag with him.

She listened for any sound as she descended the stairs, but all was quiet. Had he left? She shook her head. He wouldn't leave her stranded.

Stona wasn't downstairs either. She hurried to the back door and glanced out the window. His car was gone.

He'd left her.

She felt abandoned. The emotion was unreasonable. So was the apprehension gnawing at the pit of her stomach. She'd never been afraid of being alone—at least not since becoming an adult. The feeling didn't sit well with her. She wasn't sure she knew how to remedy the negative emotion. You couldn't just tell yourself you weren't going to be afraid.

He was gone, but she'd figure something out. She had lived with fear before she'd met Stona Jordan, and she'd do it again.

She spotted the note on the table as she walked through the kitchen toward the living room. He was a man of few words. The note read, "Call me." His card was on the table beside the note. One of the three phone numbers was circled. He'd also left her an empty teacup with a packaged teabag on the saucer. Chamomile. Was she going to need the calming influence of the herbal tea when she talked to him? She flipped the switch on the electric tea kettle he'd also filled for her.

Pulling her phone from her pocket, she punched in his number while the water heated.

He answered on the third ring. *"Hold on Willie, I'm on the highway. Give me a minute to pull over."*

"Okay." She sat down at the table. Her knees hadn't exactly gone weak at the sound of his voice, but she was shaken by the sense of well-being his voice engendered. How needy was that?

"Willie?"

"I'm here."

"Good. How do you feel this morning? Is your headache gone?"

"Yes, I'm fine. Where are you?" She cringed at the anxiety in her voice.

"I'm on my way to St. Louis. I've been called back to the Eastern District office. I haven't spoken with my direct superior yet, so I'm not sure of the reason."

"Why didn't you wake me?"

"It was early, and you needed your rest. But don't worry. I stopped by Peyton Motors on my way out of town and arranged to have a rental car delivered to you. I checked out the available vehicles and chose one I thought you'd like. I've taken care of the basic rental fees and insurance for a month. That should give you plenty of time to find a car you'd like to buy."

Her spine stiffened. "I can't let you pay for the rental car." There was a definite bite to her words.

"Calm down. I'm not actually paying for your rental. The Suttons' insurance company will reimburse me. They'll take care of your mileage fees too. I'm only making sure you get your car right away, without having to deal with the paperwork. You can call Peyton Motors when you're ready for the car. They'll bring it to you."

"All right, thank you." She laughed—a halfhearted effort at humor. "I seem to be saying that a lot lately."

"You're welcome, and don't worry about it."

"Do you think maybe there's been a breakthrough in Josh's case? Could that be why you're being called back to your office?"

"It's hard to say. My callback could be unrelated to this case. I'll let you know as soon as I find out what's going on." He paused for a long moment. *"Willie, I don't know how long I'll be away. I'm worried about you staying alone out there. If you'd have another blackout...."*

"I'll be fine. You don't have to worry." She wasn't being completely honest. She was hiding so many doubts she was sure he could hear the anxiety in her voice.

"Is there anyone—a friend or neighbor—you can check in with a couple of times a day? Someone who can alert authorities if they can't reach you?"

"Stona, I promise you I'll be all right."

"Is there anyone you can call?" There was an edge to his voice as he repeated the question.

"I honestly don't know anyone well enough to ask."

"You know one person well enough."

"I promise I don't know anyone."

"Me, Will. You know me. Until I get back you call me twice a day—no, make that three times a day. Call me when you wake up in the morning, in the middle of the day, sometime between eleven and three, and before you go to bed at night."

"You'll be at least a couple of hundred miles away. What can you do?"

"I'll contact the sheriff if I can't get in touch with you, and he won't waste time. He'll conduct an immediate wellness check."

"I don't want you to involve the sheriff. He'll want an explanation for the check."

"He wouldn't require an explanation from a U. S. Deputy Marshal. You either keep in touch with me or I'll call him. It's up to you."

He wasn't bluffing. She had one more option. "I can arrange to call Scott or Ben. You remember them, don't you?"

"They don't live anywhere near you."

"You won't be anywhere near me either."

"True, but I can get you help a lot faster than they can."

"They're paramedics. The sheriff would listen to them."

"I'm law enforcement, and he knows me. He'll get to you faster if I make the call."

He was right, but it galled her to admit it. "All right. But this is only temporary. I can't have 'Big Brother' watching me for the next month."

"Hopefully I'll be back before the month ends."

She sighed. That didn't mean he wouldn't keep watching out for her. It just meant she wouldn't have to call him if she needed help.

"And, Willie."

"Yes?"

"I'm not your brother. Keep that in mind."

He broke the connection.

———————

STONA STARED AT the phone in his hand. He knew Willie's 'Big Brother' remark was in reference to a term coined by a science fiction author and tossed around by conspiracy theorists. But he still didn't like her comparing him to a brother. Tossing his phone on the seat beside him, he restarted the car and pulled onto the highway. His feelings for her were hardly brotherly. His emotions concerning her had run from ambivalent to confused and now deep concern. How could he have allowed himself to get this close to her? *Allowed?* He couldn't have stopped it. He'd been blindsided.

He was also dangerously close to compromising his objectivity. There was no sound evidence of Willie's innocence, just as there was no evidence of her guilt. Yet he knew beyond doubt she was incapable of killing her cousin, and he intended to argue her innocence to his superiors.

His thoughts returned to last night and Willie's nightmare. He refused to admit Willie might be experiencing hallucinations. Her blackouts were already a worry. Neurological problems seldom showed up on CAT scans unless biological problems such as tumors or strokes were involved, and her doctor had pretty much ruled those out. Hopefully, her problems were stress related. It made sense. Each episode occurred directly after a high stress situation. The most recent phenomenon, the hallucination or bad dream could have been brought on by her concussion.

He signaled and merged into the left lane to pass a slower-moving maintenance vehicle, returning to the right lane as soon as he cleared the truck. Willie was never far from his thoughts. Hearing her voice when he answered the phone a few minutes ago forced him to admit he already missed her. What had it been, four hours since he'd seen her? Most married couples spend more time than that away from each other every day.

If they'd been married, he would've kissed her goodbye. Who was he kidding? If they'd been married, he would have kissed her awake and made love to her before leaving.

He'd wanted to make love to her last night. Not at first. When he pulled her against him and covered them both with the blanket his only concern had been calming her terror. It wasn't until she'd finally relaxed against him that his body began to respond to the warm woman in his arms. Her scent, a mixture of roses and the woman herself, intoxicated him. Her soft curves molded to his hard body, her gentle moans of pleasure as he rubbed her back drove him crazy with need. Oh yes, he'd wanted her.

It had been out of the question, of course. With luck, being away from her for a few days would put things into perspective, reinforce the fact that, as long as he was on this case, he had no business lusting after Ms. Wilhelmina McAllister, the Justice Department's person of interest.

TWENTY-TWO

WILLIE CALLED PEYTON Motors as soon as Stona disconnected. She wasn't sure how she felt about her promise to keep in touch with him. While she didn't like the idea of having a watchdog, it was comforting to know someone would be there if she needed help. Was she becoming too dependent on him? Maybe. Regardless, she couldn't let him interfere with her determination to find out what Josh's cryptic last words had meant.

She turned off the electric teakettle and opted for a bottle of water from the refrigerator. Stay away from Nevada. What had spooked Josh enough for him to return to St. Louis to give her that warning? Had something happened, or had he instinctively known something was wrong—or would be? She'd probably never know.

Locating her handbag, she retrieved the spearhead. Her curiosity regarding the artifact had nearly gotten her killed. The curator at the museum had offered to buy it. She should've given the thing to him and saved herself a little pain and a lot of mental anguish. Discarding the tissue, she stared down at the silver-pink flint. Parting with it wasn't an option. Even now, she was compelled to keep it close.

If she could, she'd wear it. She paused to study the artifact. A necklace, maybe? She chuckled over the absurd thought. It was at least three inches long, possibly a little more with the U-shaped base—not delicate and certainly not stylish. But then neither was she. Once the idea planted itself in her mind, she couldn't stop thinking about it. The fluted edges on the base might be deep enough to hold a ribbon or thin shoestring in place if she wrapped it tight.

She didn't have any ribbon, but there might be something useful in the cabinet's junk drawer. Rummaging through the hodgepodge of coupons, safety pins and odd treasures, she came up short on shoelaces, but the only other choice turned out to be perfect for her need. In the back corner of the drawer, she found a spool of waxed, leather thread, thick and strong enough to stitch a saddle, or sew a tear in a canvas tarp or tent. Cutting a length of thread, she made sure the ends were even then looped the thread around the base of the spearhead. After knotting it tight, she put a drop of Gorilla Glue on the back and another drop in front. Once the glue dried, she knotted the two ends, trimmed the excess and slipped the necklace over her head. The cool flint rested between her breasts, warming within minutes.

———————

HER RENTAL, A three-year-old silver Honda Accord, arrived before noon. A second car followed the Accord. After giving Willie the paperwork and keys, the Honda's driver got into the other car and left.

The vehicle looked new, the interior clean and barely worn. After listening to the motor, she decided Stona had made a good choice. If it handled well, she might consider making an offer on the car.

Anxious to see how it drove, she decided to make a trip into town. She needed a few things from the grocery store anyway. Returning to the house, she grabbed her purse and phone, made sure the doors were locked, and headed to the car.

The Honda was everything Stona had claimed. The motor hummed, everything worked, and her favorite radio station sounded fantastic. She liked the feel of the car, and by the time she'd reached town, she was sold.

The store was busy, and she noticed quite a few carts containing Halloween supplies. The seasonal shelves had been picked through and were half-empty. Halloween couldn't be that far off. She'd lost track of the days. A quick check of the calendar on her phone surprised her. Halloween was tomorrow.

November was only two days away. Still, the drive home was beautiful. The unusually warm weather must have delayed late fall defoliation though the reds and golds of early October were muted now. In the far distance, the smoky-blue tinted hills, commonly called the Ozark Mountains, offered a contrast.

She was so caught up in the splendor of fall she didn't notice the old man sitting cross-legged in the corner of the front porch until she'd stepped out of the car. Standing in the vehicle's open door, she waited to see what he would do.

The man didn't seem inclined to move from where he sat. He didn't look dangerous. No doubt she could defend herself if he gathered enough strength to attack her, though she did wonder if he had a weapon hidden beneath the woven blanket wrapped around his body. She thought about calling the local authorities but decided to wait. The old fellow looked to be in his mid-80s, and too feeble to be a threat. Reaching into her purse, she palmed the can of pepper spray just in case.

He still hadn't moved by the time she'd climbed the porch steps, though he turned his head to watch her approach. His faded jeans, western shirt, and scuffed boots didn't tell her much about him. The Stetson smashed down on top of his gray braided hair looked as old and wrinkled as he did. He embodied the Hollywood stereotype of an ancient Native American. On the other hand, if he'd worn a scruffy beard, he might have been mistaken for Willie Nelson.

Maybe he couldn't get up. She didn't know how long he'd been sitting there. She'd been gone for at least two hours. "Can I help you?"

His piercing black eyes studied her, and she was left with the distinct impression of being evaluated—no, *judged*.

She folded her arms across her waist, uncomfortable with his perusal, and edged toward the door. "Can I call someone for you?"

He didn't answer.

"Are you hungry? I can heat some soup." When he still failed to answer she got irritated. "Can I help you in any way?"

The old man held her gaze. He seemed to be waiting for her full attention. "Wilhelmina McAllister, I am here to help you. It is my destiny to guide you on your journey."

She hated being called *Wilhelmina*. "How do you know my name?"

"It is on your mailbox."

"No, it isn't."

"It should be. Makes it easier to find you."

"I don't want to be found. Why are you here?"

"I am your spirit guide."

She tilted her head and tried not to laugh. "I thought spirit guides were supposed to be animals."

He shrugged. "I'm an exception to the rule. What kind of soup?"

The shift in subject threw her. "What?"

"You offered soup. What kind?"

"I—uh...." She rattled off the first thing that came to mind. "Vegetable beef? Chicken noodle?"

"From a can?"

Of *course*, from a can. Did she look like Betty Crocker? "Canned is all I have."

He sighed. "It will have to do. It has been a long time since I've had to worry about food and drink."

That told her he had a friend or relative somewhere who took care of him. "Are you sure I can't call someone, a family member who might be missing you right now? What's your name?"

"You can call me Joe."

"Where do you live, Joe?"

"Did you say you would cook soup?"

"Oh—yes. I'll fix it now and bring it out. You're welcome to sit in the chair." She motioned to a white wicker rocking chair on the other side of the porch. "You'll be more comfortable." The old man nodded but made no effort to move.

She hesitated, undecided. Should she bring him into the house? She didn't believe he was dangerous, but there was something odd about the way he talked. Even food and drink seemed distant memories.

She was struck by his demeanor. He seemed at peace. Perhaps, at his age, he'd already faced his demons and had come to terms with them. She shook her head over her fanciful thoughts.

"You could come into the house where it's warmer." Bringing a stranger into her home wasn't something she'd normally do, but for reasons she couldn't comprehend, whatever fear of the man she had originally harbored was gone. She knew for a certainty he would never harm her.

He shook his head. "The blanket keeps me warm, and my heart finds joy in the world around me. I am content here."

She nodded and unlocked the door. By the time she stepped into the foyer he seemed to have forgotten she'd even been there.

Microwaves were a blessing. It took more time to open the can and pour it into a bowl than it did to heat the soup—well, maybe it took a little longer, but not by much. Her guest was sitting where she'd left him. She thought he might be sleeping since his head was bent so low his chin rested on his chest, but as soon as she crossed the porch, he lifted his head. "You are a good woman, Wilhelmina McAllister." He raised both hands to receive the bowl and spoon, ending her initial concern about a weapon.

A few minutes later, he lifted the bowl toward her. "The soup is salty."

She glanced at the bowl and noticed it was empty. Most canned soups were salty but apparently not so salty he couldn't finish it. "Would you like another bowl?"

"This was enough for now. You have been kind to an old man. I will teach you how to use herbs to make good soup."

Uh-oh. It sounded like he intended to stay. Great. All she needed was an uninvited house guest, or porch guest since he showed no interest in coming inside. "I'm sure your family's worried about you. If you give me a phone number, I can call and let them know you're safe."

"My people understand I am on a journey. They will not worry."

"You mentioned a journey earlier. Where are you going?"

"My destination is here. But our journey has only begun."

"Our journey? I'm not planning to go anywhere."

"Your journey has already begun. It is the reason I am here to guide you."

She was getting a little nervous. The old man made no sense. "I told you, I'm not going anywhere. You'll have to find someone else to go on your journey with you."

"The journey is not measured by miles, but by atonement."

A shiver of apprehension chilled her. "Atonement? For what? I haven't done anything I need to atone for."

"This is true, yet the burden is yours to bear. *You* are the chosen one."

TWENTY-THREE

HER CELL RANG, breaking the momentary silence stretching between them.

Without taking her eyes off the old man, Willie dug the phone out of her pocket and put it to her ear. "Hello?"

"Willie, are you all right?" Stona's voice was full of worry.

"I'm fine. Why do you ask?"

"Because it's three fifteen." His tone morphed from worry to exasperation. *"You promised to call me by three. Remember?"*

The old man got to his feet. He was much taller than she'd assumed, at least six feet. He still looked frail, though he hadn't had any trouble standing.

"Willie?" Stona sounded worried again.

She pulled her thoughts back to their conversation. "Yes—yes, I remember. I was trying out the rental and lost track of time. I'm sorry."

"You sound distracted. Are you sure you're okay?"

"I am distracted. I'm driving." She hoped the impromptu lie was convincing.

It wasn't.

"Willie you just told me you've been driving, not that you are *driving. You said, 'I was trying out the rental'—was—past tense."*

"That's right I *was* driving, and then I pulled over to get my cell phone, and now I'm driving again."

"It sounds like you're standing outside."

"I have the window down. I should go. It isn't safe to use a cell phone while you're driving. I'll call you tonight at nine. Bye." She pushed the end-call button before he could respond, shut the phone off and stuffed it into her jeans. She hated lying to him, but if she told him someone had shown up at her house, he'd send the sheriff out. She didn't want the old man—Joe—taken into custody, protective or otherwise. Anyone who came out to check on her would believe he was mentally challenged. He behaved so strangely she should believe the same thing, but she didn't.

"You did not speak the truth." Joe stared at the distant meadow when he made that comment.

"No, I didn't."

"This bothers you." It was an observation not a question.

"Yes, it bothers me. I don't lie, or at least I never used to."

"Why did you lie?"

"To keep you out of jail."

He nodded. "It is a good reason."

Of course, he'd think the lie was a good idea. But it wasn't. She was lying to a federal marshal, probably the only marshal in his district who thought she was innocent. He was the last person she needed to deceive. So why did she?

Because, if he found out about Joe, he'd be furious. She didn't doubt he would turn around and come right back to protect her, even if it cost him his job. Since the accident at the Suttons', he behaved less like a federal marshal and more like an overprotective big brother.

Her emotions, on the other hand, weren't exactly sisterly. She'd been attracted to the man since they'd first met. Even as she'd kicked him out of her house.

"You still should not lie to your man."

"He isn't my man, and how do you know who I was talking to?"

He shrugged, as though the answer were obvious. "I am your spirit guide. It is my duty to know these things."

They were back to his crazy claims. "Look... I know you mean well, but I really think we need to get in touch with your family. I'll be glad to let you stay here until they come for you. You do have family, don't you?"

"My family knows I must remain with you until you have successfully finished your journey." He adjusted the blanket closer around his shoulders. "You are not a good liar. It is too cold to leave the window down." She was beginning to think his sudden change in subjects was intentional.

She folded her arms across her chest. "You have to understand I won't be going with you on this journey of yours. I have my own journey. I'm sorry, but you need to go home. And I need to get on with what's happening in my life."

"And when our paths cross?"

"I doubt our paths will cross again."

"Have you seen him yet?"

He did it again, changed subjects on her. "Seen who?"

"He Who Walks The Earth."

Well, that certainly narrowed the field. "Does this Earth walker have a name?"

"Stone Shaper."

She needed to sit down. Staggering to the wicker chair, she collapsed into it and stared at the old man.

"So, he has made himself known to you. It is as I suspected. You have the spear point. We have waited a long time for the chosen one."

"I'm not your chosen one. I'm an ordinary person trying to hold my life together. I just want to be left alone to solve my own problems."

"Few of us are blessed with the path of our choosing." He started down the steps.

She leaned forward. "Wait. Where are you going?"

He looked around at her. "You have much to consider. I will return with the morning light. You will have questions then."

She had questions now. "Where will you sleep?"

"Your barn is warm and dry. I will sleep there."

"You'll be more comfortable in the house. I have a spare bedroom you can use."

"I do not think you will get much sleep if I am in your house. The barn will meet my needs. But I thank you, Wilhelmina McAllister."

"Please, don't call me Wilhelmina. I hate that name. You can call me Will, or Willie if you'd like, just not Wilhelmina."

"You are the chosen one. I will call you, She Who Is Chosen." He gathered the blanket around his body and slowly descended the last two porch steps. She watched him as he followed the path around the side of the house and disappeared.

Pushing her foot against the floorboards, she set the rocker in motion. She'd asked him not to call her Wilhelmina, but she wasn't sure She Who Is Chosen was any better. At least he'd be the only one calling her that. But then, he was the only one who called her Wilhelmina.

She put the small irritation aside. There was far more to worry about. How did the old man know about Stone Shaper? She hadn't told anyone about the Osage warrior. It was one more piece of a puzzle she wasn't sure she wanted to finish. The man who called himself Joe believed he was there to help her on her journey. It sounded more like a quest. At this point she wouldn't be surprised if he mentioned the Holy Grail. The only reason she hadn't decided he was a senile old man was Stone Shaper. Had he meant the ghostly figure on the hill, or did he mean the warrior in her visions? It didn't matter. Joe shouldn't have known about either one. So why did he?

She shivered. The wind had grown chilly and surely that was the only reason for the goosebumps crawling up her arms. She got out of the chair and went into the house, locking the door behind her. Was it a precaution against the old man in her barn? At this point she wasn't sure who or what she should be afraid of.

Not for the first time today, she wished Stona was here. She knew she shouldn't depend on a man who was assigned to investigate her. But since the day they'd met—the day she'd seen Stone Shaper, and experienced her first vision, he'd been an integral part of what was going on in her life. She liked him—a lot. But she didn't know the marshal well enough to trust him with her secrets. She couldn't trust anyone. Not until she understood what was going on in her life.

Regardless of what Joe told her, he was part of the problem, not a companion on her "journey"—whatever that meant. She had to face what was happening alone. The only person she would've felt safe confiding in was Josh, and he was lost to her.

Nothing made sense. Absolutely nothing.

How did Joe know about Stone Shaper? She moved to the living room window and gazed toward the meadow where she'd first seen the Osage warrior. The old man had made several cryptic remarks about his reason for being here, but he'd never been specific about what she had been chosen to do. Until he mentioned Stone Shaper, she'd shrugged him off, believing he was suffering from dementia or Alzheimer's disease. So now she had to ask herself again how he knew about Stone Shaper. Short of being a mind reader, he couldn't possibly know who the Osage warrior was. She'd never spoken his name out loud, even in the privacy of her own home. She'd never googled the name, looked it up in the library, mentioned it at the Bushwhacker Museum, or to the Suttons. And she had never told Stona. The only thing she had done related to Stone Shaper was ask the curator at the Museum about the spearhead, and at the time she hadn't made the connection between the man and the artifact. Not until last night, when she'd seen Stone Shaper in her bedroom.

She walked to the couch. The teacup Stona had brought to her last night still rested in its saucer on the coffee table. She'd forgotten to put it in the kitchen before she'd gone to bed. It had been sweet, the way he'd taken care of her yesterday, and the way he'd held her through the night....

She pushed the thought aside and lifted the spearhead from its hiding place. A picture of Stone Shaper waving the lance at her flashed in her mind's eye as she pulled the necklace over her head. She took a deep breath, then forced herself to look at the flint. Even an amateur—which was what she was—could see the fluted edges and tell it had been perfectly crafted. Had Stone Shaper worked the flint into this incredible piece of art? It stood to reason. His name had been Stone Shaper. Most early Osage carried names associated with their lives, didn't they—like She Who Is Chosen?

Stone Shaper's appearance last night had been a revelation. She should've put it together sooner. Somehow, the spearhead was the catalyst. The warrior's appearances and the visions had occurred after she'd found the artifact. But why? People found arrowheads and Native American artifacts every day. Yet there were never reports of an artifact-induced delusion, not even in the tabloids. So, what was different in her case? She turned the spearhead over in her hand, careful not to touch the edges. She already knew how sharp they were. She glanced at her bandaged finger and stilled.

Blood.

Bile rose in her throat. She had to take several deep breaths to keep from gagging. Had it only been a few short days ago? So much had happened since then. She remembered unwrapping the stained bandanna. Blood—her blood smeared the mud-covered artifact. The blood had washed away, but her connection with the spearhead had been established. Even now the urge to protect it was nearly overwhelming. And somehow her blood on the spearhead had tied her to Stone Shaper as well. Why? Was her bond with the spearhead and the warrior the reason Joe had shown up? Was that why he'd called her the chosen one? Slipping the makeshift necklace over her head, she leaned back against the couch, closed her eyes, and tried to concentrate. Nothing made any sense.

The rest of the afternoon was spent straightening her house and doing laundry, but the situation was never far from her thoughts. Feeling more than a little uneasy with her obsession over the arrowhead, she assured herself paranoia was when you worried about something that hadn't happened or didn't exist. She had cut her finger on the spearhead, which was still around her neck. At least one of her visits from Stone Shaper had basically been confirmed by Joe. But he hadn't mentioned her visions.

Yet.

She found an old sleeping bag in the storage room, aired it out and carried it to the barn. Joe was nowhere in sight. After a quick look around, she returned to the house and fixed dinner—taco salad served in crisp tortilla bowls. She carried one to the barn and found Joe sitting outside on an old bench that had been there for years. She handed him the plate of food and a travel mug of hot tea. "There's a water spigot inside the barn. Did you find the sleeping bag?"

He nodded, thanked her, and reminded her to lock her doors before saying good night.

By the time she'd finished her dinner and cleaned up the dishes it was close to nine o'clock. She checked the doors and turned off the lights before heading upstairs. Her phone was on the nightstand where she'd put it when she changed clothes that afternoon. She'd forgotten to pick it up again. Sitting on the side of her bed, she kicked off her shoes and picked up the phone to call Stona. There were three missed calls, all of them from him. The first had been at a little after six, the second at seven-thirty and the third one about twenty minutes ago. Dread shivered over her body. He was supposed to wait for her call. Something must have happened. She'd programmed his personal number into her phone this morning. Punching the speed-dial, she waited for his answer. She didn't have to wait long.

"Why didn't you answer your phone?" She held the phone out and gave it a baleful stare. He must have had her number on caller ID. He hadn't even said hello.

"Stona, stop yelling at me. My phone was upstairs, and I was downstairs. It isn't even time for me to check in with you yet."

"Didn't I tell you to keep the phone with you at all times?"

"No, you didn't." She jumped to her feet and began to pace the length of the bedroom. He was beginning to irritate her—no, he was *already* irritating her.

There was silence on the other end. *"I meant to."* He must've picked up on her mood. He'd taken it down a notch. *"Are you okay?"*

"Yes. Why shouldn't I be? Is that why you called earlier?"

"No. I wanted to let you know the reason I'd been ordered back to St. Louis." He sounded resigned and her dread was stronger than ever.

"What's wrong?"

"Your cousin's wreck happened in the Eastern Judicial District. The office I work out of is in that district. It's why I was assigned to your cousin's case.

But Nevada and your Homestead are in the Western Division. *My superiors have decided the major part of the investigation is in that district. They've reassigned your cousin's case. I was to coordinate with them, but they're taking the lead in the investigation.*"

She stopped pacing. "You said *was.*"

"*I told them I didn't believe you were involved in your cousin's murder. When I couldn't give them a substantial reason why, my boss decided I was too close to the case.*"

"How much trouble are you in?"

"*I'm not in trouble. It happens occasionally.*" She could hear the shrug in his voice. After a pause, he continued, "*But they've removed me from the case.*"

"I see."

When she didn't say anything more, he continued. "*Willie, listen to me. I'll be assigned to another case, but that doesn't mean I won't keep in touch. When I told you we'd face this together, I meant it.*"

He'd be somewhere on another case. Marshals weren't restricted to one state, were they? She walked to the window and pulled back the drapes. The night was as dark as her mood. "Do you know where you'll be assigned?"

"*It'll be in Missouri. I'll still be able to keep track of your cousin's case.*"

Pulling the drapes closed, she walked back to the bed and sat down. "Stona, I appreciate everything you've done. I know it hasn't been easy for you, but I'll be okay, and I'll call you if anything major happens."

"*Not good enough, Will. You'll call me three times a day as we agreed, or I'll send your sheriff out to check on you. If you have any problems, any at all, I want to know about them. And, keep your phone close, do you understand? If I need to call you, I want to be able to get through.*"

"All right."

"*Promise me.*"

"I promise."

"*Okay then. Call me in the morning as soon as you wake up.*" He hesitated a long moment. "*Sleep well.*"

"You too. Be safe. Good night." The tears started before the connection ended. She'd never see him again. Why would she?

Without changing her clothes, she crawled under the blankets and pulled them over her shoulders.

She was alone again. It was her last thought before the familiar dizziness took her.

TWENTY-FOUR

BETH PACED FROM one end of Stone Shaper's lodge to the other. Her captor had been gone for more than a week, and the young dark-haired woman who brought her meals and kept the fire wouldn't speak to her. One glance outside, and she'd decided escape was impossible. Someone was always near the doorway.

But she'd only seen women, children, and a few old men since her captor had left. Where were the young men? Were they hunting, or had they gone to war? Her stomach knotted. Would an entire village of warriors go after her father and his men? If they had, her mother and brothers might be caught in the middle of the fighting. Would Osage retaliation cost her family their lives?

Inactivity nearly drove her crazy. She'd tidied up the single room, neatly stacked the firewood, and straightened the mats and furs covering the dirt floor. The girl she considered her keeper had given her a buckskin dress and a pair of beaded moccasins on her first day out of bed—the bed being the pile of fur robes she'd shared with Stone Shaper.

She was given chores that paralleled those she'd done at home, mending damaged clothing, weaving reed mats. This afternoon the girl set a clay cooking pot filled with precut vegetables and meat over the fire, and handed her one of two wooden spoon-like utensils before leaving. Obviously, she was to fix her own supper tonight. She spent the rest of the afternoon keeping the fire, adding water to the pot and stirring. Herbs had already been added to the mixture and by evening the lodge was filled with the mouthwatering aroma of the savory stew.

When the flap of the lodge door was pushed back, she looked up expecting to see the girl. Instead, Stone Shaper ducked under the frame. A shiver of apprehension rolled over her body, and settled in her belly. Had he been a few minutes earlier he would have caught her at her bath.

He, too, had bathed. Droplets of water clung to his hair and muscular chest and shoulders. His breechcloth looked clean, and she wondered where he had gotten the fresh clothes. Probably from the young woman tasked with guarding her.

He sat on the bed-furs in front of the fire, picked up one of the spoons the girl had left and began eating directly from the cook pot. She wasn't surprised. She'd assumed she would be eating from the pot when the young woman failed to bring a smaller bowl. Now she understood why the girl had provided two spoons.

She walked toward a woven mat in one corner of the lodge, but he shook his head and motioned her to the furs beside him. She obeyed but wouldn't look at him. Their last encounter had been terrifying, and humiliating. He'd almost taken her virginity that night. Her face flooded with heat at the memory. She'd been terrified, but had not been unaffected by his touch. She would have fought him, but would she have eventually allowed him to take what he wanted?

"Eat."

His order startled her, and she flinched. "I—I'm not hungry."

"Eat."

"If I try to eat right now it will come right back up."

"Are all white women stubborn?"

"I'm not stubborn. I'm nervous."

"What is this nervous?"

She couldn't think of a way to explain it, so she simply raised her hands and let him see how they trembled.

"Are you afraid of me?"

"A little."

"For what reason do you fear me?"

"I'm your slave and white. Your people hate whites."

"Have I harmed you?"

"Not yet...."

"I have taken you into my home. I saw to your wounds. I provide food and a good fire for warmth. These are not the actions of a warrior intent on harming you."

"And if you become dissatisfied with my... services?"

"Eat. If you are to make a satisfactory slave, you must regain the strength the fever took from you."

That unsettled her enough to attempt to placate him. She picked up the second spoon and dipped it into the simmering pot, cautiously sipping the vegetables and broth. After a few bites, she set the spoon aside. "I'm sorry. I can't eat any more."

He nodded, set his own spoon aside and got to his feet. Walking to the corner where several woven baskets were kept, he rifled through the contents of the smaller basket, and returned with a carved walnut comb. Kneeling on the furs behind her, he gathered a handful of her hair and began working the tangles out. It was the last thing she'd expected him to do, and she didn't protest. She'd tried to finger comb her hair, but her efforts only removed a few of the snarls. She'd noticed the comb when she'd straightened the lodge but hadn't dared use it without permission.

His ministrations were a little rough, but no more so than her mama's had been upon occasion.

Once he'd removed the tangles, he continued to run the comb and his fingers through her waist-length waves. Despite her wariness, she sighed, relaxing under the gentle massage. She was wedged between his knees and when she bent her head, she noticed a reddish-brown mark on his upper thigh. The small triangular blemish looked very much like an arrowhead.

Having grown comfortable with the almost companionable silence, she asked, "Is the mark on your leg the reason you're called Stone Shaper?"

The comb paused in its descent. When it began to thread through her hair again, she thought he didn't intend to answer her. A moment or two of combing passed before he finally spoke.

"I have carried the mark since my birth. The Little Old Men considered it an omen, but they could not decide if it was good or bad. My skill with the bow and spear has convinced them the omen was good. I was given the name Stone Shaper because my spear and arrow points are strong and true."

When he finally set the comb aside, she reached up to plait the length into a single braid, hoping to prevent further tangles. He stilled her hand.

"Leave it unbound this night."

She dropped her hands to her lap and sat staring at the flames while he set the cooking pot to the side and banked the fire for the evening. No longer relaxed, she waited to see what he would do next.

A week ago, when he'd left with the men, she hadn't been fully recovered. She was now. She remembered their last encounter. Her captor had given her no doubt as to what would eventually happen between them. He considered her his slave, his possession, and held the power of life and death over her—absolute power over her body. Her stomach clenched and fluttered, and for a minute she thought she was going to be sick. Would he exercise that power tonight? She was amazed he hadn't taken advantage of her weakened state the night she'd regained her senses. Now, sitting in the absolute silence, knowing he was watching her, she wanted to scream.

Her father had given her to this frightening man without a second thought for her survival. Had his careless act taken away her right to defend her virtue? She was smart enough to know she couldn't deter the warrior. But she had to fight him, didn't she?

If she let him take her virginity without a struggle, would it make her a whore? Or had her father's words already made her one? Even if she fought him, most people in her town would believe she was dirty, no longer pure enough to marry a white man. Better off dead. She'd heard that said of other women who had been taken by savages. Some had suggested the only option for a virtuous woman used by a savage was to take her own life, especially if she found herself carrying a half-breed child. They reasoned that under the circumstances God would surely forgive a woman for the mortal sin.

Stone Shaper moved to the fur robes. He watched her for a moment, and she wondered what he was thinking.

She didn't have to wonder long.

"The sun is gone, woman. It is time to sleep." Only one pile of furs covered the ground by the fire—the furs she sat on. It was obvious he intended to sleep with her tonight.

"Remove your dress."

She shook her head.

He jerked her to her feet. "Do you defy me?" His voice, though calm, carried an edge of irritation.

Her chin came up. "I won't help you rape me."

He pulled her against him, his face inches from hers. "If I decide to rape you, I will not require your help. Remove your dress now, woman, or I will remove it for you."

Her defiance was short-lived. The question wasn't whether the dress would come off, but how many bruises she would receive if he made good on his threat.

There was only one garment to remove. The buckskin dress. She hadn't been given any undergarments. Turning her back to him, she pulled the dress over her head. Swinging around to face him, she held the garment in front of her like a shield.

———————

STONE SHAPER POINTED to the furs. "Lie down."

The woman dared to shake her head at him. His captive's defiance both pleased and displeased him. It was good to know her spirit remained unbroken. He respected her courage. Yet she was his slave and could not be allowed such disobedience. She belonged to him and before the rising sun she would understand what that meant.

With the speed of the striking snake, he yanked the dress from her hands and tossed it to the ground. She gasped and tried to cover her nakedness with her arms.

He snorted. Her effort to protect her body from his gaze came too late. He had been the one to slice the white man's rags from her body. He'd soaked a cloth in cool water and stroked her heated skin. And at night, when the chills took her, he'd climbed beneath the robes to share his body's heat. No one, not even Raven, had seen to her needs.

"You have a reason, now, to seek the protection of my robes. Do so." This time she obeyed him, scrambling beneath the buffalo hide, pulling it to her chin. With a quick nod of satisfaction, he began removing his own clothes, his gaze holding hers as he set the breechcloth aside.

She glanced away, her face flushed.

He had no doubt she'd just experienced her first view of a man in full need of his woman. The sight of her tempting body had affected him, and he didn't try to hide his desire from her. He wanted his slave to know what would happen this night, to accept what she could not change. But this woman's innocence demanded his care.

Her courage had won his respect. Had she cowered in her lodge the day he captured her, or cringed before them, begging for her life, he would have left her to die or taken her on the ground at their first camp—then let his men have her. He would not have bound her wounds and brought her into his lodge.

Her eyes betrayed her fear. She expected pain and brutality and perhaps death. The pain he could not stop when he took his pleasure of her this night. A first mating was painful for a woman, and he did not doubt this would be her first mating. That it pleased him to be the first to have her, made him uneasy. He should not care. She was only a slave and her innocence held no importance.

He dropped to his knees beside her. "I grow weary of calling you *woman*. Tell me your name."

Her eyes mirrored her confusion. "Beth—Elizabeth."

"Does your name have a meaning?"

She shook her head. "I was named after Queen Elizabeth, a great woman, a leader who lived long ago."

"Was this leader courageous and honorable?"

"Yes."

"Then it is a good name." He reached out and ran his fingers down the side of her face. She stiffened but did not cringe. That pleased him. "You will survive this night, Beth." His desire to reassure her puzzled him. He tossed the robe she huddled beneath to the side, and covered her with his body, drawing a cry from her lips. She would know soon enough that he did not intend to beat or kill her.

————————

BETH COULDN'T MOVE. The warning in Stone Shaper's eyes held her as fast as his heavy-muscled body. Breaking their gaze, he lowered his head, his lips touching her ear.

"Be at ease, little bird. Let your body remember me. You've shared my heat many times. You know my touch."

Shamed by his words, she closed her eyes. She did remember his touching her the night she'd regained her wits. But *many* times? Most of what had happened between her capture and the night she'd awakened in his arms was lost to her. Would she know if he had raped her then? Would her body feel different?

He nipped her ear. Her eyes snapped open just before he sucked the abused lobe into his mouth, teasing it with his tongue before letting go to nuzzle and nip her neck. Like a mouse caught in the claws of a cat bent on playing with her, she froze in place. He'd said she'd survive, but she wasn't convinced. He was such a big man—bigger than her father, bigger than any man in the settlement, and stronger. If he lost control….

He brushed the hair away from her face. "You will learn much this night, I think." He lifted her leg over his hip, settling his lower body more intimately against hers. His aroused length nestled in the curls at the junction of her legs and he growled his pleasure.

The savage ran his rough palm over the calf of her leg, reached her foot and he chuckled. "Were you so anxious to crawl beneath my furs that you forgot to remove this?" He lifted the moccasin she'd completely forgotten from her foot and tossed it toward her dress. Raising up, he imprisoned the opposite foot, discarding its moccasin as well before lifting that leg over his other hip.

She tried to pull her legs down, wanting to bar the intimacy but he splayed his knees and she inadvertently aided his cause when her hips lifted. He leaned over her, and she glanced between them. It didn't take experience to know his manhood was poised to breach her. She slapped both hands against his chest and shoved hard. He didn't budge. She may as well have been pushing against a stone wall.

He grasped her wrists and pinned her hands on either side of her head. "Be still, woman. You will only cause yourself more pain with your struggles."

His lips glided to the column of her neck then her shoulder, sending shivers down her body. Sucking in a breath, she tried to wriggle out from under him and heard his rumble of laughter.

He leaned closer. "Your body remembers me even if you do not—and I remember this." His mouth settled over hers, his tongue tracing the inner line of her lips before delving deeper. When he raised his head, desire burned in his dark eyes and his heart slammed against her ribs. She understood. There would be no reprieve.

Kissing seemed to be as new for him as it was for her. Mama hadn't told her much about kissing. From what she'd said, men enjoyed it a whole lot more than women did.

She had been prepared to be appalled when his mouth covered hers. And she was appalled—by her reaction. Her already racing heart picked up its pace—her breathing, as well. But not from fear or revulsion. His mouth didn't suffocate her and the way he nibbled and sucked on her lips increased her confusion, not her anxiety. His leisurely exploration of her mouth, and his calloused palms gently kneading the tension from her muscles were far from the frenzied groping of a man determined to find his pleasure at her expense.

Between kisses, he ran his fingers through her hair, holding it up to the firelight, bringing the strands to his nose, inhaling her scent. He glided his mouth down the column of her neck to the pulse point at the base of her throat, continuing down to the valley between her breasts. His nose touched her skin and he inhaled again. Was he smelling her?

They were so close, his own scent surrounded her. She wanted to be repelled by the way he smelled, like she was by most of the trappers her father brought home. But she wasn't. He smelled clean, earthy.

He cupped her breast in his big hand and gently tweaked the nipple between his thumb and forefinger. He no longer held her hands prisoner. She immediately gripped his shoulders to push him away. His warning gaze caught and held her fast as he lowered his head to the breast he'd been playing with and blew his hot breath over her nipple. Goosebumps covered her entire body. He clamped his lips over the bud, sucked it into his mouth. She jerked with each flick of his tongue, a firebrand of sensations, sizzling through her lower body. She whimpered.

His free hand plumped her other breast, his mouth taking immediate possession, nuzzling, suckling until she cried out, overwhelmed by what he was making her feel. Pressing her into the furs, he touched his lips to her ear, panting urgent promises in a language only lovers understood.

She forgot to be afraid, forgot this man was supposed to be her enemy. He made her burn, made her crave something elusive. Her mouth softened as he touched her lips again. Her tongue brushed against his. He growled and ground his lower body against hers. Moaning she writhed beneath him.

He dragged his lips away. "Be easy, little bird. We have all night to share our secrets." He took her hand and drew it down between their bodies. "Touch me." When she hesitated, he wrapped her fingers around his turgid flesh and held them there. She didn't try to pull back. He was smooth and hard and hot—incredibly hot. Instinctively, she tightened her grip and his arousal came to life, pulsing in her hand. Sucking air through his teeth, he suddenly shoved her hand away, the action almost violent. He buried his face in the hair at her neck and took several deep breaths. Had she hurt him? She had no experience to draw on. Would he retaliate as soon as he recovered? She tensed, ready to defend herself.

———————

WHEN STONE SHAPER finally had his body under control, he shook his head. "I fear we will not have all night, little bird. Too long have I waited to make you mine." He smiled at her curious expression. "Soon you will understand the mysteries of a man's body, and I will enjoy learning your secrets."

He soothed her with kisses and gentle caresses. Still, she tensed when his palm slid across her belly, down between her thighs. Two fingers delved into her moist heat. His mouth captured her cry of alarm, slanting over hers as she pushed against his shoulders.

She was so tight, so wet. All he could think about was being inside her. His fingers glided in and out, teaching her the mating rhythm as he rained kisses over her neck and breasts. Whimpering, she moved restlessly beneath him, gasping when his fingers found the barrier of her virginity.

Achingly close to losing his control, he pulled out of her and repositioned himself to take full possession.

Her hands tightened on his shoulders. "Please."

Was she begging him to stop? He wouldn't. They were beyond stopping. Her mind might not be ready to accept him, but her body thrummed with eagerness. His own body throbbed painfully with his need. She belonged to him, and this night would see his complete possession of her.

She threw her arms around his neck and pulled him closer. "Please... don't leave me."

Her whispered plea set his body on fire. He found her mouth as he sank between her thighs. Reaching between them, he positioned his manhood and pushed into her heat.

———————

BETH DIDN'T MOVE. She tightened her arms around his neck and stopped breathing the second she stretched around him. He was inside her. But only the tip of him, and she thanked God the warrior hadn't impaled her. He pushed a little deeper, forcing her body to accommodate his size. Mama had referred to that part of a man as his rod or staff—terms also given to objects of punishment. Spare the rod, spoil the child. She feared there was a reason for the comparison.

He suddenly pulled out, closed his eyes and took in deep gulps of air. Was he finished then? The niggling sense of disappointment surprised her. She should be thankful her mother's dower predictions and the terrifying stories of savage rape hadn't been true. But she still ached, wanting, needing something she couldn't explain. Her hands dropped to her sides. Flushing with shame, she planted her feet on the ground, lifting her hips, seeking the connection he'd broken.

He groaned. "Be patient little bird. We are far from finished." His hands gripped her knees, pushing her thighs farther apart, and he sank into her.

She gasped, caught in the seesaw of emotions, anticipating the worst now. More than the tip of him pushed into her this time. She was stretched around at least half of his length, or so she thought. Glancing between them, she saw it wasn't true and feared his next thrust would tear her apart. But her mind centered on what her body was feeling as his manhood mimicked the action his fingers had taken earlier, gliding in and retreating, stretching, filling her with each slow thrust. The pain that was sure to come no longer frightened her. She lifted her hips encouraging him. He responded, thrusting faster, deeper. The terrible, wonderful pleasure building in her lower body confounded her. She buried her face in his shoulder, her body tensing, as she tried to fight what was happening to her.

Stone Shaper twisted her hair in his hand, pulled her head back, and looked into her eyes. "Let go. Fly, little bird." His mouth came down on hers, his tongue thrusting deep.

Clinging to his shoulders, she cried out against his lips. Exquisite sensations shivered over her body. She soared over the precipice, throbbing around his arousal.

He grabbed her hips and thrust deep, shredding her virginity, holding her flush against him, as she fought his invasion.

His entire body was rigid, his arms trembling as they supported his weight. Each time his manhood pulsed, he groaned as though the motion caused him as much pain as it did her. She pushed against his chest, wanting him to get off her, but he wouldn't budge.

"You're hurting me. Leave me alone."

He caught her hands and held them above her head with one of his own. "That I cannot do. We will finish what we've started." He bent to kiss her, and she turned her head away. He kissed her ear instead, then grasped her jaw and brought her face back to his, claiming her lips in a ravenous, tongue-thrusting kiss.

He flexed his hips, his arousal throbbing deep inside her.

She whimpered.

His lips touched her ear. "Ahh, Beth, do not dwell on the pain. Think only of the pleasure."

He was demanding the impossible. There was no pleasure now. She wanted it to be over. "You've already taken my virginity. What are you waiting for? Finish this and be done with it."

He shook his head. "You would deny yourself much." His hand slid between them his fingers finding and stroking the sensitive nub.

She tried to wriggle free. "Don't."

His quick kiss stopped her protest. He eased out of her and slowly pushed forward, finding his rhythm again. With each deep, even stroke, the pain diminished, and the delicious tension increased. When she lifted her hips, he quickened the pace, each thrust bringing her closer to what she'd experienced before. And suddenly she was there, on the brink, her body throbbing around his again.

She cried out.

———————

STONE SHAPER ANSWERED with two quick thrusts. Roaring, he surged into Beth one last time, straining against her, allowing no separation as he poured his seed into her.

He stayed inside her until the throbbing ended and she sank, sighing, into the furs. Rolling to his side, he pulled her into his arms, holding her long after their breathing had calmed. He savored a deep sense of satisfaction. His mind had claimed her the moment she'd faced certain death to protect her family. Tonight, he had claimed her body. His arms tightened around her. It was the right he would allow no other man. He didn't question his decision. She was his woman.

Kissing the top of her head, he rolled to his feet, and crossed the lodge to the bowl used for washing, cleaned himself, then carried a dampened cloth to her.

He knelt at her side and pressed the cool cloth between her legs before she could protest. She tensed but allowed the intimacy, turning on her side away from him when he'd finished. Tossing the cloth into the corner, he covered her with the fur and climbed in behind her, pulling her against him.

His reaction to his slave surprised him. He was no young warrior experiencing his first woman. He had been married before, to Walks Beside the Water, the daughter of Brings Peace. When she'd been killed during a Kiowa raid, he'd vowed never to take another woman to his heart. To his bed, yes. He would marry again and father children. It was expected. What place would Beth have in his household then? He yawned and pulled her closer. It was a question that could wait to be answered.

SHE HAD BEHAVED shamelessly, practically begging him to…. Her face burned when she thought about what they'd done. She'd been wrong to give in to him, should have at least forced him to beat her into submission.

Her captor hadn't beaten her—hadn't needed to. He'd simply told her she belonged to him, taken her clothes, then taken her will to deny him. She hadn't been coerced, hadn't been raped. He'd soothed her with his soft words and gentle touch. He'd been careful with her. And in the end, this savage warrior she'd been taught to fear no longer frightened her.

TWENTY-FIVE

SHE HADN'T CHANGED out of her clothes last night. Dropping back on the bed, Willie closed her eyes and groaned. It had happened again. She'd been with Beth and Stone Shaper. As with every vision, she'd been in both their heads. Her face flushed with heat recalling just how personal the experience had been. Even their most intimate moments had played out before her. She was beginning to feel like a voyeur.

Stone Shaper had seduced Beth, yet *she'd* been the one in his arms. She'd known his excitement and pleasure as well. How weird was that?

Had Stone Shaper made a commitment to Beth? He might have. She'd always adhered to a moral conviction that insisted intimacy should occur only after true commitment. At twenty-seven she hadn't found a man she wanted to commit her life and body to. Having seen— experienced—the wonder of a budding love, how could she settle for anything less? She might never find a man she'd be willing to spend the rest of her life with. Unbidden, Stona's image flashed in her mind, and she admitted he might qualify.

Glancing at her phone, she remembered her promise to call Stona. She quickly showered and changed into a blue-checked flannel shirt and a pair of faded jeans. Grabbing the phone and her hiking boots, she headed downstairs. Coffee first, to bolster her for the coming conversation.

One cup of coffee later, she made the call. She still couldn't understand the reasoning behind his demand to hear from her three times a day. One daily call should be enough. Honestly, he was still acting more like a protective big brother than a federal marshal. She did have to admit it was kind of nice having someone care about you.

Stona answered on the first ring. She laughed. "That was fast."

"I had my phone in my hand. I was about to call you."

"Why, is there anything new in Josh's case?"

"No, nothing more than I told you yesterday. I'm still waiting for a new assignment. I was calling to make sure you're all right. It was getting late."

"Stona, you need to stop obsessing about whether I'm okay or not. I didn't call because I overslept. That's all. I haven't even poured my second cup of coffee yet, and trust me, you don't want to talk to me before my second cup of caffeine."

"I'll keep that in mind. And I'm not obsessing. I'd like to believe we've become friends, and friends make sure friends are all right." He sighed. *"You aren't taking what's been happening seriously. You're a nurse, Willie. You know better. Until whatever is going on with you is identified and taken care of, I'll be a thorn in your side. If that's obsessing, then I'm guilty."*

He was right, but until *she* understood what was happening to her, she wasn't about to share the details with anyone, not even Stona—*especially* not Stona. She didn't want him thinking she was having a mental breakdown.

"I'm sorry. I know you're looking out for me, and I appreciate it. I really do. But you've been removed from the case. You aren't obligated to me in any way. You never were, and I won't get used to leaning on you. It wouldn't be fair to either of us."

"Let me worry about what's fair. Case or no case, I worry about you. Now tell me why you overslept."

She was afraid he'd ask that. Nothing much got by him. She hesitated too long.

"What happened last night? Did you have another nightmare?"

She hedged. "I'm not sure."

"Willie, you either had a nightmare or you didn't. Which is it?"

"I didn't."

"Which means you had another blackout."

The concern in his voice was clear, and she wasn't going to lie to him again. "Yes."

"I want you to make another appointment with your doctor. Were you upset by something?"

"Not really. If the blackouts are stress-related, it's probably due to so much happening in such a short time."

"And if you black out again?"

"I'll make another appointment with the doctor."

His long silence told her he wasn't happy, but he didn't argue. *"Let's change things around. From now on, I make the calls. Three times a day like we arranged."*

"And if I oversleep?"

"Keep the phone beside your bed. If you're asleep when I call, you can wake up long enough to tell me you're okay, then go back to sleep. I won't call before nine. I'll call again at three and make the last call at nine in the evening. That way I don't worry."

She couldn't work up much enthusiasm for the new arrangement but decided to capitulate. "That sounds fine."

"Anything planned for today?"

"I'm staying home. The weather's supposed to be nice. I may go for a walk along the creek."

"Take your phone with you."

"All right."

"I'll call you at three. And Willie...."

"Yes?"

"Be careful."

"I will."

Her first thought after disconnecting the call was of Joe. Nights got cold this time of the year. Had the sleeping bag been enough to keep him warm? She should've taken him an extra blanket last night before she went to bed. He was probably hungry. She'd bring him a cup of coffee and offer to make breakfast.

It wasn't cold enough for a coat. She slipped on a sheepskin vest. Her waterproof hiking boots and heavy socks would keep her feet warm and dry when she took her hike.

Joe wasn't in sight when she carried a mug of coffee out to the barn. Stepping into the dim interior, she glanced around, concerned that something might have happened to him. The old man wasn't there. After calling his name a couple of times, she walked outside, and scanned the field and woods beyond. There was no sign of him.

Had he left? It wouldn't surprise her. He'd shown up out of the blue, talked about crazy things, like her being a chosen one, whatever that meant, and now he was gone. Tossing the cooling coffee on the ground, she carried the empty mug to the house. His disappearance hadn't changed anything. It probably uncomplicated her life to a degree. She wouldn't have to explain him to Stona—a definite plus. Yet she couldn't help but worry about him.

After making sure the front door was locked, she stuffed a bottle of water and a granola bar into her vest pocket and stepped out the back door into the sunshine. She made sure she had the key, then flipped the lock and closed the back door.

Taking the quickest path to the creek, she followed the ridge top briefly then descended a steep slope to a wet weather wash that intersected the live creek. The gravel-bottomed wash, dry this time of year, provided a weed-and bramble-free path to the water. Hillsides bordering the dry creek boasted a variety of trees and undergrowth.

Trees were dropping their faded leaves, but the thinning vegetation offered a better view of the area wildlife. Before she'd reached the wash, she'd startled a small herd of five or six deer. She didn't get a good count because they'd startled her, too, and were out of sight before she'd recovered. Their quick departure disturbed a gray squirrel who chattered his displeasure, his tail swishing as he scolded her.

The dry stream bed was strewn with gravel and rocks ranging from marble to basketball size, most of it washed into the bed during hard rains and flooding. She smiled. That was probably how these dry creeks got the name wash. Recently deposited rocks had sharper edges and retained the colors of the soil or clay they had rested in—muted reds and dark grays. The older stones, worn down and rounded by runoff and countless floods, had bleached white or light gray, depending on the type of stone. A good percentage of the wet-weather basin itself was made up of white flint, marbled with silver-gray and occasionally streaked with rusty red. Sometimes, when two creeks connected, flood-waters created miniature whirlpools that, over the centuries, created depressions in the layers of rock the old-timers called Indian bathtubs. They were aptly named since most were roughly the size and depth of a bathtub and held rainwater long after the creek was dry. She doubted Native Americans ever used them for bathing since the water was usually murky and smelled of rotting vegetation.

A deer path edged the live stream as it meandered west along the bank. She followed the stream to a valley that opened into a wide sunlit meadow. A shallow rivulet in the creek offered a place to cross, and she hopped from one rock to another to the opposite bank. Taking advantage of a table-high outcropping of limestone and chert, she stopped to rest and eat her granola bar before heading back to the house. After downing half of the water, she decided to save the rest for her return trip up the steep slope.

She sat for a time, arms extended behind her, eyes closed, her face raised to the warmth of the sun, breathing in the musky scent of moist earth and leaves. It was serene here. Her body seemed energized, her mind alert. How long had it been since her spirit had been this free? Free enough to hope again, though she wasn't sure what she hoped for. Closure, perhaps, or peace?

She gradually became uncomfortable with the silence. The breeze had died, and nothing moved in the trees. There were no bird calls, no chattering squirrels. A quick glance around assured her she was alone.

Closing her eyes, she concentrated on her surroundings, listening for a rattle of leaves, a footfall, anything that would explain her sudden feeling of dread. Her chest hurt, and she realized she was holding her breath. Slowly, she exhaled through her mouth, then drew in a slow breath through her nose, counting to eight and exhaling again. She repeated the process twice more, using the breathing technique to calm her anxiety. It was beginning to work. Her heartbeat slowed, and the tension eased out of her body. One last deep breath and—

"*I -shta' tha -btha.*" Willie jumped and her eyes snapped open. Stone Shaper stood directly in front of her. She shook her head, denying what she was seeing and closed her eyes again to rid herself of the vision. "*I -shta' tha -btha.*" He was still there. She hadn't been able to banish him from her mind. Her eyes were closed so tight the lids hurt. *He wasn't there, he wasn't there,* she silently chanted. He couldn't be. That would mean she really was crazy, and she refused to be crazy.

"He is telling you to open your eyes and see." She swung her head toward the new voice and squinted.

Beth.

God help her, she *was* losing her mind. It wasn't a nightmare. She hadn't been asleep. It wasn't a vision, either. She hadn't gotten dizzy and blacked out. Stone Shaper and Beth had both spoken to her. They'd never acknowledged her existence during a vision.

Beth seemed to be patiently waiting for her to recover her senses. Willie glanced back at Stone Shaper. He looked every bit as angry as he had the other night when he'd appeared in her room.

She glanced back at Beth. "What's happening? Why is he—why are you both here?"

Beth shrugged. "He seems to expect something from you, though why he is speaking Osage is puzzling. He speaks English when he chooses. He used English to communicate with me. He hated doing it. He hated anything to do with the whites." Beth's gaze fell on the warrior still frowning at Willie, her expression tender. "I am amazed that he loves me."

"Who do you speak to?" Stone Shaper's demand brought Willie's eyes back to him. "Are you so frightened of me, woman, that you babble?" He'd spoken in English.

She shook her head. "I'm talking to Beth." Stone Shaper's frown intensified, and Willie turned to Beth, "What did I say wrong?"

"You've confused him. He can't see or hear me." The pain in Beth's voice magnified the sadness in her eyes.

"How can he not see you? He sees me. He's even spoken to me."

"Woman...."

She gave him a sharp look. "Please be patient. I'm trying to figure out what's going on and as soon as I find out I'll tell you."

Her honesty seemed to appease him, and he nodded, apparently willing to give her time to sort out her thoughts. He folded his arms across his chest, bent one knee forward in a more relaxed stance and waited.

Willie looked at Beth again. "Why are you here? What do you want from me?"

"I am here because Stone Shaper is here. I have been with him since my death, though he has never known of my presence. I don't know why he has chosen to reveal himself to you. He may not have control over it."

Chosen. Joe had told her she'd been chosen.

"Woman...."

Willie swung around to face him, her anxiety revealing itself in irritation. "Don't call me *woman.* It's demeaning. I have a name, use it."

She swore if he'd had eyebrows, he would have raised one as he contemplated her.

Beth laughed and Willie glared at her. Stone Shaper drew her attention right back to him. "I have no name to put to you." Now he was irritated.

She sighed. "Willie—you can call me Willie."

"That name has no dignity.

"Neither does woman."

"I will call you *Zyˆka.*"

Willie looked at Beth and raised her own eyebrows—she couldn't manage just one. Beth was grinning. "He calls you squirrel."

Willie rolled her eyes heavenward. "Yeah, that *reeks* of dignity."

"I'm sure he means no insult. The Osage often name a person after an animal, especially if that person's behavior somehow reminds them of the animal."

"He thinks I act like a squirrel?"

"Squirrels often scold those who disturb them."

"Maybe, but at least they're smart enough to stay in the tree while they're doing it."

"Zy´ka, do you chatter at nothing? Has your mind left you?" The warrior was back to issuing insults and demanding answers she didn't have.

"I told you before, I'm talking to Beth."

There went the non-eyebrow again, and he growled something she was glad she couldn't understand.

Beth gave her a loose translation. "He wants to know why you insist you are talking to me when I am not here. He is angry now."

Beth didn't have to tell her he was angry. She saw it in those dark eyes, in the tenseness of his stance, and in the way his fists clenched and unclenched. Willie wasn't sure how much power an angry ghost really had, and she didn't want to find out. She needed to appease him but didn't know how.

"I can't explain why, but I promise you I see Beth. She's standing beside you wearing the buckskin dress and moccasins Raven gave her. You sometimes call her little bird."

Suddenly the warrior roared and came at her.

She jumped up from the rock, ready to run. Stone Shaper's and Beth's images wavered and snuffed out. Willie's heart fluttered, beating erratically with every breath she took. Her legs buckled. Strong hands grasped her shoulders from behind and dragged her back onto the large rock.

TWENTY-SIX

WILLIE WASN'T FRIGHTENED. Her mind couldn't process the emotion, not after everything she'd just experienced.

Once she was off her feet, she regained her strength. Joe moved around to face her. She'd half expected it to be Stona and was surprised by the strength she'd felt in the old man's hands.

He peered into her eyes. "Are you feeling better?"

She nodded. After a deep, steadying breath, she glanced in his direction. "You saw them?"

The old man sat down beside her and sighed. Apparently, he needed the respite as much as she did. "Yes."

She waited for him to elaborate, and when he didn't, she prompted. "Do you know who they are?"

Again, he nodded.

"Why did he attack me?"

"You knew too much about his woman, I think. It confused and angered him."

"What do you know about them? Are they ghosts? Am I haunted?"

He turned his attention to the woods beyond the stream before returning her gaze. "I do not know the answers to all of your questions. Some things we will have to learn together.

"They are *not* ghosts—not as you believe ghosts to be, and they do not haunt *you*. I believe Stone Shaper's spirit is tied to this land and to the plane on which his spirit exists. I do not understand why he cannot see Beth, though she is aware of him. Their spirits may reside on separate planes."

"So why am I being haunted—*visited* by spirits that obviously come from another time?"

"Time is different in the spirit world. It is measured not in its passage, but in the memories retained. Stone Shaper's spirit may not remember everything that occurred before he died. He may only be aware of the force that keeps him in this place and that you are connected to the reason he cannot leave."

"How?"

Joe shrugged. "It is one of the mysteries we have yet to resolve. I only know you are the chosen one and I was sent to aid you in your quest."

"Who sent you?"

Joe considered her question for a moment then looked confused. "I have no memory of being told. I am here because you are the chosen one. I know I am your spirit guide in the same way I know the sun will come up when the day begins—as I know it is your obligation to free Stone Shaper's spirit." His fist gently thumped his chest over his heart. "This was told to me here."

Basically, they were both clueless. The blind leading the blind. Neither of them knew what to do next. "I've seen Stone Shaper before."

Joe nodded. "I have suspected as much. Tell me."

"The first time I saw him he was standing in the meadow on the ridge top watching me. I looked away, and when I looked back, he was gone. The second time was in my bedroom. I woke up, and he was at the foot of my bed. He was angry and came at me, then simply popped out of existence. Both times he was there for no more than a few seconds. Today was different. He talked to me, and you're right, he did seem confused and frustrated. When he lost his temper, I stood to run, and both he and Beth disappeared. I don't understand why he keeps disappearing. Don't misunderstand me. I was relieved to see him gone."

"It must take a considerable amount of energy to make himself known to this world. He may not have a choice when he disappears. I don't know what source of energy he drew upon before, but I do know there are places of power on this earth. I believe the slab of stone we sit on is such a place. Can you feel it?"

Willie's eyes widened. "I did feel it at first, but after I'd spoken with Stone Shaper, I felt drained."

"Perhaps he drew his strength through you."

"Are you saying he used me like a conduit, drawing energy from this place through me?"

"It is possible they both did, and you broke the link when you stood. What little energy they used just before disappearing belonged to you."

She nodded. "That would explain my sudden weakness."

He reached into her pocket and handed her the half-empty water bottle. "Drink this. If you need more, I will refill the bottle."

She glanced down at the stream where minnows darted in and out of the rivulets and gave him a wary look.

He chuckled. "There is a rock ledge not far from here. A spring trickles from an opening high above my head, its source deep within the earth. The water is pure, and for many lifetimes has quenched the thirst of man and beast."

She took the bottle from him and drained it before handing it back. It did help. "Thank you."

"Have you regained your strength?" He stood, offering his hand. Taking it, she cautiously scooted off the rock, testing the muscles in her legs before nodding.

Neither spoke as they climbed the steep hillside. Once they'd reached the house, she invited him in for lunch. "I know you didn't eat break-fast. I can fix some sandwiches and make a salad."

"A sandwich will be enough. Thank you." He followed her into the kitchen and sat in the chair she offered at the table.

"I can make coffee or tea." She opened the refrigerator and glanced inside. "There's orange juice, milk, or soda."

"Do you have root beer? I like root beer."

Retrieving two cans of root beer and packages of thin sliced beef and Swiss cheese, she smiled. "I like root beer too." She set one of the sodas in front of him and carried the other to the counter. "Would you like a glass and ice?"

He'd already popped the top on the can. Shaking his head, he lifted it to her in salute and took a long swallow. They ate their sandwiches in silence, and when they were finished, she suggested they sit on the porch to enjoy the afternoon sunshine.

Her phone rang, and she pulled it out of her pocket to check caller ID. Stona. She glanced at the readout on her phone, three o'clock—exactly.

"Hello?"

"Hi, Will. Just checking in."

She couldn't believe how good it was to hear his voice.

"Did you take your walk?"

"I got back about an hour ago. Have they reassigned you yet?"

"Not to a specific case. They have me researching a couple of cold cases Justice would like to close."

"I don't suppose you've heard anything about Josh's case?"

"Nothing new." He paused for a minute and then spoke again, sounding concerned. *"You need to understand something, Willie. Your cousin's case is at a standstill. We know he was murdered. We even know how it was done. But the rest is supposition. We suspect the man who tampered with your cousin's car is a ghost."*

A shiver ran the length of her spine. Strange he would say that after her experience this afternoon. "A what?"

"A professional hitman who goes in, does a job, and disappears is sometimes called a ghost. Because the jobs are random, law enforcement never has a clear pattern to follow. Ghosts never make amateurish mistakes that might catch them up, and once they've gone to ground, they're impossible to find."

"Do you think that's what happened with Josh's case? Has his killer gone to ground?"

"It's too early to tell, but the longer it takes, the greater the chance any evidence out there will be compromised."

"I see."

"Don't give up hope. Your cousin's murder isn't a cold case yet."

"Okay."

"I mean it. I'll make sure they search out every lead."

"I know you will. Thank you."

"I worry about you out there alone."

"I'm fine, really."

He was silent for a long moment. *"I still worry."*

His admission warmed her. She suddenly wanted to set his mind at ease. She glanced at Joe. "You don't have to worry about me. I have a... friend staying with me."

"What friend?"

She should've known he'd want details. "He's someone I've known for a while." Two days could constitute a while, couldn't it?

"He?"

"His name is Joe."

"Joe who?" When she didn't immediately reply he asked again. *"Joe who?"*

"Stona, we're not playing knock-knock. Like I said, he's a friend."

"Trust me, Willie, I'm not playing games. I want a last name." He'd gone from sounding like a friend to sounding like a U.S. Marshal.

She didn't know Joe's last name. Covering the phone's speaker with her palm, she glanced in the old man's direction. "He wants to know your last name."

Joe looked as nonplussed as she felt. Didn't he know his last name? After a moment's hesitation, he shrugged. "Sage. Joseph Sage."

Stona was shouting her name through the phone. She put it back to her ear. "Sorry."

"What's going on?"

"Nothing. I'm just a little distracted, that's all. Joe's full name is Joseph Sage."

"Is he spending the night?"

She didn't like his tone. Her houseguests were none of his business. "Probably, I'm not sure."

He must have sensed her irritation. *"Look, I'm not trying to invade your privacy, Willie, but until we have some answers in your cousin's case you need to be very careful. I can't protect you if I don't know the people around you."*

He was right, but he wouldn't understand why Joe was here. She barely understood herself. "I promise you don't have to worry about Joe. He isn't a threat. In fact, I feel safer with him here."

"Just be on guard."

"I will."

"I'll call tonight."

"Okay, I'll talk to you then. Bye."

"Goodbye."

Before Willie could put her phone back in her pocket it rang again.

"Miss McAllister?"

"Yes?"

"This is James Sutton. How are you this afternoon?"

"I'm fine, Mister Sutton. How are you and Missus Sutton?"

"We're doing well. I called to let you know the insurance papers are ready to sign whenever you can make it back to Nevada."

"Will you be available tomorrow?"

"I can be, but you'll want to come in early. They're calling for snow to move in by late afternoon."

"I can be there by ten if it's convenient."

"Ten would be fine. We can meet at my insurance company's office in Nevada." He gave her the address and quick directions. *"Bring the spearhead. Maybe we can figure out its origin."*

"I will. I think I know the tribe it came from now, but I'd like your opinion, as well."

"I'm looking forward to seeing it. I'll let Mary know you'll be here tomorrow. She'll want to join us."

"I'd like that. Until tomorrow then."

———————

STONA STARED AT his laptop screen in pensive silence. There'd been several Joe Sages in the DOJ's massive database—some upstanding citizens and a few not so upstanding. Willie's Joe could fall into either category. Why hadn't he asked how old the man was or where he lived?

His need to get to Willie was nearly overpowering.

It didn't take a Sherlock Holmes to know something was going on with her. She'd been a little distracted—her words—and evasive. He mentally kicked himself for not setting up a safe-word between them, some innocuous word or phrase that would warn him something was wrong.

She hadn't sounded frightened, though. That was the only reason he hadn't gotten in his car the moment he'd disconnected the call and headed back to southwest Missouri. He was tempted to do it, anyway.

The idea of a man he didn't know staying in the house with her unsettled him. Any man spending the night bothered him. He didn't like admitting that. Not even to himself. Maybe he was being obsessive. Was he the only person worried about her safety?

Her cousin and his fiancée had been murdered, but nothing linked Willie to their murders, not as a conspirator or potential victim. She should be safe. Still, something didn't feel right. He didn't know what was wrong, but he wasn't going to wait around St. Louis to find out. He'd finish the research tonight, turn in his report in the morning, and take a leave of absence.

TWENTY-SEVEN

WILLIE WAS HALFWAY to Nevada when Stona called at nine the next morning. He could tell she was driving and asked why. She told him the truth. "I got a call from the Suttons yesterday and I'm on my way to Nevada to sign the insurance settlement papers."

"Why didn't you tell me what you were planning when I called last night?"

"I knew you'd try to talk me out of it, and I was too tired to argue with you. You knew I had to make a trip to Nevada to sign the papers."

"Yes, I did, but I intended to go along. Your cousin warned you away from that town for a reason."

"Josh was nearly out of his head at the time. And I don't need a babysitter every time I step out of the house. Don't worry about me. I've recovered from my concussion, and I haven't had a blackout for two nights. If I didn't feel well enough, I wouldn't make the trip."

"There's a weather front moving in your direction."

"Yes, I know, but it's not due here until this afternoon. I should have my business finished and be on my way home before then."

"These fronts can move in faster than expected. Keep checking the updates. You don't want to get caught on the highway in the middle of a snowstorm."

"I will, and Stona?"

"Yes?"

"Thank you for worrying about me." She disconnected before he had a chance to reply.

———————

JAMES AND MARY Sutton were just climbing out of their car when Willie pulled into the insurance company's parking lot. Mary surprised her with a warm hug, which she returned. After everything that had happened the night of the storm they didn't feel like strangers.

The paperwork went fast and in less than half an hour the settlement check was in her hand.

James suggested she join them for an early lunch. It would give him an opportunity to examine the spearhead. She agreed and followed them as they drove to a small restaurant located close to the center of town.

The eating establishment was less than a block from the public library and Bushwhacker Museum. If there was time, she'd drop by and ask Greg Brandon, the curator, a few questions about Josh's visit. She should have enough time to get her questions answered and be on her way home before the bad weather set in.

The small restaurant looked more like a fifties diner complete with booths, tables, and seating at the long counter—and chrome, lots of chrome. A jukebox in the corner completed the effect. She glanced at the workspace behind the counter. Swinging doors separated the kitchen from the rest of the diner. There was a wide window for orders, but as far as she could tell, most of the cooking was done by the fry cook in front. Burgers sizzled on a long grill, the buns toasting beside them, and a basket of fries dripped hot grease while the cook ladled steaming bowls of chili from a large vat simmering over low heat.

They took their seats in a booth along the wall, and the waitress brought them menus and water.

James set his menu aside and smiled at Willie. "I come here for the chili. You can't beat it."

They all ended up ordering the chili, and she ordered a glass of cold milk to go with hers. While they waited for their food, she pulled the spearhead necklace over her head and handed it to James. The anxiety she experienced whenever she allowed another person to touch it hadn't faded. It heightened as she watched him turn the artifact over in his hands examining the fluted edges.

"This is a perfectly-crafted piece." He held the point out in his palm, angling it in one direction then another, weighing it in his hand. "See how straight, and well-balanced it is? Look at how even and precise the flutes are? I'm fairly sure it's an Osage point, though it's possible someone from a different tribe could've lost it. A spearhead of this quality could have been used for barter with other tribes. Then, too, if a point were lost during a hunt or skirmish, it might have been found and used by someone totally unknown to its original maker. If you ever decide to part with this, I suggest you donate it to a museum. It's a fine example of Osage craftsmanship."

He handed the necklace to her. She took a deep, relieved breath as she slipped it around her neck.

After their food arrived, the topic turned to the night of the storm.

Willie sipped her milk. "Has anyone been able to identify the remains we found?"

James nodded and leaned forward. "Our friend was male, somewhere between fifty and sixty-five. His height and the etchings on his arm bands indicate he was Osage, like your spearhead. But the manner and place of his burial don't fit with Osage traditions. The Osage of his time were buried sitting up. His grave would've been covered with stones rather than dirt."

He took a sip of his water. "Our front yard is a ways from either of the Osage villages and their burial sites. Even if he had died away from the village, his companions would have brought his body home for burial. The skeleton was so tangled in the tree roots there was no way of knowing how he was buried. The most telling fact that this wasn't a traditional Osage burial is the lack of stones in the immediate area. The number of stones should've been significant, yet no more than a handful were found around the uprooted tree." He shrugged. "I doubt we'll ever know what really occurred."

"What's going to happen to the remains?"

"I don't think it's been decided yet. It may take years to sort everything out."

"He should be laid to rest with the traditions he lived with."

Mary tilted her head. "You sound like it's personal for you."

"It feels personal. I don't know why. Maybe it's because I came so close to dying that night."

They sat in silence until James changed the subject again. "We haven't seen the face in the window since the night of the storm—after they took the remains away."

Willie nodded. "That doesn't surprise me. It stands to reason there would be a connection. I hope he finds peace." Neither Sutton questioned her newfound belief in spiritual beings.

"Miss McAllister, I didn't expect to see you here."

A tall, broad shouldered, young man strode toward her. She smiled, realizing she'd met him before. It took a few seconds more to recall from where. "Jake. It's good to see you again." She reached out to shake the fireman's hand. "I'm happy to see you, too." He nodded a greeting to the Suttons before turning back to her. "What are you doing in Nevada?" He glanced at the table. "The marshal isn't with you?"

"No. I'm here to finish the paperwork on the insurance claim."

"Of course. The accident with the tree. How are you feeling?"

"I'm fully recovered. I appreciate everything you and your crew did for me that night."

"Hey, you're one of us. You deserve the royal treatment." He tossed her an incredibly sexy grin. "The guys and I are doing routine maintenance on all of our equipment today. Since I'm the youngest man on the team, I get to be the gopher. That's a piece of luck. They send me here for take out, and I get a second chance to invite you to dinner." He gave her a smoldering, wide-eyed, hopeful look she suspected was well practiced.

She honestly hated to tell him no. "I'm sorry, Jake. I won't be staying in town much longer. They're predicting heavy snow this afternoon. I don't want to get caught in it on the drive home."

The grin faded. "Another time, maybe."

"I'd like that. I'll be coming back to Nevada to do some research. Maybe then."

His smile returned. Grabbing a pen from his pocket, he tore a corner off the paper placemat under her bowl and squatted beside the table to write a phone number. "Cell service is sketchy at my house. This is my captain's number. If you call him the next time you're in town, I'll get the message."

He glanced toward the counter and stood. The waitress was setting two large carryout bags beside the cash register. "That's probably my order." He nodded toward Mary and James Sutton and smiled at her again. "Hopefully, I'll see you soon." He didn't wait for her reply, but hurried to the counter and paid the bill. Grabbing the bags, he gave her one last nod before leaving the restaurant.

"He seems like a nice young man." Mary folded her napkin and set it beside her plate.

Willie had to agree. Jake was nice, but as soon as he'd disappeared through the door, her thoughts returned to the man who spent more time irritating than charming her. Stona Jordan had become the proverbial thorn in her side. So, why did she miss him?

After lunch, Willie drove the short distance to the museum and parked in the lot. It was nearly empty, so she pulled close to the building and used the library entrance, taking the stairs down to the museum.

Mr. Brandon sat behind his desk at the foot of the stairs. When he spotted her, he stood. "Miss McAllister, it's nice to see you again."

She extended her hand. "It's nice to see you, too."

"What can I do for you today?"

"Do you remember my asking about my cousin, Josh?"

"Vaguely. He was the deputy who stopped by here a few months ago, wasn't he? The young man who was killed in that unfortunate car accident."

"Yes, that's right. I didn't have enough time to go over any specifics the day I stopped by. Do you happen to remember what Josh seemed interested in?"

"I can't remember exact details, but as I recall, he was interested in the areas around the two Osage village sites. He asked about maps. I think he was interested in visiting places like Bluemound and some of the bluffs along the river. Many sites, like Haley's Bluff, are privately owned now. We have an extensive research department here, and your cousin spent quite a bit of time looking over old maps while his fiancée looked around the museum. I'm sure we can find a few of the maps if you'd like."

"If it isn't too much trouble."

"No trouble. It's one of the reasons we're here." Leading her to a room with tables, shelves of books, and dozens of file cabinets, he had her sit at a table piled with large, heavy tomes. She spent the next couple of hours poring over maps and reading about places of interest while employees and a couple of volunteers silently worked around her.

Even on vibration, her cell phone buzzed overly loud against the table where she worked. Grabbing for it, she glanced at the clock on the wall. Three o'clock. She didn't have to look at her caller ID.

"Hi, Stona."

"Hi. How'd your trip to Nevada go?"

"Actually, I'm still here. I'm getting ready to leave right now."

"Haven't you been paying attention to what's going on outside?"

"I've been in a basement for the past couple of hours. I haven't had a chance to look outside."

"If it isn't snowing where you are, it will be soon. The front's moving fast. You might want to consider renting a room and staying the night. Let me know if you do. If you don't, call me when you get home."

"Okay, I will."

"And Willie?"

"Yes?"

"Be safe."

"I will. Is it snowing where you are?"

"Yes, but I'm fine."

"You need to be careful, too." Disconnecting, she wondered how safe the roads in St. Louis were.

She stood up, grabbed her purse, and reached for one of the large books intending to replace it on the shelf. A worker put his hand on the book and smiled. "We've got this."

She smiled back. "Thank you."

It wasn't what she'd call blizzard conditions, but the snow was coming down faster than she'd like. The ground and parking lot were already white, and there was about a quarter inch of the heavy stuff on top of her car.

A vehicle had been parked beside hers not too long ago, the snow between the two cars disturbed. She imagined the driver brushing snow off the windows before pulling out of the lot. The footprints and tire tracks were already filling in.

She considered Stona's suggestion of finding a room after cleaning the snow off her windshield and watching how fast it built back up, but the salt trucks and plows were already out. With luck, she could get home before the highways became a problem. If she and the weather front were headed in the same direction, she might be able to drive out of the worst of it.

After gassing up and getting a couple of bottles of water, she started home. The roads weren't bad. The highway department had salted the pavement early on, and interstate traffic kept them reasonably clear. Her main problem was the slush thrown on her windshield when cars passed.

She didn't outrun the weather front. Snow built up on the secondary roads, and by the time she turned onto her farm road, she was grateful only three miles separated her from home.

A red light lit the dash-panel in front of her. Unfamiliar with the readouts, she didn't recognize what the warning indicated, and couldn't take her eyes off the road long enough to get a better look. Pulling over was out of the question. The problem would have to wait until she got home.

She reduced her speed but didn't slow the car as much as she would have liked. Any slower, and she might not make it over the next hill. There was probably four inches of snow on the road now, with only one set of tire tracks to stay in. People in this part of the country planned ahead and stayed home when the weather got bad. She was beginning to wish she'd done the same.

Less than a half mile later a deer leapt the fence that ran parallel to the road and darted in front of her car. Instinctively, she hit the brakes and cut the wheels to avoid the animal. The Honda slid out of control, slamming into the low bank on her right. The brake pedal sank all the way to the floor.

Momentarily stunned, she watched the deer jump the fence on the other side of the road and bound over the next rise. Shaking herself out of her stupor, she opened the door and stepped ankle-deep in the snow to survey the damage. The entire passenger side of the car was plastered against the barbed wire fence and the row of saplings lining it. The front fender had crumpled against a large corner post, the tire and wheel setting at an odd angle. It must've hit hard. Odd. She didn't re-member the impact—and apparently hadn't been hurt. No doubt she'd be sore in the morning.

Fishing the cell out of her pocket, she climbed back into the warm car. The motor was still running, the heater going full blast. She was about to dial Triple A when the phone rang. Startled, she dropped it in her lap and had to scramble for it.

She raised it to her ear. "Hello?"

"Willie, it's Stona. Are you home yet?"

"Almost." She really didn't want to tell him she was stranded in a snowbank at the side of the road. He couldn't do anything about it from St. Louis, anyway.

"How far away is almost?"

"A couple of miles." He was silent for a moment. That worried her.

"Will, your voice is shaky. What's wrong?"

Frustrated, she hit the steering wheel with her palm. How could he read her so easily? "I slid into the ditch. I'm all right but I'm going to need a tow."

"You're sure you're all right?"

"I'm fine. Honest."

"Why didn't you tell me you were stranded to begin with?" He sounded as frustrated as she felt.

"Because I'm not really stranded, and there's nothing you can do about it."

"Has someone stopped to help you?"

"No. The road's deserted. I'll call Triple A, then walk home. It isn't that far."

"No. Stay in your car. I'm about fifteen minutes behind you."

"What?" She practically strangled on the word. "How can you be—"

He cut her off. *"I'll explain in a few minutes. Right now, I need to concentrate on my driving. Stay in the car and lock your doors."* He disconnected.

Lock her doors? No self-respecting bad guy would consider coming out in this weather. He was being obsessive again. She did as he'd asked, though. It didn't hurt to be careful.

Ten minutes passed, and another ten before she saw the headlights through her rearview mirror. He pulled in behind her car and turned on his emergency flashers. The pre-dusk haze combined with the swirling snow distorted her vision, and she couldn't be sure it was Stona's car until he got out and walked toward her. With recognition came a surge of relief and she unlocked her door. He opened it, and leaned in, his eyes reflecting concern.

She wanted to throw herself into his arms. "Why are you always turning up when I need you?"

He reached in and gave her a hug. "Just lucky I guess." Releasing her, he stepped back. "Stay in the car where it's warm. I'll check the damage." He closed the door and walked to the front of the Honda, knelt to look at the passenger tire, then stood and shook his head. The saplings her car had plowed into prevented him from checking out that side of the vehicle. Retracing his steps, he walked along the driver's side to the back, looking at something in the snow, then bent to peer under the rear wheel well. Straightening, he sloshed to his car, opened the trunk and retrieved a large flashlight. He followed her skid marks from where she'd started sliding to where her vehicle had stopped, shining the light back and forth between the tracks. When he reached her car, he knelt and shined the light under the car again.

What on earth was he doing? She was about to get out and ask that question when he stood and walked to her door.

"Turn off your car and get in mine." She did as he asked, pocketing the keys and cell phone and grabbing her purse. He took her elbow so she wouldn't slip as they walked to his car then opened the passenger door for her. Shaking his head, he pointed to the Nikes on her feet.

"Were you planning to walk home in those?"

She objected to his tone. "No, I didn't want to get them wet. I planned to go barefoot." She didn't give him a chance to comment on her sarcasm. "Why are you upset with me? I didn't intend to slide off the road."

He closed her door, walked around his car, and slipped into the driver's seat, slamming the door in obvious agitation. "I'm not upset with you because you slid off the road. I'm irritated because you didn't take my advice and stay in Nevada until the roads cleared."

She folded her hands in front of her chest. "The roads weren't bad. I'd have made it all the way home if a deer hadn't jumped in front of the car. And I could've taken care of the situation. I was about to send for help when you called me."

"Have you called Triple A yet?"

"No. I decided to wait and see if you thought we could get it home by ourselves."

"Don't call them."

"Can the car make it home?"

"Even if we could get it home, which I doubt, we aren't going to." He pulled his cell phone out of his pocket.

"Then why can't I call for a tow?"

"I'll make the call."

"But it's my insurance company. I'll have to make the call."

"I'm not calling Triple A."

"Then who are you calling?"

"The Highway Patrol."

"Why?"

"Because they'll need to take it."

"I don't understand, Stona. Having the car moved off the road is my responsibility."

"Not this time, Will."

"Can you be a little less cryptic and explain what's going on?" She was beginning to feel the day's stress. She'd been so tense on the way home her muscles were aching. The near miss with the deer had frightened her, and the crash had rattled her nerves. Now, he was frustrating her with his non-answers.

He took a deep breath and exhaled slowly. "I don't mean to be cryptic. I just don't want to upset you unnecessarily."

"I'm already upset."

"All right. I noticed what looks like a residue of brake fluid in the snow under the rear wheel. I think there's more on the road but the snow's covering most of it. I won't know until an expert checks it out."

"Won't know what?"

"If someone tampered with your brakes."

TWENTY-EIGHT

STONA WATCHED THE color leave Willie's face. She was already
shaking her head.

"No. You're wrong. You have to be wrong."

"It's always a possibility."

"But you don't think so."

"We'll know more after they've checked out the Honda, but no, I
don't think I'm wrong."

She shivered. He reached into the backseat for the blanket he'd
tossed in the rental before leaving his apartment in St. Louis. He usually drove the car assigned to him by the U.S. Marshal's office, opting for
rental vehicles for personal use.

Wrapping the blanket and his arms around Willie, he pulled her as
close as the console would allow.

"I won't let anything happen to you. You know that, don't you? I
won't leave your side until we get him."

She nodded, and he retrieved his phone to call the Highway Patrol.
Explaining the situation, he asked for assistance. His second call was to
one of his superiors in St. Louis, giving her a brief explanation of the
potential escalation in Josh's case. He promised to keep her updated
before disconnecting.

Shoving the phone in his pocket, he turned to Willie. "Okay. Tell me what happened."

She shook her head. "I want some answers first."

He didn't care who asked the first question, as long as his got answered. "Okay."

She leaned forward. "How did you end up fifteen minutes behind me on the road?"

"I took a leave of absence and came back."

"When did you decide that?"

"Yesterday afternoon. I didn't feel right about leaving you."

"Before or after you talked to me?"

"After." He held his hands up to forestall the argument he saw coming. "Look, Will, I didn't like the idea of anyone staying with you if I didn't know anything about him. I checked your friend out—or I tried to, at least."

"You couldn't find him?"

"Oh, I found Joe Sage—more than one as a matter of fact. Athletes, architects, high school students, and several rather unsavory characters. Now which one do you suppose is your friend?"

"Stona, I—"

He shook his head. "That isn't the only reason I'm here. I told you, I couldn't shake the feeling that I shouldn't have left you alone. The longer I was away from you the stronger it got. So, I finished my research assignment and turned it in this morning. That's when I took a leave of absence. You're stuck with me, especially now."

He didn't give her a chance to ask any more questions. "Tell me what happened."

She sighed. "Most of the trip home wasn't so bad. The secondary roads were snow-covered, but they were still drivable. Even the farm road was passable. I did notice a red light on the dash as I turned onto this farm road but couldn't spare a glance down to see what was wrong. I had to concentrate on my driving and figured whatever the problem was could wait a couple of miles for me to get home. Then the deer jumped out in front of me. I hit the brakes hard and the car went into a skid just before the brake pedal sank to the floor." She waved a hand toward the Honda. "You can see where I ended up."

He nodded. "It makes sense, now. I'd guess the warning indicator on your dash was the brake alert. There isn't much fluid under the car, so most of it was gone by the time you hit the fence. I couldn't see an obvious problem with the line. But your cousin's vehicle didn't have an obvious problem, either. If your brake line was slit, like Josh's, every time you stepped on the brake pedal, you lost a little fluid." He drew a deep, almost shaky breath. "He miscalculated this time, probably thought you'd be hitting the brakes more often in this weather. I doubt he intended your accident to happen on an empty farm road."

"You're saying the same person who murdered Josh is...."

"... after you now."

Crossing her arms against a sudden shiver, she stared up at him. "But why?"

He pulled the blanket close around her shoulders. "I don't know yet, but I promise you I'll find out. We'll get him, Willie. And when we do...."

———————

WILLIE WAS GLAD Stona hadn't finished the thought. The chill in his voice matched his cold, deadly eyes. Red and blue flashing lights broke the tension. The Highway Patrol hadn't wasted any time getting to them.

She waited in the car while Stona walked the two patrolmen through the accident scene. The snow didn't seem to bother the men as they knelt to look under her car's rear wheel well. They talked, occasionally looking in her direction, and after a few nods and a little headshaking, one of the officers returned to the patrol car. He retrieved a camera and snapped several shots of the road and Honda.

Stona trudged to his car, opened the driver's door and leaned in. "Do you need anything from your car?"

She shook her head. "I've got my purse. It's all I had with me."

"Give me your keys. I'll leave them with one of the patrolmen." Returning to the officers, he handed over the keys and shook their hands, then headed in her direction, while the two men sought the shelter of their own vehicle. After knocking the snow from his boots, he climbed in and closed the door.

"They'll let the sheriff know what we've found. The car will be held until they can determine whether it was tampered with. If we're right, and someone tampered with the brakes, the car will be impounded and used as evidence in the attempt on your life."

She shuddered. He'd said it so matter-of-factly. But then he was in law enforcement. These things happened all the time in his line of work.

"Are you cold?" He reached over and adjusted the heat vents, aiming the warm air in her direction.

"I'm all right. How long do we have to wait here?"

"We don't. Local law enforcement will begin the investigation and the FBI and U.S. Marshals Offices will take over if there's a connection with Josh's case. I'm on leave, but I have friends who'll keep me in the loop." He shifted the car into gear and pulled out from between the Honda and patrol vehicle.

She touched his arm. "Is it okay to drive over the tire tracks?"

He patted her hand and grinned. "Yeah, it's fine. The snow's compromising the evidence, anyway. That's why the patrolman took pictures. The dealership's insurance company will need that information.

"The skid marks aren't that important to the Highway Patrol's investigation. It's the brake line that will provide the hard evidence if there was tampering."

He drove home slow and easy, his car cutting fresh grooves in the deepening snow.

She tensed as he pulled to a stop behind her house. She'd left the door unlocked for Joe and wasn't sure how Stona would react to that.

But the back door was locked, and she suspected the front door would be, too. Taking her key, Stona opened the door and hurried her inside. He took her coat and hung it in the mud room. She removed her

snow-covered shoes and wet socks, stepping into a pair of warm slip-
pers. Stona borrowed her broom and went outside to brush the snow
off his boots.

After looking in the parlor, Stona made her wait in the living room
while he checked the rooms upstairs.

He returned a few minutes later. "Where's your friend?"

"Joe?" She shrugged when he nodded. "I don't know. He was here
when I left this morning."

"In the house?"

"Of course, in the house—but he might be in the barn now. That's
where he stays at night."

"If you were such good friends, why would he sleep in the barn?"

Good question. One she couldn't explain without admitting she had
no idea who the man really was, or why she instinctively knew she
could trust him. "He likes roughing it, claims beds are too soft."

"Do you have any idea where he is now?"

"Like I said, he may be in the barn. It's got to be cold out there." She
headed toward the mud room. "I'd better go check on him."

He was already rebuttoning his coat. "No, I'll go. Lock the door
behind me."

———————————

STONA STOPPED BY the car for his flashlight, then walked to the
barn. He had no idea who he was looking for. Willie hadn't offered a
description and he hadn't asked. She'd been a little defensive about the
man over the phone. He'd wondered why at the time and thought he
might be a former boyfriend. The idea of an old flame staying with her
rankled. Not good. Not good at all. He was getting a little too close to
the case—no, not to the case, to Willie.

The interior of the barn was as dark as ebony and smelled musty.
After a couple of sweeps, the light's beam settled on a frail, old man. He

sat cross legged on a moldy bale of hay that looked as old as he did. This was Joe? His mental image of a thirty-something bodybuilder evaporated. His feeling of relief was almost physical.

Hunched forward, the man's chin touched his chest. The tattered blanket draped over his shoulders couldn't be very warm, and Stona suspected something might be wrong with the old guy.

"Joe?"

The gray head bobbed up, but the man didn't say a word.

"Are you Joe?"

Nodding, he unfolded himself, and got to his feet. Despite his years, he was still tall, only a couple of inches shorter than Stona's six-foot-four frame.

"Are you all right?"

Again, the nod.

The old man looked as if a good sneeze would topple him, but he wasn't about to let him in Willie's house before he knew it was safe. Stona shined his light on the badge and identification he held up. "I'm Deputy U.S. Marshal Stona Jordan. Do you have any identification?"

"In my wallet."

"Where's your wallet?"

"In my back pocket. Do you want to see it?"

"Remove the blanket and turn around." Joe didn't argue. He tossed the blanket over the hay bale and did as he'd been instructed. As soon as Stona was sure there were no hidden weapons he relaxed a little. "You can turn around. May I see your identification?"

Joe fished his billfold out of his back pocket and handed his ID to Stona. The information surprised him. After using his phone to confirm what he'd read, Stona returned the driver's license to the older man. "You're an ordained minister?"

"I am retired."

"Do you still live in Nevada, Reverend Sage?"

"Yes. Please call me Joe."

"Why are you here?"

"Because Willie needs me."

"Did she ask for your help?"

"She did not need to ask. I know I am supposed to be here—as you are. We will watch over Willie together."

Stona wasn't sure what to make of the old man. He'd keep an eye on him, but for now Joe looked as though he was the one in need of care. He picked up the blanket and handed it to him.

"Come to the house. Willie's worried about you."

Joe slipped the blanket over his shoulders and angled a look at Stona. "She worries too much about what does not matter and not enough about what does." His voice sounded as brittle as late November leaves.

"You're talking about her safety."

"Yes. It is good you have come to protect her."

"What makes you think I'm here to protect her?"

"The snow will end soon."

The abrupt change in topic threw Stona for a moment. Apparently, Willie's friend was done with the subject.

"We need to get to the house before Willie decides to come after both of us." Stona stepped back and Joe, pulling the blanket closer, led the way.

Willie opened the door and they stomped into the mud room, shaking the snow from their feet. She smiled. "You found him."

Joe moved into the kitchen with her. "I was not lost."

Stona followed. "He was in the barn."

She tilted her head toward the old man. "Why didn't you stay in the house? You should have at least left the door unlocked when you went out."

"I did not wish to stay inside. I locked your house when I left, to keep you safe."

"What if I had been delayed in Nevada?"

"The barn is warm and dry."

She took Joe's hand and shivered at the touch. "Your hands are ice cold. We need to get you warmed up fast." She turned to Stona. "Go upstairs with Joe and show him where the bathroom is. A hot shower will take away the chill. I'll find some clothes he can use."

Stona gave the old man a sidelong glance to see how he was taking her mothering.

His stoic expression gave nothing away, but he tilted his head in her direction. "She likes to take care of people. It is her gift." A hint of a smile touched his lips. "I think you are the same." His gaze fell on Willie before he started up the stairs. His voice trailed in his wake. "She is in need of your strength. You are here for a purpose."

TWENTY-NINE

JOSH'S CLOTHES WEREN'T a perfect fit for Joe, but they would do. Willie went through a couple of the boxes in the storage room and found jeans, T-shirts, heavier long-sleeved button-ups and a warm jacket. Stona had just come downstairs when she sent him back up with a change of clothes for Joe. She packed the rest in a cardboard box and set it at the bottom of the steps.

She suffered only a twinge of pain when Joe descended the stairs twenty minutes later in jeans and one of Josh's favorite shirts.

She threw together a quick meal of soup and sandwiches. After they ate, Stona helped Willie clean the kitchen, then went out to the car to retrieve his suitcase and laptop. He hadn't asked if he could stay and the look in his eyes warned her not to argue with him about it.

Joe was standing at the foot of the stairs when they moved into the living room. He held the box of clothes in his arms.

"I have decided to accept the room you offered me last night." With no further explanation, he started up the stairs. Suitcase in hand, Stona followed him up. She wasn't far behind.

Joe walked into the room across from hers—the one Stona had previously occupied and closed the door. She wondered how he'd known it was the room she'd intended to give him last night. Without missing a step, Stona continued down the hall and turned right, into the bedroom that adjoined hers. He gave her another, don't-argue-with-me, look before moving inside.

She was still standing outside Joe's door wondering what had just happened when her self-imposed mentor—or maybe she should call him her tormentor—appeared in the doorway.

"It is as it should be."

She glanced in his direction. "What?"

He didn't answer directly but shrugged. "He is your protector. It is good he sleeps beside you."

An instant memory of falling asleep in Stona's arms, his warm body surrounding hers, made her knees weak. "Our rooms adjoin, but he won't be sleeping beside me. He isn't... we aren't...." She shook her head, turned, and headed for the stairs. Joe had purposely manipulated their sleeping arrangements. A quick glance into his room had proven that. He'd used the bedding to make a pallet on the floor. His decision to move upstairs had nothing to do with a comfortable bed. What was he up to?

STONA SET HIS laptop on the dresser and his suitcase on the bed. Joe was a strange duck. With his antiquated speech and Willie Nelson braids, he seemed a man out of time and place. There was little doubt the man was a member of a tribe, probably from Oklahoma. He'd guess Osage from the man's height.

Opening the suitcase, Stona transferred his clothes to the closet and empty chest of drawers. With or without Willie's approval, he intended to be here for a while. Even if the problem with the brakes turned out to be mechanical instead of man-made, he was staying put. He'd learned to trust his instincts over the years, and he knew beyond doubt Willie was in danger.

Joe was right about Willie. She mothered the old man, giving him clothes and a warm place to sleep. She'd seemed confused by his sudden decision to take her up on her offer of a bedroom. When he'd taken the room across from Willie's the only remaining option was the room connected to hers.

He'd staked his claim to this room before she could suggest he sleep on the couch. She'd been irritated enough to do just that.

After putting the empty suitcase in the closet, he sat on the side of the bed and dialed his office, leaving messages for his superior, asking her to return his call as soon as she got into the office. Hopefully, by the time she called, he'd have an update from the Highway Patrol. He was convinced someone had tampered with Willie's car—someone who wanted her dead.

———————————

THEY WATCHED THE ten o'clock news and weather report on her flat screen in the living room. Joe sat in the wing-backed Queen Anne chair. Stona had taken the seat next to her on the couch. The meteorologist promised the snow would end before morning with an accumulation of between six and eight inches by the time it stopped. Willie was glad she had a well-stocked pantry and freezer. The curves and hills of Ozark back roads were more of a challenge to navigate than the highways and streets around St. Louis. Besides, she was without a car again.

Joe had drifted off during the program. His head lulled against the wing of his chair, and his eyes were closed. She was about to wake him and suggest he go up to bed when his eyes suddenly opened.

"Why did your protector bring you home? Where is the car you left with this morning?"

Was he only now realizing her vehicle wasn't parked behind the house? "I had car trouble, and my—*Stona* brought me home." She wasn't about to call the marshal her protector.

Joe glanced toward the couch. "It was good that you were close enough to assist her."

Stona nodded. "Yes, it was."

Exhausted, she pushed to her feet. "I'm going to bed. Stona, please get the lights when you're ready to come upstairs. Good night, Joe."

Deciding a hot bath would ease the tension out of her neck and shoulder muscles, she grabbed a warm cotton gown from her dresser, and went into the bathroom. She locked the door connecting Stona's room, removed the necklace and got undressed while the tub filled, then eased into the hot water and submerged to her chin.

The moist heat relaxed the tension from her body but couldn't calm her mind. The day had kept getting worse. Visiting with the Suttons had been interesting, but spending time in the museum had been a mistake. She'd lost a couple of hours poring over books and maps, hours that could've gotten her home before the snow started—and maybe before someone got to her car.

Stepping out of the tub, she dried off and slipped into her nightgown. After pulling the necklace over her head, she walked into the bedroom, dragged the quilt off the bed and climbed in, leaving the lamp on—her habit since Stone Shaper's visit. Settling against the pillow, she pulled the covers over her shoulders and closed her eyes.

THIRTY

STONA WAITED UNTIL Joe made his way up the stairs before checking the doors and windows and turning off the lights. Upstairs, he grabbed clean clothes and headed for the hall bathroom to shower.

There'd been little doubt in his mind the Honda's brakes were compromised, confirming his worst fears. Willie was the killer's next target. But why? What had she seen? He could understand Josh's murder. Her cousin had been in law enforcement, might have discovered something incriminating about the killer. But Willie was as much of an innocent bystander as Patricia Collins had been. Why did the killer need her dead, too?

He threw on a ragged pair of sweatpants before making one final sweep of the house.

Joe's door was closed, with no light showing beneath it. The dim light under Willie's door told him her bedside lamp was still on. Downstairs, he double checked both doors and the ground floor windows. Satisfied everything was secure, he headed to bed.

Halfway up the stairs he heard a crash.

"Willie!" He took the stairs three at a time, gained the landing, and slammed through Willie's door. She lay on the floor, unmoving. The broken lamp, its light still burning, lay on its side next to her.

Her open-eyed stare was glazed and fixed on the ceiling. "No!"

Dropping to his knees beside her, he touched the pulse point at her throat with shaking fingers. Her heart beat a strong, steady rhythm, and he sagged with relief, but her transfixed stare worried him. People occasionally lost consciousness with their eyes open. It didn't always happen, yet it wasn't an uncommon occurrence. But this was his Willie and seeing her like this unnerved him. He brushed his hand over her eyes to close the lids. "Willie, honey, can you hear me?"

She didn't respond.

He checked her limbs for broken bones before lifting her into his arms. She sagged like a life-sized ragdoll. *Deadweight.* He suddenly hated the term.

Placing her in the center of the bed, he sat by her side. "Please hear me." He brushed the hair away from her face. "Wake up, sweetheart. Please wake up."

"You cannot call her back." Joe walked into the room and stopped beside the bed.

Stona looked up at the old man. "What?"

"She is no longer in this place. We must wait for her return."

"We need to get her to a hospital." He reached for Willie's cell phone still in its charger on the nightstand.

Joe's hand on his shoulder stopped him. "What are you doing?"

"Calling for an ambulance."

"She does not need assistance, only patience."

Stona shrugged the old man's hand away. He didn't have time for riddles. "She needs medical care."

Joe shook his head, frowning. "You must not remove her body from this place. Her spirit will not be able to find its way back if you do."

The old man was babbling nonsense. He couldn't waste any more time on him. Stona reached for the phone again.

"You love her."

Stona froze. "What did you say?"

"You love her."

He didn't argue. "Yes."

"Then trust me. Her body must stay where it is. And you must be here when she wakes. It is time for truth between you."

"Joe, she—"

"Willie is in no danger. Her body waits for her spirit to return. You can watch over her and call for help if it becomes necessary. But it will not become necessary."

"Is this what she calls a blackout?"

Joe nodded.

"How long has she been having them?"

"I cannot say."

The old man could be as cryptic as Willie when it came to her blackouts. "How long have you known Willie?"

"Two days."

"Two days! You've only known her for two *days?*" He picked up the phone. "You don't know any more about what's wrong with her than I do."

"I know she will not come back to us if her body is removed from this place." There was a thread of iron in the ancient voice, and a conviction that couldn't be ignored.

Crazy or not, Joe believed every word he said—believed enough to make Stona pause in the middle of dialing. "Why are you so certain you're right? What's she told you?"

"She shares no more with me than she does with you. I did not know her spirit traveled until tonight."

"But you believe you know what's happening to her. Why?"

"Three, maybe four times I have seen this happen. Only once did a spirit lose its way. The man had been moved to a clinic. It took a long time for the man's spirit to find him."

Stona closed his eyes and prayed for patience. "You do know what a coma is, don't you?"

"She is not held by that deep sleep. She is in a place unknown to us, and we must give her time to return." Joe walked back to his room, leaving Stona to make the final decision.

He stared at the empty doorway and then down at the phone in his hand. Common sense told him the old man didn't know what he was talking about, but there was something about his certainty....

THIRTY-ONE

STONE SHAPER LAY on his back, one arm under his head, watching the smoke from the fire drift up and disappear through the smoke hole in the lodge roof. Beth lay on her side away from him, facing the embers. He couldn't see her face, but knew if she turned to him, he would see tears—as he did each time he mated with her. It wasn't because he hurt her. Only once had he drawn a cry of pain from her lips—the first night she lay beneath him. He had been the first man to touch her. His sudden smile was hidden by the darkness.

He did not blame her for weeping. As an obedient daughter, she had honored her father's decision to give her to him. It was the same with his people, though he could not imagine an Osage father delivering his daughter into the hands of an enemy.

Jackson LaRouche had tossed his daughter aside with no more thought than a man would give a stray dog, and he hadn't asked for assurance that she would be safe or treated well. He suspected the man never thought of her again after he'd turned and walked into the woods, leaving Beth to the life of an Osage slave.

Her father no longer fouled the land with his presence. His death had not been quick. His friends had suffered the same fate. Her mother and brothers had not been in camp and there was no talk of further retribution.

Rolling to his side, he pulled Beth against him and nuzzled her neck. "Do you still weep, little bird?" When she didn't answer, he turned her in his arms and brushed the hair out of her face. "The cries I drew from your lips tonight were not of pain. You were caught in the same storm as I. We found joy together." When she remained silent, he lifted her face. Her lips were swollen from his kisses—an intimacy he'd known only with her.

"Did I hurt you tonight?"

Her eyes widened at the question, and she placed a hand on his bare chest as she shook her head. "You are always gentle with me."

"Tell me why you weep each time we come together."

She closed her eyes and shook her head. "It isn't important."

"Then why do you cry?" When she tried to push away, he tightened his grip and threw a muscular thigh over her legs. "Answer me."

She gave up the fight and took a deep breath. "I was given to you as a slave. I could've lived with the disdain and submitted to a heedless master whose rutting caused me pain. I understood pain. It was what I expected and prepared my mind for."

He rested his cheek against the top of her head. "Are you crying because I do not abuse you?"

"No, of course not. I'm grateful for your care of me. Truth be told, I fare better in your home than I did in my father's. The first time we... came together, I was afraid, but you didn't beat or humiliate me as I feared you would. You've always been gentle, even when you took my innocence."

"I ask you again, why do you cry?"

"I was taught a man and woman were never supposed to... do what we just did without being married first. There are no exceptions. Even if a woman is forced to submit to a man's lust, it's considered shameful."

"You cry because of what your people will think of you?"

"I'm not concerned with what people think of me."

"Do you somehow believe you could have stopped me from making you my woman?"

She shook her head. "There was never a doubt in my mind. I expected to be ravaged, but I got your patience instead. You didn't have to force me. You made me burn with a need I couldn't understand. I still don't. You made me crave your touch. Instead of bearing your caresses with quiet dignity, I have shamed my family by *willingly* giving myself to you."

"You shame no one. I am your family now."

She looked away from him. "I'm your slave. Nothing more."

He rolled on top of her, bracing his weight on his arms. "You and Joseph are not the only whites in this village. You've seen the old man who gathers wood and tends the corn and squash. He works from the time we greet the morning until the light has left the sky. And the woman Bear captured carries fresh bruises every morning. *They* are slaves. You are not. You do not go hungry, or sleep outside shackled to a post, as an offering to any warrior who passes. You have enough to eat and I share you with no man. You are my woman, not my slave."

"But I'm not your wife. To your people—to Raven, to Brings Peace, even to Joseph, I am your whore."

He was suddenly furious with her for belittling herself. "You are my woman."

Her eyes filled with fresh tears and the pain reflected in their depths touched his heart. She lifted her hand and gently touched his cheek. "I am your woman, yes, but not your wife. In my heart there is a difference."

He moved to her side, taking her into his arms again. "I will not send you back to your people."

"I know." She rolled to her side away from him.

———

IT SEEMED AS if Beth had just dozed off when Stone Shaper nudged her awake. "Get up, little bird. Dress yourself." He tossed the buffalo robe aside and pulled her to her feet. The cool night air chilled her body and she hurried into the dress he'd insisted she remove before going to bed. She looked up at him while pulling on her moccasins. He was already dressed. "What's wrong?"

"All is well. Add wood to the fire and braid your hair." He walked to the lodge opening and paused. "I will return with guests."

"Guests? It's still dark...."

He was already gone.

She laid twigs on the fire's glowing embers, blowing on the coals until a small flame caught, then added larger chunks of wood. Retrieving the comb, she quickly plaited her hair, tying the ends with strips of rawhide. After straightening the furs and robes they'd slept in, she huddled close to the fire for warmth and waited.

Stone Shaper finally returned, stepping back from the lodge opening as Brings Peace and Joseph entered. From their disheveled appearance she knew both men had been roused from their own beds, and Brings Peace seemed upset. She sent Stone Shaper a worried glance.

"Be at ease, little bird. They are not here to cause you sorrow." He'd never used the endearment in front of others. She glanced from one man to the other, gauging their reaction. Neither seemed surprised.

Brings Peace placed a hand on Stone Shaper's arm. "If you propose *O me ho*, Bear will claim you and Beth were already *Ka shon le Me gro ka*, that you have married recklessly."

He spoke mostly English, obviously wanting her to understand what was being said. She still didn't understand and moved closer to Joseph. "Married?"

"*Ka shon le Me gro ka* is the Osage term for a common-law marriage without ceremony. It is not acceptable to the people. *O me ho* is a marriage ceremony used when the bride or groom has been married before. Stone Shaper has decided to make you his wife."

She was stunned. "Wife? Why would he—"

Stone Shaper interrupted her to confront Brings Peace. "Bear keeps his own captive, and, as it is in my lodge, no family members share his fire. By condemning me, he risks condemning himself."

Brings Peace shook his head. "No one questions what Bear's captive is. She wears rags and cowers like a slave. Beth does not. The

Little Old Men will see the difference. Bear's clan considers him a leader. He is gaining power with the people. The Little Old Men listened when Bear claimed the daughter of their hated enemy was not worthy of being adopted into the tribe and denied my request to do so. You and Bear have equal standing in your clans, and in the tribe, but Bear craves power and wishes to be more than your equal. He wants to destroy you."

Stone Shaper nodded. "I am aware of what he wants."

"Yet you have called for the *O me ho.* And have asked me to be your messenger. As your friend I agreed, but I must remind you of the dangers of your decision. The people have accepted Beth as your slave, though your treatment of her speaks otherwise. She does not have her own lodge for you to enter, or family members to give their approval in keeping with tradition. For this reason, Bear could challenge your right to O me ho, claiming you were *Ka shon le Me gro* ka first. If The Little Old Men are persuaded, you could be severely punished."

"Punished how?" She hadn't meant to interrupt but couldn't help herself. The men didn't seem to take offense and Brings Peace answered her.

"Stone Shaper could lose the title of Good Man, and never become a Little Old Man. You both would no longer be considered humans, and your children would be treated as the young of animals."

Horrified, she looked up at Stone Shaper. "Why would you take such a risk?"

"Brings Peace believes what we do tonight will give Bear the opportunity to accuse us of being *Ka shon le Me gro ka.* Bear does not need an opportunity to bring this matter before the people. He will do it soon. Short of giving you up, the *O me ho* is my way of keeping you safe, and I will not give you up."

Joseph gained her attention when he faced her. "You must freely accept him as your husband. Are you willing to do this?"

She didn't have to think about it. She had nowhere else to go, and no one to go to. The fierce warrior at her side had protected and cared for her, and his gentleness had won her heart. Her throat tight, she could only nod.

It was enough.

Brings Peace instructed her to sit on the furs in front of the fire. Stone Shaper stepped out of the lodge. Joseph moved to one side.

Brings Peace stood before her on the opposite side of the fire. "I have been chosen as a messenger. The warrior, Stone Shaper, gifts you with this lodge and all it contains and wishes to become your husband. Do you accept?"

"Yes."

Nodding, Brings Peace left the lodge. A moment later, he returned with Stone Shaper, who sat beside her on the furs. She waited for one of them to do or say something.

Stone Shaper finally stood, pulling her to her feet and touched his forehead to hers. Was that the Osage version of the wedding kiss? No vows had been exchanged between them. Were they married? She supposed they were. Her new husband moved from her side and spoke with Brings Peace, handing the older man a buckskin pouch.

Curious, she stepped closer to Joseph. "What are they doing?"

He bent to her ear. "Your new husband is giving Brings Peace the messenger's fee for his assistance. The pouch probably contains tobacco."

"And you were here as witness?"

"Yes, and for the ceremony to come."

"There's more? What ceremony?"

"The one I will perform."

It took her a minute to realize what he was saying. She shook her head. "You're Osage now. Can you still perform a Christian marriage ceremony?"

"I'm an ordained minister. Adoption into the Osage tribe doesn't change my beliefs or my standing with the church. Your marriage will be valid—accepted by the whites, ignored by the Osage."

"But why would Stone Shaper want a Christian ceremony? It won't change our situation."

He lifted his shoulders. "You should ask him that question."

Stone Shaper pulled her to his side. Brings Peace gave Joseph a nod and the minister took his place before them.

Her new husband reached for her hand. She caught her breath at the tender look in the fierce warrior's eyes. She understood then.

This ceremony was his greatest gift to her.

THIRTY-TWO

HE'D FALLEN ASLEEP with Willie in his arms. Stona's sleep-drugged mind couldn't process more than that. He tightened his arms, buried his face in her hair, and nuzzled her neck, inhaling her wonderful feminine scent.

"What—"

He covered her mouth before she could scream. She clawed at his hand with both of hers. "Willie, stop. It's me, Stona. I'm not attacking you. I promise. Calm down before Joe wakes up. Stop gouging me. I swear your fingernails are lethal weapons." He released her mouth and put some distance between them.

She rolled to face him, closing most of the space he'd given her. "What do you think you're doing?"

He didn't think she'd appreciate knowing he was smelling her. "Waking up. Do you always come out of one of your blackouts ready to do battle?"

"Only when I'm being manhandled. What are you doing in my bed?"

"Comforting you." He grinned. "How am I doing?"

"I'd be more comforted if you got out of my bed."

He laughed. He couldn't help himself. She had a smart mouth and gave as good as she got. He liked that about her—liked a whole lot more.

The thought propelled him out of her bed. He grabbed his shoes from the floor and headed for his bedroom. "When you're dressed, come downstairs. We have a few things we need to discuss. I'll start the coffee and make breakfast."

Joe was already sitting at the kitchen table, mug in hand. He'd taken the initiative and made coffee. Lowering the cup, he looked up. "She is well?"

Stona nodded. "I'll take a guess and say she's fully recovered. She'll be down in a few minutes." He retrieved a couple of cups from the cabinet, poured coffee into one, and set the other beside the coffee maker. Resting against the counter, he took a cautious swallow. "You really weren't worried about her, were you?"

Joe set his cup on the table and leaned back. "Only when you wanted to take her away from this place, did I worry."

"I still question my decision to let her stay here. You have to know what happened last night isn't normal. She needs help."

"Your help, yes, and mine. She cannot walk her path alone."

Stona carried his cup to the table and sat down. "If your plan is to make me crazy, it's working. You talk in riddles, and Willie doesn't tell me anything. How am I supposed to help her—no, let me rephrase that. Other than keeping her alive, how am I supposed to help her?"

"She needs your trust." Joe stood, went to the cabinet, and pulled three bowls from the shelf. After setting places at the table, he made a second trip for spoons and milk. Stona patiently waited for him to explain as the old man searched the cabinets until he found a box of granola cereal and one of Cheerios.

"Are you going to tell me what you mean by trust?"

Joe shrugged. "You need to trust her. To accept what she tells you as truth."

Stona paused, his cup halfway to his lips. "At this point I'm not sure she knows what the truth is."

"So, you believe I'm delusional?"

He sighed and shook his head. Willie just had to walk in at that moment. He wasn't about to back down but decided to let her start the argument that was bound to happen. She'd changed into a lavender pullover sweater and snug-fitting jeans and looked too good for his peace of mind. She also looked irritated.

Moving to the coffee maker, she filled the empty cup and carried it to her place at the table. The woman actually glared at the cereal and milk. "I see you made breakfast."

He tilted his head toward Joe. "He cooked."

She turned a smile on the man. "That was nice. Thank you."

Joe slid Stona a sly glance before returning her smile. "I made coffee, too."

It took every ounce of control Stona possessed not to roll his eyes. He nudged the granola in her direction. "You need to eat. Then we need to talk."

She pushed the box away. "I'm not hungry. I'll make a piece of toast."

"I'll get it." He was surprised Joe didn't try to beat him to the toaster. The man seemed content to sit beside Willie and, in fact, held his cup out to be refilled after the bread was in the toaster. Stona carried the carafe to the table, filled Joe's cup, and topped off his own before returning it. The toast popped up. He put it on a plate and set it in front of her, along with a knife and what passed for butter in her house. He finally sat at the table and sipped his coffee while she ate. No one said a word. When she'd finished, she carried her plate to the sink, grabbed the carafe and filled their cups before draining the last of the pot into his.

Finally, it was time to talk. And way past time for truth.

She cleared her throat. "What do you want to know?"

He was relieved she didn't make him force the issue. "Tell me about the blackouts. I know we've been over this before, but you weren't very forthcoming. We're going over it all again, and this time don't hold anything back."

"Not even if I sound crazy?"

"Not even if you sound certifiable. I want to know every detail of what's been happening to you, including the episode before I left for St. Louis—the one that ended with me in your bed the first time."

Her cheeks reddened when he emphasized 'the first time,' but she did as he ordered. "I didn't have a blackout then. It was—something else."

"All right. Do you want to talk about what happened that night first, or the blackouts?"

"The blackouts."

Nodding, he leaned back, took a sip of his coffee, and tried to act as though they were having a normal conversation. She looked ready to bolt, and he wanted to put her at ease. "You're a nurse. I assume you know what constitutes a blackout. Do you believe that's what's happening to you?"

"Not exactly."

He held his patience. "Explain *not exactly*."

"I'm not sure I can explain." She took a minute to think about it, then continued. "When a person blacks out, they're not aware of anything until they wake up. It's why they call them blackouts."

"But you don't really black out."

"No. I get dizzy and lose consciousness—and this is where it gets bizarre. I experience something like a dream." She shook her head. "But it isn't a dream. It's like I'm there."

"Where?"

"I don't know where—or when, for that matter. These visions—that's what I call them for lack of a better description—revolve around two people, Beth, the daughter of a French trapper, and Stone Shaper, an Osage warrior. Every vision concerns some pivotal event in their lives. If I were being fanciful, I'd guess I traveled back in time about two hundred years. It's like walking into a Western movie."

"Could they be recurring dreams?"

"They don't feel like dreams and they aren't recurring. The visions are about the same people, but the events change."

"They could still be dreams."

She shook her head. "No. I wasn't just watching something happen. I experienced their fear and anger, knew their rage and despair and sense of betrayal. When Beth was shot with an arrow, I saw it coming and felt the shock and agonizing pain. It burned white-hot."

She took a sip of her coffee, grimaced, and carried the cup to the microwave. A minute later she returned to the table. "It's weird, but I can be in both of their heads at the same time. I understand what they think while they're thinking it. I experience every word, every touch."

Stona looked from Willie to Joe. "And you knew this was happening to her?"

She interrupted him before Joe could speak. "He couldn't have known." She set her cup down. "I've never told anyone."

"He must know something. He stopped me from calling an ambulance last night when I found you on the floor. He said if I moved you to another place, you'd never wake up. He insisted your spirit wouldn't be able to find its way home."

Her eyes widened and her attention swung to Joe. "My visions?" She shook her head. "How could you know?"

"I did not know about your visions until last night, but I have seen this happen before, and know the dangers. That Beth and Stone Shaper appear to you in more than one form does not surprise me."

Stona paused with his cup halfway to his mouth. "What do you mean by more than one form?"

Joe tilted his head toward Willie. "She can explain better than I."

Glancing in her direction, he waited.

She lifted her shoulders. "I've seen them when I was awake too—three times."

He set his cup on the table and leaned forward. "You're telling me you see ghosts?"

"I don't know. Aren't ghosts supposed to show up at night when it's dark and scary? I've seen Stone Shaper and Beth twice when the sun was shining."

"Let me guess. You saw them once in your bedroom—the night you screamed."

"Not both, that night. Just Stone Shaper. He's appeared alone once in the meadow, and once in my room. The only time Stone Shaper and Beth appeared together was beside the creek when I'd gone for a hike."

Her story was too fantastic. He was beginning to fear for her mental health. Stories of schizophrenia and dementia raced through his mind and he prayed he was jumping to conclusions. "Willie, don't take offense. You know I have to ask this. Is it possible you were hallucinating?"

Joe folded his hands on the tabletop. "I saw them as well."

Stona sat forward. "What?"

"I have also seen Stone Shaper and Beth."

"Where?"

"At the creek with Willie."

He glanced at her. "Joe was with you at the creek?"

"Yes."

His law enforcement experience kicked in. "Come with me." He took her hand and led her out of the kitchen. "Joe, stay here. We'll be back in a few minutes." The old man nodded and poured more Cheerios into his bowl.

Stona didn't say anymore until they'd climbed the stairs and gone into her room. He closed the door behind them, leaned back against it, and crossed his arms over his chest.

"I want you to tell me exactly what happened at the creek. I want to know every detail you can remember."

If she believed he was acting paranoid, she didn't mention it. In concise detail she described her trip to the creek, and her interaction with both Stone Shaper and Beth. "I don't know how long Joe had been standing behind me, but it was long enough for him to see them." She took a deep ragged breath and laughed. There was no humor in the sound. "Until Joe told me he saw them I questioned my sanity. But I'm not crazy, Stona. I have no idea what's happening to me, but it is happening, and I don't know what to do about it." She was vulnerable—and in need of a friend.

He dropped his arms to his sides, walked to where she stood in the middle of the room, and pulled her to him, gently rocking her back and forth. She hugged his waist and held on.

He liked the feel of her against him. Lifting her face, he stared into her beautiful dark blue eyes. Her ivory skin, tinted gold by the sun, beckoned his touch, and her lush red lips, slightly parted, were a temptation he couldn't resist. He lowered his head slow enough to let her pull away if she wanted to. She didn't move, and in fact tightened her hold on him when his lips slanted over hers. His tongue slipped in to taste her as he deepened the kiss. She moaned her pleasure and he knew she enjoyed the intimacy as much as he did.

When he realized he was urging her toward the bed, he broke off the kiss and held her at arm's length. They were both breathing hard. He couldn't help his smile, so pleased was he with her reaction to him. "I think we'd better go back downstairs."

"I think so, too." Her voice was whisper soft, her cheeks tinged with pink.

Slipping his hand around hers, he walked her into the hall. "Come on. Joe's liable to lose patience and wander out to the barn, and I'm not finished talking to him yet."

"Why?"

"I want to hear his version of what happened at the creek."

She stopped at the head of the stairs. "You don't believe what I told you?"

"I believe it's what you think you saw. I want to hear what Joe has to say without his being influenced by you. Then I can compare the two versions and get a clear picture of what happened."

Joe had cleared the table and was rinsing the dishes when they walked into the kitchen. Willie pulled free of Stona's grasp and walked to her friend. "Leave those, Joe. I'll take care of them later. Stona wants to talk to you." He nodded and sat at the table.

When everyone was seated, Stona asked Joe to explain what he'd seen and heard. The older man's account was nearly identical to Willie's.

"Did you follow her to the creek?"

"I did."

"Why?"

"As her spirit guide, it is my duty to be close during her spirit quests should she need me."

Stona's eyes narrowed. "Why didn't you interfere when the warrior tried to attack her?"

"Stone Shaper's spirit walks a different plane. He cannot physically harm her. I sense he struggles to even make himself known to her."

"Does he want to hurt her?"

Joe shook his head. "I do not believe so. He is confused and frustrated, but he wishes her no harm. She is the chosen one. She is destined to aid the warrior, but I am not sure how."

Stona admitted they made a sound case for the ghosts' existence. But his main concern was for her protection—not from a restless ghost, but from a madman who had already murdered her cousin and his fiancée. Now, he was after Willie. Her mental well-being was his concern as well. He couldn't and wouldn't leave her to face the bizarre situation with only an old man for support.

Decision made, he glanced from Willie to Joe. "All right, where do we begin?"

THIRTY-THREE

"I THINK WE should start with the first time I saw Stone Shaper. It was also the first day you came to see me."

Stona smiled. "I remember that day." He glanced at Joe. "She threw me out of her house."

Willie's spine stiffened. "He accused me of killing my cousin." She shook her head before either man could comment. "I had decided to plant a tree in Josh's memory and was digging a hole for the tree when I cut my finger on a piece of flint." She touched the lacing of the necklace. "It turned out to be the spearhead.

"After Josh's death, I'd developed an aversion to blood. As soon as my finger started bleeding, I experienced a wave of nausea and dizziness and closed my eyes to regain control of my senses." She gazed out the window. "When I opened them, Stone Shaper was standing in the far meadow at the edge of those woods. He was watching me. I looked away for a moment, and when I looked back, he was gone."

Joe folded his hands in front of him. "It's interesting. The spearhead draws your blood and in the next moment you see Stone Shaper."

Stona nodded. "What happened next?"

"That night I experienced my first vision. I woke the next morning sprawled across the bed clutching the spearhead."

Stona touched her hand. "Let me get this straight. You were holding the spearhead when you saw the warrior and again when you experienced the vision, right?"

"Yes, but I wasn't holding it when I had the second vision—at the Osage village."

"But it was still in your possession?"

She nodded. "I kept it in my purse. It's always with me."

"Joe, did you know about the spearhead?" When he shook his head, Stona glanced at Willie. "Would you mind if we look at it?"

She hesitated, then realized how obsessive she was acting. Stona was trying to help her. She couldn't imagine anyone else she trusted more, not even Scott and Ben. Lifting the spearhead from its hiding place, she pulled the heavy thread securing it over her head.

"I know it's obsessive, but I need it close to me." She handed it to Stona with all the care a person would give a delicate porcelain antique.

He must've picked up on her anxiety and was equally careful when he examined it. A few minutes later, he passed it to Joe.

The minute the artifact touched his hand, Joe stiffened. The color drained from his face. His fingers clenched around the fluted piece of flint as he tried to stand. Clutching his chest with his free hand Joe fell back with an anguished cry.

"Joe!" She lunged to his side, grabbing his shoulders to keep him from falling out of the chair. Stona moved to his other side to steady him.

"Take it," the old man cried, raising his arm. "Take it! I can't turn it loose." He was still clutching his chest and gasping for breath between each word. My fingers won't move."

She steadied him as Stona carefully pried each finger open. The spearhead clattered to the tabletop and Joe sighed as if a great weight had been lifted from him.

Willie squeezed his shoulder. "I'm calling an ambulance."

Joe caught her hand. "There is no need."

"Joe, you were clutching your chest. I don't want to frighten you, but your reaction to the spearhead might've triggered a heart attack. Let me make the call."

He shook his head. "The pain is gone."

Still anxious, she hurried to the refrigerator and opened the cabinet above it. Pulling a small medical bag from one of the shelves, she rushed back to Joe.

"I keep this handy in case of emergencies." Unzipping the bag, she pulled out a portable blood pressure kit and stethoscope. Joe looked disgruntled. She held up a hand before he could say anything. "I'm going to have my way, Joe. You may as well indulge me."

Inserting the stethoscope's ear tips, she placed a hand against Joe's back to steady him and pressed the diaphragm to his chest. His heartbeat was a little rapid but strong with a steady rhythm. After the scare he'd just given her, she imagined her own pulse was as erratic.

Straightening, she leaned back "Are you sure you're not in pain?" She paused in the process of putting the blood pressure cuff around Joe's arm waiting for his answer.

He shook his head. "There is no pain."

She glanced at Stona after checking the reading. "It's a little elevated, but considering what I witnessed a few minutes ago, I'm surprised it isn't higher."

Stona brought Joe a glass of water while she put the medical kit away. Resuming her seat, she patted Joe's hand. "I had a similar reaction. Twice. It was like holding a firebrand, and, like you, I couldn't open my fingers. The first time it happened I saw Stone Shaper in the meadow. The second time I saw him in a vision. Did you see or hear anything while you were holding the spearhead?"

Joe shook his head. "I experienced no spirits, no visions. Only pain." He tapped his chest with a closed fist. "Here."

She glanced at Stona. "Our reactions were different, but there's a connection, isn't there?"

Picking up the artifact, he turned it over in his hand. "Between you and Joe?"

She nodded. "And the spearhead. Yes."

"It's possible." He hefted the piece, clasping and releasing it, gauging its balance. "I don't feel anything unusual. Has anyone else handled it?"

"Two, maybe three people. The curator at the museum and Mister Sutton both held it. I don't remember if Mary Sutton handled it or not."

"Did they show any signs of an adverse reaction?"

"No. But I've only reacted to the stone three times, and I'm wearing it."

He set the necklace on the table in front of her. "What triggered your reactions?"

"The first time was while I was planting the tree. That was when I saw Stone Shaper in the meadow. The other reactions were related to visions."

She reached for the spearhead but hesitated. Joe's violent encounter made her wary. Would she feel the searing heat again? Holding her breath, she picked it up. Nothing happened. Her heart slowed its frantic rhythm. She hadn't realized it was racing.

"Willie, are you all right?" Stona had moved from Joe's side to hers.

"I'm fine."

"Are you sure? You look like you've seen a ghost."

She stared at him for all of ten seconds before bursting into laughter. "I can't believe you said that." It took him longer to recognize what he'd said. The corner of his mouth turned up in a wry grin.

Willie started to slip on the necklace, but Stona shook his head. "Since I seem to be unaffected, maybe I should keep that with me."

When he reached for the spearhead, she snatched it away. "Don't! It stays with me."

He raised both hands, backing off. "Okay, I won't argue. If you need to keep it close there must be a reason. But you need to understand. From this point on, when you're in the same room with the spearhead, I'm going to be in that room, too. I swear, Willie, I'm afraid to let you sleep alone."

THIRTY-FOUR

"I WILL RETURN before the new moon." In the privacy of their lodge, Stone Shaper pulled Beth back against him, stretched his arms around her and stroked her rounded belly. "Because Brings Peace goes with us as guide, we will use the ponies. You will see me long before my son greets this world."

She turned in his arms and smiled up at him. "Are you so sure it will be a son? I could as easily give you a daughter."

He nuzzled her neck. "A daughter will please me, as well." His arms tightened, pulling her closer. "You must take care while I am gone. Joseph will make sure all is well with you, and Raven will be close if you need her."

Her eyes filled with concern. "The babe and I will be fine, husband, but I worry for you. Raven tells me your ponies will be easier to see. You'll be safer if you go on foot."

"Our ponies are necessary. The Little Old Men have decided our summer hunting camp will be to the south and east of our village, where the grasslands give way to wooded mountains and deep-spring rivers. The very old remember this place. Brings Peace made the journey in his youth and can show us where the buffalo are plentiful. But he is no longer young and cannot make the trip on foot. We must respect his age and use the ponies."

"I know." She sighed. "I also worry knowing Bear and his friends go with you. When The Little Old Men ignored his accusations and declared our *O me ho* marriage acceptable, he became your enemy. He has never forgiven you and Brings Peace for besting him."

"Do not concern yourself with Bear. He will not endanger his standing with the tribe by challenging us. I am pleased to know he will be with us and not in the village where he can cause further mischief." He touched his lips to her forehead. "It is time for you to put aside your fears and bid me safe journey."

She lifted her hand and touched his cheek with the back of her fingers. "Do you know how much I love you? Almost a year ago, when you took me from my home, I feared for my survival. Instead of making me your slave, you made me your wife and, despite the seeds of mistrust Bear tried to sow among the Osage, I have found my place here. I doubt I would be as content among my own people. It is fortunate my father gave me to you. He could have as easily given me to one of his friends, if the man made it worth his while. You saved me from the life my mother suffers, and I will always be grateful."

He held her face in his hands, gazing into her beautiful gray eyes, and touched her lips with his. "You saved *yourself,* little bird. Your courage gained my respect and the respect of many Osage. Even Bear cannot deny this is so. But your loyalty and devotion to me, and your gentle spirit have won my love."

―――――――――

THEY MOVED TO the lodge entrance. He slipped his bow and quiver of arrows over his shoulder and lifted his spear. She reached out to touch him one more time and the side of her hand brushed the spearhead. She flinched but was too caught up in his leave-taking to give the paltry scratch more than a passing notice.

"I wish you could go on foot. You would be safer."

"Do not regret the ponies. They will speed me home to you." Kissing her, he rested his hand on her belly one last time. "Take care of our child." He wiped away the single tear on her cheek and left their lodge.

She watched him walk out of sight then turned to add more wood to the fire. It was then she noticed the blood on her hand. It was fanciful, she knew, but she imagined her blood on his spearhead somehow connected them. Maybe she could keep him safe.

EVEN WITH THE ponies their journey took three risings. Brings Peace lamented the number of new white settlements they cautiously avoided.

Evidence of recent campsites caused them to wonder if their enemy, the Kiowa, also sent scouts to seek new hunting grounds.

Brings Peace proved his memory was true. He led the small band to a plain of lush, undulating grasslands reaching so far to the west they could not see its end. Deep forests of ancient trees bordered the plain to the south and east. The old warrior told them the level prairie gave way to steep hillsides, ragged bluffs, and shadowed valleys in those directions.

"I remember a spring at the foot of a tall bluff, not far from this place. The water is cold like snow melt and comes from a source so deep it is not possible to find the bottom. The stream flowing from this spring is wide and clear enough to watch the fish dart in the current."

Stone Shaper's cousin, Raven's younger brother, Winter Storm, glanced at the older man. "If there is grazing in the valley for our ponies, it would make a good place for our camp." The young man would soon see his fifteenth summer and was no longer considered a child. It was an honor to be included in the scouting party and he was eager to prove himself.

Brings Peace shook his head. "The ponies would find grass in the valley, but there are also caves and crevices in the bluffs offering shelter to predators like the wolf and mountain lion. And a camp so deep in the valley could not easily be defended from an enemy's attack."

He led them to a rise overlooking a wide, grassy basin. The high ground was full of large flat rocks giving grass and other vegetation little room to grow. A small campfire could be easily contained. The old warrior decided it was a good location for their camp. After unpacking the buffalo robes and pouches of food, they released their mounts to graze. Brings Peace spread his robe on an outcropping of rock to rest and watch the ponies while the younger warriors scouted the area.

The sun was low in the west before the last warrior returned. Stone Shaper and Winter Storm had followed a deer trail through the woods to a dry wash and eventually a clear stream close enough to provide water for the camp and the ponies.

Bear mentioned a sunken place in the ground not far from where they stood. "There is an opening wide enough for a man to crawl through at the base of a large tree. The hole is too deep to harbor predators."

Brings Peace got to his feet. "You will show us this place." The men followed Bear into the shadow of the trees, the scent of moist, decayed vegetation rising from every footfall.

The opening was as Bear had described, and the warriors agreed it posed no danger. The medicine chief nodded. "Our ponies will not venture into the woods when the grass is plentiful where they are."

That night, Stone Shaper lay awake long after the others found sleep. Though he would not admit it, even to Beth, he did not sleep well unless she lay by his side. He was already looking forward to returning home.

The warriors traveled on foot the following day, allowing their mounts to rest and graze. Brings Peace offered to remain in camp to guard the ponies. "I, too, can use the rest. These bones are not as willing to make long journeys as they once were."

Since there had been no fresh sign of buffalo in the area, Bear suggested the men split up in order to cover more territory in their search for the herd. They would meet in the valley of the big spring Brings Peace had recalled.

Winter Storm boasted he, Stone Shaper, and another young war-rior, Stands Alone, would catch enough of the large fish the medicine chief had spoken of to feed the party that evening.

Stone Shaper shook his head. "Do not wait for me at the spring. I search for the herd in the north and west. This camp will be closer than the spring when I return. Brings Peace will have many questions."

Since a single buffalo would supply more meat than they could pre-serve, the warriors left their bulkier spears in camp. Armed only with their bows and quivers of arrows, the men left the camp.

BRINGS PEACE WOKE with a start and glanced around the campsite wondering what had disturbed his nap. A moment later Bear walked into the camp.

THE BRISK SPRING morning had lengthened into warm afternoon when Stone Shaper skidded down the steep incline leading to the small spring he'd found earlier in the day. Lying on his belly, he quenched his thirst in much the same manner as any wild animal of the forest. Sated, he rose to his knees, removed the water skin from his belt, and filled it. He hadn't found the buffalo herd but had spotted several large herds of deer. He'd seen signs of wolf, fox, and bear, as well as bea-ver dams. Brings Peace would be interested to know this land could provide a successful winter's hunt. Satisfied with his discoveries, he returned to camp, looking forward to a few minutes alone with his friend to share their day.

He came across the ponies a good distance from the camp and wondered why Brings Peace had allowed them to wander so far. At his approach, the ponies' heads came up, ears flicking in his direction. Nostrils flaring, they tested the wind, prancing a few steps before turning to snort and stomp the ground. Something besides him had unsettled them.

Crouching in the deep grass, he pulled an arrow from his quiver and notched it to the bowstring, alert for an enemy or predator. He sprinted in the direction of the camp, avoiding the open meadows, preferring the cover of the woods.

————————

THE CAMP WAS empty. Apparently, none of the warriors had returned yet. Brings Peace wasn't in sight. Wary, he moved into the clearing—and saw the blood—a thick, dark puddle of it, soaking into the ground. The blackish red stain trailed over a low outcropping of rock. Stone Shaper prayed the blood was from an animal Brings Peace had encountered and slain—not from his friend. A slight rustling came from the other side of a thick clump of small trees ahead of him. A low menacing growl warned him away.

He stiffened. The huge, tawny cat slinked out of the brush, teeth bared in a snarl, ears flat against its head. The animal's hindquarters bunched, prepared to leap. Stone Shaper planted his feet and raised his bow.

The mountain lion twitched its ears, flicking the tips forward, and its head cocked slightly. It glanced toward the foliage, hissed its defiance, and bounded into the dense undergrowth. Stone Shaper wasted only a second in surprise before running to the lion's hidden victim, praying he'd find the carcass of an animal.

Brings Peace lay on his back, eyes wide, his head tilted, with one arm outstretched above his body. An agonized howl of denial rent the air as Stone Shaper sank to his knees.

Deep gashes in his friend's hand and wrist evidenced the lion's effort to drag the old man into the concealing scrub. The beast left no other marks on the medicine chief's body. Like any predator, the big cat was not averse to stealing the kill of another. It had simply been drawn to the camp by the scent of blood.

The spearhead embedded in his mentor's chest had felled the old man. *His* spearhead.

Tossing his bow to the ground, he raised his face to the sky and bellowed his rage. Brings Peace would never have allowed an enemy into his camp. The man who had taken his life had walked into the clearing as a friend. A deep sense of betrayal enshrouded Stone Shaper like the robes of the dead.

Fearing moving his friend would somehow cause the old warrior pain Stone Shaper lifted his friend, carrying him to the center of the camp where he could remove the spear without further damage. Blood, from the wounds Brings Peace had suffered, glistened on his own arms and chest. He felt humbled by it. Groaning from the pain tightening his chest, he carefully placed Brings Peace on an outstretched buffalo hide and knelt to straighten his arms and legs. This man had been his mentor and advisor, his father when he gave his daughter to him as wife—and he had been his friend.

Someone had dared to use the weapon he had crafted to take the life of the tribe's peacemaker.

Reaching for the shaft, Stone Shaper mentally prepared himself to remove the spearhead from the medicine chief's heart. Brings Peace would never know of its removal, yet it seemed like another insult.

Ponies galloping in the distance alerted him. The lion's keen ears had picked up the animals' approach long before their arrival. He stood, his hand on the hilt of his knife, until he recognized the warriors astride their mounts. The men had also come across the herd and taken time to catch them.

Grasping their animals' manes, the warriors kneed their ponies to a skidding stop and gaped at the sight of their medicine chief at Stone Shaper's feet, the lance jutting from his chest.

No one moved. No one spoke.

Roaring, Bear suddenly leaped from his pony, lunged forward, and grasped the spear's shaft. He carelessly jerked the spearhead from the old man's chest.

And plunged it into Stone Shaper's heart.

THIRTY-FIVE

WILLIE SCREAMED, AND screamed again and again, fighting the arms that came around her, pounding her fists on the chest she was pulled against.

"It's okay, Will. It's Stona. I've got you."

She clutched his shoulders. "He killed him!"

He pressed her against the pillow. "Sweetheart, Josh is—"

"Not Josh—Stone Shaper. Bear killed him! He used the spear—*my* spearhead. He never gave Stone Shaper a chance to explain. There was so much blood—Brings Peace was covered with it. His blood smeared Stone Shaper's body." She gagged and suddenly found her head dangling over the edge of the bed, while dry heaves wrenched the strength from her body. Stona's strong arm supported her, and he pulled her hair away from her face. Her retching eased and he lifted her back into his arms.

"The visions come closer together." Joe stood in the open doorway.

Stona switched on the lamp. "Too close together."

A moment later, Joe stood over her, holding out a damp washcloth. Stona took it and gently wiped her face.

She wilted against him, caught between two worlds. "We have to do something. Bear killed Brings Peace, too. I know he did. He killed them both."

He tossed the washcloth on the stand and tilted her face up. "Willie, look at me." His eyes were filled with concern. "There's nothing we can do. They've been dead for hundreds of years."

She cautiously shook her head, fearing the awful retching would begin again. "For you, maybe, but I just watched them die." She glanced at Joe. "You're my spirit guide. Tell me what to do."

Her mentor was quiet for several minutes before meeting her gaze. "The marshal is right. There is nothing we can do now to stop what happened then."

"If we can't help them, why am I having these visions? Why do you call me the chosen one if I can't stop what happened?"

He lifted his shoulders in a heavy shrug. "There is a purpose for what is happening. Each vision draws us closer to the mysteries of the past. We must be patient."

She sighed and pushed the hair out of her eyes. "I'm not sure I can handle much more."

Joe placed his hand on top of her head. It felt like a blessing. "You're stronger than you believe. If you were weak, you would not have been chosen."

"Chosen for what?" She shoved out of Stona's arms. "What do they *want* from me?"

Stona wouldn't let her go far. He took her hand and brought it to his lips. "Don't think about it right now. Give yourself time to process what's happening. We can talk about it in the morning."

Nodding his agreement Joe moved to the hall door. "She should not be left alone. The past yet holds her."

"She won't be alone." He lifted her to the center of the bed and turned off the lamp. When the room darkened, he stretched out, drawing her against his hard body and covered them both with the quilt.

She didn't object to the intimacy. She didn't want to be alone any more than they wanted her to be. Stona's presence calmed her. Even now the horror of the vision was easing, allowing her mind to slip out of the past into the present. Her heart settled into its normal rhythm—well almost.

Stona's presence didn't leave her unaffected. He'd wrapped himself around her like a shield. Grateful for the security he offered, she tried to ignore the occasional flutter low in her belly where his hand rested, and told herself the pleasant tingling had nothing to do with his possessive touch. This sudden breathless feeling was simply part of the aftermath of her trauma.

Stona wasn't making her uncomfortable. Wrapped in his arms with the front of his thighs cradling the back of hers, she felt safe.

Safe from the world? Yes. Safe from her own reaction to his body touching hers? Not so much.

She'd worn a short, light-cotton nightgown to bed. The hem had worked its way up to just below her hips. They were skin to skin except where her gown separated their bodies.

He wasn't wearing his sweatpants.

"Stona?"

"Uh-huh?" It was a sleepy response.

"What are you wearing?"

"Boxers. Why?"

"Just curious."

He snuggled even closer, brushing his lips across her ear. "Try to sleep, sweetheart."

"You can go back to your own bed now." She tried to sound casual.

"I wasn't in my bed. I've been here all night."

She turned in his arms and tried to see his face. "Why?"

"After tonight it would seem obvious. I need to be here, to stay as close as I can." He leaned up on an elbow. "You need me here and this is where I'll be every night until you resolve whatever is going on—and until we catch the psychopath trying to kill you. Do you understand me?" His declaration had been whisper-soft but emphatic.

She nodded. "Can we at least put some distance between us?"

After a moment, he rolled away, giving her his back.

She suddenly felt bereft. His warm arms had been her sanctuary tonight. Straightening her clothes, she pulled the hem of her gown as far down as she could stretch it. She didn't need a sanctuary.

"Willie?"

"Yes?"

"I'll never take advantage of our sleeping arrangement."

"I know."

It wasn't him she was worried about.

THIRTY-SIX

WILLIE SHIVERED FROM the chill in the morning air as she walked to the back door. After a warm fall, late November was proving to be cooler than normal.

When she hung her coat on the wall hook beside the door, she noticed the jacket she'd given Joe. At the time, the garment had been sufficient. Now, though, she doubted it was enough.

She remembered packing a heavier coat in one of the boxes she'd marked for donation.

Switching on the light in the storage room, she spotted the box marked winter donation right away. Pulling it out of the stack, she carefully dug through the folded clothes until she found what she was looking for.

Shaking the coat out, she smoothed her hand over the front of the sheepskin-lined garment, remembering the time she'd spent with Josh and Trish. Something white caught her attention. Reaching into the pocket, she retrieved an opened envelope. It was addressed to Josh. The return address was a street in Ottawa, Canada, but she didn't recognize the sender's name.

Setting the coat aside, she extracted the letter and began to read.

Dear Mr. McAllister,

My name is Joan McCaffery. I'm sure you've never heard of me,
but we are fourth cousins on your father's side of the family.

They had relatives in Canada? Why hadn't Josh mentioned the
letter to her? She smiled. Josh was methodical. He wouldn't have said
anything until he knew more of the facts. What had he discovered? A
fourth cousin in Canada. It was comforting to even suspect there was
family out there somewhere. She continued reading.

While settling my mother's estate, I came across a chest that had
apparently belonged to my father. It was filled with documents and
letters, some dating as recently as nineteen ninety-eight and others as
far back as the early eighteen-hundreds.

Included was a detailed family tree. I was surprised to discover my
father's side of the family migrated to Canada from the United States.
With the help of our local genealogy group, I was able to locate you.

I have enclosed a copy of our family tree. You may recognize the
names of some of our mutual relatives. Our two families branched off
after Frank and Iona McCaffery's generation. They had two sons and
a daughter. My great-grandfather was Jonas McCaffery, the oldest
son. Their daughter, Wilhelmina McCaffery, was your great-grand-
mother. She married Isaias McAllister.

Another Wilhelmina? Had her aunt been named after Wilhelmina
McCaffery? She must have been. Had she disliked the name, too? Willie
wouldn't have been surprised. Had Isaias called her Willie, or Will as
Stona sometimes called her? She read on.

As you can tell by the diagram, I haven't yet finished your branch
of the family tree. You might find it interesting to do so.

I discovered something else in the trunk. Iona McCaffery's per-
sonal Bible was all but buried in the bottom corner of the chest. It was
so fragile I was almost afraid to touch it but was too curious to leave it

where it was. Several sheets of paper separated the pages toward the middle and I carefully opened the well-used book to reveal a long-hidden, long-forgotten family secret.

It's fortunate the three-page letter to Iona from her mother, Jennifer, wasn't folded. I doubt the brittle parchment would have survived being opened. I used extreme care as I separated the pages.

The letter reads like a deathbed confession. It seems Jennifer had been taken captive during an Osage raid. Her captor was a brute of a man who chained her to a lodge-post in his longhouse. He beat and raped her whenever he took the notion.

Jennifer's survival depended on a young Osage woman who visited each day bringing food, water, and a means of relieving herself. In broken English, the woman warned Jennifer to be submissive and not anger the warrior or she might find herself shackled to the post behind his longhouse with his other slave.

Jennifer wrote that she'd never seen the pitiful woman chained behind the Lodge, but she'd heard her weak whimpers along with the grunting satisfaction of the men using her. Apparently, her captor didn't mind sharing a woman who was out-of-favor. That fear prohibited her from fighting the man when the sounds from the other side of the wall spurred his own lust.

Our distant grandmother was rescued within a month, and though she was shunned by most of the community, her fiancé married her immediately, and moved with her to St. Louis.

I don't understand why Jennifer didn't spare her daughter the details of her captivity. Maybe she believed Iona needed to know everything in order to protect herself.

Can you imagine how devastated the girl must have been when she discovered the father who'd raised her as his own wasn't her blood relative, that the man who'd fathered her was an Osage warrior known only as Bear?

The story is fascinating, and I would appreciate any information you might have....

The words blurred and the letter fluttered to the floor. Willie staggered and sank to her knees, knocking over a stack of boxes.

Bear.

She was related to the man who had wounded Beth, murdered Brings Peace, and stabbed Stone Shaper in the heart. She existed because her Osage ancestor brutally violated an innocent girl.

Like Iona, she was the byproduct of rape.

She hadn't been chosen because of some grand scheme in life. She had been called to do penance for the vile sins of a man she already hated.

———————

STONA HAD JUST closed the back door behind him when he heard the muffled noise in the storage room. On guard, he cracked the door and peered in.

Willie sat on the floor, head bent, legs pulled to her chest, arms gripping her knees. He knelt, almost afraid to touch her. "Willie, honey? Are you hurt? Did you fall?"

She shook her head.

"Sweetheart, I need to know if you're hurt."

She refused to look at him. "I'm all right. I need to be alone."

He couldn't and wouldn't leave her on the floor. Scooping her into his arms, he stood and turned to leave. When she started to protest, he shook his head. "You can't stay in this chilly room."

She didn't argue. Wrapping her arms around him, she buried her face in his neck. Silent, hot tears wet his skin and he pulled her closer, wanting to shield her from whatever torment she was experiencing. Joe hovered in the doorway, his eyes full of questions. When Stona shook his head, the older man began restacking the boxes.

He carried her into the living room and placed her on the sofa. Sinking into the cushions she clutched a pillow to her chest and turned her face away from him. The anguish he'd seen in her eyes compelled him to stay. He'd leave her alone, but he couldn't abandon her, and that's what he'd be doing if he left her now. Sitting in the overstuffed chair a few feet away, he waited until she was ready to talk to him. It was as much privacy as he was willing to give her.

She'd been fine when she'd gotten out of the car after a quick trip to town for a few groceries. Unlocking the door, she'd gone into the house ahead of him. Since Joe had elected to remain home, he hadn't worried about Willie entering the house without him. He'd checked the barn and shed and circled the perimeter of the house before carrying the groceries into the house. It couldn't have taken more than fifteen minutes—twenty tops. What had happened in that short window of time? Another vision?

He didn't know.

Willie leaned her head against the couch back and drew a deep breath, exhaling slowly. Her eyes were closed, and though her tears were gone, she wasn't ready to talk to him yet.

Joe nudged his arm and handed him an envelope and a couple of sheets of paper. "You need to read this."

Stona glanced at Willie. She hadn't looked up when Joe came into the room, and seemed oblivious to what was going on.

The envelope was addressed to Josh. He turned his attention to the letter. After reading it twice, he looked at Joe. "Did you read it? "

The old man nodded. "She has been given a heavy burden."

"It isn't her burden."

Joe placed a hand on Stona's shoulder. "I agree, but you must convince *her* of that truth." The old man turned and left the room. A minute later, the back door opened and closed.

"What am I going to do?" Willie's whispered question tore at his heart. He wanted to hold her until the pain went away.

He didn't move. She wasn't ready to be comforted—held the pillow like a shield between them.

Tossing the papers on the coffee table, he leaned forward resting his arms on his thighs. "You need to forget you ever read that letter."

"I can't do that."

"The man may not be your ancestor. Bear was probably a common name for warriors of that time."

"He is. In one of my visions, Stone Shaper spoke of the woman chained behind Bear's lodge."

He wasn't sure how to console her. Logic seemed to be the best way of reaching her. "Would you be as devastated if the warrior who'd violated Jennifer had gone by another name?"

She was silent for so long he thought she wouldn't answer him. Then she took a deep, shuddering breath and shook her head. "If he'd been no more than a name out of the past, I could have accepted what happened as a part of my heritage. I would have regretted what happened to Jennifer, but not been devastated."

"If you're going to get through this, you need to forget Bear was involved, and remember the incidents that happened two hundred years ago have nothing to do with you."

"Bear isn't just a name out of the past. I watched him commit murder and get away with it. He's as real as the crazy man out there who wants to kill me." She threw the pillow across the couch. It bounced against the arm and landed on the floor. "I exist because Bear raped a girl barely old enough to be called a woman. I may never come to terms with that."

He did go to her then, sitting close and pulling her against him. "Sweetheart, most of us are fortunate enough to never know about the villains in our ancestry. It doesn't matter who they were. What matters is who we are, what we become. You're a good person—a nurse who's chosen to spend her life saving others. How many people have you kept alive on their way to the hospital? How many people would be dead today if you didn't exist? You have nothing to be ashamed of."

She breathed a sigh and shook her head. "I feel contaminated."

He pulled her onto his lap. "Do you believe Jennifer was soiled or ruined because of Bear?"

She shook her head. "She was victimized by Bear and by the people who shunned her."

"What about Iona? Was she less of a person because of her parentage? Think of Josh, and your dad. Do you think any less of them since you found out about Bear? Were they contaminated?"

"No."

He lifted her face to his. "Neither are you." His lips touched hers. "Remember that."

THIRTY-SEVEN

STONA STUFFED HIS phone into the back pocket of his jeans. He didn't care for the news he'd received from his boss. Willie had been taken off their person of interest list. *That* was a good thing. What he hadn't expected was to have his leave of absence canceled and to be reassigned—as Willie's bodyguard.

While he was relieved the assignment had gone to him, the action complicated matters. It took the decision-making out of his hands. The major decisions, anyway.

Since he was already protecting her, the assignment was, for the most part, simply a formality. He couldn't tell his superiors he was already keeping an eye on her. They'd know then he was too close to the case, and Willie—and go with their original plan of placing her in protective custody.

As it was, he'd barely convinced them not to do it.

She wasn't going to like his assignment for an entirely different reason. Not that she had any more choice in the matter than he did. His superiors had wanted him to take her to a safehouse in St. Louis. While normally he'd be in full agreement with the plan to keep her safe, it would only complicate her unique situation.

She'd balk. He'd probably have to cuff her to gain her cooperation.

He grinned. Knowing Willie, he'd end up being the one in handcuffs. His grin broadened. That was an interesting thought.

He'd managed to forestall his superiors in St. Louis, but it hadn't been easy. He couldn't very well tell them Ms. McAllister had two ghosts and an old man depending on her to solve a mysterious, two hundred-year-old problem. Yeah, that would get him an extended leave of absence and a stint with the department's psychologist. In the end, St. Louis had compromised, and he'd been assigned to her case as a personal bodyguard.

His holster and Glock were back in place. He hadn't worn the firearm while he'd been off duty, but he'd kept it close. His new assignment had put the weapon back on his hip.

"Why are you wearing your gun?" Willie stood in the adjoining bedroom doorway. He was surprised she'd risen this early. After last night he'd expected her to sleep past noon. "You're not required to wear it when you're on leave, are you?"

He watched her gracefully move from her room to his. Even in the shapeless robe she'd tied around her nightgown, she looked utterly feminine. And sexy.

He closed the duffel and set it on the floor beside the bed "I got a call from my office this morning."

She paled and glanced from the gun on his hip to the bag he'd just closed. "You've being reassigned. You're leaving." There was a note of panic in her voice.

"Don't jump ahead of me, Will. This is a good thing. The department doesn't believe you had anything to do with your cousin's death. Since you're no longer considered a person of interest, I'm no longer investigating you."

"You still haven't explained why you're wearing the gun."

"I *have* been reassigned—as your bodyguard."

Her expression went from panic to relief and then irritation. "I don't need a bodyguard."

"Well, you have one." He folded his arms over his chest. "Or you can choose their original plan."

"What plan?"

"They wanted me to take you into protective custody and bring you to St. Louis." He held his hands up when she started sputtering, to ward off whatever she was about to say. "Now, sweetheart, calm down."

"Don't you dare threaten to arrest me in one breath and call me sweetheart with the next."

"Who said anything about arresting you?"

"You just said you were taking me into custody."

"*Protective* custody. There's a difference. And I'm not taking you anywhere. I've managed to convince my bosses you only need a body-guard. Since you're not a witness to any crime, and our suspect has always used the same mode of assassination, they believe you're safe enough with a bodyguard."

"What if they change their minds?"

He walked to where she stood and rested his hands on her shoulders, gently kneading her tense muscles. "If I can't talk them out of it, I'll go with you to St. Louis."

"And if I refuse to go?"

"You won't have that option."

"I'll leave before that happens. You can't force me if you can't find me."

He walked back to his bed, picked up the overnight bag and opened it. When he returned, he carried his handcuffs, and held them up in front of her face. "If I even suspect you'll run I'll cuff you to me. We'll be as inseparable as newlyweds. We'll eat and sleep in these things." He smiled. "I hope you like cold showers."

WILLIE STORMED THROUGH the kitchen, opened the cabinet, and plunked a mug down beside the coffee maker. She didn't close the cup-board door quietly. After filling her cup with the dark, steaming brew, she headed for the back door.

"Something troubles you?"

Her abrupt stop sloshed coffee out of the mug and onto the floor. She glanced at Joe. "I didn't see you sitting there." Apparently, she had a gift for stating the obvious this morning.

Joe waited, as stoic as ever, while she wiped up the mess, refilled her cup, and joined him at the table. He gave her a few minutes to study the swirling liquid in her cup before repeating his question. Only this time it wasn't a question.

"Something troubles you."

She lifted her shoulders. "Stona and I are having a difference of opinion. That's all. Nothing to concern yourself with."

"Tell me."

She guessed he was playing her mentor, now. She wasn't in the mood to see reason. "I don't really want to talk about it."

"Tell me."

She looked up. "Did you know the marshal's office has canceled Stona's leave?" When Joe shook his head, she continued. "They've decided that since I'm not the killer, I need protection. They've made *him* my bodyguard."

"And this upsets you?"

"No, but they wanted to put me in protective custody, and might still do it. If so, Stona will have to take me to St. Louis, and his superiors will put me someplace where I can stew in my own juices until it's safe to come out."

"You're afraid he will leave you there, alone."

"He *will* leave me alone. I won't be his problem anymore. He can get on with his life."

"Have you told him you love him?"

"I didn't say I loved him."

The old man's only comment was a raised eyebrow.

"You don't believe me?"

"I believe you're avoiding the question."

"I haven't known him long enough to love him."

"You sleep in his arms each night."

"We both know the reason for that."

"We speak not of reason, but of feelings. What does he make you feel when he holds you close in the night?"

"Not what you're implying."

There went that eyebrow again. "I ask you once more, have you told him you love him?"

He wasn't going to let it go. He was forcing the issue, making her face the internal turmoil Stona Jordan had set in motion. The marshal had gone from adversary to champion in a matter of weeks.

And now he....

Stona was a good and honorable man who'd made seeking justice his life's work. He was kind, compassionate—and more than a little sexy. She sighed in resignation.

What wasn't there to love?

"No, I haven't told him."

THIRTY-EIGHT

BEAR JERKED THE spear from Stone Shaper's chest before the warrior fell and turned, defiantly holding it in the air. "This weapon belonged to Stone Shaper." His attention fixed on Winter Storm and Stands Alone. "The blood of Brings Peace stains Stone Shaper's body. Do you deny it?" The younger men remained silent, but the two warriors from Bear's clan shouted their support of their leader. "The spear and the blood condemn him. He dared to take the life of our medicine chief. It was my right to avenge Stone Shaper's betrayal with swift punishment."

Bear glared at his rival, who had fallen across the old chief's legs. With a sneer, he shoved his foot into Stone Shaper's ribs, rolling him off his mentor. Winter Storm gasped at the callous treatment of one who had been an honored member of the tribe and his friend.

Bear swung around, transferring the spear to a throwing position. "Do you question my decision?" There was a warning edge to his voice. Bear's friends said nothing.

Winter Storm and Stands Alone shook their heads.

The fierce warrior nodded his satisfaction and tossed the spear into the brush. "Gather your possessions. We leave this place of death." He glanced at the young warriors. "Wrap Brings Peace in his robe and tie him to his pony." They immediately jumped from their mounts, and carefully laid the old chief's body on his robe, tying it around him. Bear caught the elder's pony, grasping the forelock, and slipped the halter-like bridle over the animal's head while they secured Brings Peace on its back. When they'd finished, he handed the reins to Crooked Tree and vaulted onto his own mount. His friends followed as he led them toward the northwest.

Winter Storm turned his attention from his cousin's crumpled form to the retreating group. "What of Stone Shaper?"

Bear reined his pony around. "Leave him for the wolves."

"We cannot." Winter Storm stood his ground. "He must have a ceremony, or he cannot—"

"He does not deserve an honorable burial." Bear all but snarled his opinion, then shrugged as if the matter no longer concerned him. "Do what you want, but we leave now. Join us soon, or you will be left to find your own way home." He swung his pony around, kicking it into a gallop.

Winter Storm knelt beside his fallen comrade and stared up at Stands Alone. "I will not believe my cousin murdered our medicine chief. Brings Peace was his father-by-marriage, his mentor, and his friend. He had no reason to cause him harm."

"You saw the spear." Stands Alone tilted his head toward the brush where Bear had tossed the weapon. "The markings on the lance proved it belonged to Stone Shaper."

"The spear may have been his, but it doesn't prove he used it against Brings Peace. Bear was too quick to retaliate. He denied Stone Shaper the right to defend himself. I will make sure the council understands this. I may be an untried warrior, but I believe the Little Old Men will listen to me."

Stands Alone finally nodded in agreement. "Do not let Bear or anyone in his clan suspect you intend to seek the council. He has proven today his retaliation is cunning and swift."

Winter Storm glanced at the gaping wound in his cousin's chest. The blood that had poured from his heart melded with the heart blood of Brings Peace. "We have to take him back with us."

Stands Alone shook his head. "Bear will never allow it. You chance his reprisal."

"We cannot leave him here. Stone Shaper deserves better than to be left for the animals."

"What else can we do?" Stands Alone glanced toward the northwest. "We don't have time to honor your cousin with a proper burial. We must catch up with the others or risk not finding our way home."

Standing, Winter Storm glanced toward the woods. "We can at least keep wild animals from scattering his bones. Help me get him on my horse. We'll use the sunken hole Bear found. It's too deep for animals to crawl into. Once we've lowered him through the hole, we can seal it with large branches and stones to protect his grave."

Struggling under the weight of the large warrior, the two lifted him onto Winter Storm's pony and led it into the woods.

The hole was barely wide enough for a big man's body. The young warriors lowered him feet first through the opening until only his shoulders and head remained aboveground.

"I'm sorry, my friend," Winter Storm whispered, his voice tight. They let go of Stone Shaper and listened as his body bounced off the steep-angled walls until only the scattering of small pebbles could be heard.

They made quick work of sealing the grave but stood together in silent respect for long moments. Taking only enough time to wash Stone Shaper's blood from their bodies, they gathered their belongings, and mounted their ponies to follow the others.

No one questioned what they had done. As though the men feared his spirit's retaliation, Stone Shaper's name was never mentioned.

The warriors pushed their ponies hard and were less than a day's ride from the village when the Kiowa attacked. The small band had given them little warning. Crooked Tree rode last in the single file line, leading the pony bearing Brings Peace. He took the first arrow. The others turned at his surprised cry and saw him slump over his mount's neck, dropping the reins of the pony he led. They scattered, seeking the shelter of the trees.

———————

THE PONY STEPPED into the clearing, directly in the path of the grizzled old man on horseback. Grabbing his Brown Bess from its scabbard, the lone rider scanned the trees on either side of the trail he followed.

Satisfied no one waited to ambush him, he dismounted. Still watchful, he looped the pack-mule's reins over his mount's saddle horn and cautiously approached the pony. He stopped to pull his bandana over his nose and mouth as he got closer to the skittish animal. Grasping the dangling reins, he smoothed his fingers over the mare's neck, tracing the painted handprint. A moccasin-shod foot dangled from the hide-wrapped pack secured to the animal's back. Using his knife, he cut the bindings and dragged the cumbersome bundle off the pony, laying it at the side of the trail.

Tugging his bandana down around his neck, he secured the pony's reins to the mule's packsaddle. Giving the animal a calming pat, he moved to his horse and mounted. Leaning against the saddle horn, he studied the mound of furs, then scanned the surrounding woods. Several minutes passed before he sighed, shook his head and dismounted. He walked to the mule, retrieved a short-handled shovel from his pack and began digging.

Dragging the robe-shrouded body into the shallow hole, he covered it with dirt and stacked rocks on top of the fresh-turned soil to prevent animals from getting to the body.

Hat in hand, he bowed his head for a moment before remounting his horse and guiding the three animals over the next hill.

THIRTY-NINE

STONA ABSENTLY STIRRED his half cup of cold coffee with a tea-spoon left over from lunch while he considered the stubborn woman upstairs. As soon as he'd come into the kitchen, Willie had gone to her room claiming she needed to rest. After ten minutes, he'd checked on her, assuming she'd used exhaustion as an excuse to keep from being in the same room with him. But when he'd found her sound asleep, he'd been forced to reconsider his assumption and returned to the kitchen. He'd been sitting and stirring and thinking since.

"What are your intentions toward Wilhelmina?"

Stona glanced up at the old man, who sat, arms crossed over his chest, silently observing him.

"I'm sorry. What did you say?"

"She has no father to protect her. As her spirit guide, the responsi-bility for her well-being falls on me. So, I must ask the question. What are your intentions toward Wilhelmina?"

"I wouldn't use that name to her face if I were you." At Joe's raised eyebrow, he shrugged. "I intend to protect her."

"You sleep with her every night."

"I can't protect her if I'm not close to her. You can rest easy. I'm not taking advantage of our situation."

"She is a beautiful young woman. You do not desire her?"

Stona didn't like the conversation's direction. "My desires have no bearing on our situation. I've never taken advantage of her—and I won't."

Joe wouldn't let it rest. "Tell me, if another man is sent to replace you, will he also sleep beside her?"

The thought of another man holding her close through the night, set his teeth on edge. "No."

"You would not be here to protect and comfort her. She would be forced to depend on another."

"Willie wouldn't let him in her bed."

"She has allowed you to sleep beside her."

"She trusts me."

Joe leaned forward. "The thought of Willie depending on another man displeases you?"

"Why don't we change the subject?"

"You've already admitted you love her." Joe was as tenacious as a justice prosecutor.

"I was afraid she might be dying." He took a deep breath. "Look, Joe, I can't afford to become emotionally involved with Willie. I wouldn't be able to protect her."

"Yet you cannot stay away from her. Is it not already a problem?"

"What's your point?"

"You must leave her, my friend." Stona pinned him with a glare, and the old man held up his hands as if to ward off a blow. "Or, you can make her yours in fact as well as in your heart."

"What's that supposed to mean?"

"Marry her."

Willie walked into the kitchen. There was a vagueness about her, an almost ethereal persona. "I know who he is."

Stona nearly knocked his chair over in his haste to stand. "Willie?"

She glanced up at him. "I know who he is."

Taking her arm, he guided her to the table, gently pushing her into a chair, scooting his close. "Tell me what you're talking about."

Joe placed a cup of coffee in front of her, and she thanked him before turning her attention to Stona. Her eyes had lost their dazed expression. "The skeleton at the Suttons—the one tangled in the tree roots—I know who he was. I watched a man bury him."

Stona shook his head. "Willie—" Joe's hand on his shoulder made Stona pause.

"Tell us his name," Joe urged.

"Brings Peace. His name was Brings Peace."

She and Joe stared at each other—her eyes questioning, his inscrutable. Stona suddenly felt like he'd been left out of the loop. "Who is Brings Peace?"

She dragged her attention from Joe to answer in a subdued voice. "One of the people in my visions." Her gaze returned to her mentor. "He was a good, wise man."

"Wait." Stona took her hand, drawing her attention back to him. "Are you telling me you've had another vision?"

"Yes, but that isn't important right now."

"It is to me."

She patted the hand that held hers. "I know, and I'm sorry you're worried, but this is a breakthrough. It's the first time I've been able to connect the dots. But I still feel like I'm missing something." She leaned back in her chair and sighed. "I'm too tired to focus."

Stona didn't like her gray pallor. "You missed lunch. I'll fix you something to eat."

"I'm not hungry."

"Fix her soup from a can." When Stona glanced over at him, the old man shrugged. "She likes soup from a can."

A FEW MINUTES later, whether she wanted it or not, a microwaved bowl of chicken noodle soup sat in front of her. Stona personally handed her the spoon. She wasn't irritated with them. They were looking out for her. It was really kind of sweet, but she doubted she could keep anything in her stomach and pushed the bowl aside.

Stona pushed it right back. "You need to eat."

"And if it won't stay down?"

He answered by retrieving a plastic pail from the mud room and setting it beside her chair. She guessed she wasn't going to win this round.

She finished her soup, then rinsed the bowl and spoon, setting them in the sink. A cup of chamomile tea sounded good, and she filled the electric kettle. Stona grabbed a can of root beer and a Coke from the refrigerator. He handed the root beer to Joe and popped the top on the Coke, taking a long swallow before settling into his chair at the table. They were so comfortable with one another it almost felt like family—almost.

Family members didn't keep secrets from one another.

Willie could've been alone in the kitchen for all the attention she paid the men. She didn't speak to them until she'd carried her cup of tea to the table.

"Something's puzzled me. Well, two things, actually. I thought Brings Peace was just another person in my visions, like Raven. Then he was murdered. His blood touched the spearhead. But Brings Peace never appeared to me outside of the visions like Beth and Stone Shaper did. I wondered why."

She turned her attention to Joe. "You puzzled me, too. I couldn't figure out why you were able to see Beth and Stone Shaper and Stona wasn't. I still hadn't put it together an hour ago when I realized the skeleton at the Suttons' home belonged to Brings Peace." She shook her head. "But the pieces have finally connected. I know why Brings Peace didn't take physical form to contact me." She leaned toward the old man. "He didn't have to, did he?"

She crossed her arms on the table, and pinned Joe with an intense frown. "Tell me, am I talking to Joseph Sage or Brings Peace?"

FORTY

JOE DIDN'T BLINK, not even when Stona shot him an incredulous look. "We both watch over you."

"Who am I talking to right now?" She wasn't challenging him. She simply needed to know.

Joe seemed to understand and smiled. "Most of the time you speak to me, Joe, but Brings Peace is always near."

Stona drew their attention by scooting his chair back to stare first at Joe, then Willie. "Are you telling me Joe and this Brings Peace are the same person?"

Willie shook her head. "Not exactly. I think Brings Peace is temporarily sharing Joe's body."

Stona glanced at Joe. "And you're okay with this?"

"His presence does not distress me. We are both here to aid the chosen one."

The men turned to stare at her.

It was Stona who finally broke the silence. "How long have you known about this?"

"Not until this last vision." She stood and moved to the window before facing them again. "It wasn't exactly an *aha* moment. At times I seemed to be speaking with two different people." She glanced at Stona. "Didn't you notice how his speech patterns changed occasionally? I didn't understand why. Now I do."

Joe folded his arms across his chest. "When I first came to you, I was confused and a little uncertain of my place in your journey. Brings Peace spoke to you then. As I became more aware of our connection, he became my mentor, and I, in turn, became yours. He seldom speaks directly to you now, but we share the honor of being your spirit guide."

She looked through the window to the wide expanse of meadow, noting how tall the grass and brush had gotten this year. Her neighbor might like to rent the field again. She'd need to put a small fence around Josh's tupelo sapling first.

A splash of color in the distance caught her attention. She saw him then, standing exactly where she'd seen him the afternoon she'd found the spearhead. Stone Shaper. Even from that distance she knew he was watching her.

"He's out there." The men pushed away from the table to join her at the window. "Do you see Stone Shaper? He's standing across the meadow, beside the fence."

Joe nodded.

Stona unsnapped his holster and leaned into the window. "I don't see anyone."

"He is there." Joe's voice was firm with conviction.

"He's moving." She grabbed Stona's arm in her excitement.

"In which direction?"

"Away from us. He's across the fence now, walking into the woods." She let go of his arm and ran toward the back door, grabbing her jacket from the hook.

Stona was right behind her. "Oh, no you don't. You're not chasing after that—whatever it is. Not by yourself."

Joe followed them into the mudroom. "We'll all go. But we must hurry." He took the lead. The day was warm for late November, and most of the snow had melted over the past three days.

By the time they reached the fenceline, the apparition was nowhere to be seen. She whipped around. "We've lost him."

Joe shook his head. "Remember, he cannot hold his form for long. He has led us in this direction and moved beyond the fence. Perhaps he wishes us to be on the other side."

Stona glanced at the trees lining the fence. "I don't see any no trespassing signs or paint marks indicating we shouldn't cross. Do you know the owner of the property?"

"The land belongs to Robert Tensile. He and Josh went to school together. He won't mind if we go over the fence."

Three strands of barbed wire stretched between tall metal T-posts. Careful not to stretch the wire, Stona held the middle wire down with his foot and lifted the top wire high enough for them to climb through. Joe did the same for him.

There was a feeling of familiarity about the place. She stared back at her house for a moment, then swept her gaze in a half circle, taking in the wide meadow of rolling hills and valleys. How would it have looked two hundred years ago?

Suddenly, she knew exactly how it had looked, and what had happened here. Her quick, indrawn breath alerted both men.

Stona slipped his arm around her waist. "What is it?" He looked around, his free hand on his Glock. "Let's find a place where you can sit down."

She shook her head. "I'm okay. I just realized I've seen this place in my vision. I think I understand what I'm—what *we're* supposed to do." She was already climbing through the fence. Stona scrambled to keep the barbs away from her clothes and skin. She didn't seem to notice. "We need to go back to the house and check the toolshed." She sprinted toward the house, leaving the men to catch up.

Stona grabbed her elbow, pulling her to a halt, allowing Joe to catch up. "Let's stop at the house, grab a bottle of water, and give Joe a chance to rest."

She glanced at the older man's flushed face. "Okay."

By the time they were seated at the kitchen table and Joe had caught his breath, she was calm enough to explain her revelation.

"Two hundred years can make a big difference in the lay of the land, but if you ignore the house and the fences, the meadow and woods haven't changed all that much." She stared out the window. "I think Stone Shaper's remains are buried in a sinkhole somewhere in those woods."

Even the unflappable Joe looked stunned. "You are sure?"

In her excitement, she took his hand. "It isn't an opening in the side of the bluff like you might think. Animals would've gotten to him if that had been the case, and there wouldn't be much left to find. In my last vision, I was with Winter Storm and Stands Alone—Stone Shaper's cousin and his friend. They lowered his body through the sinkhole and covered it with brush and rocks."

She glanced at Stona. "We need to look for a shallow depression in the ground with a hole that goes straight down from the surface." She worried her lower lip with her teeth. "I can't be sure the opening is visible now. After two hundred years, trees could have fallen into the sinkhole and blocked the entrance."

Her gaze shifted Joe. "I'm supposed to find him. It's why I was chosen, isn't it?"

He raised an eyebrow. "Perhaps. And when you've found him?"

"I have a feeling I'm supposed to help him find peace." She shrugged. "We can solve that riddle when we come to it. Right now, I'm more concerned with finding him."

Stona didn't look happy. "So far, your search for answers has made you a target." He took her hand in both of his and squeezed gently. "I'm willing to help you find your warrior, but if I have an inkling you're in danger, I'm taking you to St. Louis. Understand?"

She looked directly into his eyes, needing *him* to understand. "I know you want to protect me, and I'm grateful for it, but you need to accept I have to do this. Two good men died."

Stona was already shaking his head. "That was two hundred years ago, Willie."

"You keep saying that, but as far as I'm concerned, it was yesterday. They're as real to me as anyone I've ever met. Their lives matter to me. I wonder about Beth." She waved her hand to forestall him when he opened his mouth. "I want to know what happened to her, and to her baby. I need closure, not only for myself, but for them, so they can find peace at last."

She sank back against the chair, suddenly drained of energy. "I love you, Stona, but I won't let you stop me from helping them."

He straightened and the intensity in his gaze was mesmerizing. "I won't let you take that back."

He wasn't making any sense. "Take what back?"

"You said you love me. I won't let you take it back."

She shook her head. "I'm not ready to talk about this yet."

He agreed with a quick nod. "But we *will* talk about it."

FORTY-ONE

THE DOOR TO the old tool shed sagged, scraping the floor as Stona forced it open. Dust motes, kicked up by their invasion, sparkled in the ray of sunlight streaming through the entrance. Cobwebs, probably as old as Joe, hung low enough to brush their heads. A small animal skittered behind a broken orange crate in the corner. Stona laughed when Willie moved a little closer to him.

Unfortunately, the dilapidated shed failed to yield much of use—only a long iron bar used for wedging larger rocks out of the ground. It probably weighed more than she did. The only shovel had a cracked handle, and the rusted pick had no handle at all.

Stona carried the bar out and pulled the shed door closed behind them. "We'll need to buy some rope, a pick, and a couple of long-handled shovels."

They made a trip to the farm store in town. Besides the tools and rope, they bought heavy-duty work gloves and a large canvas tote bag to hold Stone Shaper's remains if they found him. Stona double-checked the strength of the handgrips. The skeletal remains of an average adult male ranged from fifteen to twenty-six pounds in weight. That piece of information came in handy when working missing persons cases. However, the Osage were known for their height—many had been as

tall as seven feet. He was sure the warrior was no exception. His remains might weigh close to thirty pounds.

The trip took just under two hours, and they were already losing
daylight. Tomorrow would have to be soon enough to begin their
search. That evening, after dinner, the three sat in the living room,
discussing their plan of action for the next day. Stona had been quiet,
leaving most of the planning to Willie and Joe.

The older man noticed and gave the marshal a quizzical glance.
"Something is wrong?"

Stona shook his head. "I'm curious. How is it you can see our friend
out there? You had a reaction when you handled the spearhead, but you
never cut yourself. Your blood never touched it. Am I wrong about the
blood connection?"

Willie touched his sleeve. "It *was* the blood. Joe is linked through
Brings Peace. Beth sliced her hand on the weapon. Hers was the first
blood to touch the spearhead." Holding up her hand she exposed the
white, half-moon scar on her index finger. "Now I'm in their heads.
Blood connects us all."

Despite her nap earlier in the day, Willie looked exhausted. Stona
suspected the stress was getting to her. He stood, stretched, and walked
to the mud room to make sure the back door was bolted. He checked
the front door as well.

Returning to the living room, he grasped Willie's hand, pulling her
to her feet. "Come on, sweetheart. Time for bed."

She didn't balk at the suggestion or the endearment and allowed
him to lead her up the stairs to her room.

He walked through the adjoining doors to his room. "I'm going to
grab a quick shower. You might enjoy a leisurely bath. It might help
you sleep."

Willie nodded as she crossed to the dresser for a fresh nightgown.
"That does sound good."

"Leave the doors unlocked. No one will intrude." He grabbed boxers
and a tee from the stack of folded clothes on the bed. Someone—and
he doubted it was Joe—had done his laundry. When had Willie found

time to wash clothes? He grinned as he moved to the bathroom across the hall. Stacking his clothes with his holstered gun on the counter, he stepped into the hot shower. Joe probably had fresh clothes in his room, too. She was treating them like family. It didn't surprise him. As rough as their relationship had been in the beginning, he'd soon realized she was a warm, giving woman with a tendency to mother those she deemed in need of mothering. Joe was proof of that.

He, on the other hand, had no desire to be mothered by Willie. He wanted to be *loved* by her. She'd already admitted she loved him, and he wasn't going to let her take the words back. Soon, when she was ready to hear it, he'd give her his own words of commitment and a proposal of marriage.

Joe's little pep talk had forced him to evaluate his feelings for her. The wily old man had known what buttons to push, too. All it took was Joe's outrageous suggestion of another marshal sleeping with Willie, and he'd reverted to a caveman mentality. She belonged to *him,* and he'd challenge anyone who dared interfere. How barbaric was that— and how telling?

He knew exactly when she became his exclusive person of interest—when he'd lifted her out of that metal coffin of a car. She'd been vulnerable yet strong, frightened, yet brave, and compassionate. Her concern for the privacy of the remains of a man who had been dead for two centuries was proof of that.

Drying off, he pulled on his clean clothes, grabbed his gun, and went into the hall.

Joe had just reached the door to his room and stopped to wait for him. "Is she all right?"

"I think so. Hopefully, she's relaxing in a hot bath." He moved to Willie's door, placing his hand on the knob when he noticed Joe eyeing his choice of nightclothes. "You don't have to worry. I promised not to take advantage of her vulnerability, and I won't."

Joe stood a little straighter. "If I thought otherwise, you would not enter her room tonight."

Stona didn't laugh at the old man's warning. It would have been disrespectful. And he might be surprised. Joe appeared frail—he looked as if a summer breeze would knock him over—he would find a way to protect her.

Joe stepped into his room. "Guard her well tonight. Her visions are closer together now, more vivid." He rubbed the back of his neck and sighed. "I think we are close to the end of this journey. She will find peace soon."

Stona's hand fell away from the doorknob. "I'm more concerned with the man trying to kill her. He's out there waiting to catch her alone, and if he's who we think he is, he won't stop until she's no longer a threat."

Joe paused at the door. "You believe she is a threat to him?"

"No, I don't. But I think the killer does. Josh was asking specific questions about the area surrounding the Osage village. Since he was in uniform at the time, the killer probably suspected the authorities were looking for him again."

"What do you mean, *again?*"

"He hasn't been active for a decade. His previous murders were considered cold cases, and law enforcement had all but given up finding him. I'm sure he thought he was safe. Then Josh starts asking questions, and Willie shows up after her cousin's death, asking the same questions. It sent up red flags."

"Do you believe he will tamper with your car next?"

Stona shook his head. "Not likely. As far as we know he's never used any other method for taking out his victims, but he has to know we're on to him. He'll try something different this time—something we won't be expecting."

"You're worried."

"I'm more than worried. I'm scared. I want to drag her out of here, lock her away somewhere safe, somewhere he won't ever be able to find her." He pushed himself away from the frame. "You and I both know she'd never stand for it. I'd have to physically drag her away from this place—not that I won't do it if it becomes necessary."

He turned away from Joe. "I'll keep her safe." He tapped on her door twice, waited a moment, then went inside.

———————

WILLIE HAD JUST climbed into bed when she heard the murmur of voices outside her room. The sound was clear enough to identify Stona and Joe, but she couldn't make out the words. Propping the pillow up behind her back, she straightened her nightgown, pulled the covers up under her arms, and affected a stern expression. There was no reason for Stona to sleep with her tonight, and she was determined to make him admit it. Not that she didn't trust Stona. There was no question of his integrity. She worried more about her own response when his big warm body surrounded hers in the middle of the night. She liked it a little too much.

He knocked and opened the door a crack. "It is safe to come in?"

She almost laughed. Considering the direction of her thoughts, it might not be. She cleared her throat. "I'm in bed."

He must've interpreted her response as an invitation. He walked into her room and closed the door behind him. "Did you enjoy your bath?"

"Yes. I feel better." She decided to get right to the point. "In fact, there's no reason for you to spend the night with me. I'll be fine."

He moved to the bed and sat on the side, placing his gun and holster on the nightstand. The strap securing the Glock was unsnapped. He didn't say anything, she thought he might be considering what she'd told him.

His quiet voice finally broke the silence. "I'm glad you're better, but it doesn't change anything. I need to be close enough to protect you from whatever's out there. Your visions are more intense, now. Have you forgotten Stone Shaper's visit to your bedroom? You ended up in hysterics."

"Sleeping with me won't stop my visions or prevent any visit Stone Shaper decides to make. They're not something you can wrestle to the ground and cuff. You can't keep me safe from something you can't see."

"I'll admit your visions scare me—because I am helpless. You're right. I can't stop them. But I can keep you safe in this world. And I can keep you from being alone when they haunt you."

She started to argue, but he shook his head. "Have you forgotten the flesh-and-blood man out there trying to kill you? If he makes it into the house, I intend to be close to you—real close. Move over, sweetheart."

Heaving a sigh intended to let him know she wasn't happy with his overbearing attitude, she scooted out of his way as he climbed in beside her. The dark red mark on his upper thigh caught her attention. She stopped him from pulling the cover over them.

"What's that?" She nodded toward the mark.

"My leg." He said it with a straight face.

She laughed. "No, you idiot, the red spot on your thigh. What is it?"

"A birthmark."

"Are you sure?" Melanoma was always a concern. "May I see it?"

He lifted the leg of his boxers a little higher, exposing the perfect image of an arrowhead. She stiffened and caught her breath.

Frowning, he tilted his head toward her. "It bothers you?"

"No. It took me by surprise. I've seen that mark before."

"I've never tried to hide it from you."

"No, you don't understand. I didn't see it on *you*. But it was in the same spot."

He half smiled. "Whose thigh have you been looking at?"

"Stone Shaper's."

"Who?"

"Stone Shaper. That same mark was on Stone Shaper's thigh—an almost perfect arrowhead, identical to yours. When Beth asked him about the mark, he told her his people believed it was an omen." Willie leaned back against the headboard and took a deep breath. "I wondered if it foretold his murder. He was killed with my spearhead. A spearhead and an arrowhead are similar in shape." She glanced at the birthmark again.

He must have read the worry in her eyes. Shaking his head, he pulled her down beside him. "Don't let your imagination get away from you. The idea of a birthmark foretelling a person's future is pure superstition. It's a mark on my leg. That's all. My grandfather has the mark, and he's still alive at ninety-three. It shows up once or twice in every generation, and I don't know of a single family member who's been killed with an arrowhead."

"You do now. At least with the spearhead."

"Are you talking about Stone Shaper?"

"It makes sense."

"You believe I'm related to Stone Shaper?" He shook his head. "Isn't that a bit of a stretch?"

"There's no doubt in my mind. If you carry his mark, you carry his blood."

"You can't be sure, and it isn't likely my birthmark and Stone Shaper's are identical."

"Is yours identical to your grandfather's?"

"Yes, but we're not separated by half a dozen generations. And you're trying to remember something you saw in a dream state."

"My visions aren't nebulous. I remember them as if they were imprinted on my mind. Your birthmark and his are identical. There's no doubt in my mind. You are Stone Shaper's direct descendent."

"And if I am?"

"I have to believe your involvement in all of this was no accident." She yawned and scooted closer. "We'll need to talk to Joe about this in the morning."

"Agreed." He pulled the covers over them both, turned off the light, and stacked his hands under his head. "Try to get some sleep. You need your rest."

Tonight, she was in the mood to let him order her around. She turned her back on him, wrapped her arms around her pillow, and the world and her troubles faded away.

———————

STONA WAITED UNTIL Willie was asleep before pulling her against his body. She snuggled her backside against his groin. He considered himself a strong, in-control man, but he was also human. The desire to nuzzle her neck was almost overwhelming. He needed to get out of her bed.

Joe had asked him what his intentions were. The question had been old-fashioned, and a bit naïve for this age of sexual freedom, but appropriate for Willie.

When she was safe again, he would make his intentions known. Until then, her safety was his primary concern. He would die before letting anyone hurt her. Cradling her in his arms, he covered her head with his hand in a protective gesture. The little spitfire who had thrown him out of her house would eventually face the truth—they were meant to be together.

FORTY-TWO

THE AGONY WAS almost physical. Beth staggered and would've fallen if she hadn't grasped the sturdy poles of the lodge's doorway.

Stone Shaper.

Sinking to her knees, she wrapped her arms around her swollen belly, cradling their child as she rocked back and forth, keening. He was gone. The light had gone out of her life. No matter how hard she tried, she couldn't call him back to her. He wasn't there to call back. He was beyond her reach.

Tears wet her cheeks as she tried to convince herself it wasn't true. The baby was making her emotional. Her natural worry for the man she loved had somehow turned into a fear that was eating her alive. It made no sense. There was no reason she should be experiencing this devastating sorrow. He was fine. He *had* to be fine....

Raven found her kneeling in the dirt. Once she knew it wasn't the baby causing the problem, she sent for Joseph.

Beth wouldn't speak to either of them.

Lost in a fog of sorrow, Beth turned inward, unwilling to share her devastation. Voicing the fears would make them real. She existed in the void between hope and despair, denying the emptiness lodged in her heart that bespoke the truth. He wasn't coming home. She would never touch him again, never hear his voice in the dark hours of the night, never see the love in his eyes. And he would never see his child, never hold his son or daughter. And his child would never know him.

One day faded into the next, and the next. She left the lodge only when her body demanded she do so. Raven kept the fire burning and brought her food, urging her to eat for her baby's sake. Stone Shaper's cousin all but hand-fed her.

She didn't know how many days passed before a commotion on the fringe of the camp pulled her from her stupor. Sorrowful wails and cries blended with angry shouts. Something was wrong, and she steeled herself against the pain of the truth that was to come.

Raven was the first to enter the lodge. Any lingering hope that she'd been wrong died when she saw Raven's ravaged face. Barely contained tears brimmed in her dark, anguished eyes.

"Stone Shaper?"

The girl nodded. "And Brings Peace."

Though she had braced herself for the agony of knowing beyond doubt that Stone Shaper was dead, the shock of learning Brings Peace too had died staggered her. Stone Shaper's father-in-law had been kind to her over the past few months. In many ways he had become more father to her than Jackson LaRouche ever had.

"How?"

"I don't know. Maybe there was an attack. Only four warriors returned. Most of our people came out to meet them, and I was at the back of the crowd."

"Then you can't be sure Stone Shaper and Brings Peace—"

"They're dead. Joseph was one of the first to greet the returning warriors. He found me in the crowd and gave me the sorrowful news. He told me to come to you and make sure you stay in your lodge. He is worried about something. I can hear Bear shouting over the grieving cries, but I couldn't understand what he was saying. Joseph will come to you soon and explain everything. I am to stay with you until then."

"What of Winter Storm?"

"Joseph tells me my brother and his friend were among those who returned. But they won't enter the village until the purification ceremony is complete. They do not wish to bring the ghosts of the dead into our midst."

Beth nodded, though in her heart she wondered how anyone could fear a person they'd loved in this life even when their loved one passed into the afterlife. She would be comforted knowing Stone Shaper's spirit remained close to her. She wouldn't feel so alone.

Only a short time passed before Joseph came to the lodge. She and Raven had been sitting on the furs in front of the fire. The girl helped her to her feet when he entered. His eyes reflected shock and sorrow, but his intense frown and the urgency in his step frightened her.

"Bear has accused Stone Shaper of killing Brings Peace. He also claims he retaliated in our medicine chief's stead and took Stone Shaper's life."

She staggered and would've gone down if Raven hadn't supported her. "My husband would never have killed his friend. Bear lies."

Joseph nodded. "Winter Storm tried to defend his cousin, claiming no one saw Stone Shaper kill Brings Peace. He also accused Bear of not giving Stone Shaper the chance to defend himself." He looked at Raven. "I fear this night your brother has made himself a powerful and ruthless enemy."

He took Beth's hand. "Are you well enough to travel? Bear is accusing you of having caused a rift between your husband and Brings Peace."

"Why would he say that? You know there was never any conflict between them."

"I know, and under different circumstances most of the tribe would not take Bear's accusations seriously. But tonight, the people are filled with grief and anger. Though you have made a few friends, your only connection with the tribe was through Stone Shaper, who is now considered a murderer. You're no longer safe here. We must leave."

"Joseph, this is your home. These are your people. I can't ask you to abandon your life here. If you take me away, Bear will make sure you are never allowed to return."

"As Brings Peace and Stone Shaper's friend, I can do no less. I've hidden two of my best horses in the woods below the spring. Raven, go and join the crowd. No one must believe you were here."

Raven nodded and hugged Beth. "I hope we will see each other again."

Joseph sprinted to the lodge entrance and looked out, then beckoned to her. "Everyone is listening to Bear. No one will see you if we hurry." He watched Raven leave then turned to Beth. "The air is cold. Put on your robe and let's go."

She quickly slipped the fur covering over her shoulders and moved toward the entrance, but stopped and hurried as fast as her condition would allow to the corner where the baskets were kept. Reaching into the smallest basket, she retrieved the walnut comb Stone Shaper used to comb her hair. Clutching it close to her heart, she followed Joseph out into the dark night.

FORTY-THREE

WILLIE CAME AWAKE crying and clutching Stona's neck as she returned to reality. He was rubbing her back while he murmured nonsensical words of comfort.

"Willie?" His voice was gruff against her ear.

"I'm awake." She released his neck and tried to pull away from him. He wouldn't let her go far. "Why are you crying?"

"Beth." She blinked back fresh tears. "I was with Beth. She knew Stone Shaper was dead and grieved for him long before the warriors returned to the village. It was heartbreaking."

He pulled her back into his arms and gently forced her head against his shoulder, his fingers combing through her hair. "It's okay, sweetheart."

She tried to shake her head. "I'm not your sweetheart."

"Yes, you are. Now, finish telling me what happened."

She didn't feel up to arguing over the endearment. "Bear accused Stone Shaper of killing Brings Peace and blamed Beth for causing trouble between the two friends. Joseph got her out of the village in the middle of the night." She caught her breath on a sob. "It's so tragic. I don't know what she'll do now."

He rolled her onto her back and raised up on an elbow to peer down at her. "Willie, listen to me. Whatever happened to her is in the past.

These people you're so worried about lived out their lives long ago. If you believe the mark on my leg makes me Stone Shaper's descendent, you have to believe Beth survived long enough to have his baby. Her friend, Joseph, would've made sure they were safe. You need to remember centuries have passed since they were alive.

"I know you're right, but please understand I was with them minutes ago. I've been with them for months. They're a part of my life. I care about them."

"It tears me up inside to watch you grieve for someone who died before your great-grandparents were born."

Taking a deep breath, she tried to gain control of her emotions. "So you believe you are Stone Shaper's descendent?"

He settled back against the pillow, taking her with him. "I didn't have the benefit of seeing the birthmark on Stone Shaper. It's going to take a while to get used to the idea, but yes."

Glancing toward the bedside clock, he pulled her closer and drew the quilt over her shoulders. "It's only six. You should try to go back to sleep. We don't need an early start, and you can use the rest." His mouth brushed across hers, his kiss feather light. "Close your eyes."

His hand rubbed her back in slow circles. It felt so natural, being held by him. His wonderful scent surrounded her. His strength too. She was safe in his arms. Sleep had nearly overtaken her when his lips touched her forehead.

It was after nine when she came downstairs. Stona was in the living room, using his phone. He looked up and smiled. At least whoever was on the other end wasn't giving him bad news.

He disconnected and met her at the bottom of the stairs. "Are you feeling better?"

She nodded. "Who was on the phone?" Too late, she realized it might have been a personal call. "Never mind. It's none of my business."

"I was checking in with the office."

"Oh, okay. I didn't mean to sleep so late."

"I'm glad you did." He walked her into the kitchen and pulled out a chair for her at the table. "Do you want coffee or tea this morning?"

"Coffee. I need the fortification. Where's Joe?"

"Outside somewhere." He set a steaming cup in front of her. "He's getting the tools together. What do you want for breakfast?"

Lifting her cup, she took a sip of the hot liquid. "Nothing right now. I'll grab something later."

"Later will be lunch. You need to eat now."

"All right," she conceded, knowing he was in the mood to be obstinate. "I'll have a piece of toast."

"Toast it is." A few minutes later he set a saucer of toast in front of her. The bread was smothered with peanut butter.

She frowned at him. "How do you know I like peanut butter?"

"You have a half-empty jar of the natural stuff in the refrigerator. Eat up."

Joe waited beside the car. Stona had given him the keys earlier and he'd removed the tools from the trunk. The iron bar they'd taken from the old shed rested at his feet with the coil of rope. He'd tied a knot every three or so feet along its length, probably to aid Stona's descent into the cave.

Stona pulled the flashlight from the console and clipped it to his belt. He shrugged the rope over his shoulder, grabbed the iron bar and pick and tilted his head toward the meadow, waiting for her to take the lead. She smiled in anticipation, handed Joe a pair of work gloves, and stuffed another pair into Stona's jacket pocket before picking up a shovel and the canvas bag. Joe retrieved the second shovel and fell in line behind her as she set a brisk pace toward the opposite side of the meadow.

Stona suggested they leave the tools at the fenceline while they searched for the sinkhole.

She nodded her agreement. "I don't think the sinkhole is far from here." She glanced toward the house, then scanned the meadow. "The trees would've changed, but the way the land lays would stay the same. If we separate—"

"We stay together." Stona's frown suggested she not argue the point.

She didn't try. "Let's get started, then."

Willie had been right about the location. Less than an hour later they came to a sunken area that might hide a cave opening. The shallow sinkhole wasn't as deep as she remembered from her vision, but it was close enough to check out.

She was surprised no one else had noticed the slight dip in the landscape. Her neighbor allowed hunting in these woods. She'd often glanced across the meadow and seen men dressed in camouflage come and go during hunting season. They usually parked along the blacktop fronting their two properties. She glanced in that direction, but an overgrowth of buckbrush and sassafras sprouts prevented her from seeing the road itself. It couldn't be more than a couple hundred yards away, though.

After retrieving their tools, the men walked into the bowl-shaped depression with the bar and pick. She remained on the perimeter as a safety precaution. If there was a problem, her nursing skills might be needed. At least that was Stona's explanation for the decision. She had a feeling he was more concerned with her safety and would have argued if Joe hadn't been in full agreement.

Joe watched as Stona jabbed the heavy bar into the soil, testing the ground's stability in several locations. After deciding on a possible soft spot, he traded the bar for a pick and began loosening the root-bound soil at the edge of the sunken area. Joe grabbed a shovel to scoop out the soil and loose rocks.

The bottom dropped away suddenly, nearly taking Stona with it. Both men scrambled from the depression and stared at the fresh opening. She reached for Stona's hand. The hole looked as it had in her vision—a vertical shaft wide enough for a large man's body.

Stona grinned at her. "I think we found your cave." Her heart raced from the scare she'd been given. It had been a close call. Stona could have been hurt, or worse.

Now, it was pounding from fresh adrenaline surging through her system. They were about to discover Stone Shaper's remains. She was sure of it.

Stona studied the trees surrounding the sinkhole, chose a sturdy red oak growing a few feet from the opening and secured the rope. Unwinding the coil, he approached the opening, bent on one knee, unclipped the flashlight and aimed the beam into the black abyss. She held her breath when he leaned into the hole. Finally, he stood and shook his head.

"The shaft's too narrow for rappelling down. It looks like it goes straight down for about twenty feet, then widens as it angles to the right. I can't see anything beyond that point." He finger-combed his hair away from his face and frowned. "Can't tell how deep it is. I hope we have enough rope." Clipping the flashlight to his belt, he dropped the rope through the opening, shaking it occasionally, probably to prevent it from catching on rocks.

He'd be out of their sight and hearing once he reached the bend in the shaft. The thought sent chills down her spine. She grabbed his arm. "How will we know you're okay? What if the rope isn't long enough?"

He clasped his hand over hers, squeezing gently. "Don't panic. If the rope isn't long enough, I'll climb out and we'll buy a longer rope. Once I've made it to the bottom, it shouldn't take long to find Stone Shaper—*if* he's there. If he is, I'll return to the surface and we can decide the best way to bring him out."

"What if something happens to you?"

"From what I can see, the shaft is mainly chert."

"Chert? I don't understand."

"Flint, like your spearhead. Caves in this part of the country are mostly limestone-based. It's a softer rock, but there's a lot of chert in Missouri, too, and chert won't crumble away underfoot. There shouldn't be a problem getting in and out."

"I still don't like the idea of you being alone down there."

"If it'll make you feel better, we'll set a time limit for my return. If I don't make it back in thirty minutes, call fire rescue. They'll take it from there."

She grudgingly nodded.

He gave her a fierce hug. "Nothing's going to happen to me. I've climbed around in caves before. I know how to be careful."

Nodding, she stepped out of his arms and sighed. "I'll be glad when we're finished here."

Joe moved beside her and placed an arm across her shoulders. "Let's get out of his way. He can't finish this if you keep talking to him."

Willie looked at her watch. "Okay, thirty minutes starting now."

Stona laughed. "How about thirty minutes starting from the time I enter the cave?"

Joe grinned. "Makes sense." He led Willie to the red oak. "We will wait here for your return."

Stona walked to the cave opening, grasped the rope and slid feet first into the narrow hole. Glancing up, he gave her a wide smile and a wink before lowering himself out of sight.

IT HAD BEEN a few years since he'd done any spelunking and had to admit the ragged walls closing in on him were a little unnerving. He used the knots in the rope for hand and footholds as he climbed straight down from the surface.

As he suspected, the shaft widened as it angled to the right and leveled off a bit, but the ceiling was low. Gripping the rope for balance, he backed down the incline, keeping his head bent. Loose pebbles and dirt rolled under his feet as he descended. After another few yards, he was able to stand upright. No light penetrated this section of the cave, and he unclipped his flashlight.

He paused a moment, experiencing the ultimate darkness. Without sight, his other senses took over. The air was damp, and cool, and carried an earthy scent. The echo of dripping water surrounded him. He was in a good-sized room. Geologists and spelunkers would call this a living cave—their nickname for a cavern with active formations fed by the mineral-rich drops of mildly acidic water.

Knowing he was on a time limit, he switched on his flashlight and looked around. The narrow entrance had opened into a domed room filled with slabs of rock and rubble that had once been part of the cavern's original ceiling.

Several fair-sized stalagmites stood sentinel within his light's beam. Glistening flowstone glazed the rocks. He aimed the light higher and panned it across the arc of the ceiling. The beam's distance was limited, but hundreds of soda straw formations and stalactites gleamed white.

Dragging his attention from the natural wonder, he pointed the light at his watch. Ten minutes had passed. He figured he had about ten minutes to look around before he was forced to return to the surface.

The chance of Stone Shaper's body making it all the way to this level was slim. Light from the surface hadn't offered much illumination as he descended into the cave. He could've turned on the flashlight dangling from his belt, but it was easier to spot something when he was on his feet and not hanging off a rope. Turning, he aimed the light toward the narrow shaft as he grasped his lifeline. He'd considered the possibility of stepping on the remains once he'd found his footing and moved into the cave. There was also a slight chance the warrior's body had rolled to the bottom of this steep-angled room. If that were true, he would need more than a knotted rope and a flashlight.

Grasping the rope for support, he began a slow assent, panning the light ahead of him. He was standing on a wide, collapsed shelf near the ceiling. Red, clay-rich dirt covered almost everything. It was dry for the most part, but not dusty. He was only twenty or so feet from the surface at this point. Soil as well as rock had fallen into the domed room at the time of the collapse. He was standing under the low ceiling when the flashlight's beam caught something to his right.

Using the rope for balance, he sidestepped to a slab of rock jutting out of the debris like a broken seesaw. Kneeling, he aimed the light under the lip of the shelf.

He vowed never to doubt Willie again. Snug against the upturned rock lay the skeletal remains of an exceptionally large man.

Stone Shaper.

FORTY-FOUR

ANY LINGERING DOUBT he'd harbored about Willie's visions and ghostly visitors were dispelled. For reasons none of them understood, she had known this man, had in some way been a part of his life, and grieved for him. This centuries-old warrior had been as real and vital to her as any person living today—including himself. It was a humbling thought.

The bones had a reddish cast, having absorbed iron oxide from the clay-mix soil they'd rested on. Still, he should have seen them earlier. If he hadn't been concentrating on his footing and the low ceiling, he might have.

As if he'd entered an ancient, sacred tomb, he bent his head and sent up a prayer for Stone Shaper's lost and tormented spirit. This man had been robbed of life before he'd seen his own child born.

Willie had convinced him he was Stone Shaper's descendent. It was ironic that circumstances had brought him to this place—or had a more powerful hand guided their paths?

He stared down at the remains of the man who was responsible for his own existence. "I pray you find peace."

Stepping back, he hooked the flashlight to his belt. The allotted thirty minutes was probably long past. With a final nod to the remains, he grabbed the rope and climbed to the surface, a subtly different man from the one who had climbed down.

———————

"DO YOU THINK Stona's all right? He's been down there for almost half an hour." Willie hadn't been able to sit still. She'd paced the perimeter of the sinkhole, checking her watch every couple of minutes. She glared at Joe, who appeared to be dozing. His calm irritated her. "Don't you think we should do something?"

He rolled his shoulders before looking up at her. "You worry too much. We will give him a little more time."

A grunt from the cave entrance drew her attention away from Joe. She scrambled down the slight incline. An arm reached out to grasp the rope above ground. Stona half-lifted out of the hole and levered himself out of the cave.

Rolling onto his back, he waited until his breathing had calmed before sitting up. Dirt and red clay covered his clothes and skin.

She knelt beside him, pulled a bottle of water out of her jacket pocket, and handed it to him.

He chugged the water down before handing her the empty bottle. "Thanks."

"Do you need more?"

She reached into the other pocket, but he shook his head. "No. I'm good. Aren't you going to ask me if he's down there?"

"I'm almost afraid to."

"He is."

She gasped and threw herself into his arms, nearly bowling him over. "He's there? He's really there?" She pushed away from him. "We have to get him out as soon as possible—after you've rested."

"Give me a few minutes and I'll be fine."

"Are you sure?"

He laughed. "It wasn't that far down."

She jumped to her feet. "I'll get the canvas bag. There's an old blanket in it to wrap him in. The bag's bound to bump against the rocks when we pull him out."

"Good idea."

———————

FIFTEEN MINUTES LATER, Stona climbed back into the cave. The second trip down didn't take as long. He was more familiar with the cavern's layout—at least the entry.

The steep grade of the cave floor made his job more difficult, though. He positioned the canvas bag beside the body and braced the low end with a couple of brick-sized rocks to keep it from sliding down the embankment and out of reach. He nested the blanket inside the bag with the surplus hanging over the outside.

When the bag was ready, he paused to stare down at Stone Shaper's remains. His body had rested in this natural sepulcher for nearly two centuries, maybe more. Now that it was time to bring him out, he hesitated, suddenly feeling like a grave robber. Was this truly what his ancestor wanted, or had they mistaken the reason for his connection with Willie?

Why Willie? Was her blood on the stone enough to bind their spirits and bridge the centuries? Would anyone else's blood have triggered the visions, opening their minds to the injustice of the past?

He didn't know.

In the end, Willie's wishes took precedence over any of his doubts. With meticulous care and a sense of reverence, he began placing the bones on the blanket, inside the bag. When he was finished, he folded the edges of the blanket over Stone Shaper's remains and zipped the bag closed. He double tied the rope to the corner of the handle so the bag could be pulled up lengthwise in order to prevent it becoming wedged in the narrower sections of the passage.

Climbing to the surface, he pulled the rope out of the hole, going slow to prevent ripping the bag as it bumped and dragged over the ragged walls. Against Stona's better judgment, Willie waited at the entrance to guide it out.

ONCE THE BAG was on the surface, Stona carried it out of the depression, setting it on a level piece of ground. Willie knelt in front of the canvas duffel and carefully drew the zipper across its length. Stona and Joe stood on the opposite side, silently watching. She glanced up, giving them a tremulous smile, needing to share this moment with the two men who'd helped make it possible.

Had it only been a day since the warrior's last appearance—since she'd finally realized what was expected of her? It seemed a lifetime.

Tears rolled unchecked down her cheeks as she folded the blanket back, exposing the remains to the light of day. Could Stone Shaper's spirit feel the sunshine warming his bones? She shook her head. It was a fanciful thought.

Without hesitation, she touched his bones. Her shiver wasn't due to dread or revulsion. Here was the physical evidence of her ethereal experience. Proof she'd been privileged to share their lives. And now, she could right a grievous wrong.

STONA WALKED AROUND the satchel to gently lift Willie to her feet. She threw her arms around his waist, holding him close.

He almost missed the man rising out of the brush growing along the blacktop.

"Get down!"

Pivoting, he placed himself between Willie and potential danger. White-hot pain seared his upper arm. The impact propelled him into her. They both went down.

FORTY-FIVE

STONA ROLLED ON top of Willie, unsnapping the safety strap on his holster at the same time. He pulled the Glock free, and scanned the area where the man had been. The brush along the outer fenceline was too thick to see anything from his position on the ground.

"Joe!" The old man was face down on the ground beside them.

"I'm okay. Can you see him?"

The roar of an engine and the squeal of tires on blacktop told them their attacker had fled. Stona moved away from her and raised his head.

"Stona, your arm!" She crawled to her knees.

"Stay down!"

"Look at your arm!" She grabbed his hand, ignoring the gun he held.

"Willie, let go. Do you want to get yourself shot?"

Her fingers moved from his hand to his arm. "Stona! Pay attention. Your arm—"

"Doesn't concern me right now."

Joe crawled over beside them. Both men kept low as they scanned the woods.

Stona glanced at the older man. "Did you count more than one?"

"No." He nodded toward Stona's arm. "I think you should probably take care of that."

Stona glanced down. The triangular point of a hunting arrow had gone completely through the muscle of his upper arm. The long shaft extended out behind him. An arrow. Now he understood why he'd felt the impact but hadn't heard a gunshot.

Joe steadied him as he got to his feet. Willie scrambled up beside them, her attention on his wounded arm. "Can you make it to the house? No, maybe you should lie down." Her voice had a take charge edge to it. Apparently, her trauma training had kicked in.

He moved to place himself between her and the road. "Don't make me an invalid, Willie. The arrow's in my arm, not my heart." She paled, and he realized too late the parallel between the events in her visions and his injury. "Aw, honey, I'm sorry." He holstered his gun and wrapped his good arm around her shoulders. "I wasn't thinking."

She shook her head. "It's all right. Don't worry about me. We need to get you to the hospital."

He would've shrugged if his shoulder hadn't been throbbing. "We need to make sure you're safe first. My arm isn't bleeding much. You're a nurse. You take care of it for now."

She gave him what he assumed was 'the look.' "You have an arrow sticking out of your arm. That isn't something I can put a Band-Aid on. There are five arteries in your arm, weaving in and around the bones. The arrow might not have done much damage yet, but it's capable of nicking one of those arteries if it moves around."

"You're overreacting."

"I hope you're right—you probably are, but for all we know the shaft could be pinching off a damaged artery. You need to be where you can get immediate help if something goes wrong."

Joe nodded. "You should listen to her."

Stona continuously scanned the surrounding woods. There was always a chance the killer had circled back to take another shot at her. "We need to get you out of here." He pulled his car keys from his pocket. "It isn't safe for Willie to cross that open meadow. The ground between here and the house is rough, but I think the car will make it." He pushed her toward Joe. "Stay with her and keep down."

He started toward the fence when Joe's hand on his good arm stopped him. "You cannot drive the car. The arrow will not allow you to sit behind the wheel."

Stona couldn't argue the point, didn't waste time trying. He handed the keys to the older man. "If the killer is out there, I don't think he'll give himself away by taking a shot at you. He wants Willie. Stay low, just in case."

"I'll need my medical kit. It's in the cabinet over the refrigerator." She glanced at Stona. "I have to stabilize your arm for the trip to the hospital."

He nodded, then ordered her to crouch down, keeping a large oak between her and the road. He knelt beside her. Joe climbed between the strands of barbed wire and headed to the house, angling toward the back yard. A few minutes later they saw Stona's car emerge from the other side of the house, moving in their direction.

Joe pulled the vehicle in front of the fence. He carried the pair of fence pliers she'd remembered seeing in a box of old tools in the barn. "Does your neighbor have any cattle in this section?"

Willie shook her head.

"Then he won't mind if we make a hole in his fence. Stay back." The specialized pliers were generally used to build a fence, but they were also adept at cutting heavy strands of barbed wire. Joe opened the plier handles and positioned the jaw-like blades snug against the strand, close to one of the fence posts. She'd begun to suspect her friend wasn't as old and frail as she'd believed. He was stronger than he looked. With the flex of his hand, taut fence wire strands whipped back with the speed of a lightning flash. Obviously, he had built a fence or two in his lifetime. In less than a minute Joe had opened the space between two posts. Using the pliers, he dragged the clipped wire out of the way, then pulled the car into the cover of the trees.

———————

WILLIE CUT STONA'S shirt sleeve away to get to the arrow's shaft. After cleaning his arm, she packed gauze pads around both the entry and exit wounds, securing the packing with adhesive tape before immobilizing his arm against his body with a long gauze strip. His gun was out, and he constantly scanned the surrounding area while she worked.

Joe stowed the tools and the canvas bag with Stone Shaper's remains in the trunk while Willie finished up.

Getting into the car proved tricky. Fortunately, Stona's rental was a four-door sedan. He ordered Willie into the backseat on the passenger side, closed the door and walked to the driver side. Holstering his gun, he opened the back door. With the arrow protruding out of both the front and back of his arm, it was impossible to sit normally. Kneeling on the seat, he ducked his head under the door frame while keeping his back straight to avoid bumping the shaft. Then he inched forward until his feet were inside the car.

Willie leaned toward him, reaching for his seatbelt. He shook his head. "Not gonna work." As soon as Joe closed the door behind him and got into the front, Stona leaned his good shoulder against the seatback and looked down at her. "Come over here."

"There isn't much room."

"There's enough. I want you close."

His eyes were constantly moving as Joe backed the car away from the fence and turned it around.

Willie scooted next to Stona. "You think he's still here?"

"There's always a chance he is. When we get to the hospital you stay by my side—no questions, no arguments. Do you understand?"

He was always asking her if she understood. It irritated her at times, but not today. She nodded her agreement.

"Stay in the car and down out of sight until I get out and come around for you."

"You don't think he'll be at the hospital, do you?"

"He probably knows he got one of us. If he wants to finish this tonight, the hospital will be the first place he tries. When we get there, do what I say, no hesitation."

"Okay, yes."

Stona practically wrapped his body around Willie on the ride to the hospital, continuing to make himself the target. Joe pulled into the ambulance bay next to the emergency doors and stopped.

Joe opened Stona's door, steadying him as he backed out of the car. Both men surveyed the parking lot and the side of the building as they moved around the vehicle. Stona retrieved his wallet, opening it to expose his badge.

Joe slapped the button activating the emergency entry then opened her door. When she stepped out of the car, Stona moved behind her to protect her back as they quickly walked into the building.

Joe stopped inside the doors. "I'll move the car." He turned and left.

Stona's gun activated the alarm and a security guard came running from one of the side halls, skidding to a halt in front of them. She wasn't sure if the badge or the Glock on Stona's hip had captured his attention. Then again, the arrow in Stona's arm might have been responsible for his stunned reaction.

Stona took advantage of the silence. "Call the sheriff. Tell him Deputy Marshal Jordan needs backup at the hospital."

The man hesitated, still staring at the Glock.

"*Now!*"

That got him moving. He reached for the radio on his shoulder as he stepped aside for a nurse and an orderly with a wheelchair.

Stona ignored the orderly and looked at the nurse. "Where?"

She pointed toward a curtained area. "Bay Three." She looked at Willie. "There's a waiting area down the—"

"She stays with me." The emergency doors opened, and Joe walked through. He couldn't have moved the vehicle far. Stona nodded in his direction. "He stays, too."

"The sheriff's on his way." The security guard still had his eyes on the Glock.

Stona glanced around before returning his attention to the guard. "Stand outside the emergency entrance. Make sure only paramedics and patients on gurneys get through those doors. Send anyone on foot to the front." The guard nodded and took up a position outside the automatic doors.

"Joe, keep an eye on anyone coming into the Emergency Room from inside the hospital. He took Willie's arm as they entered the exam room. "Willie, don't leave my side under any circumstances."

She nodded.

The nurse shook her head. "Once the doctor gets here, she'll need to wait on the other side of the curtain."

"No. She stays." Stona's tone left no room for discussion. The woman frowned, then shrugged, and began lining up instruments on the side stand.

Sheriff Devenson arrived before the doctor. Stona introduced Willie and Joe and filled the man in on the details of the attack. The hospital was immediately placed on lockdown and a deputy took over the security guard's watch.

The sheriff had removed his hat when he shook Willie's hand. He replaced it and gave her a worried glance. "I imagine the marshal's office will want to find a secure place for Miss McAllister."

Stona nodded. "Until it can be arranged, we'll need extra manpower. Can you spare a couple of men to watch the house, and a car to patrol the farm road?"

"I can arrange that. When you've finished here, a patrol car will follow you home."

Doctor Jeffries's arrival interrupted their conversation. The sheriff tipped his hat toward Willie and shook Stona's hand. "Keep me informed, Marshal."

"I will. And thanks for your help."

The precautionary scan indicated no arteries were at risk, and it was safe to remove the arrow without surgery. Once the area was numb, the doctor unscrewed the point and slid the shaft free.

Dr. Jeffries was in a talkative mood. "I've seen my share of arrow wounds. They don't happen often, but they do happen. Most of the time, we get smaller bullet-points generally used by amateurs for target practice. Makes a small hole. This one," he nodded toward the bloody point in the tray, "this one is a different story. It's designed to kill—deer mostly. They call those points broadheads. You're lucky it only caught the fleshy part of your arm."

Eight tight stitches on each side of his arm closed the wounds, and after a tetanus shot, Stona was given a list of instructions and a prescription for pain medication, and antibiotics to prevent infection. For security's sake, the doctor had the prescriptions filled in the hospital and brought to the emergency room.

Stona's holster was unsnapped and his hand on the butt of his gun when they walked out of the hospital. Their car was parked at the emergency entrance. Two deputies in a patrol car waited in the parking lot to follow them home.

Willie sat close to Stona on the trip back. He made her stay low for the duration of the trip and didn't relax his guard until they were safe inside the house with the doors bolted. She glanced at the clock in the kitchen, surprised to discover it was only a little after two in the afternoon. She felt as if she'd been caught in a time warp.

FORTY-SIX

THE WOMAN WAS driving Stona crazy. Willie had gone into nurse-mode as soon as they'd entered the house. The doctor had suggested he take it easy. She insisted he go to bed. The wound wasn't serious, and she needed to leave him alone. They finally compromised and he sat on the couch with his feet propped on the ottoman.

She didn't know it yet, but the attempt on her life necessitated decisions she wasn't going to like. He didn't much care for them, either, but her safety was his main concern.

When she brought him a bottle of water, he took it and patted the place next to him on the couch. "Sit down. We need to talk." He turned his attention to Joe, who was leaving the room. "You need to stay, too. This concerns all of us."

He steeled himself against the dread he saw in her eyes. No, she wasn't going to like what he had to say.

Stona waited until Joe had taken his seat across from them before giving Willie his full attention. "I've underestimated our adversary. Until now he's kept his distance. His method was simple and clean, easy for him to get the job done and be a hundred miles away when the supposed accident happened. Today he changed the game." Stona's voice turned deadly cold. "He tried to kill you."

He shook his head when Willie started to speak "I don't know what he thinks you have on him, but it's obvious he isn't going to be satisfied until you're silenced."

She leaned toward him shaking her head. "You can protect me, like you always do."

"We were lucky today, but we both know I can't always be there." He lifted her hand to his lips. "He could have taken aim at you while I was in the cave. You might have died while I was down there, and I would never have known you were in danger. I'm not chancing that again. We leave for St. Louis first thing in the morning. You're going into protective custody."

"You can't be serious." She started to jump to her feet. He wouldn't let go of her hand, keeping her beside him.

She tried to pull away. He tightened his hold. "Calm down."

His clipped command infuriated her. "Calm down? You're asking me to *calm down?*"

"No, I'm *telling* you." He glared at her a long moment then sighed. "Take a deep breath and we'll talk about this rationally."

"I'm not the one being irrational, and I shouldn't be the one hiding. He's the criminal. Why should I be put away somewhere?"

"No one's putting you away. You'll be taken somewhere safe and comfortable until we catch him. And we *will* catch him."

"I'm *not* overreacting!" She realized she was shouting and took the deep breath he'd suggested a minute ago. "All right, we'll talk about this." She tried to tug her hand free. He still wouldn't turn her loose. She tried for a calmer tone. "How long will I be forced to stay 'somewhere safe and comfortable?'"

"I've already told you."

"Tell me again." Could he hear her teeth grinding?

"Until we've caught or killed him. I don't care which."

She was already shaking her head "Oh, no. It could take years. You told me you've been chasing him for over a decade."

"We've never been this close before. He slipped up when he went after you today. He'll slip up again, and when he does, I'll have him." His hand gently tightened over hers and his voice softened. "But first you have to be safe."

She sank back against the cushions. "If I do agree to go into protective custody, what happens?"

"Like I said, you'll be taken somewhere safe. Only a handful of people will know where."

"Will you be with me?"

He shook his head. "No. You'll travel with someone trained for this type of assignment."

"But you'll know where I am. We can stay in touch?"

"Only your handlers and their superiors will know where you are."

"My *handlers!*" She pulled free of his grasp and jumped to her feet. "I'm not an animal in a zoo. I don't need handlers."

"It's the only way to be sure you're safe."

And alone. She'd be alone again.

"So, I wasn't overreacting. I'll be forced to leave my home, and my friends, become someone else, while he lives life as usual."

"Willie, you're going into protective custody, not witness protection."

"What's the difference? I'll still be alone." The thought terrified her.

"Someone will be with you twenty-four-seven."

"That's not what I mean, and you know it."

"When this is over, we'll see each other again." He got to his feet and reached for her.

She jerked back, refusing to let him comfort her. "How long?"

His arm dropped to his side "How long what?"

"How long before we see each other?"

"I don't know."

"And that's all right with you? You're fine with not seeing me... I thought. . .." She turned her back, refusing to let him see her humiliation.

He pulled her around to face him. "Fine with it? You honestly believe I'm fine with never seeing you again?" He half-dragged her into the privacy of the kitchen, pulled her into his arms and showed her exactly how he felt. The kiss was demanding, passionate, and full of frustration.

She melted against him, slipped her arms around his waist, and kissed him back. His fingers slid into her hair, cradling her head as his lips slanted over hers again and again.

When he pulled back, they were both gasping for air. He held her face in his hands and kissed her again, a quick touch of his lips against hers and looked into her eyes.

"The thought of not seeing you, not touching you, not being able to protect you, for even a day unmans me. Never doubt my motives for wanting you in protective custody. I love you, Willie, and I need to spend the rest of my days with you—but not at the risk of your life. I'd rather never see you again than put you in jeopardy for an hour." He used his thumbs to wipe the tears from her cheeks. "You have to go."

"There must be another way to stay together."

"Marry her!" Joe shouted from the other room.

Stona grabbed her hand and pulled her into the living room. "What did you say?"

"Marry her. I doubt the marshal's office will separate a husband and wife." He shrugged at Stona. "You'd probably end up in protective custody with her. That's what you want isn't it, to be close enough to protect her?"

Stona dragged her back into the kitchen. Pulling their clasped hands to his chest, he gazed down at her. "Will you marry me?"

"To protect me?" She shook her head. "Marriage is a lifetime commitment, not a short-term answer to a problem. We can't—"

He kissed her silent. "Don't misunderstand me. If we get married it won't be a short-term anything. Do you love me?"

"Stona, I—"

"Do you love me?"

"Yes."

"Enough for a lifetime?"

FORTY-SEVEN

JOE JUST HAPPENED to have the necessary papers, which led Willie to wonder if he'd anticipated this outcome. It didn't surprise her. The man who'd appointed himself her mentor often surprised her with his insight.

Joe made a trip to town. No one would tell her the reason, and Stona insisted she remain safe in the house when they walked out to the car. She watched from the mud room window as they paused to speak with one another.

A man emerged from the interior of the old barn. Her stomach clenched and she was about to shout a warning when she recognized his uniform. Stona turned, his hand at the gun on his hip. The stranger raised both hands and said something she couldn't hear as he retrieved his ID. They talked for a few minutes then Stona and Joe shook the man's hand.

Stona remained outside after Joe left. The officer grabbed his jacket from the unmarked car she'd only just noticed and returned to the barn. Her future husband glanced around the back yard before moving out of sight toward the front of the house. She assumed he was checking the area for anything suspicious, though he might only need some time to himself. He was, after all, about to be married.

And so was she. Suddenly a long, relaxing soak in a hot bath sounded good.

———————

WILLIE WIPED THE fog from her bathroom mirror and stared at her reflection. Did every bride have misgivings on her wedding day? She imagined most did. Marriage was one of the most important decisions a person made, or it was supposed to be. The decision to spend the rest of your life with another person shouldn't be hurried. Both parties needed to be sure the commitment was right for them.

She doubted many brides were forced into a hurried wedding because a killer rushed the courting process. Maybe in time she would have considered a life with Stona. She smiled to herself. She probably had. Visions, ghosts, and a madman bent on killing you tended to take precedence over everyday thoughts and emotions. Her life had been put on fast-forward. Stona had gone from being her adversary to her protector in a matter of weeks. And now she was about to marry him. He would be her husband, her lover. How was she supposed to feel about that?

She glanced at the simple, knee-length dress of eggshell-white with wisps of lace on the collar and cuffs—an impulsive buy she'd never found an occasion to wear. Until now. It would be her wedding dress.

Her attention returned to her reflection in the mirror. Was she doing the right thing? This wasn't just her life-changing event. Stona's life would be changed too.

Not for the first time, she wished she had Josh to confide in.

———————

STONA STOOD AT the foot of the stairs and watched Willie come to him. She was breathtaking. Her hair was pinned on top of her head. Delicate ringlets of deep auburn fell around her face. No bride had ever been more beautiful. When she reached him, he handed her the small bridal bouquet of white carnations and pink roses he'd been hiding behind his back. Her eyes widened in surprised pleasure. She inhaled the blossoms' fragrance and smiling, whispered her thanks.

The uncertainty lingering in her gaze prompted him to lift her hand to his lip. "Don't be afraid, sweetheart. I promise neither of us will ever regret our commitment to each other." Slipping her hand through his arm, he led her to the hearth where Joe and the deputy he'd coerced into being a witness waited.

PLAYING BEST MAN as well as minister, Joe surprised her when he held a delicate gold wedding band out to Stona. Accepting the ring, he lifted her left hand as he gave her his vow.

"I've never believed in fate, but I am convinced we were destined for this moment. I have no doubt we would have found each other under different circumstances." He slipped the ring on her finger. It was a perfect fit. "I will remain at your side until my dying day. I will love you, Wilhelmina McAllister, forever and always."

Joe gave her a ring to slip on Stona's finger. She repeated her vows, her voice so low the older man leaned close to hear the words. Her friend smiled and glanced at Stona when she omitted the word obey. She might be a little uncertain, but she wasn't stupid.

She barely heard Joe pronounce them husband and wife. Nor did she note the deputy's departure. The depth of Stona's love had been in his words, in his eyes as he promised to love her forever and in the gentle touch of his lips on hers, sealing his vow. Their wedding had been perfect. She even forgave her new husband for calling her Wilhelmina.

Joe surprised them with the wedding supper. Apparently, he'd ordered carry-out while he was in town. He set the table, heated the roast and vegetables, and placed them in serving dishes on the table. When they saw he'd only set two places at the table, she set another, and insisted he join them. After all, the wedding had been his idea. Stona carried a plate out to the deputy.

By silent agreement, no one mentioned this morning's attempt on her life, or Stona's near brush with death. This was their wedding day, after all, and tonight…. Her cheeks suddenly warmed.

Stona noticed. "Are you all right? You look a little flushed."

She had the most insane desire to laugh. "I'm fine." She frantically searched her mind for a change in topic. "The ring," she blurted out. "Where did you find our wedding rings, and my bouquet?"

Stona leaned back in his chair and grinned. Was drop-dead gorgeous still a term used to describe an exceptionally handsome man? Her new husband was certainly that. She was so busy drooling over him she almost missed his explanation.

"I found the local jewelry shop online and checked out their wedding bands. A couple of the basic styles were stocked in a variety of sizes for men and women. I purchased the rings online and Joe picked them up. He stopped by one of the florist shops for your bouquet."

"How did you know my ring size?"

Still grinning, he reached into his suit coat pocket and produced one of the dinner rings she kept in her jewelry box. She raised a questioning brow. "You went through my stuff? When?"

Laughing, he shrugged. "When I realized I was out of my element. Joe suggested I find one of your rings for comparison."

The old man grunted and shook his head. "He wanted to tie a string around your finger."

Stona shrugged. "It would've worked, though I have to admit it would have ruined the surprise." He reached for her hand and rotated the ring on her finger. "When we have an opportunity, you can choose a band you prefer."

"I prefer this one. It's the ring you put on my finger when you said your vows. No other ring could be more beautiful or more precious."

He placed a chaste kiss on her lips. "Then we'll find a matching engagement ring."

They shared the task of cleaning the kitchen. Even Joe grabbed a dishtowel, and together they made short work of it.

By eight o'clock, Joe declared he'd put in a long day and was tired. He also insisted he was too exhausted to climb the stairs and asked Stona to bring his pillow and blankets downstairs. He would make his bed in the study for the night. Since he seldom slept in the bed anyway, no one argued with his decision. A few minutes later, clutching his bedding to his chest, he bid them good night and closed the study door.

Stona put his arm around Willie's shoulders and slowly led her up the stairs to what was now their bedroom. Her heart rate increased with each step. Her concern wasn't what would happen in the next few hours. She wasn't a naïve virgin—well, a virgin, yes, but not naïve. She wasn't afraid of their physically coming together. She instinctively knew Stona would be a gentle lover.

Her worry stemmed from the enormity of what they were doing. Had circumstances forced them into a commitment neither was truly ready for? They'd only known each other for a handful of weeks and their situation had drawn a line in their relationship neither had felt comfortable crossing—not even in the dark hours of the night when he'd shared her bed.

And now they were married. Would there be regrets?

FORTY-EIGHT

"MISGIVINGS?"

Sometimes he was a bit *too* perceptive.

They'd stopped in front of the bedroom door.

"Sweetheart?"

She flinched.

He gently pulled her into his arms and lifted her chin. "Baby, look at me." She did and was warmed by the tenderness in his gaze. "You know we won't do anything you don't want to. If it's too soon, if you're not ready, we can wait." He cupped her cheek and bent to touch his lips to hers. The kiss was tender, brief, and soothing. His fingers slipped into the hair at her nape and began to rub her neck.

She leaned into his embrace, enjoying his gentle massage. He'd mistaken her hesitance for wedding night anxiety.

"Better?"

"Yes." She gazed up at him. "But I'm not worried about tonight." Then she shook her head. "That's not entirely true. I'm worried *you'll* have regrets."

"You can't believe I'll be disappointed. You're open and kind and gentle and giving and passionate. How can you keep from pleasing me?"

He was still getting it wrong, but his kisses distracted her.

"So passionate," he whispered, nuzzling her neck.

"How can you know I'm passionate? We've never...."

"I've seen you spitting mad. If you're as passionate in loving as you are when you're angry, you'll probably kill me." He nipped her shoulder. "But I'll die with a smile on my face."

He was being outrageous, and she was about to tell him so when he swooped her into his arms.

She grabbed his neck. "Stona, your wound."

"I'm being careful." He carried her into the room, kicking the door shut as he walked to the bed. Her body slid down his until her feet touched the floor. He bent and gently kissed her until she was breathless. The pins and clips that held her hair were suddenly gone, and his fingers threaded through the thick auburn mass, capturing a handful to hold her still while he nibbled and licked her lower lip.

He gently lifted her chin and waited for her to look up at him. "From the moment I saw you standing on the porch steps I couldn't get you out of my mind."

She grinned. "I didn't like you much then."

He laughed. "I could tell. You threw me out of your house."

"You practically accused me of murder."

"I was doing my job, and you weren't making it easy."

The zipper at the back of her dress lowered, seemingly of its own volition. He teased the garment off her shoulders.

"You like me well enough now." His teeth nibbled a path from her ear to the spot where her neck and shoulder joined. Goosebumps followed in his wake. She felt like purring.

He lifted the necklace over her head. She tried to stop him, but he caught her hand, raising it to his lips. "Only for tonight," he promised, setting the spearhead on the nightstand. "The necklace is part of your past. This night we celebrate our future."

His mouth covered hers for a deep, drugging kiss she never wanted to end. His fingers loosened the clasp of her bra, his hands shivering down her body. She dragged her mouth free when the wisp of lace fluttered to the floor, with her dress.

She grabbed the quilt on the bed and pulled it in front of her. "Wait. We need to talk first."

He stared at her, his eyes glazed with passion. "Talk? Now?" He drew a shuddering breath. "About what?"

"You have to be sure you want this."

He tried to pull her into his arms again. "Sweetheart, I've never wanted anything more in my life than I want you."

She stepped back, tangled her legs in the quilt, and would have landed on the floor if he hadn't caught her. She grasped his arms and righted herself. "I'm not talking—I *know* you want me. It's not what I'm asking."

Concern tempered the desire in his eyes. "What are you so worried about?"

"Before we commit ourselves completely, I need to be sure you didn't marry me out of a misguided sense of duty."

He clasped her face in both hands and kissed the bridge of her nose. "Willie, sweetheart, weren't you listening when I gave you my vows? I promised to love you forever. If I'd had any reservations, we wouldn't be standing here now." His mouth covered hers in a thorough, tongue-thrusting kiss that weakened her knees.

Their eyes met and held. "Now tell me, have I rushed you into marrying me? Is that really what this is about?"

She shook her head. "We've only known each other a matter of weeks, but I can't imagine spending the rest of my life without you."

He pulled her against him, his hand gliding lower to caress her throat. "Wait."

He heaved an exasperated sigh. "Baby, if I don't get to touch you soon, I'll go crazy."

"I should've brought this up sooner—much sooner. I know we're married, and someday we'll want children... but right now...." She knew the minute he understood.

Smiling, he reached into his pocket, extracted several small foil-wrapped packets, and tossed them on the bedside table. "I intended to protect you."

Her eyebrows rose at the number of packets he'd tossed down, and she angled a questioning look in his direction.

Chuckling, he bent to nuzzle her neck. "A man can always hope."

Stona rained kisses from her lips to her throat as he unbuttoned his shirt. She thought she might have helped him slide it off his shoulders. She did remember unbuckling his belt. By the time he stepped back to kick out of his shoes and pants she was breathless.

He was magnificent.

Powerful shoulders and chest, sculpted abs, muscular hips and thighs—the man was every woman's fantasy—and more. She might have drooled over him if her mouth hadn't suddenly gone dry.

He sat her on the edge of the bed, removed her shoes, then skimmed his palms up her calves and thighs. His fingers hooked the band of her panties, peeling them down her legs and over her feet. He kissed her toes before lifting her to the center of the bed. After a moment to see to her protection, he rolled onto the bed and his hot sexy body came down on top of her. They were skin to skin, his body touching hers everywhere. The light spring of hair on his chest teased her sensitive nipples into hard nubs. She couldn't catch her breath.

"Am I too heavy?" He raised up, easing his weight from her upper body, his thighs settling between her legs, his arousal pressing more intimately against her heat. She moaned.

Chuckling, he kissed her eyes, her lips, her throat, and all the while his hands glided over her, caressing her hips, lifting first one thigh then the other, inching his hard length closer until the tip of his arousal sought and found her.

He groaned.

She nearly choked on her indrawn breath.

"It's okay, baby, I only want a taste. We'll go slow. I promise."

His mouth covered hers, his tongue wild, seeking. He kissed a path to her throat and lower, teasing and stroking first one nipple then the other, until both glistened with moisture. His breath fanned across the sensitized peaks. The buds tightened and puckered. She nearly came off the bed, inadvertently taking in a little more of him.

He groaned. "Ahh, sweetheart, you're perfect." His lips closed over a taut peak and sucked it into his mouth. Her fingers grasped his shoulders and she arched her back in response. He slipped a little deeper.

His hand skimmed down her belly, his fingers splaying across her pelvis, pressing her hips into the mattress to hold her still as he paid homage to the other breast. He leaned up to kiss her, slanting his lips across hers again and again. She could feel him throbbing inside her, his primitive hunger igniting primal passions in her. Grasping his hair, she returned kiss for kiss.

His hand glided down her body, his fingers slipping through the curls at the junction of her legs to find and tease the most sensitive part of her.

"Stona!" She grasped his arm and tried to pull his hand away.

He stilled. His mouth touched hers in a gentle, teasing kiss. "I'm not hurting you, am I?"

She shook her head. It was all she could do. He was inching into her, pulling out, inching inside again in a slow, shallow rocking rhythm.

"We'll stop if you want to."

"No. Don't stop yet."

He laughed. "We won't, sweetheart." He increased the rhythm, delving a little deeper with each gentle thrust. Her mind and body centered on the exquisite pleasure he was giving her.

"Stona, please!" She wasn't sure what she was asking of him. Only knew she wanted more. He bent to kiss her, his tongue rubbing against hers, exploring her mouth, taking her out of time and place until there was only him. His hands caressed her thighs, lifting them, his arousal throbbing, gliding deeper. She moaned as her body stretched around him and pushed forward, drawing a groan from him. "I didn't expect it to feel so…."

"Tight?" He managed.

"Perfect."

He touched his forehead to hers. "Same difference."

———————

HE BARELY GOT the words out. She was so tight, his path so slick. The sexy little sounds she made were shredding his control. He pressed forward, retreated, pressed forward again. Each thrust deeper and agonizingly slow—each retreat an anticipation of the next thrust.

Her virginal barrier ended the game. Without giving her an opportunity to fret over what would come next, he thrust through the membrane, planting himself in her liquid heat, catching her cry with his kiss.

He knew he'd hurt her. "I'm sorry, baby. Give it a minute. It'll be all right in a minute." He hoped he was right. The need to move was killing him. He throbbed with the urge to finish what they'd started. He wouldn't though. Not until she was ready to join him in the bliss.

THE GUILT IN Stona's voice pulled Willie from the haze of pain. Her virginity was a gift she could only give once. She had given it to him, and with it her love and loyalty. Grasping his shoulders, she touched her lips to his ear. "Don't regret being my first lover—my only lover. Make me forget the pain. Make me forget everything but loving you."

He lifted his head to look at her. She was nearly mesmerized by the intensity in his beautiful brown eyes. "Do you know how much I love you?"

She touched the bandage on his bicep. "Enough to take an arrow for me." She locked an arm around his neck, pulling him down and pressed her lips to his. He deepened the kiss, rocking forward, sinking deeper until his pelvis rested full against hers. The tingle of pleasure caught her by surprise. She whimpered.

"Baby?" He started to pull out.

She lifted her hips, fully embedding him. "Don't leave me. You... I... do it again."

And he did, each thrust and retreat intensifying the sweet pressure. His strength surrounded her, his scent and taste pushing her over the edge. She stiffened, tightening around him, her body pulsing with every thrust.

"Stona!"

Air hissed through his teeth as he increased the tempo. His mouth covered hers. She was mindless to everything but Stona's husky promises, his body driving her beyond control. She cried out, lifting her hips to meet his thrusts, squeezing him as wave after wave of exquisite pleasure engulfed her.

He roared her name and drove deep, thrusting again and again before fusing their bodies as they found release together.

Collapsing on top of her, he buried his face in her hair, gasping for breath. He lifted his head, and brushed the hair away from her face to gaze into her eyes. "Are you all right?"

She smiled and nodded. Her body still thrummed. "It was uncomfortable at first, but when you began moving it felt...."

He rolled to his side, taking her with him, and nuzzled her neck. "Was it good?"

Snuggling close, she sighed. "Amazing."

Chuckling, he began rubbing her back in slow, soothing circles. "Yeah, amazing."

He slipped from the bed and went into the bathroom, returning a few minutes later. She was awake enough to see him wince when he braced his arms on the mattress to climb in beside her.

Sitting up, she pulled the sheet over her breasts, and glanced at the bandage on his bicep. Flecks of dark red dotted the gauze. "You're bleeding."

"Not enough to worry about." He reached for her, but she scooted away, dragging the sheet with her as she slipped out of bed.

"I'll be right back." She smiled before closing the bathroom door behind her. After washing, she traded the sheet for a robe hanging in the bathroom.

That afternoon, she'd set Stona's antibiotics and pain medication in the adjoining bathroom cabinet thinking he'd have easier access. He'd taken the antibiotic at dinner, but refused the Tylenol/codeine medication Dr. Jeffries had prescribed for pain. Opening the container, she shook a tablet into her palm, and filled a paper cup with water. Returning to bed, she held out the cup and white pill. "Take this."

He tilted his head in question. "What is it?"

"The pain medication Doctor Jeffries prescribed for you."

"I don't need it."

"Yes, you do. I saw the grimace on your face when you climbed into bed."

"Let me put it another way. I don't want it."

She didn't care for his tone of voice, but held her patients—barely. "Stona, I don't care how paltry you think that wound is. We both know you're hurting right now, especially after we...."

He leaned up and took the cup and pill from her, setting both on the stand. Pulling her down on top of him, he nuzzled her neck, nipping her ear, before sucking the abused lobe into his mouth, tickling it with his tongue.

He made short work of removing her robe and rolled her to her back surrounding her with his hot, hard body. "What about you?"

She was having a hard time concentrating on the conversation. "What about me?"

"I know I hurt you. Are you still sore?"

Her cheeks warmed but she shook her head.

"Promise?"

She nodded. "I promise."

He reached for one of the packets on the stand and rolled to her side. "If you're sure," he whispered against her neck.

FORTY-NINE

HOW COULD TWO people so in tune twenty minutes ago be at such odds now?

"I'm not going anywhere until we've buried Stone Shaper." Willie rolled away from Stona, intent on leaving their bed. He rolled her right back around to face him and towered over her.

"This isn't open for debate. You are not going *anywhere* near Nevada."

"The burial site Joe told us about isn't near Nevada."

"It's close enough and you aren't going there."

"We've only been married, what, a few hours, and you already think you can tell me what to do? It won't work, Stona. I am not going to play the obedient little woman to your I-always-know-what's-best man. This marriage is already in big trouble if that's how you think it's going to be."

He shook his head. "You know me better than that. This is an exception. Whether you like it or not, I won't let you endanger your life."

"An exception, huh?" She nodded toward the white tablet sitting beside the cup of water on the nightstand. "And was your refusal to take the pain medication another of your reasonable exceptions?" She didn't give him time to answer. "I'm a nurse. I'm trained to know more about your body's reaction to trauma than you do. But did that stop you from deciding you knew more about it than I did? I'm beginning to think in this marriage your exceptions are the rules."

"Fine." He leaned over, popped the pill into his mouth, drained the cup of water, and tossed it toward the small waste can "Satisfied?"

"That you've taken your pain medication? Yes, I'm satisfied, but I haven't changed my mind about leaving. We need to bury Stone Shaper without delay. It's disrespectful to leave him in a bag in the trunk of your car."

"Sweetheart, he's rested in a cold dark cave for two hundred years. He can wait a little longer."

"If it were only his body, I might agree, but we're dealing with his spirit, and with Beth's, too. He's been in limbo for those two hundred years, tied to the Earth, to this piece of land so far from his home and people. And Beth. She loved him enough to seek out his spirit and watch over him through the years."

She pulled back enough to look into his eyes. "Who knows how long it will take to catch the killer. That madman has managed to elude you for more than a decade. I can't wait another decade."

"If it means your life, yes you can."

She shoved against his chest. "The ring you put on my finger doesn't make you my master. The honeymoon will be over real soon if you believe that. I'm your wife, not a prisoner to be carried off to who knows where."

"You may be my wife, but that won't stop me from personally dragging you to St. Louis."

"You wouldn't do that."

"Don't test me." He sighed, clearly frustrated, rolled to his back, and stared at the ceiling. In a calm, still firm voice he said, "I'll do whatever it takes to keep you safe, but I'll be there to see you through it."

She lay beside him, as stiff as an over-starched shirt. The silence made her want to scream. This wasn't how her wedding night was supposed to end. She fought the tears welling in her eyes. You weren't supposed to cry on your wedding night. She blamed her sorry condition on the seesaw of emotions she'd experienced in the last few hours—finding

Stone Shaper at last, being attacked, nearly losing Stona, and finding herself married. She sniffed.

He groaned and pulled her into his arms. "Let's not fight, baby. This is our wedding night. I don't want to mar it with anger. Tomorrow, when our heads are clear, will be soon enough to discuss this. Tonight, we should be thinking about how much we love each other."

She slipped an arm around his waist and snuggled against him. He was right. An argument was no way to begin a marriage. Yet she couldn't escape the need to right the centuries-old sin that had been laid at her feet. She doubted she'd ever be free of the guilt, but she could at least make sure Stone Shaper found peace.

STONE SHAPER'S LONGHOUSE lay in shadows. The fire in the center of the room burned low, the embers glowing gold. Beth sat close to the heat on a buffalo robe, her gaze on the flickering flames.

"Why are you here?"

Beth was alone. Who was she talking to?

Beth swung around, her angry blue eyes pinning Willie with a glare. "Answer me! Why are you here?"

Caught off guard by the woman's fury, Willie shook her head. "I don't know." Something wasn't right. She was never directly addressed in her visions—had never been aware of being in a vision.

She was now.

Beth got to her feet. "How long will you wait to give my husband peace? It is your obligation as the chosen one."

She moved closer, and Willie resisted the urge to back up. "Why do you consider your own safety when my husband suffers confusion and anguish? He has been bound to this plane far too long. His spirit grieves. My heart breaks because I cannot comfort him as a wife should. You must not allow others to decide your actions. Go now."

WILLIE JERKED AWAKE. Stona's arms tightened around her, but he didn't rouse. The pain medication she'd goaded him into taking must have been strong enough to keep him from waking.

She slipped out of bed and walked into the bathroom. After splashing water on her face, she gazed at her reflection in the mirror. *'Go now.'* Beth's mandate replayed in her mind. Forget her own safety, forget everything but her family's obligation—to right the wrong her ancestor had caused.

Returning to the bedroom, she slipped the necklace over her head and quickly dressed, glancing at her husband more than once. His deep, even breathing reassuring her. After penning a quick note to Stona, she crept down the stairs in her stocking feet, her shoes, purse, cell phone, and Stona's car keys in hand.

The humiliation she'd experienced when she'd discovered the papers tying her to Bear hadn't diminished. But the need to free Stone Shaper was stronger. She couldn't ignore Beth's plea. And she couldn't wait for the marshal's office to find the man who wanted her dead. Heading for the mud room, she hoped Joe was a sound sleeper. After slipping on her shoes, she shrugged into her heavy jacket, buttoned it to her chin and quietly left the house.

No one had thought about moving the canvas bag from Stona's trunk. Before her argument with Stona, she had assumed they would be taking Stone Shaper's remains to the burial site the following day. She glanced at her watch. Today. The attempt on her life had changed that—as far as Stona was concerned. At least she didn't have to worry about loading the bag in the car.

She *did* have to worry about making it past the guards watching her home. Moving cautiously into the back yard, stealth gave way to speed the minute she opened the car door and the interior light came on—a dead giveaway to any guard looking in her direction. Lunging into the driver's seat, she slammed the door and activated the locks. Someone yelled as she started the car, threw it in reverse, and angled around to face the lane. The car hadn't come to a complete stop before she shoved the gear into drive and stomped the accelerator, throwing gravel as the vehicle fishtailed away from the house. More shouts—the harsh tone making her glad she couldn't hear the words.

Darkness forced her to turn on the headlights. How many deputies had been assigned to watch them? She knew about the one in the barn. He probably did the yelling. And the sheriff had mentioned at least one patrol car. Were they still out there keeping an eye on what little traffic traveled the farm road this time of night? She skidded onto the blacktop without slowing down. There was an intersecting farm road on the right less than a mile from her driveway. The sheriff's men weren't likely to patrol it. If she could reach the turn before being seen, she could bypass the town and connect with the state highway at the other end.

What happened after that would be up to Stona. She blinked back tears of remorse—and guilt. She'd been suffering a lot of that particular emotion recently.

Was she betraying the man she loved? Shaking her head, she reminded herself this wasn't the eighteenth century. Married or not, she was her own person capable of making her own decisions—though, she conceded, marriage was a shared endeavor. She prayed he would understand. There really wasn't any choice. She owed this to the man her ancestor had murdered.

FIFTY

THE INCESSANT KNOCKING grew louder. Stona rolled over and reached for Willie. She wasn't there. "Sweetheart?"

Still the knocking.

He swung his legs over the side of the bed and reached for his pants. "Hold on. I'm up. Give me a minute." Slipping into his shoes, he stumbled to the door, and found Joe on the other side, looking agitated.

"What's wrong?"

"Someone took your car."

"My car?" He rubbed the back of his neck, trying to rid himself of the lingering thick fog in his brain. "Did you see who took it?"

"No. Deputy Collins woke me. He didn't get a look at the driver."

"Where's Willie?"

Joe seemed confused. "She isn't here with you?"

"No." He switched on the light, and glanced around the room, his gaze stopping at the nightstand. He'd dropped his keys beside his wallet and gun last night. The keys were gone. So was Willie's phone—and the spearhead necklace he'd placed there. A folded piece of paper rested against the lamp.

Moving to the bed, he scooped up his shirt and put it on before reading the note. A few seconds later he crumpled the paper and tossed it aside.

Considering their argument last night, he knew *exactly* where she was. In his car on her way to Nevada. Bending, he tied his shoes then buttoned his shirt and tucked it in. The woman was certifiable taking off in the middle of the night knowing a killer stalked her. He was tempted to call his office and have her picked up.

Clipping on his gun, he shoved the wallet in his back pocket and grabbed his phone, punching her speed dial number as he walked into the hall and headed for the stairs. The call went immediately to voicemail. He left a clipped message ordering her to let him know where she was.

"Find a public place and wait for me. I'm right behind you."

"What was in the note?"

Stona glanced over his shoulder at the man puffing after him. "Three words. Come after me."

"Smart girl."

"I swear, I don't know if it was a challenge or a plea." He didn't even try to hide his anger. It was all he could do to keep from shouting his frustration.

He dialed the sheriff's office. Sometimes being a Deputy U.S. Marshal had its perks. The dispatcher didn't argue when he told her to get the sheriff out of bed. Five minutes later, the man was on the line. "What's the problem, Deputy?"

"I want a statewide APB put out on Willie McAllister."

"I thought she wasn't a suspect. You were protecting her—"

"I still am. She… panicked and ran. I want you to handle this yourself. Make sure every agency knows this is a safety protocol only. If she's spotted, contact me. No one is to approach her unless she's in trouble."

"Is there anything else?"

"Nothing now. I'll be in touch. Thanks for your assistance."

Stona disconnected and glanced at Joe. "Where's the deputy?"

"In the barn." Joe shook his head. "I don't think he'll be much help, though."

Grabbing both coats from the hooks in the mud room, he tossed one to Joe "Oh, he'll be helpful. I'm taking his car."

WILLIE SPENT MORE time looking through her rearview mirror at the vehicles behind her than she did the road ahead. She was fairly sure she wasn't being followed yet—by friend or foe. She wasn't certain how many friends she had now. Joe, of course, would understand. But Stona... Stona was another matter. No doubt she had an irate groom pursuing her by now. She shook her head. He was more than her groom. He was her husband... her lover... the man who at the very least thought she was crazy, and might now believe she had betrayed him.

She hadn't betrayed him. Manipulated? Perhaps. She was desperate to have him understand the rightness of what she was doing—before he dragged her to St. Louis, and protective custody.

It was still dark when she took the first exit at Nevada. She hadn't dared stop before now, not even for a bathroom break. It had been crucial for her to make it this far before Stona caught up with her. Now she could relax—maybe. The note she'd left him was brief, and a little cryptic. She'd been afraid he'd wake before she got away.

The reason she'd taken off in the middle of the night was obvious and smacked of pure defiance. It was desperation, though. She prayed he'd realize the difference. If he didn't, he'd be livid.

It wouldn't stop him from coming after her, but he might be angry enough to make sure every department of every law enforcement agency in the state was looking for her. If so, and if someone else found her before Stona, they might take her back home, or worse, send her to the US Marshal's Office in St. Louis. It was what he'd intended to do this morning. Would they confiscate the car? If they did, what would happen to Stone Shaper's remains? Her sense of urgency returned.

Pulling into a busy truck stop, she drove to the back lot where most of the big rigs were fueled. Finding a pump with both diesel and regular gas, she hid her car between two semis and hurried inside to the restroom, then grabbed a breakfast-sandwich and coffee. She paid for everything, including the gas, with cash—no credit card trail. At the car, she fueled up, then took a moment to check Joe's map.

Fortunately, she'd taken the precaution of going online and adding county road numbers to the lines Joe had drawn. At the time, she hadn't thought she'd need them. But old habits were hard to break, and two years as a paramedic before becoming an air-vac nurse had taught her to make sure of the numbers. Without Joe's guidance, the farm road numbers would be indispensable.

Leaving Nevada without being noticed turned out to be easier than she'd anticipated. Turning east onto Highway 54, she left the lights and traffic of the town behind, the road stretching dark and lonely before her. A couple of cars followed but were too far behind to pose a threat.

She finally spotted the first junction, County Road 1900, to her left. After making the turn, she kept an eye on her rearview mirror. The cars behind her didn't leave the highway. She was both relieved and disappointed. Stona couldn't be too far behind her now.

She followed a maze of county roads and curves, stopping at every intersecting road to double check the road signs or landmarks Joe had provided. Several times she thought she'd seen headlights a ways back, but none had gotten close.

After turning onto the final county road marked on the map, she watched for the narrow drive with the blue and white cattle gate. The lane, Joe had explained, wound up and around a high hill. There, hidden within the forest, were the ancient burial places of Stone Shaper's people.

A gleam of white in the distance caught her attention. She slowed the car to a crawl, prepared to turn. A milk can, holding a short post with a mailbox mounted on top, seemed to materialize out of the darkness, its reflective, light-colored paint making it impossible to miss.

Headlights in the rearview mirror caught her attention. Could it be Stona, or someone he'd sent after her?

She almost missed the gate. There, on the right, at the end of a long curve. She braked, skidding past the weed-covered drive, raked the gears into reverse, and shot back far enough to make the turn. Nudging the front of the car close to the blue and white gate, she killed the lights and motor and waited for the car rounding the curve to pass.

The vehicle skidded to a stop, its red brake lights bright in the dark. Her heart caught in her throat. If it were a law enforcement vehicle there would be lights flashing right now, wouldn't there?

It might be Stona. Please God, let it be Stona. The silent prayer became a chant in her head as she dug through her purse and found her phone.

The road behind the vehicle suddenly flooded with light as the car backed up, pulling across the drive, blocking her only escape. She couldn't breathe. A cry barely passed her lips, escaping as a strangled whimper.

She hit Stona's speed dial. Her hand shook as she lifted the phone to her ear. Someone was walking toward her car, a large-beamed flash-light aimed through the back window spotlighting her.

"Where are you?" Stona's angry voice through the phone startled her. She almost dropped it.

"Stona, is that you behind me? Please tell me it's you."

"Someone's behind you? Who?"

"You aren't walking behind my car with a flashlight?"

"No. Willie get out of there, now!"

"I can't. He's blocking the road."

"Where are you?"

"At the gate—at Joe's gate. He's running now. Stona, he's here, he's trying to break into my car!"

"Who?"

"I don't know. I can't see his face. He's big and so strong he's shaking the car."

"We're close, Willie. Just a few minutes away. Where's your gun?"

"I didn't bring it. I didn't think about it."

The large light her attacker had been shining in her face suddenly arced high over his head and rocketed down toward the window.

"Stona!"

FIFTY-ONE

A LOUD CRASH and breaking glass merged with her scream.

"Willie!"

No answer.

"Willie, talk to me." She still didn't say anything, but the line wasn't silent. He heard her groan and a metallic click. A door lock or maybe her seatbelt latch? He couldn't tell.

Joe slapped his shoulder, pointing to the right where the road forked. Stona jerked the wheel in that direction, sliding into the ditch and back out. He slammed the accelerator to the floorboard and lifted the phone to his ear again.

Silence.

"He's got her." Stona didn't try to hide the tremor in his voice. Terror? Anger? He didn't have time to identify the emotions tightening his throat.

He'd never been so helpless—or scared.

She was alone out there with a killer, and he was powerless to stop whatever was happening to her. He slammed his fist so hard against the steering wheel the old man jumped.

"It isn't far now, three, maybe four miles."

Joe's calm reassurance did nothing to ease his mind. He kept telling himself she was alive. She had to be alive. He wouldn't be able to hold it together long enough to save her if he thought otherwise.

The sun was lighting the eastern sky when they made what Joe promised was the last turn. After a couple of minutes, the road arced into a long curve.

"There, on the right. I see her car!" Joe's normally calm demeanor evaporated into an anxious excitement. "Pull in."

Stona swerved in behind the rental, threw the vehicle in park, and hit the emergency lights. The squad car was still rocking when he jumped out and ran to the other vehicle.

Willie wasn't in sight. The driver's door hung open, the window broken. Inside, blood spattered the safety belt, seatback, and steering wheel—*her* blood.

"She is alive." Joe's stoic voice broke through Stona's haze of fear and anger.

Taking a deep breath, he nodded at the older man. "I know. He's decided not to kill her, at least not right now."

It was completely out of character for the man. He'd never kidnapped a victim before. He'd come close to killing Willie twice—would have if things had gone as he'd planned. So why keep her alive now? Stona was both relieved and terrified by the killer's irrational tactics. Relieved because he was giving them time to find her, terrified by what she might be suffering while they searched for her.

"We have to find her." He pulled out his phone and hit her speed dial number. Holding the phone away from his ear, he listened intently. If she had the phone with her and was close by, they might hear her ringtone.

And they did.

His hopes soared for no more than a second or two before plummeting into despair. The familiar sound came from inside the car. Brushing the fragmented glass out of the way, he leaned in, located the source of the sound, and ran his hand between the seat and console. He found her cell. Straightening, he stuffed the phone into his coat pocket and looked around. Walking to the front of the car, he studied the ground and fence rows on either side of the gate.

Joe came to stand beside him. "What are we looking at?"

"The weeds." He pointed to the area he'd been scrutinizing. "Nothing's been disturbed up here. No one came this way." He pivoted and headed toward the squad car. "Back here, the overgrowth tells a different story. The dried vegetation's been trampled, and not just by us." The sky was getting brighter, but he still reached into the police car for a flashlight and swept the beam over the crushed, mostly brown vegetation.

"There!" He knelt by the side of the road, shining the light where the pavement and ground joined.

Joe dropped down beside him. "What?"

"Blood. Look at the stain. It isn't smeared like it would be if she were struggling. The grass is compressed here. I don't think Willie's conscious." He sucked in a quick, involuntary breath. "She has to be unconscious. He wouldn't take her with him if she were...." He couldn't finish the thought. Standing, he panned the light across the immediate area.

"Here, on the blacktop." Stona knelt again and centered his light on the pavement. "It's hard to tell, but...." He touched a discolored spot of moisture. His finger came away smeared with blood.

Getting to his feet, he moved to the driver's side of the patrol car. "Get in."

Joe paused at the passenger door. "What are we doing?"

"Going after Willie."

"Do you know where she is?"

"Not yet, but I intend to tear every inch of this county apart until I find her." He glanced at his rental and shook his head. "I swear, every car she drives becomes a crime scene. We'll call it in on our way."

Joe had started to climb into the car. He stopped and looked over the top of the car at Stona. "We cannot leave Stone Shaper's remains in the trunk of your car."

"We don't have time for this. Get in the car."

Joe shook his head. "If Stone Shaper's remains are found they will be confiscated. We may never have the opportunity of giving him the burial he deserves. Willie has risked much to give him peace. For her sake we can do no less."

Without a word, Stona reached into the squad car, pushed a button on the dash, then moved to the rear of the car and opened the trunk. They transferred the canvas bag, and Stona's government-issued ballistic vest from one car to the other. Stona was propelling them down the road minutes later, praying they were going in the right direction.

They'd gone less than a mile when Joe shouted, "Stop!" Stona slammed the brake pedal to the floor and the car skidded to a halt, crossways in the road facing an intersecting blacktop. The headlights flickered and Stona revved the motor to keep the car running.

Joe pointed straight ahead. "Do you see him?"

Stona squinted in the direction he'd indicated. "See who?"

"Stone Shaper. He's standing in front of us."

Grasping the wheel, Stona leaned forward and stared through the windshield before shaking his head. "We both know I've never been able to see him. What's he doing?"

"Nothing. His back is to us." A moment later Joe shook his head. "He's gone."

Stona pulled the car to the side of the blacktop before glancing at his friend. "What's going on?"

"I'm not sure. I think Stone Shaper wants us to take this side road."

"To find Willie?"

"Yes, I think so."

"Why?"

"You forget she is the chosen one. It is her duty to see his remains are given the proper Osage burial." Joe tilted his head and studied Stona. "Do you also forget you are Stone Shaper's descendent? Willie is your wife, and you love her even as he loves Beth. That alone would give him reason to help you find her."

"So we follow him?"

"We can drive around, blindly following one road after another, or we can...." Joe shrugged his narrow shoulders.

"Blindly follow the ghost of my great-great-great grandfather, who, fortunately, you can see." Nudging the car onto the blacktop, he increased the speed as they moved forward.

Handing Joe a pen, he nodded toward the glove compartment. "Find something to write on and mark down the road numbers. We'll call this in when we're sure it isn't a wild goose chase."

Early-morning streamers of sunlight caught the tops of the trees, diminishing the shadows as they drove on, following their only lead to saving Willie. Joe pointed out another turn, and Stona wondered if they were going in circles.

Joe pointed to the left. "He's standing there, on that grassy slope. This time he's facing us. He hasn't moved. I think he wants us to stop."

Stona pulled to the side of the road, released his seatbelt, and opened the door. "Is he still here?"

"About twenty feet ahead of us." Joe followed Stona out of the car. "What are we looking for?"

"Tracks." He'd walked about ten feet from the car and knelt to examine the dried grass, then jumped to his feet. "Get in the car." He sprinted to the vehicle.

Joe was still closing his door when Stona swung the car onto the grass. "What did we find?"

"Tire tracks. They're heading up the hill."

Joe nodded. "It is good Stone Shaper has taken spirit form. You drove through him."

The incline became steeper, the trees closing in on both sides of the narrow lane. Following an arc in the tree line, they spotted a dark blue sedan in a small clearing.

As Stona maneuvered the car through brush and around trees, he used the deputy's radio to call for backup. After identifying himself and giving the dispatch a brief summary of the situation, he handed the mic to Joe.

"They need directions."

Stona loosened the seatbelt and unsnapped his holster strap. "Stay in the car and keep your head down." He didn't wait for Joe's agreement. Palm on his Glock, he opened the door and cautiously stepped out. Crouching low, making himself less of a target, he approached the sedan, his heart slamming against his ribs. Willie could be in the car.

He refused to allow himself to think about the worst-case scenario. She was alive. He'd know if she wasn't.

The killer could be hiding behind any tree surrounding the clearing. Lifting the gun from its holster, he aimed it toward the ground a few feet in the distance, while constantly scanning the woods.

The car was empty. The horrific images his mind had conjured were dispelled in that moment. He exhaled the breath he'd been holding and glanced around. The grass behind the vehicle had been trampled. His stomach tightened when he spotted a red smear on the bumper. A long, dark red strand of hair was caught in the now-dried blood.

FIFTY-TWO

THE EXCRUCIATING HEADACHE made it impossible to concentrate on anything else. The side of her head above her left eyebrow throbbed. Willie tried to touch the place but couldn't move her arm. Confused, she tried again.

Understanding came in a flurry of realizations. Her hands were bound behind her back. Something covered her eyes—and her mouth. Her outstretched feet were bound, too.

He hadn't killed her. *Yet.*

Rocks scattered. Something or someone was out there, wherever 'out there' was. Something stopped in front of her. She could almost feel its heat, could smell a hint of aftershave. A man. She might have fared better with a wild beast.

Warm fingers touched her face and she jerked upright. "I'm going to remove the tape from your mouth. If you scream, I'll kill you here and now. Have I made myself clear?"

His voice was vaguely familiar, though she couldn't remember from where. The threat was clear.

She nodded.

He ripped the tape away, drawing a surprised cry. The man chuckled. "Sorry about that."

She licked her lips and swallowed, trying to force moisture into her mouth. "Who are you?"

"Ah, you can't see me, can you? At this point it isn't going to matter if you can identify me." He pulled the blindfold over her head.

She blinked a couple of times before looking up at her assailant. "You?"

Jake Arnold squatted in front of her, a satisfied smirk on his face.

It *couldn't* be him—not the good-natured fireman who'd helped rescue her the night of the tornado. He'd saved her life. She couldn't wrap her mind around the possibility. Why would he save her life and then try to kill her?

"Remember me, do you? I remember you well enough. You've been a thorn in my side since the day you first walked into the Bushwhacker Museum. You didn't see me that day, did you? I noticed you and liked what I saw—until you started asking questions I didn't want answered. Your little brush with death that day offered me the perfect opportunity to be rid of you. I thought I was first on the scene. I couldn't believe my luck when I recognized your car. I thought the storm had saved me the trouble of killing you." He shook his head and heaved an exaggerated sigh. "But you weren't dead. I could have made sure you didn't come out of that wreck alive. A thick blanket pressed over your face would've done the trick. But your marshal friend beat me to you, and I ended up playing the hero. No matter. Good things come to those who wait, don't they? And here you are."

His taunting half smile thinned. "How did you find me?"

Confused, she shook her head and winced. The pain was close to unbearable. "I didn't find you. You found *me*."

He grabbed her chin. "You know what I mean. What gave me away?" There was an urgency in his voice.

Clarity struck her with the speed and intensity of a bolt of lightning. He wanted his curiosity appeased, wanted to know what he'd done wrong, find out who else was involved, tie up loose ends. It was the only reason she was alive.

"I had a sweet deal here before you and that deputy interfered. I'd bought a few secluded acres in the middle of the county. Nice place to retire. I should've bought an estate somewhere out of the country, maybe Greece. I have the money. You'd be amazed at how much people are willing to pay to have someone killed." He laughed. "I don't usually get to brag about my work, but I'm good at what I do—the best, in fact. I earn top dollar. One precise cut to a brake line will see the job done. A deadly accident on a major highway that couldn't be attributed to my client or myself."

He sighed, almost wistfully. "Yeah, it was sweet. I nodded to the neighbors in passing, went to church on Sunday morning, even volunteered at the Bushwhacker Museum and Fire Department. Made it real convenient for keeping track of what went on around me." He chuckled, but there was no humor in the sound. "Volunteer firemen monitor scanners for emergency calls."

He ran a finger down the damaged side of her face, smiling when she jerked away. "Did you know Marshal Jordan put an APB out on you?" He tilted his head. "Surprised? Don't worry about it. No one was supposed to stop you—just contact him. Made it easy for me, didn't he?

"So, now I have to wonder what gave me away? What made that deputy come nosin' round the museum a few months ago, asking about a certain area on the county maps? The area where I live. And you... you show up asking your own questions, wanting to see the same maps the deputy asked about."

She had trouble following his line of thought. *Deputy?* Did he mean Josh? Did he think Josh had been looking for him? She was suddenly horrified. Had Josh and Trish been murdered because this man jumped to the wrong conclusions?

He bent closer, his voice a whisper. "I followed you that day, to see what you were up to."

He laughed. "You surprised me when you went to the Osage village. I would've taken care of you then, but I spotted a black sedan parked on the road. You don't live outside the law as long as I have without recognizing a stakeout."

He jumped to his feet and kicked her outstretched legs. "Did you try to set a trap for me? Was that Jordan?" He shook his head. "It didn't matter. I drove away nice and easy with one eye on the rearview mirror." He began pacing, his head barely missing the rock overhang they were beneath.

Willie kept a cautious eye on him. There hadn't been time for her to figure out where she was. She'd been too frightened to care. She was still scared. Glancing around, she realized they were in a small clearing nearly surrounded by woods. The vegetation and trees ended about fifty feet from where she sat. There was nothing beyond that point, until she saw ledges and more trees a short distance away. Were they on the edge of a cliff? How would Stona ever find her in this wilderness?

Jake squatted in front of her again. "You still haven't told me how you knew."

She glared at him "You got it wrong."

"Got what wrong?"

"The deputy you murdered was my cousin, not someone I worked with. Use your head. You know I'm an airevac nurse, not a member of law enforcement. Josh and his fiancée were in Nevada for a funeral. Their visit to the museum concerned our family history. It had nothing to do with you. You killed two innocent people that day. Two people I loved."

He leaned closer and shrugged. "Mistakes happen."

"You murdered the only family I had left, and all you can say is, mistakes happen? You godless, psychopathic slime." She screamed in outrage and lunged forward, butting his face with her forehead. He teetered back, blood gushing from his nose.

Roaring, he reached for her throat, his fingers curling around her neck, cutting off the air. Black swirled like smoke in her vision. She was going to die.

Suddenly he released her.

Struggling to draw a breath, she tried to focus on the man standing above her, his attention on the woods.

He knelt and grabbed the tape he'd tossed on the ground, smashing it against her lips. "Someone's here. You get to live a little longer." He wiped his bloody nose on his sleeve and winced. Growling, he backhanded her.

FIFTY-THREE

"DID YOU HEAR that?" Stona glanced up the hill before popping the trunk on the patrol car and grabbing his bulletproof vest.

Joe jumped out of the car. "Hear what?"

"Screaming. From up there." Holstering his gun, he slipped off his coat and strapped on the vest. Tossing the deputy's flak jacket to Joe, he slammed the trunk hard. "I can't wait for backup." He was already sprinting toward the hill. "Stay by the radio. You'll need to guide the sheriff in. No lights or sirens."

Retrieving the Glock, he stayed low, stopping often to listen for any sound that might give the killer's position away. The hill grew steeper before leveling off and opening into a grassy terrace flanked by a huge limestone bluff. The trees had thinned, providing less cover. Ducking behind a large oak, he scanned the clearing. Ancient cliff fall had created a low overhang in the bluff. Most of the debris consisted of flat limestone slabs—none tall enough to conceal a man.

Where was Willie?

His gaze constantly shifting from one side of the expanse to the other, he crossed the open ground, and came to the edge of a sheer precipice that ended at the bank of what he assumed were the murky waters of the Osage River. He backed away from the drop off and turned. He was a target out in the open. But nothing moved in front of him, and anyone behind him would have to have wings.

Bending low, he sprinted toward the nearest cover—the rockfall under the low hanging ledge. The niche didn't offer much protection, but he didn't plan to be there long.

He crouched against the back wall, wondering where to look next when he spied a bit of plaid material sticking out from under a tilted slab of rock. He edged closer for a better look.

"Willie!"

Holstering his gun, he dropped to his knees in front of her. Bruises colored her head and cheek. Duct tape covered her mouth. Her wrists were taped behind her, but he found a pulse. She was alive. He could breathe again.

As gently as possible, he scooted her out from under the rock. The fresh scrapes on her arms told him her kidnapper hadn't been as careful when he'd shoved her in the niche. Cradling her in his arms, he peeled the tape away from her lips and kissed her despite the sticky residue.

"Sweetheart, can you hear me?"

She groaned and blinked up at him. "Stona?"

"I'm here. Are you all right?" Stupid question. She looked as if she'd walked out of a war zone. He brushed her hair away from the bloody bruise on her forehead. She winced when he touched the swelling on her jaw. He wanted to kill someone.

"Help me sit up."

He lifted her against his chest and glanced around. "Where is he?"

"I don't know. He hit me, and when I opened my eyes again you were here."

"We need to get out of here before he comes back." Stona tried to free her wrists, but the bindings were wrapped too tight. "I can't slip my fingers under it." He reached into his jeans pocket, then checked his coat. "I've lost my pocketknife. I'll have to carry you down."

"Wait. Use the spearhead. I'm wearing it."

Reaching into her shirt, he slipped the necklace over her head, and used the fluted edge to slice through the tape binding her hands and feet.

She moved her arms out from behind her. "I recognized him."

"What?"

"I recognized him." She grabbed his shirt front. "It's Jake Arnold. Remember him? The fireman who helped get me out of my car the night of the storm. The one who found my purse."

He remembered. Arnold was tall, wiry and strong. He'd seen him toss limbs the size of small trees out of the way so they could get to Willie. He'd worked hard to save her life that night. Now he wanted to kill her?

Pulling Willie to her feet, he steadied her as they moved out from under the ledge. She stumbled, but he caught her before she fell. He was handing her the necklace when she glanced over his shoulder.

"Stona, watch out!"

Her warning shout came a second before he felt the Glock being lifted from its holster. Stona pivoted, slashed out with the hand holding the spearhead. Clipping Arnold's wrist, he sent the gun flying into the tall grass.

Jake cried out, grabbed his hand, and staggered backward, blood oozing from a long thin gash. His eyes narrowed and he lunged at Stona, the force of his weight knocking them to the ground.

Both men rolled to their feet, and Stona grunted with satisfaction when he landed a punishing blow to his opponent's midsection. The man had dared to touch Willie. Her bruised and swollen face flashed hot in his mind. Bellowing, he grabbed the man's shirt and hauled him closer for an uppercut to the jaw that sent him sprawling on his back. Stona advanced. Jake raised his arm and aimed the Glock—at Willie.

Stona froze.

Arnold slowly climbed to his feet, staggering once before regaining his footing. Blood poured from the corner of his mouth. "Get over there." He waved the gun toward Stona and Willie ran to his side. He shoved her behind him.

"I think we're finished here." Jake took aim at Stona. "As much as I'd like to see the look on your face when I kill her, I should probably shoot you first. Safer that way. I haven't had a gun in my hands for a decade or so. They're too noisy, makes people ask unwanted questions." "I'll try to make this quick." He smirked. "It will probably be messy and painful."

Stona pivoted, swinging Willie toward the trees. "Run!" He pushed her forward, shielding her with his body.

The Glock fired. The first bullet missed.

The next one didn't.

FIFTY-FOUR

THE BULLETPROOF VEST saved his life. The impact ripped the breath from his body. His feet rolled out from under him and he went down hard, landing on his hands and knees.

"Stona?" Willie slowed, turning her head to look at him.

"Keep running." He surged to his feet, caught her around the waist, and half carried her to the safety of the trees. Bullets sizzled past their heads. Arnold hadn't exaggerated his inability with firearms. The faster he pulled the trigger, the wilder the shots.

They ducked behind a large oak. Stona glanced back at their pursuer, and stilled. Everything—the pain, the anger, the fear—vanished.

In front of him, stood an image straight out of the past.

Willie edged closer, grasping his arm. "It's—"

"Stone Shaper." Eyes wide with amazement, he held up his hand, exposing the bloody gash on his palm. "I can see him."

The killer backed away from the huge, silent warrior. Hunched for battle, the apparition slowly stalked his quarry, swinging his lethal war-club from side to side.

"He sees him, too." She glanced up at Stona. "How?"

"It's the spearhead. We were both cut during the fight."

JAKE ARNOLD WAS big, but Stone Shaper dwarfed the man. By the look on her kidnapper's face, the warrior terrified him. Was it the apparition's size or the bullets passing through him? Stone Shaper advanced one slow step after another. His prey stumbled back, his arm outstretched, weapon discharging.

She pressed her lips close to Stona's ear so he could hear her. "How many bullets were in your gun?"

"A full clip." He never took his eyes off the killer. "Eighteen rounds."

"Shouldn't he be running out—"

Silence.

Stona grabbed her shoulders. "Stay here." He moved to intercept the killer.

Emitting a bellow of rage, Stone Shaper raised his weapon and lunged. Arnold threw the empty gun at the warrior. It passed through, landing on the ground behind him.

Raising his hands defensively, Arnold pivoted and ran—off the edge of the embankment. His long, strangled scream ended with the sickening thud of flesh striking rock. Small pebbles scattered after him.

She ran to Stona, throwing herself into his arms. He pulled her against him, never taking his eyes off the warrior who had turned and was striding toward them. She stiffened, moved out of her husband's grasp and waited for what the warrior would do.

Stone Shaper's proud demeanor, so familiar to her, was nonetheless intimidating. He'd never been overly friendly, had, in truth found her a source of irritation.

Stona took her hand, pulling her into his side.

Less than ten feet separated them. Cradling the war club in his arms, he stood with one leg bent forward—a relaxed, nonaggressive stance—and nodded toward her battered face.

"He will not hurt you again." Straightening, he bowed his head in what she interpreted as a sign of respect. "You have acted with honor and bravery."

She understood. He no longer held her responsible for Bear's sins. "Thank you."

His attention shifted to Stona. There was pride in his eyes. With a quick, single nod, the warrior vanished.

Stona shook his head, then squeezed her hand. "Stay here. I need to check on Arnold." She wouldn't let him pull away. He patted her hand. "It'll only take a minute."

"I know, but I can't seem to let go of you."

"Okay."

She walked with him to the edge of the bluff and peered over the side. The sheer drop-off had to be over a hundred fifty feet, ending at the foot of the cliff where the ground angled into the muddy water. Jake Arnold's bloodied body lay at the river's edge, a foot bobbing in the swift water. His neck tilted at an unnatural angle. Even at this distance, she could see his lifeless eyes staring up at them.

She gagged.

Stona hauled her away from the edge. "Don't look at him."

Willie drew a deep, ragged breath and snuggled against his chest, finding comfort in his strong, steady heartbeat.

"It's over, sweetheart." His arms tightened around her. "Come on, let's get you off this mountain. Joe's probably worried."

For a few minutes, when the bullets were flying around them, she thought they were going to die. It amazed her they hadn't been shot. Stona had used his body to protect her. Watching him now, she was amazed by his calm, nothing-to-see-here attitude.

"I need to get my handgun." He pulled her with him to where Arnold had hurled the weapon.

There was something vaguely familiar and unsettling about the stiff way he moved. She'd seen the stiff-gated walk before, in patients at the hospital and at accident scenes—they moved as though they steeled themselves against the pain.

"Stona, what's wrong?"

He didn't bother to look at her. "With what?"

"With you. Tell me what's wrong with you."

"Wait a minute. I have to mark my gun's location." He let go of her hand and walked into the deeper grass. One glimpse of the gaping hole in his vest made her forget her own pain. She scrambled after him.

"You've been shot!"

He turned and caught her before she plowed into him. He shook his head before she could say anymore. "My vest was shot, not me."

"Take it off."

"Willie—"

"Take off your vest. I want to see your back."

He gave her an exasperated look. "The bullet didn't penetrate the vest. I'd have known if it had."

"Take it off, anyway. I need to make sure you're okay." Frowning, he released the Velcro straps holding the vest in place and dropped it on the ground.

She carefully lifted his shirt and wished she hadn't insisted. The point of impact was unmistakable. The blood red, half-dollar sized abrasion was below and slightly right of his left shoulder blade. If he hadn't worn the vest....

She gently touched the outline of the bruise with her fingertips. When he flinched, she pulled her hand away. "I'm sorry. When did this happen?"

"Just before we reached the trees."

"When you fell?"

"When I was knocked off my feet by the impact."

"I didn't realize.... Your back's going to be one big bruise." She dropped his shirt. "You'll need an x-ray to make sure you don't have any cracked ribs. The pain must be terrible." What about your arm?"

"It's fine."

"We'll need to check it out at the hospital, too."

He brushed the hair away from her face. "How's your head?"

"It's been better. We could probably both use a Tylenol about now."

"I'll mark the spot where my gun landed, then we can head down."

He pulled a small evidence bag from one of the pockets in his vest and opened it. Gathering a few good-sized stones, he mounded them beside the Glock before picking the weapon up by the barrel and slipping it into the evidence bag.

He pulled her into his arms, his eyes lingering on her bruised face. "I'm sorry I didn't stop him from hurting you."

Leaning up, she brushed her lips across his. "You kept him from killing me."

Rocks scattered in the distance. Stona shoved her behind him again and pulled his identification and badge from his pocket. A sheriff's deputy walked into the clearing from the crest of the hill, gun drawn.

Stona raised both hands high, the badge with his picture ID evident as the man approached. "I'm Deputy U.S. Marshal Stona Jordan."

The officer eyed his credentials before lowering his weapon and shouting over his shoulder. "I've got 'em! The marshal and Miss McAllister are up here!"

When she stepped out from behind Stona, the deputy frowned. "Ma'am, are you okay?"

Stona shook his head. "No, she isn't. She needs a doctor."

She patted his arm. "I can wait until we finish up here."

Two uniformed men crested the hill. The older of the two identified himself as Sheriff Wingate. Stona shook his hand, then introduced her. "Sheriff, this is my wife, Willie McAllister Jordan."

The sheriff tipped his hat then gave her an assessing look. "There's a paramedic team on site below. Currently, they're caring for an older gentleman, but they can see about your injuries, too."

"Joe's been hurt?" She grabbed Stona's hand. "How bad?"

The sheriff shook his head. "I'm not sure. He was unconscious when we found him, but he's awake now and sitting up. It looks like he received a blow to the head."

Stona glanced at her. "That's probably where Arnold was when I found you. He must have circled the area and found Joe. We're lucky he didn't kill him."

Sheriff Wingate agreed with a nod. We'd have been here sooner, but we lost radio contact, probably when your friend was attacked. Fortunately, we were close enough to hear the gunfire."

Seeing the ruined vest at Stona's feet, the sheriff whistled and glanced up. It looks like you've had your share of trouble, Marshal."

"You'll find Jake Arnold at the bottom of that cliff." He tilted his head toward the place the man had gone over. "He kidnapped my wife and tried to kill her." Stona lifted his vest, exposing the damage. "He attempted to shoot us in the back."

Wingate couldn't hide his astonishment. "Jake Arnold? The fireman?"

"The same."

"I've known Jake for years. He's well-liked in the community." He glanced at Stona. "You shoot him?"

Stona shook his head. "I'm ashamed to admit he was the one doing the shooting." He handed the evidence bag with the Glock to the sheriff. "Arnold's prints should be on the grip. With any luck, they'll be in the system and we'll discover who he really is. Justice may be able to connect him to a few related cold cases and the people who hired him."

The officer and his men walked to the edge of the embankment and studied the area below. After a brief conversation, they returned. One of the deputies continued past them, descending the hillside with cautious speed.

Sheriff Wingate stopped. "Deputy Brinkley will secure the death scene below. He'll take one of the paramedics with him to confirm the suspect's status."

"The marshal's office will be working the case with you. This is the culmination of an ongoing investigation."

Wingate removed his hat and rubbed the back of his neck before sighing. "Any idea of how he ended up going over the cliff?"

Stona shook his head. "He admitted he was a terrible shot, and it was true. Only one bullet found its mark while we were running for cover. Fortunately, my vest absorbed the impact. He kept firing even after we'd ducked behind a large tree. I expected him to circle around and come at us from a different direction, but he didn't. He stayed where he was and kept firing."

"Why didn't he rush you?"

Stona shrugged at the Sheriff. "I guess we'll never know what he was thinking. After the clip emptied, Arnold threw the gun away. I don't think he realized how close he was to the edge of the embankment. He stepped back and went over."

Willie shivered and he pulled her into his arms. "If you don't mind, I'd like to get my wife to a hospital."

The officer nodded toward a break in the woods several feet to the right. "There's a decent path over there. She'll find the going easier."

Stona took her hand and headed in that direction. The pace was slow and not just for her. From the stiff angle of her husband's body as they walked, it was obvious he was in as much pain as she was.

The sheriff noticed. "Looks like the hospital's emergency staff will be busy tonight."

FIFTY-FIVE

STONA AND WILLIE climbed the stairs together after bidding Joe good night. As he had done the night before, he opted to sleep on the pallet in the study. His excuse was the one he'd used then—the climb to his bedroom was more than he was ready to take on. Considering the knot on Joe's head, Stona didn't doubt it.

Switching on the light in their bedroom, Stona sagged in relief. The nightmare was over. Willie was no longer in danger. They staggered toward the bed like two drunken sailors and sank together on the side. She leaned into him. "Joe looked so tired tonight. Do you think he's all right?"

Stona began unbuttoning her blouse. "The doctors assured you twice he was fine." Leaning in, he kissed her nose—one of the few places on her face that wasn't bruised. The left side of her head and cheek were turning blue. She'd probably have a black eye by morning.

He shook his head. "You're as beat up as Joe, and I imagine I look worse than either of you."

"With reason. You were shot."

He kissed her again, on the lips this time. "Sweetheart, I've told you before, my *vest* was shot. The bullet didn't touch me. I'm a little stiff, but the soreness will work itself out."

She helped him slip the blouse from her shoulders. "I've seen your back. You're lucky the impact didn't crack a rib." She reached for the buttons on his shirt.

He smiled at how like an old married couple they acted. His smile faded though, when she brushed the hair out of her eyes, exposing the small, white bandage on her head. He skimmed a finger along the edge of the gauze.

"When I think of how close he came to killing you...."

She touched her fingers to his lips. "But he didn't. You stopped him." Standing, she eased the shirt away from his back, and helped him free his arms.

He unfastened her jeans and slid them down her legs, enjoying the silken feel of her thighs and calves as he helped her step out of the garment. Her bra and panties were little wisps of black lace. He forgot how to breathe.

Standing, he gently pulled her into his arms for a long thorough kiss. When he stepped back her bra dangled from the crook of her elbows. One tug of his finger, and it drifted to the floor, her panties quickly following. She looked at him in question.

He unfastened his jeans and lowered the zipper before grinning at her. "I thought you'd appreciate a hot shower after what you've been through today. You have dirt, dried blood, and what looks like a smear of grease in your hair."

He slipped out of the rest of his clothes.

Her cheeks pinkened. "You could've waited until I finished showering before you undressed."

His grin widened. "The shower's big enough for two." Her blush deepened to a lovely dark rose. He sighed in appreciation and laughed. "How can you be embarrassed after last night?"

She shrugged, trying to look everywhere but at him. "It's going to take me a while to get used to this."

"Can't think of a better way to get to know each other. By the time we're squeaky clean, you should be over your shyness. Come on, I'll help wash your hair."

———————

STONA DID WASH her hair, taking care not to get water on her bandage. They'd have to change his. The shower's hot spray eased the aches, and stiffness she'd acquired that day. Soaping his hands, he lathered her body, turning her away from him, drawing her back against his arousal to slowly skim his hands over her breasts, his fingers teasing her nipples into hard, sensitive nubs. His hand slid down her stomach, into the curls between her thighs, long fingers finding her heat. He delved deeper, and she groaned with the pleasure he gave her.

He stilled. "Am I hurting you?"

Caught up in his magic, she could only shake her head.

"Good." The word was a caress shivering over her body, making her knees go weak. His tongue traced the delicate shell of her ear. He kissed the side of her neck, his free hand cupping a breast, as she rode his fingers.

Pulling out, he turned her to face him, his mouth claiming hers, his tongue sweeping in to taste her. "I need you."

"Not yet."

Grabbing the bar of soap, she lathered his powerful shoulders and chest, her hands inching down, to circle his navel. He was fully aroused, had been since they'd stepped into the shower. Playing the seductress shouldn't be daunting. Yet she hesitated. Her eyes swept up his magnificent body to gauge his reaction. He didn't say a word, simply tilted his head and waited.

Dropping the soap, she lathered his lower belly. He tensed, his hands fisting at his sides. Her fingers closed around his arousal, squeezing and stroking him. Air hissed through his teeth. He pulled her hands away and reached for the packet he'd brought with them.

After seeing to her protection, he lifted her against him. "Put your legs around me, sweetheart." The second she moved to obey, he thrust into her, embedding himself fully.

She threw her head back and groaned.

"Willie?"

She was incapable of speech, could feel every powerful inch of him. When she didn't respond he started to pull out. She tightened her legs around his hips. "Stay."

He pulled out a little more. She thought he hadn't heard her demand, thought he was going to end it. Before she could protest, his arms tightened and with one agonizingly slow thrust he glided deeper, the delicious friction taking her breath away. She whimpered, circled his neck with her arms and kissed him, her tongue tracing his lower lip until he opened his mouth inviting her to taste him.

His exquisite, gliding thrusts quickened. She was mindless to everything but the feel of his hot, hard length driving her over the edge.

"Stona!" She tightened around his hard shaft, knew she was on the verge of losing control, of splintering into a million shards of light.

"I'm here, baby. I'm with you." He buried his face in her wet hair, kissed a path from her neck to her shoulder and thrust again, harder.

Her world exploded. She cried out as her body throbbed around him. He shared the moment, shouting her name, climaxing deep inside her.

"I love you, Willie." He sealed his vow with a sweet, lingering kiss.

Breathless, she leaned her head on his shoulder, and kissed his neck. "I love you, too."

WILLIE SNUGGLED INTO Stona's side, using his chest as a pillow. After they'd dried each other off and she'd redressed the bandage on his arm, he'd carried her to their bed. But sleep didn't come easy.

She lifted on an elbow and gazed into his shadow-darkened eyes. "The nightmare's really over, isn't it?"

He pulled her back into his arms. "Yes, it's over. Arnold can't hurt innocent people like Josh and Trish anymore."

"They've finally found peace."

"What about you? Have you found peace?"

"I'm not sure. So much has happened in such a short time. It will take me a while to process it all." She drew a deep breath and exhaled slowly. "How soon do you have to report to the St. Louis office?"

"Next week. I'm not sure how long I'll have to wait before my next assignment. The office has a decade of paperwork to wrap up on this case." He rested his cheek on top of her head. "We don't have to live there, though. I work out of the St. Louis office, but my assignments take me all over the state. Do you plan to return to the hospital in St. Louis?"

"If I do, it won't be as an airevac nurse. I was beginning to burn out, and after Josh...." She paused a long moment before finally smiling up at him. It was time to put the past aside and look toward their future together. "I'm considering pediatrics. I like working with children."

He gave her a squeeze. "You'll be good at it."

"If I do go back to the hospital, we'll need to live in St. Louis. But I'd like to spend as much time here as we can. I'm considering asking Joe to move in permanently. What do you think?" She chuckled. "If we buy a radically firm mattress he may even sleep in a bed."

He laughed. "Sounds like a plan." Brushing the hair from her face, he touched his lips to hers. "I hope he decides to stay."

"Me, too. He feels like family."

She yawned, but refused to give in to sleep, until she'd broached the subject that had already proven contentious. "How soon can we bury Stone Shaper? I'd hate to have another visit from Beth. She's getting impatient."

"You had another vision? When?"

She leaned up to look at him. "Last night, after you fell asleep. I was dozing off when the vision came." She shook her head. "I'm not sure it was a vision. I'd always been a watcher, experiencing their lives, but never directly involved. It was different this time. Beth spoke directly to me. We were alone together in Stone Shaper's lodge. She was angry because we were taking too long to bury him."

"That's the reason you left? Why didn't you wake me?"

"Because you would have insisted we wait until Arnold was captured. I couldn't wait—not after Beth's visit."

"I probably wouldn't have agreed." He pulled her close again. "You took a terrible risk." His voice lowered to an anguished whisper. "I almost lost you."

He rolled to his side and settled her head on his arm. "You'll have to explain what you were doing in Nevada."

"To the Marshal's office?"

"To everyone involved—Justice, FBI, and any other law enforcement agency since day one. Arnold is dead. Killer or not, his death will be investigated. You'll have to explain why you were alone in the middle of nowhere at that time of morning."

She shook her head. "I can't tell people about Stone Shaper. They'll think I'm crazy."

"When you left last night, *I* thought you were crazy. I swear, the only times in my life I've been terrified involved you. You'll make me an old man before our first anniversary."

She took a deep breath. "I can't lie, but I can't tell the truth either. If the authorities discover we have Stone Shaper's remains…. They can't take him away from us, can they?"

Responding to the tremor in her voice, he began rubbing her back. "Not if we take the control away from the government."

"How can we do that?"

"Once he's laid to rest, I doubt the Osage would give him up without a fight."

"We have to do something fast."

"I know, but I have an idea. We'll talk to Joe and see if we can set some things in motion." He drew the covers over them, and planted a gentle kiss on top of her head. "There's nothing we can do tonight. Try to get some rest. And sweetheart?"

"Yes?"

"If Beth comes to call, ask her to be patient a little longer. Stone Shaper's about to join her."

AT DUSK, A small solemn group watched as Stone Shaper's remains were placed in a hand dug grave on the south facing hillside. There was no coffin. The Osage warrior was laid to rest according to the traditional practices of his time, with one exception. The age and condition of his bones prevented the group of mourners from sitting him upright facing the east as had been the custom, but they had made sure his body faced the east and the rising sun. Representatives from each clan piled rocks around and over Stone Shaper's bones, filling in the grave until he was completely covered.

Joe led the mourners in the Song of Sorrow. Many of his people still sang this song each morning, so their ancestors knew they were remembered, and their people were full of sorrow because they had passed over.

The ceremony finished, the Osage mourners nodded their goodbyes and began to leave. Each mourner placed a final rock on the grave as though it were a flower. Willie leaned toward Joe. "What are they doing?"

"It is our tradition. A friend or relative of the deceased will place a rock on the grave whenever they pass by. It is a sign of respect. In the past, some Osage graves had stone towers several feet high. Unfortunately, many graves fell prey to early white settlers who desecrated the burial sites, looking for anything of value. This is no longer a common occurrence. My people own this cemetery site. Stone Shaper will be well protected."

Joe placed a hand on Stona's shoulder. "As Stone Shaper's descendent, you will be welcome here." He nodded to Willie. "You have fulfilled your obligation to Stone Shaper and are free of Bear's sin. You, too, will be welcomed."

She blinked away the tears blurring her vision. "Do you think Beth and Stone Shaper are truly at peace?"

Stona drew her into his side. "Do you have any doubts?"

Smiling, she shook her head. "No. Not really. Beth seemed pretty determined."

Joe handed her a smooth, palm-sized rock and gave another to Stona. The men added their rocks to the grave and stepped back to allow Willie a final goodbye. She knelt and rested her hand on the mounded stones. She'd shared an almost intimate bond with this warrior and his wife. Placing her stone on the mound, she closed her eyes and offered a silent prayer.

––––––––––––

THE SONG OF Sorrow beckoned… welcomed Stone Shaper into the light, its stark brilliance surrounding him. Holding his war club at the ready, he circled in place, searching for… what? He did not know.

The weight of ages slowly fell away. His earthly body no longer trapped him in the dusky void. Anger, so much a part of his dark existence, faded like dying sparks from a campfire. He was free.

"Husband, I am here." She spoke with silent words his spirit understood instantly.

"Beth?" He swung around, drawn to the achingly familiar voice of his love, the woman he'd thought never to see again.

She appeared in a shimmering golden haze, still beautiful, as he'd remembered in his seemingly endless banishment. He did not reach for her, sensing a barrier between them, a great invisible force preventing him from moving forward.

She came to him instead, dissolving the barrier, releasing the ties binding him to the earth, walking into his embrace. He held her close, never wanting to let go. His spirit rejoiced. She who had been lost was now returned to him.

He was whole again, strong, complete.

He was at peace.

THE LIGHT FADED until only darkness surrounded the gravesite. Willie reached for Stona's hand. His fingers tightened around hers.

"Did you see them?" Her whispered question seemed overloud in the black silence. In that moment, they might have been the only people on earth.

Joe touched her arm. "They have found peace." His voice was rough with emotion.

She thought about the man whose skeleton had been exposed the night of the storm. A man she had come to know well. "What will happen to Brings Peace?"

The old man smiled. "Soon the Medicine Chief will be given his own resting place and ceremony. Until then, we will walk the path together." Pulling a pen light from his coat pocket, he switched it on. "I'll meet you in the car." He followed the foot trail to the small parking lot.

Leaning into Stona, Willie sighed. "I suddenly feel at a loss."

He drew her around to face him, pulling her into his arms. "Why? What's wrong?"

Responding to the concern in his eyes, she shook her head. "Nothing's wrong. It's hard to explain, but for the past few months, I've been under tremendous pressure to right a wrong I wasn't even aware of until I read the letter explaining my relationship to Bear. Now it's over— no more solving ancient mysteries, no more running from killers. I should be rejoicing. Instead, I feel like I'm in limbo, like there's nothing more for me."

He rested his cheek on top of her head. "It may feel like an ending, but it's simply the closing of a chapter in your—in our lives. We have a lifetime ahead of us, filled with love and dreams."

She leaned back to look up at this wonderful man and marveled that he belonged to her. "I love you, Stona," she whispered, "more than words can tell."

Careful of her bruises, he held her face in his hands. "Your warrior has found his love at last." His warm lips, softening against hers, lingered. "Just as I have found mine. Forever and always, sweetheart. It is my promise to you. Forever and always."

Rose Sartin was born in Illinois, raised in Iowa, and has spent most of her life in the Missouri Ozarks. She and her late husband, Gary, raised three daughters, Melissa, Angela, and Faye, while building businesses as beekeepers, leathercrafters, and managers/tour guides in a show cave. Ms. Sartin is also proficient with the mountain dulcimer, performing in radio, television, and documentaries. Today she lives in their family home on an Ozark ridgetop that overlooks the Mark Twain National Forest. She is currently finishing the third novel in her Centallian Guardians trilogy. Her life is filled with family and friends, music, good books, and plotting adventures for characters who show up on her mind's doorstep.